MISTRESS NANCY

* * * * * * * * * * *

MISTRESS NANCY

* * * * * * * * * * *

Barbara Bentley

McGRAW-HILL BOOK COMPANY

New York   St. Louis   San Francisco

Düsseldorf   Mexico   Toronto

1 2 3 4 5 6 7 8 9 BPBP 8 7 6 5 4 3 2 1 0

Library of Congress Cataloging in Publication Data

Bentley, Barbara.
Mistress Nancy.
1. Morris, Anne Cary (Randolph)—Fiction.
I. Title.
PZ3.B44397Mi   [PS3503.E5714]   813'.52   80-14264
ISBN 0-07-016722-2

Book design by Andrew Roberts.

For Ruth and Roger

Author's Note

This is a work of fiction, based on
events in the life of Nancy Randolph.
No major character or situation
has been invented.

A copy of John Marshall's notes on
the murder trial of Richard and Nancy Randolph
is in the collection of the Virginia
Historical Society.

Copies of John Randolph's letter to Nancy,
and her reply, are in the New York Public Library.

Dramatis Personae

At Tuckahoe

COLONEL THOMAS MANN RANDOLPH
ANN CARY RANDOLPH, his wife
     Their children:
NANCY, later married to Gouverneur Morris
JUDITH, later married to Richard Randolph
MOLLY
ELIZABETH
THOMAS, later married to Martha Jefferson
WILLIAM
JOHN
HARRIET
VIRGINIA, called JENNY
JOHN LESLIE, tutor to the younger Randolphs
GABRIELLE HARVIE RANDOLPH, second wife of Colonel
     Randolph
AGGIE, personal servant to Nancy Randolph
CICERO, CATO and CLIO, servants
     Visitors from Richmond:
ARCHIBALD CARY, Speaker of the Virginia House and
     Ann Randolph's father
POLLY CARY, Ann Randolph's sister, later MRS. CARTER
     PAGE

At Bizarre and Williamsburg

RICHARD RANDOLPH

THEODORIC RANDOLPH

JOHN RANDOLPH, Republican leader in Congress

ST. GEORGE TUCKER, stepfather and guardian of the three Randolph brothers

ST. GEORGE AND TUDOR RANDOLPH, Richard's and Judith's sons

SYPHAX AND PSYCHE, servants

At Glenlyrvar

RANDOLPH HARRISON

MRS. RANDOLPH HARRISON, SR., his mother

MARY HARRISON, his wife

At the Trial

PATRICK HENRY, defense attorney, former Governor of Virginia

JOHN MARSHALL, defense attorney, later Chief Justice of the United States

In New York

GOUVERNEUR MORRIS, former Ambassador to France and chief drafter of the United States Constitution

DAVID OGDEN, his nephew

SALLY OGDEN, David's wife

* * * * * * * * * * *

The Letter

* * * * * * * * * * *

On Christmas Day, 1809, at the manor of Morrisania, New York, Gouverneur Morris's guests dined exceedingly well. The oysters had come fresh that morning from Morrisania's own beds, the pheasants had been properly hung and redressed in their own feathers, the beef was roasted to a pink and brown untouched by gray. Morris himself was not satisfied with the claret. It's what comes of not being able to manage the stair to the cellar myself, he thought. But if the wine indeed fell short of the perfection their host required, none of the guests appeared to notice it. His old friends Mr. Beecher and Commander Decatur fairly glistened with pleasure, and even that unlikely guest the local vicar seemed a bit flown.

Sally Ogden, wife of Morris's nephew David, had fully intended that her uncle-in-law should know how displeased she was that her usual and proper place opposite him at the long table was today filled by Miss Randolph, his housekeeper. "He can call those women 'housekeepers' if he likes," she had said to her husband. "I know what I'd call them." She managed to sulk through the oysters, but the sliver of pheasant she took undid her, particularly since Morris determinedly ignored her pouting. Fortunately, although no lady could possibly take a second helping of a fish course, game did not come under the same restriction. Neither did wine, and after her second glass she was able to think almost kindly of the usurper. Miss Randolph seemed more of a lady than her uncle's usual run of housekeepers, and her dress was at least ten years behind the fashion and patched at the elbows, an indication that she was no great expense. Gouverneur Morris was of that most delightful breed of uncles, well over fifty, unmarried, very rich, and without a direct heir. All his nephews and nieces, by blood and marriage, considered it their duty to protect him from the sin of extravagance and that far more dangerous vice, philanthropy.

Dessert was a *crème brulée.* Bardolin, the steward, and Alfred, the cook, had both come back from Paris with Morris after his tour of duty as Ambassador, and although they were in constant and noisy disagreement on all other matters, they had found common ground when one of the previous house-keepers had tried to explain to them a Christmas boiled pudding. "An absurdity," Bardolin had said. "No, no, no, an abomination," Alfred had corrected.

When the nuts and apples and winter pears were served and the claret glasses cleared away, Morris himself stumped over to the sideboard on his wooden peg and brought back the thin-necked green bottles waiting there.

"This is a special wine." He carefully cut away the seal with Bardolin's pearl-handled knife. "A Tokay, as you see, and a true Imperial Tokay with the Empress Maria Theresa's seal in the wax. It was a part of a wedding gift from the Empress to her poor unfortunate daughter, Marie Antoinette, and came to me at the Versailles sales. I have been holding it for a great occasion, and I am delighted to say that the day has arrived. Are your glasses charged? Then, dear friends and relations, I ask you to join me in a toast to Miss Nancy Randolph, who this morning did me the very great honor of becoming my wife."

"Thank God," murmured Commander Decatur to Beecher, "that explains the vicar. I was afraid Morris had had bad news from his medical men." The two old friends were quick to recover from their surprise, to congratulate the groom and claim their kisses from the bride. The Ogdens were perceptibly slower and their words did not carry quite the warmth that their uncle might have liked or felt was due him.

"How old would you guess she is?" David Ogden asked his wife in their carriage on the way home.

"Not old enough. She can't be over thirty-four or five. Young enough to have half a dozen brats." They rode on in gloomy silence, broken by Sally when they reached the ferry crossing. "What I don't understand is, if she's from such a splendid old Virginia family, where were they today? And where were they all the months she's been working as Uncle's housekeeper?"

In their bedroom Nancy Morris read aloud to her husband the text she wished to send to the Virginia newspapers.

" 'Announcement is made of the marriage at Morrisania, New York, of Miss Ann Cary Randolph of Tuckahoe, Virginia, to Gouverneur Morris of Morrisania, former American Ambassador to France, former member of the United States Senate, and author of the Constitution of the United States.' "

"No, no, my dear. That won't do. We'll just say Morris of Morrisania and stop there."

"But I want everyone to know who you are."

"Anyone to whom those titles would mean anything already knows who I am, and I never claim authorship of the Constitution."

"Then it's time you did. You were chairman of the committee, after all. Cousin Tom always claims to be the author of the Declaration of Independence and never even mentions Mr. Adams or Mr. Franklin."

"Trust me, Nancy, the cases are not comparable. The newspapers will have the simplest announcement and, if you like—" he smiled at her—"you may write privately to your friends and tell them what a splendid marriage you have made."

"You think you're making a joke, but that's precisely what I would do and tell them all how kind and generous and wise and forgiving and strong and . . ."

"Come, come, Nancy, I'm far too old to have my head turned by flattery."

"But it's all true." Nancy knelt beside her husband's chair and took his hands in hers. "You know, it's the strangest thing. I should feel grateful to you for what you've done, making me safe at last from all the old scandal and gossip, making me mistress of this house and everything else that goes with being your wife, but I don't feel that way at all. Instead—" she hesitated—"I feel things I never thought I'd feel again." She looked up at him and went on in a breathless rush. "Shall I tell you something, Gouverneur? I am in love with you."

"My darling girl, you're the only one here whom that surprises."

* 2 *

On the day that the wedding announcement appeared in the Richmond and Williamsburg papers it was the chief subject of conversation at a great many Virginia dinner tables. It was read with particular interest in three households—the Randolph's at Tuckahoe, Monticello, and Bizarre.

From Nancy's brother Willie at Tuckahoe came a brief note offering scant congratulations and a pompous warning to avoid extravagance and ostentation in her new position. She crumpled it up and put it on the bedroom fire and decided that she would, after all, permit Gouverneur to order the new phaeton for her.

From Monticello her sister-in-law, Martha Jefferson Randolph, wrote most affectionately for herself and for Nancy's brother Tom and added that she was sure that when "the President" heard the news he too would want to express his warmest good wishes, for although "He has had his political differences with Mr. Morris, he has always said that Mr. Morris was at heart one of the best of the Northern men."

"Isn't that just like Martha," Nancy said. "Imagine calling your own father 'the President' in that affected way. And he isn't even in office any more."

"I must say she knows her father well, though. That's just the sort of thing he would say about me." Morris shrugged. "He has a head like a feather bed himself, so he puts great store in purity of heart."

"Gouverneur, you may be cross with Cousin Tom because of the embargo and all that, but when I was in the worst of my troubles and had very few friends he was one of them, and he saw to it that his daughter and my brother stood by me as well."

Her husband was contrite. "Well then, history will call Tom Jefferson the worst President this country ever had—at least I pray God that Jemmy Madison won't be worse—but against that in the scale we will put that he was kind to my Nancy and that will always weigh heavier with me."

At Bizarre, Nancy's sister Judith was at her prayers when her late husband's brother, Jack Randolph, rode up from Richmond. When she came down the stairs he was waiting in the hall with the newspaper folded back to the column of announcements. She read the notice through without expression and then read it again aloud. "Ann Cary Randolph of Tuckahoe," she smiled. "She hasn't so much as set foot on Tuckahoe land for eighteen years . . . well, it's as the Book says, 'the wicked shall flourish like the green bay tree.' " She handed the paper back to her brother-in-law. "I didn't expect you until tomorrow. I'm afraid there's only a bit of cold mutton for supper."

"Will you write to Nancy?"

"I think not."

* 3 *

After the first flurry of calls and dinner parties for the new bride, the Morrises settled very happily into comfortable domesticity. It was soon made clear to the hostesses of New York in the politest fashion that the new Mrs. Morris had very little interest in going about in society. For himself, Morris was quite content to lead a quiet life. His old friends were still frequent guests at his table, his days were filled by the management of his business affairs, the remnants of the Federal Party, and the plans for the Erie Canal. Occasionally he worried aloud that Nancy might find it dull living in such an exclusively masculine world, but she assured him that she had had a full ration of the company of women and their gossip in her life and was happy to be without it.

There was only one flaw in their marriage and that was remedied early in its fourth year when Nancy presented her husband with a son. There was never a more joyous father or a more pampered and cosseted mother. The birth of Gouverneur, Junior, gave Nancy the impetus to try to mend the breach between herself and her family. Her nephew Tudor spent some months at Morrisania. Her sister Judith came to visit and, when she trailed a hand over the back of one of the drawing-room chairs that had once graced the private apartments at Versailles and said that they were pretty, "but the Randolphs have always preferred the English style," Nancy found that instead of the helpless wave of rage that her sister would once have inspired, she felt only amusement and a little pity.

"If you'll forgive my saying so, your sister's a damned dreary woman," Gouverneur said later when she quoted Judith to him. "She told me that the Beauvais tapestries in the hall 'must be useful against these dreadful drafts even if they are shocking dustcatchers.' I tell you, I won't be sorry to see the back of her."

"Patience, darling. Just one more day and Jack will take her away."

"Now there is someone who does surprise me. A much pleasanter companion than when we met in Washington. I believe he must be coming to terms with his infirmity at last. Made him less thorny."

"Perhaps." Nancy shrugged. "Jack has always been as charming as anyone could wish when he chose to be, or his

(8)

devils or the drink would let him be. But I've known him all sunshine and smiles one day and so dark and broody and touchy the next that you couldn't call a horse a gelding in front of him without his taking it as an insult."

When Nancy went to her bed on the night that her relations left Morrisania she thought that every woman in the world must envy her if they knew her. She had made her peace with her sister, not just a façade of civility, but in her heart. She had a generous and loving husband, a son she adored, and they lived together in perfect amity in a house fit and furnished for a queen. She could have a commanding position in society any time she cared to take it up. She thought perhaps she would, now that young Gouverneur was a little older.

On the last night of September 1814, Nancy Randolph Morris was a supremely happy woman. There was no reason to suppose that she would not continue so for the rest of her life.

At half after eleven by the *régulateur* of M. Lépine, on the first true frost day of November 1814, Nancy Randolph Morris was halfway down the carved main staircase of Morrisania when her carefully ordered, gentle and happy world was blown apart.

The French parquetry still gleamed, the Roman Republican on top of Mr. Petit's clock stayed firmly in place. Alexander, Aristotle, and Aspasia remained frozen in the Beauvais. From the kitchen wing came very faintly the sound of Alfred's and Bardolin's regular morning quarrel. Upstairs her son was squirming only a little as his nurse washed his hands and face before his tray came up. A riding cloak was thrown across a chair in the hall; a hat and crop lay on the table beside it.

The door to the library burst open and David Ogden sidestepped through it. He fumbled for his hat and cloak, shying away as his uncle followed him into the hall.

"Get out. Get out of my house."

"I am trying to do you a service."

"Can you not understand simple English? Get out before I call someone to pitch you out."

Ogden backed toward the door and caught sight of Nancy on the stairs. "Your servant, madam," he said.

Startled, Morris turned and looked up at Nancy where she clung to the banister.

"What is it?" she asked. "What's happening?"

"It's nothing, Nancy, nothing at all. Our nephew has been impertinent, but he will trouble us no further."

"Oh no, no, that won't do, Uncle. Tell your whore of a wife and watch her face and then see who's the liar in this."

"I've warned you, David." Morris reached for the bell pull.

"I'll go. But you think about what you've been told before it's too late to save yourself."

When the door closed behind Ogden, Nancy ran down the stairs and into her husband's arms.

"Careful, girl. You'll knock me off my pin."

"What's happened . . . something dreadful . . . to make you quarrel with David? You know you mustn't get so angry. You'll make yourself ill."

"It's nothing that need worry you. David overstepped himself, that's all, and exhausted my patience."

"Gouvero, I am not a child that you can put off by telling me that what I just heard was of no account."

"Indeed you're not. You're an extraordinarily handsome woman who shouldn't be troubling her head over a matter of business."

"Nor am I fool to be turned off by soft talk. What kind of business matter is there between you and David that makes him call me a whore and demand that you tell me . . ." She pulled away from him. "Tell me what?"

"It's nothing to do with you. The man was in a rage and simply lashed out at you because you were there."

"Darling, I begin to believe that I have given you more credit than you deserve for always being honest with me. It's simply that you are no earthly good at lies."

"Can't you accept that if I don't wish to tell you something it's for your own well-being?"

"And can't you see that you'll have no peace until you tell me what this is about? I don't choose to be left wondering all manner of things."

Her husband sighed, took her arm, and led her into the library. There was a fire in the grate against the cold outside, and he stumped over to it. It was funny, she thought, how easily she could tell his mood from the sound of his peg across the floor. He poked angrily at the fire, scattering embers out on the hearth. "I should have thrown the damned thing in here when it came," he said.

"What thing?"

"Nancy, I want you to listen to me very carefully. Whatever you hear, whatever happens, you must always remember this. I love you and our son above all other things. I had thought I would go to my grave unwed and childless. Having you and Gouverneur has been the greatest joy of my life. Nothing has changed and nothing will ever change that."

"You are frightening me."

"I meant to reassure you."

"Why do I need reassurance? I see your love about me every day. It is not a thing that needs words between us."

"I'm glad. Just hold fast to that and we'll come through." He walked away from her to his desk and put his hand on the deed box that sat at the corner. "It seems that you are as ill-served by some of your relations as I am by mine. About a month ago I received a letter from your cousin Jack enclosing another letter addressed to you. The one to me was civil enough, simply saying that there was information that he felt I should have. It was the sort of letter that an honorable man might write to an opponent if he had damaging political information or some hint of fraudulent practice. It was a bit overblown, but I put that down to his style."

"He sometimes forgets that he isn't addressing a public meeting. It comes from going to Congress at too early an age."

Her husband didn't smile. He took a key from his watch chain and unlocked the deed box. "As I say, the letter was civil enough, and in it he required me to read the enclosure before passing it on to you. I thought he might be making some disclosure that would be upsetting for you for family reasons, to do with your brothers perhaps, and he wanted me to prepare you for the news." From the box he took a thick sheaf of closely written pages, holding them gingerly as if their weight in his hand was somehow corrupting. "I am still of two minds whether to show it to you."

"You cannot go this far and then not go on."

"The letter to you is the raving of a madman. At first I thought that he must have been drunk, that he would soon regret having written it, and that within a few days or even hours I would have a second letter asking me to destroy it without your eyes ever having seen it. That we could call it a temporary aberration of a sick man and put it behind us."

"Jack never apologizes. He insults people and then promptly forgets it and is forever being surprised when they treat him coolly afterward."

"Only the accident of your overhearing Ogden this morning persuades me even to tell you of the letter's existence. . . . And I still wish very much that you not read it."

"Surely you can see that I must."

"Nancy, he accuses you of unspeakable crimes. He rakes up all the old scandal about you and Richard and the death of the baby and he brings new charges against you."

"Let me have the letter."

"Only if you insist. I withhold it out of love. I would not have you think for a moment that I kept it from you because I believed any word of it."

"Please, must I come and take it from your hand?"

Slowly he crossed the room and gave her the closely written pages. He sat beside her as she read. It was a long letter and took even longer to read. Several times she turned back a page to read it over as if her mind refused to believe the message her eyes brought her. When she at last finished she sat quite still, all color and life drained from her.

From the decanter on the serving table her husband poured a glass of brandy and, with his arm about her shoulder, forced the glass to her lips. She pushed it away. "No, no, I don't want it. It would only make me sick. It's very strange . . . I feel as if this were not happening to me at all, as if I were up somewhere in the corner of the room watching a person I know reading a letter about some other people that I can't quite remember. And yet I can feel my body. My arms are so cold. . . ."

"Drink the brandy. It will help bring you back to yourself."

"I'm not sure I want to be brought back to myself. . . . Who am I? The Nancy Randolph in that . . . that thing? A lewd, incestuous double murderess, plotting still another crime? The vampyre that has its harpy fangs in an infirm old man? That's how he says he sees us."

"He is insane, Nancy."

"Someone is mad, certainly. At the moment I think it may be me. I cannot make myself understand what has happened. Look at the date on this thing. October fourteenth. Less than two weeks before he was our guest, we laughed together. When he left he took me in his arms and kissed me goodbye. He said remember the past and I thought he meant the good times. Now he says that it was to remind me that I am too hardened a criminal to be disturbed by the eye of God. . . . It's such a strange mixture, outright lies and ravings and half-truths and distortions . . . all that hatred . . . stored up for twenty years and then bursting like a boil. Oh my God, Gouverneur, I swear to you that I am not what he says."

"Dearest Nancy, no one who knows you would believe any of it for a moment. Decatur and Beecher assure me that they put no credence in it at all."

"You showed it to them? How could you?"

"Of course I didn't. What do you take me for? Under the pretext of consulting them as to what he should do your cousin went to them and told them the substance of it."

"And how many others?"

"I can't be sure. Wilkins heard something of it in the town and went himself to Randolph to hear the story."

"So for all you know the whole town may be buzzing with it while I am kept in ignorance."

"I wanted to protect you."

"To protect me? Or to wait and watch me and see if I were really planning your murder, the way he says?"

"Now stop. Remember the promise you gave me when I let you read this thing. I am not your enemy. I am your husband and your lover. Come here and let me hold you."

And then at last she began to cry. Clinging to his shoulder, she sobbed, "Oh God, I thought it was all over, all behind me. So long ago, so long ago."

* * * * * * * * * *

Tuckahoe

* * * * * * * * * *

* I * * * * * * * * *

Thomas Mann Randolph did not attend the birth of his seventh child and fourth daughter at Tuckahoe. Instead he sat in one of the back pews of St. John's Church in Richmond, listened to Patrick Henry beg heaven to grant him either Liberty or Death, and cheered as the Virginia Convention voted to arm themselves and took one more step toward war.

"She's a pretty little thing," Randolph said, leaning over the cradle. "Let's call her after you. Ann Cary Randolph. How does that suit you?"

"Whatever pleases you, Tom," his wife said.

"Then that's settled. Nancy for short. The last Randolph born a loyal subject of George the Third. The old fool doesn't know what he's losing."

"Do you really think it'll go that far?"

"Just a matter of time. Meeting in the convention itself is an act of treason to the Crown, but it might have been passed over if there was a reconciliation. Now they've voted to arm themselves, and even the most indulgent monarch couldn't let that go by."

Nancy took her first staggering steps on the day in July a little over a year later when her cousin Tom sat up all night in a Philadelphia tavern to put the final touches on the document that announced the colonies' independence and tried to justify rebellion to the nervous governments of the rest of the world.

(17)

She was nearly six when she and her older sister Judy leaned out the window of the nursery to see if they could see the smoke from the fires that the British soldiers, led by the turncoat Benedict Arnold, had set in Richmond. The hall downstairs filled with friends and relations fleeing from the troops, Cousin Tom, now Governor of Virginia, among them. She swore that she could smell the smoke that day and managed to convince herself later that she had seen the flames. Perhaps there had been a slight darkening of the haze that always hung in the air downriver. It was enough for a heart that thirsted for adventure to embroider.

She liked to frighten herself and her younger sister Hattie at night with tales of what would have happened to them if Papa had not stopped the ravening hordes of redcoats before they could advance the miles to Tuckahoe, until poor Hattie ran screaming to Judy. Judy took her into her bed and told her to pay no attention to Nancy, who was a wicked, wicked liar.

"You should be ashamed of yourself, frightening Hattie so," she told Nancy.

"Don't be so soft. She likes it. She begs me to tell her about it."

The defense of Richmond was the last action that her father, a colonel in the militia, was to fight. The British retreated and her father came home. He hung his sword back up on the pegs in the hall, but he would keep the title of colonel for the rest of his life.

Except for those few days the war was no more than an irritation for Nancy and her brothers and sisters. Her older sisters, Molly and Elizabeth, fretted that all the eligible young men were too preoccupied with war to think of courting, and they had both passed their seventeenth birthdays and were in imminent danger of withering on the vine. Her brothers chafed at a war which kept them at home to share a schoolroom and a tutor with their little sisters and still did not look to be long enough for them to join it.

With time the villainy of the redcoats faded. Nancy was not overly surprised when her father brought home two young officers, on parole after General Cornwallis's surrender, to find them mild and homesick boys, not at all the ogres she had frightened Hattie with. One of them fell an easy victim to her six-year-old charms and gave her one of the epaulets that he was no longer permitted to wear. "There you are. You can grizzle it and wind the thread and when you are a young lady you'll have a gold-embroidered petticoat. I'll take the other one home to my little sister, and when you meet at a great ball in London, your petticoats will nod at each other."

"I would be ashamed to go around begging things off guests in the house," Judy said to her later. "Besides, it was a waste to give it to you. You haven't the patience. You'll get tired of it and lose it before you have it half unwound."

"And if I do, what of it?" Nancy said airily. "Someone else will give me another one. If you didn't go around so dark and scowly you might get one too."

Randolph of Tuckahoe was not the only Virginian to offer friendship and hospitality to the British officers who had surrendered at Yorktown, but he was the most prominent of them and attracted the most criticism, most particularly from his father-in-law, Archibald Cary.

Grandfather Cary's visits were always exciting for the children at Tuckahoe. He would descend on the house with a roar and continue to bellow until his daughter was lying down in her room with a cloth wrung out in vinegar over her eyes and his son-in-law, normally the most amiable of men, had turned quite purple in his struggle between rage and good manners.

"Goddammit, Tom, I don't understand you at all. It's one thing for a tavernkeeper to serve whoever comes in the door, but for someone who calls himself a soldier and a patriot to entertain the same men he was fighting not a year before . . . If you have no care for your own reputation you might have some for mine."

"It has nothing to do with your reputation. No one in Virginia thinks that my actions are controlled by you."

"We'd all profit if they were. I don't know what you can have been thinking of. I hear you even mounted them from your own stable. They could have broken parole and been in the Carolinas for all of you."

"They came for the hunting. Would you have had me let them follow the hunt on foot like black boys?"

"And who in hell's name invited them for the hunting? This isn't olden days when you fought all morning and then sat down to dinner and a glass of wine together. This is modern warfare and those men are your enemies as long as they still stand on the soil of Virginia."

"Oh come, Archie. They were boys not that much older than my Tom and Willie. And as for standing on the sacred soil of Virginia, they would like nothing better than to feel the wooden deck of a London-bound ship under their feet. The war's over, the glory's gone out of it."

"And when they come back and try to burn Richmond again, the way they burned New York?"

"It was my understanding that it was our forces who put the torch to New York and General Howe who put the fires out."

"And sometimes I think you lack understanding all together."

"Please, Father, and you too Tom. It's Christmas Day," Mrs. Randolph intervened in distress. "Please don't provoke each other so. I'm sure if Father had seen what very pleasant and well-mannered young gentlemen they were he would feel differently."

"I would not," her father said stubbornly. "It's a matter of principle."

"Then we must agree to disagree, sir." Colonel Randolph beckoned to Cicero. "And we'll have a cup on that."

Gentlemen's quarrels, Nancy observed, were often resolved by a claret cup or a toddy. It seemed a pity that the cure was not available for the nursery. Her sister Judy's quarrels with her could last a fortnight, with sulks and black looks long after the original cause was forgotten.

Not that they battled much when Grandfather Cary was visiting. When he arrived all the younger members of the household were as one, united in a common loathing. Not for their grandfather, he might terrify them with his roar, but he could always be melted by a smile from his granddaughters. Unfortunately, he brought with him his daughter Polly, plump and self-important at sixteen, insisting that she be called Aunt and treated respectfully despite her years. The older girls thought her silly and ignored her, but the boys and Judy and Nancy despised her as a meddler and a tale-bearer and pulled faces behind her back when she boasted about how much better things were at Ampthill than at Tuckahoe and how important her father was as Speaker of the Virginia House.

Moreover, although their older sisters sometimes spoke wistfully of the Christmases before the war when the shops of Richmond were full and the wharves piled high with goods from London, Polly managed to complain about the scarcities of war in a manner that made the younger Randolphs feel that in some obscure fashion it was all their fault.

All in all the household gave a great sigh of relief when the Carys went home again. Even that gentlest of women, Ann Randolph, could turn to her husband and say, "He's my father and she's my sister, but it's downright miraculous how much better my headache is when I see their carriage going down the drive."

*   2   *

Just as the war had come gradually to the country over a period of a year or years, so too did peace creep in. A state of war still existed until such time as England would acknowledge the colonies' independence, but the soldiers who had gone to fight it had come home to stay, to pick up their old lives or get off to a delayed start on new ones. The houses and wharves that had been burned in Richmond were rebuilt and the ships came back up the James. In some parts of the country life came completely back to normal, the peace treaty that Franklin struggled to negotiate in Paris no more than an unimportant detail, but for the Virginia planters bound by long custom, convenience, and mutual trust to their factors in England, the war could not be over until trade was reestablished. However much they owed the French for their assistance to the cause of liberty, they did not think them reliable trading partners, and any man who shipped his crop off to a Spanish broker was thought a fool who might just as well place his cargo aboard a ship with a gaping hole in the hull.

So, for Nancy Randolph and her brothers and sisters, the war was not over until the day that their father told them that they might bring him the lists of what they most wanted to order from his broker in London. The Treaty of Paris was signed, and he would ship his first crop in eight years. "But remember," he cautioned at the dinner table, "I'm not a rich man. Have a little mercy on me."

"You always say that." His wife smiled at him.

"But this time it's true. Leastways I don't know whether I'm rich or poor. I don't even know for sure whether I'm in debt or credit to Barbour, or even whether he's still alive. I don't know what price tobacco is fetching in London, though it should be a good one. Lord knows they've been starved of good Virginia leaf for long enough. On the other hand there's such a battle for shipping space that I'll have to take what I can get in a ship at whatever price they choose to charge me and then not even be sure that it hasn't a damp bottom that'll ruin my leaf. And after all that, Mr. Rockford must have what he needs for the place before everything else. He tells me that if he doesn't have some of the tools he needs there won't be a crop next year."

Molly and Elizabeth, with their heads full of wedding plans, ordered a barrel of china apiece. "With a pattern of leaves or fruit, whatever Mr. Barbour thinks we'd like."

Tom and Willie and John drew round their feet on pieces of paper as patterns for the London bootmaker and solemnly swore that they would not allow their feet to grow more than the allotted extra half inch at the toe. Their mother ordered lengths of Turkey cloth and nankeen, lace edgings and ribbons of all colors, and sprigged muslins in colors suitable for young girls.

"And for yourself? Not the girls."

"Don't worry, I'll find enough to make a new cap at least. But what I really want is two dozen of the claret glasses with the baluster stem. Those things they make up north aren't fit for a gentleman to drink out of, and try as you will things do get broken. Especially claret glasses."

Judy put on her most pious look and said that all she really wanted was a new prayerbook bound in Morocco leather and whatever other books of an improving nature Mr. Barbour should select. Her father raised his eyebrows and wrote it down, but when Nancy said that she wanted most of all a red riding cloak with a triple row of shoulder capes and a crop with a silver handle, he asked Judy if she would not reconsider.

"I didn't wish to be thought extravagant. But if it's possible I would like a riding cloak too. Only not red. That's babyish. A dark gray . . . with silver buttons."

"I am surprised you think red's babyish," Nancy said. "I would have supposed you thought it wicked."

Judith smiled at her in a pitying and particularly aggravating way, and Nancy wished that she had thought of asking for silver buttons.

In the end it didn't matter. The Randolph crop arrived in London in prime condition in a dry hull and fetched a price that not even an optimistic Tom Randolph had hoped for. The buttons on the red riding cloak were silver with a wash of gold. To Nancy the end of the war would always mean two things— the feel of a new riding crop in her hand and the way that all

Richmond glistened as the boats from London brought in the lead for paint.

It seemed, on the whole, that the coming of peace made much more difference to the household at Tuckahoe than any war ever could. First Molly and then Elizabeth married and moved away, but they had always seemed to Nancy, because of the differences in their ages, to be more aunts than sisters. The departure of the boys made a much greater hole. Tom and Willie were sent off to Edinburgh escorted by their tutor, John to a tutorial school in Williamsburg. No one thought enough of John Randolph's capabilities to consider him worth either a voyage abroad or the cost of a tutor at home. In a less exalted family he might have come close to being considered simple.

Nancy and Judith had shared the tutor, Mr. Elder, with their brothers. They could write a fair hand and figure well enough to make sure that the shopkeepers didn't cheat them. It was in the eyes of everyone concerned quite enough. Their mother engaged to teach Hattie until she reached her sisters' level and to help Nancy with her music, but the door to the schoolroom was shut for two years.

Mrs. Randolph had borne nine children and raised eight of them. She was tired. From time to time she would scold herself for inattention. Surely Nancy was spending far more time at the stables than was wise, and her sister Polly had commented on how pert her niece was growing. Polly blamed it on the books she read. Privately, Ann Randolph knew that her husband was spoiling his favorite daughter, but she knew why his preference lay in that direction and was flattered. Besides the very thought of trying to discipline Nancy made her head hurt.

Into the disciplinary void stepped Judith. Now at twelve the oldest child in the house, a grave, prosy, pious little woman at best, she became to Nancy a scourge, a source of unwanted instruction on the proper behavior for a lady and a Randolph. In part the role that Judith took on was that of any older child trying to command the obedience of younger members of the family, but with Judith there was something more. She truly believed that it was her duty, spiritual or religious, to correct and guide her sisters, particularly as it became more and more apparent that her mother and father lacked either the energy or the interest for it. In this view she was supported by her favorite reading matter, those books of parables and advice for young women that were beginning to settle like a plague of pious platitudes on the household of every gentleman in England and America.

She was particularly enamored of a heavy volume called *Virtue in Humble Life* by a Mr. Hanway, two hundred and nine conversations between a Farmer Trueman and his daughter who was about to leave home to go into service in the wicked city. The idea that advice for a servant girl in England might differ mightily from the information required for the life of a daughter of one of Virginia's richest families never seemed to occur to Judith. When Nancy pointed it out, Judy stated firmly that the principles were the same. "Mr. Hanway says it is a sin to be discontented with your station in life, and surely that is true whether your station be high or low."

"Sometimes I wish that I did have a low station in life. I could start on my adventures sooner. Actually, what I shall be in my life is so beautiful that everyone will fall in love with me and I will refuse them all, but gently so that they will not die of it but only linger and pine."

"What a great many fools you expect to know," Judith said shortly.

Eventually Judith despaired of ever bringing Nancy under control by any direct means and concentrated on the more malleable Hattie. For Nancy she developed a special weapon. Night after night she knelt and asked God's forgiveness, not just for her own sins of the day but for Nancy's, listing even the smallest errors of omission in a clear, firm voice designed to reach her sister's ear as well as Heaven's.

Nancy complained in vain to her mother. "Surely you can't expect me to ask your sister not to pray for you. I can't think what you're making such a fuss about."

Ann Randolph herself had begun her slow progress away from her family. After a difficult pregnancy, the birth of the last of her children, Virginia called Jenny, who would become Nancy's special pet, seemed to exhaust all her strength. She stayed longer in her bed than ever before, and to Judith fell the task of managing the household, and Nancy became her father's companion.

For a few glorious months in her eleventh year Nancy had the nearly undivided attention of the man she considered the handsomest and bravest of any gentleman in Virginia. She was too old now to ride in front of him on Shakespeare, but every morning Cato saddled Lady for her when he saddled Shakespeare for her father, and they made his morning rounds together. She missed her brothers and she was sorry that her mother still felt too ill to come to the table, but she had never been happier. It worried her father not at all that her lessons seemed to be permanently given up. She could write a clear enough hand to make the entries in his stud book for him. She read every book in his library and could play a fair tune on the spinet. He asked no more of a daughter, especially one as beguiling as this one.

Tom and Willie had gone to Edinburgh as boys; they came back in June of 1786 as young gentlemen, at least in appearance. They had been to Paris and seen Cousin Tom and particularly his daughter Martha. Willie talked of meeting the Marquis de Lafayette again, but Tom talked of Martha.

With the return of her sons, Ann Randolph found a new source of strength. There were dinners and dancing parties again at Tuckahoe. Sometimes there was even a dancing master brought up from Richmond. Nancy was still so young that she could be permitted to dance only with her brothers or cousins, but nearly every young man they knew was a cousin of some sort from one side of the family or the other, so there was no great restriction.

John had come home from Williamsburg as well. There was nothing to be gained by having him tutored there when Tom and Willie had brought a new tutor home with them from Scotland. John Leslie was young and fervent, burning with his commitment to republicanism, mathematics, and the Scottish kirk and lacking the slightest leavening of humor. Nancy and Willie escorted him down to the schoolhouse to see what needed doing before he could begin work, and Leslie went into what Nancy thought a rather unbecoming fit of ecstasy.

"These hallowed walls," he breathed, "the vairry walls where Jefferson learned his letters."

Willie and Nancy exchanged glances. They were seldom friends but they were in agreement now. It was a given among the Randolph children that Cousin Tom tended to put on airs now that he had acquired an exaggerated reputation outside Virginia. Still, Mr. Leslie could not be expected to know how little considered Mr. Jefferson was here, and it seemed both ill-mannered and unkind to tell him.

For Nancy the return to the schoolroom after two years of freedom was in itself a trial, made more severe by the personality and regimen of their teacher. Only a few days after he had begun work he approached Colonel Randolph.

"There was something you wanted to speak to me about, Mr. Leslie? One of the children been acting the fool? Something you need? Books? Whatever it is, you give your list to Mr. Rockford, and if it can be had in Richmond or even Williamsburg you shall have it."

"Thank you, sir, there's nothing I need and I would think myself a poor sort of teacher if I could not manage five students without running to their parents. It's only—" he paused—"I cannot help but be surprised that you do not lead your family in prayer in the morning."

Randolph laughed. "There'd be a great many more people flat out astonished if I did do so. I do my praying on Sundays when the weather's fair in the pew I paid for in the church. As for the rest of the time, let's just say that I worship God by tilling the soil. I've always thought that good scripture. Don't you?"

"I beg your pardon, Colonel Randolph, I'm afraid you find me impertinent. I would not have spoken of it except for my deep concern for the well-being of your children."

His employer did, in fact, find him impertinent. He also felt sorry for the young man blushing and stammering before him. It had taken some courage to approach him. Obviously Leslie felt deeply on the subject. Randolph was not only a generous spirited man but also above all else anxious to have a quiet household. "Look here," he said. "I'm too old a dog to change my ways, but if you'd like to start the day in the schoolroom with prayer I'd have no objection. Might even be useful. Quiet them down so they can get to their lessons."

Nancy was sure that her father had thought that morning prayers would be a reading of the Collect and the lesson for the day and an Our Father, that he had never anticipated the half hour of kneeling on a drafty hard wooden floor while Leslie begged God's forgiveness not only for the sins they might have committed but for some that none of his students had even contemplated. It was an advanced version of Judy's nightly prayers, comments addressed less to Heaven than to earthly listeners.

She quickly learned to cope with the worst of the morning ordeal. If she bundled her petticoat up under her knees the floor was not so hard, and she found that if her eyes were demurely downcast there was no way for anyone to know how far away her thoughts were. With practice one could manage to hear nothing at all until the general stir that preceded "Our Father . . ."

But there came a morning when she could not ignore Mr. Leslie's prayer.

"Almighty God, we humbly beg that you may grant true repentance for their many sins to those you see here before you. Purge them of all error and grant them the strength to carry the message of repentance to their father, who in ignorance damns himself eternally for the souls he keeps in bondage away from the light of your love and has now all unwittingly brought one of his own children into a sinful state. Grant that your child Nancy, here kneeling before you, be given the strength to turn away from the evil path trod by her father and grandfather . . .."

From behind her Nancy heard Willie draw his breath sharply. She heard the thump as he came up from his knees and sat down again on the bench. After a moment she did the same. Mr Leslie's eyes flicked over them briefly before he turned again to Heaven and launched into a sermon on the evils of slaveholding, ignoring their hostile stares.

She knew what had inspired their tutor. Grandfather Cary had sent her a girl from Ampthill. Called Aggie, she was a year or two younger than Nancy, light-skinned and intelligent. Nancy supposed that she might be willing to confess to the sin of pride that Aggie had come to her instead of Judith, but only if her sister would admit to the sin of envy. As for Mr. Leslie, she heartily agreed with Willie, who burst out almost before the final amen had died away. "I think it's a bit too much for you to pray against a man who gives you your living."

"I am not praying against your father. I am praying that he may be brought to the light before it is too late. It is a mystery to me how men who were willing to die for their freedom a few short years ago can keep a whole race in chains."

"You never saw a servant in chains at Tuckahoe," John observed. He was not quite sure what the quarrel was about, but he knew what he knew. Mr. Leslie's reply so puzzled him that he lapsed back into his usual silence.

"I am speaking metaphorically, John. Surely none of you can deny that there is something inherently evil in the placing of one child in the possession of another only because they differ in the circumstances of their birth."

"What would you have me do?" Nancy asked. "Send her back to Grandfather? She wouldn't be any less of a slave than before, and she doesn't want to go back to Ampthill. Polly is cruel to her. For that matter, what would you have any of us do? Everybody knows the slave trade is wicked, but we have

(29)

nothing to do with that. I don't think you understand the first thing about us, and I don't think you ever will."

"I think Mr. Leslie is perfectly right," Judith said.

"You would," Willie and Nancy chorused. "But I don't remember ever seeing you carry out your own slops," Willie added.

Aggie was the cause of comment in the master bedroom as well as the schoolroom. "I can't think what Father was thinking of sending that girl here to Nancy," Ann Randolph said. "She's far too young to have a personal servant, and it'll only make trouble with Judith. He's getting old and confused."

"Maybe he is," her husband said, "but he wasn't all that old ten years ago, and it's easy to see why he wanted her out of Ampthill."

"I don't know what you mean."

"Oh yes you do. Look at the nose on the girl. Barring the color, it could be yours. He wanted her well away before there were any questions about her. She'll be better off here with Nancy and your father knew it."

* 3 *

Gentlemen came from all over Virginia to the Richmond summer race meeting in 1787, but to Nancy's disappointment the table talk at Tuckahoe was all politics and no horses. All of the Randolph guests were much exercised over a convention being held in Philadelphia. "It's a damned Northern conspiracy to destroy Virginia," one of the guests said. "And if you don't believe me, why are they being so secret with the doors locked and no dispatches in the papers?"

Colonel Randolph said it was clear that the delegates must be discussing more than just some revisions of the Articles of Confederation but that with General Washington in the chair Virginia's interests would be protected.

"In any case something must be done," another of the guests added. "It's all very well for you planters who trade across the ocean, but if you have to trade between the states it's damned near impossible."

Mr. Leslie cleared his throat. "I think that Americans must be on guard that they not exchange the tyranny of the Crown for the tyranny of money."

The gentlemen at the table were startled. It was as if one of their horses had volunteered a political opinion, but Judy looked at him adoringly and Willie gave Nancy a savage pinch to call her attention to her moon-struck sister.

Judith wrote *Judith Leslie* and *Mrs. John Leslie* all over her slate and rubbed it out with her finger but not before Nancy saw it. When she walked with the solemn young man in the garden John and Nancy followed behind and strained to listen but never heard anything more interesting than theological discussion.

"I would rather not have an admirer at all than have one who talked religion at me all the time,' Nancy said to her brother.

"Then you have your wish. You have no admirer at all."

"Really, Johnny. You are so stupid."

John nodded placidly and smiled. "Yes, I know."

"It's time to send Leslie packing," Colonel Randolph said.

"Darling, I don't think that's necessary. Judy's very young and I don't believe he would ever take advantage."

"I'm not worried about that. I don't believe he knows what his thing's for except pissing. If all the Scots are like him it's a wonder to me that the race survives. I only meant that it's time Willie went off to join Tom at the College, and there's no profit in trying to pound any more learning into John's thick head."

"You mean for the girls and John to just run wild then?"

"I'd as soon they ran wild as spent their time praying over me."

But Mrs. Randolph was too tired even to think about starting again with the girls' lessons, and although her husband grumbled about the needless expense and the dampening effect that Leslie had at the dinner table, he agreed that the tutor could stay on for at least another year.

Spring came round again and Nancy was thirteen, caught between a child and a woman. Beautiful and willful, spoiled and enchanting, she did not as yet really know her power. She knew that she could make her father obey her with the gentlest of spurring, but she judged the rest of the male world by her brothers and, like all brothers, they were not just immune to her charm but completely unaware of it. There were others who were not. Her cousin Archie Randolph found that more and more often he was drawn to her side. True, they still never spoke of anything other than horses, but now he sometimes found himself blushing and stammering when he talked to her, quite as if she were a real girl and not familiar Cousin Nancy. Archie was as far removed from the dashing lover that Nancy fancied in her future as it was possible to be, but she was fond of him, not least of all that spring, because he was the only male she knew, man or boy, who seemed to have anything on his mind other than politics.

The Virginia delegates to the Constitutional Convention of 1787 had returned home divided and uncertain. The fierce debates of Philadelphia were transferred to Virginia, to Richmond and the state convention, and to the dinner tables where policy was more often made than in public debate. It seemed to many Virginians that the Constitution was nothing more than a scheme to force Virginia to pay the debts that other states were too improvident to manage. "I may very well be my brother's keeper," said one of the Randolph guests, "but I'm damned if I'll be Rhode Island's."

Edmund Randolph had led the delegation to Philadelphia, but he had refused to sign the final product. General Washington had chaired the convention and signed the draft, but now he sat above the battle at Mount Vernon. Jemmy Madison said he had a letter from Thomas Jefferson in Paris supporting the new Constitution, but there were others who had letters that they maintained said just the opposite. It was generally held at the Randolphs' that Cousin Tom was so changeable he probably wouldn't make up his mind until it was all over.

There was one leader who had no doubt at all where he stood. Patrick Henry was violently opposed. He considered the Constitution the undoing of the Revolution, the exchange of one tyranny for another. He carried with him all of Henrico Parish, but he was also burdened with a major disadvantage. As another of the guests of the Randolphs put it, "If it comes right down to what Edmund Randolph decides to do, I'll put my money on ratification. I never yet heard of a Randolph getting aboard the same horse as Patrick Henry."

Politics in Virginia was an intricate web of family connections, of old alliances and old feuds. Into this maelstrom, Gouverneur Morris limped warily. He had come down from Philadelphia to help Madison in the fight for ratification and soon discovered that he could best serve the cause simply by being himself, demonstrating that a Northerner could be as honest a gentleman as any Virginian and no more eager to exploit them. He was heard to point out that if Virginia failed to enter the Union by ratifying, Washington would be ineligible for the Presidency of the new nation and that old John Hancock in Boston had already ordered the gold buttons for his inaugural waistcoat.

For the rest he made himself an amiable guest, telling Hattie when she stared at his missing leg that he considered it a blessing because in his old age he could have the gout in only one foot. Nancy thought he must have lost it heroically in the Revolution until Willie told her that everyone knew he had injured it leaping from a married lady's window as her husband came in the door. On the whole, Nancy found that more intriguing than a war wound. Morris did what he could and then sensibly decided that the fate of Virginia would after all have to be thrashed out by Virginians and went back home.

In Richmond the debate raged on. Every Virginia gentleman with the slightest interest in political matters came to the capital that spring, either as a delegate to the convention or as a spectator to history. The guest wings and bachelor houses of every family within twenty miles were overflowing.

"I met those stepsons of St. George Tucker in town today," Colonel Randolph said to his wife. "The oldest is about to start farming his father's land himself. Thought it might be helpful to have them visit for a few days, see how we do things here. After all, they are Randolphs. Some sort of cousins. I'll leave you to figure out just how."

"It seems to me," Nancy grumbled, "that we already have more than enough cousins without adding any. Certainly we have more than enough boys in the house."

"We must be kind to them," Judy said. "Tom says they are poorer than church mice. It's an act of charity on Papa's part and he will be remembered in Heaven for it."

*   *   *   *   *   *   *   *   *   *   *

Three Brothers

*   *   *   *   *   *   *   *   *   *   *

On the hottest day of July 1788 the ladies of Tuckahoe and Mr. Leslie were all together in the main hall, whose windows were open at either end to catch what breeze might happen to come up from the river. Mrs. Randolph was playing at noughts and crosses with Hattie, who crowed with delight at every game she won.

Nancy was reading, the book propped on her chest. She sprawled across a couch crosswise to the windows, one of her feet on the floor so that she could kick Jenny's ball back to her when the youngest Randolph rolled it to her.

"Look at her," Nancy said, "that baby plays just like a puppy playing fetch."

"Please, Nancy," her mother protested without much conviction, "that's not a very ladylike way to lie about and not a very kind way to talk about your sister."

"It's far too hot to be ladylike, and Jenny knows I would never be unkind to her. She's my very own fat little puppy dog, aren't you, baby?" Jenny abandoned her ball and climbed up to sit astride her sister, squealing with delight as Nancy bounced her. "She's my very own, very own puppy dog, and she's going to follow me wherever I go. Say yes to your Nancy, baby, say I love you Nancy, say I love you best of all."

"You always want people to say that," Harriet said.

"So I do, and so they always will, except Mr. Leslie of course. I don't believe Scotsmen ever say I love you."

Tormenting Mr. Leslie had long been a favorite pastime of his younger students and now Hattie quickly picked up her cue. "Why don't we ask Judy?"

"What an excellent idea," Nancy said. "I'm sure she's listening. She hasn't turned a page of that book for ages. Tell us, Judy, do Scots say I love you?"

John Leslie's thin freckled skin turned a red to match his hair, to the immense gratification of both Harriet and Nancy.

"Oh Nancy, I do believe he's blushing."

"You know, you're right. Isn't it interesting the way he becomes all one color? Would you call it salmon? Scotch salmon, of course."

Now Judith closed her book with a bang. "You children have the worst manners in the county. Mama, speak to Nancy and Harriet, make them apologize."

"I'm sorry, darling. I wasn't listening."

"They called Mr. Leslie a fish."

"We did no such thing. Mr. Leslie isn't angry with us, are you, Mr. Leslie?"

"No, no, it's just high spirits, Mrs. Randolph, the girls mean no harm."

"Nevertheless I apologize for them. What you kindly call high spirits can come dangerously close to incivility, I know."

"Dear Mr. Leslie," Nancy said, "you know we wouldn't want to hurt your feelings for a minute. But it's a matter of great importance to all of us. Especially Judith."

Judith stood up angrily. "Mama, if you can't control these girls' tongues, at least I don't have to listen to it. I'm going upstairs where I can read in peace."

"You'll perish of the heat up there," her mother protested. "The girls will behave. They're just bored."

"Then let them find something useful to do with themselves for a change." At the foot of the stairs she turned, her voice breaking with tears of rage. "Hattie's still a little girl, but Nancy is old enough to know better and I think she is a p-p-perfect abomination."

"Well," Nancy shrugged, "how pleasant that Judy thinks I'm a perfect something."

Mrs. Randolph, either from fatigue or normally placid nature, rarely lost her temper, but now she came near to it. "Nancy, really now. Judy is quite right, you are impossible. Now you've made your sister cry and upset Mr. Leslie, although he's too much of a gentleman to say so, when he's been so kind and patient with all of you, and you've disturbed my rest when you knew I needed it and with guests coming too."

"'Darling Mama, let me get the flower water and I'll rub your forehead."

"You'd be more use to me if you would go up and apologize to your sister."

"I will later on. Right now she wouldn't even answer her door to me. And poor Mr. Leslie, Hattie and I are truly sorry. We really don't mean to be so unkind, but it is such a temptation to tease you, because of the way you color up. But I'll give you my solemn promise not to provoke you any more."

'I would settle for a solemn promise from both of you to come better prepared to your lessons."

"All right, that too, but not," she added quickly, "not the mathematics. I cannot see the use of that for girls."

"Perhaps not the use . . . but the enjoyment . . . mathematics is the most beautiful of disciplines."

"I know, you've told us so, but you also said that it was much like music, and some people just have no ear for music, Willie for one, and I think I must be like that with mathematics. I mean I can figure all right. Like how much a dress length comes to at two and nine pennies a yard and things like that. It's when you brought all those letters and things in."

"Can you not think of it as one of your games, a puzzle?"

"No, I can't."

"But they are just symbols, like the notes on a page of your music."

"I don't have to solve the notes. I just play them, it's not the same at all."

"But it is the same, that's what I am trying to teach you. One is an abstraction just like the other."

"Ah, but when my fingers hit a wrong note, I can hear it right away. And I can spend all day with your letters and do the set work over and over and I still don't know whether it's right or wrong or why, until you tell me."

"The trouble with you," Hattie said, "is you can't bear for things to come slowly. You must have them all at once or you can't be bothered."

"You know, you're exactly right and I have just had a marvel of an idea. What if there were a magic way of learning, you just mixed up a toddy of mathematics and drank it down and before it hit bottom you'd know as much as Mr. Leslie."

"There could be a Latin one for Johnnie."

"And a music one for Willie."

Mr. Leslie smiled. "Ah, but then how would we poor tutors live?"

"Why, you'd live like a lord," Nancy cried. "You'd be the only one who knew the secret ingredients and how to mix them up. And you could sell it to all the lazy students in the world, which is practically everybody. And be rich as Croesus himself."

"And when I am very rich what should I do with myself? I'm afraid Scots were not made for idleness."

"You do think of the strangest ways to make a problem. Hattie, what do you think Mr. Leslie should do when he is very very rich?"

"He could give balls and suppers and small dancing parties and go to the theater whenever he wished and have very beautiful clothes and houses and a great many servants."

"And horses," Nancy added, "don't forget the horses. A stallion like Shakespeare to ride and matched grays for his carriage. You could even have a racing stable, would you like that, Mr. Leslie?"

"I am sorry to disappoint you, but it all sounds rather alarming to me. And you know my religious principles forbid me the theater and dancing and all worldly display."

(40)

"Really, Mr. Leslie," Nancy said impatiently, "why must you have such a very dreary religion?"

"Nancy," her mother intervened sharply, "now that is excessively ill-mannered. No lady discusses a person's religion."

'I thought that was just at dinner and besides we weren't really discussing it."

"I am not offended. I know that my religion seems harsh to you, but that is only because you have no understanding of it."

"Perhaps you could teach me."

"I'm afraid that would be even further from my abilities than teaching you mathematics."

"I'll tell you what. I'll make a bargain with you. I'll let you teach me about the Scottish kirk if you'll let me teach you to dance before our next supper party. Judy wouldn't half be pleased," she added slyly.

"I couldn't possibly. It would be using an ill means even to a good end. I mean the end, of course, of making Nancy Randolph somewhat less ignorant of the church."

"I quite took your meaning. But I can't understand why it should be evil to dance. You like music. I've watched you when the fiddlers are playing and you stand against the wall. Your head moves and sometimes your fingers tap out the time. All that's left are your feet. Dancing is just moving about while the music plays. What could possibly be wrong about that? Here, let me show you." She took his hands in hers. "Just follow me. Right, one two, and left, one two, and right, one two, and turn me about ..." But Leslie stood immovable, and as Nancy tried to swing him about she lost hold of his hands and sat down very abruptly on the floor, her petticoats flying.

"I truly think you must be the clumsiest man in Virginia as well as the dreariest," she said angrily.

Hattie was laughing, Jenny began to cry, Mrs. Randolph said, "Oh, dear" faintly. From behind Nancy a strange voice said, "If you will permit me to assist you," and a firm hand under her elbow hoisted her to her feet.

"Mr. Randolph of Bizarre and Mr. Theodoric and Mr. John," Cicero said from the doorway.

"Perhaps," said Richard Randolph, "we should go out and come in again."

"I beg you, don't do that," Mrs. Randolph said. "With these girls Heaven only knows what you would find a second time. These are your cousins, my three youngest daughters. Nancy and Harriet, and that caterwauling is Jenny." Mr. Leslie cleared his throat. "Forgive me, this is Mr. Leslie, who very kindly does his best to teach my young savages."

Mr. Leslie and the brothers bowed, Nancy and Harriet curtsied, and Jenny increased the volume of her wails.

"Hattie, would you please take Jenny up to Clio so we can hear ourselves think. Cicero, would you send a boy out to help the young gentlemen's servant with their things and show him the rooms that are ready." Cicero acknowledged her request with a bob of his head, knowing that it was said purely for form's sake. Both he and his mistress knew that the rituals of hospitality at Tuckahoe were far too well rehearsed for him to need instruction.

Mrs. Randolph was eager to settle down for a good gossip about old friends in Williamsburg, particularly Frances Tucker, the boys' mother, before the men of the house returned and the conversation became all farming and politics and horses. When the brothers protested that they were traveling without a groom and must go first to the stables, Nancy quickly offered to go in their stead and her mother rather uncharacteristically agreed.

"But, Nancy," she said, "don't hang about down there too long. You have that matter to take care of with your sister before dinner."

* 2 *

Despite her mother's caution, Nancy stayed at the stables long enough to be able to report back that her cousins' horses were well in hand, in their stalls, watered, fed, and being brushed down. "The black was a little fractious, but Cato gentled him down."

While she was gone her father and brothers had returned to the house and the party had broken into three groups. Her father and Tom and Richard Randolph with sherry flips in their hands were earnestly talking politics. Her mother and Hattie on the couch with Theodoric were still talking about family matters, earnestly trying to determine what degree of cousinship they shared. "Let's see," her mother was saying, "we are all Turkey Island Randolphs, but you come from the Pocahontas line through the Rolfe marriage, and we do not. So we are quite distant cousins through the Randolphs, but I think there's a closer connection through the Carys. Wasn't your mother . . ." In Nancy's opinion trying to disentangle the Randolph family lines was like working with a basketful of fishhooks and no more rewarding, so she joined her brother Willie and the two Johns at the far end of the room.

"Good God, Nancy," Willie said, "it's easy enough for anyone downwind of you to tell where you've been. You smell like old boots."

"I really despise you, Willie. I wish Papa would send you back to Edinburgh and the ship would be captured by pirates and they would hang you and keel-haul you . . ."

"Surely not both," Cousin John said. "Hanging is so final that keel-hauling afterwards would be a tremendous waste of effort."

"Our sister is often excessive," John said. "Where's Judy?"

"Upstairs sulking."

"I'll bet you I know why. You've been after poor old Leslie again."

"You're a fine one to talk. You are worse than Hattie and I put together." Nancy laughed. "But, Johnnie, you should have been there. He turned absolutely purple."

"There isn't a penny's worth of difference between the lot

of you," Willie said. "You'll make the poor man sorry he ever decided to come back with us."

"Not any sorrier than I am that you brought him home." She turned to her cousin. "Tell me, Cousin John . . ."

"Please call me Jack. Everyone does."

"Oh good. It will be much less confusing. Do you have sisters?"

"Hundreds of them, or so it seems. But of course they are very small. They are only half-sisters, you see."

Nancy groaned. "And do you torment them in other ways than punning?"

"Only when they deserve it."

"And your brothers? Are they as unkind to their little sisters as my brothers are to me?"

"I am not sure that Theo even knows that they exist, and Richard has never found it possible to be unkind to anyone in his life."

"Goodness," Nancy said, "what a very model young man he must be."

Jack frowned. "Cousin Nancy, if you want to be friends with me don't ever by word or look make light of my brother Richard."

Nancy looked at him. "I believe you're serious."

"About Richard I am always serious. Anyone who can't see that he stands miles above everyone else hasn't the sense of a goose."

"And I suppose I don't . . ." Nancy broke off as Willie gave her upper arm a savage pinch. "Stop that, Willie."

John cleared his throat. "Uh, Nancy, Mama has been giving you rather meaningful looks."

"Just meaningful or threatening meaningful?"

"Right on the edge, it seems to me."

"She wants me to go up and sweeten Judith."

"If she got a whiff of you," Willie said, "she'll be wanting you to change before you come to table, and you'd better hurry it up."

In their room Nancy found Judith sitting in her shift before the open window. "What on earth are you doing? Mama would kill you if she saw you sitting like that when anyone might look in."

"Never mind that. No one can see. The sun's round the other side. Tell me about him at once."

"I don't know. I haven't seen him. He must have left while I was down to the stables. He's all right. We made it up, and he's probably in his room or down at the schoolhouse."

"Not Mr. Leslie," Judy said impatiently. "Our cousin."

"Well, they must be poor as Tom said, because they are traveling with only one servant for the three of them. Only I heard Papa talking and he said he remembered when Syphax—that's the servant's name—was their father's body servant and everyone conceded he was the best body servant in Virginia. They don't have a groom, but their horses are good and they have very handsome boots. That would be Syphax's work, I guess."

"Who cares about their horses or their boots?"

"I do. What else do you want to know?"

"Everything."

"Let's see. There are three of them. The youngest is John called Jack. He's about Willie's age, I think, but his voice hasn't altered yet and he hasn't any beard. He has very strange hands, the longest fingers I've ever seen, and there is something rather odd about him in general. But I suspect he is very intelligent and a little witty but hot-tempered. And Theodoric, isn't that just like a name in a book? They call him Theo and he is dark too and thin with deep-set eyes. I scarcely spoke to him."

"And the eldest? The fair-haired one in the blue coat?"

"Judith Randolph, you were leaning out the window watching. Aren't you ashamed? Mama would give you fits for that. It's really common. Like a tavern maid."

"I was not leaning out the window. I was simply sitting by it to get a breath of air."

"Why aren't you dressed anyway? It's about dinner time."

"Never mind that. Tell me about the last one."

"There isn't much to tell. His name is Richard and he is very well turned out and has pleasant manners. His brother Jack thinks he is the marvel of the world."

"What did he say?"

Nancy shrugged. "Nothing."

"He must have said something. Tell me every word."

"He said permit me or something like that when he helped me up, and he asked to be excused to see to his horses, and then I went down to the stables instead and when I got back he was talking with Tom and Papa and I wasn't listening."

"That's all? That's all you took any notice of?"

"Why, yes. He seems pleasant enough. But Jack is the interesting one."

"I don't understand you. The most beautiful man you have ever seen walks in the door and all you can say is that he has pleasant manners and good horses."

"Men aren't beautiful."

"This one is."

"How far out that window were you leaning? I think you've had a rush of blood to the head. You'd better be getting dressed before the bell goes." While they talked Nancy had changed her dress, decided that her slippers were the source of Willie's complaint about her, and was now scrambling around the bottom of the armoire looking for another pair.

"I can't. I don't know what to wear. And I've used about two pounds of rice powder and I'm still soaking through."

"Wear anything you want to. It's only three cousins for dinner. There are always cousins for dinner. You're acting like General Washington was waiting downstairs."

"The new one ... the muslin with the rose sprigs ..." Judith took it out and laid it across the bed. "Do you think it's really becoming ... or maybe I should wear something simpler ... I don't want him to think I'm making a special fuss over him. ... And, Nancy, what shall I do about my hair?"

"Just comb it. I think the heat has gone to your head

completely. Get dressed and come on downstairs. There's sherry flip going round and I think you could use some."

There was a round dozen at table for dinner. Mrs. Randolph, despairing of seating a party of four ladies and eight gentlemen, simply placed Richard on her right and left the rest of them to sort themselves out. Her eldest son promptly took the place on Richard's other side so that they could continue their conversation, and Judy, who had made what Nancy considered a rather unseemly dash for the place her brother took, was trapped on the wrong side of the table. Between Theo and faithful Mr. Leslie, no matter how she craned her neck, she could get only an occasional glimpse of his hands or a bit of his profile.

Leslie launched into a carefully prepared speech of apology. Never for a moment would he have caused her any discomfort or by any act of his caused a quarrel with her sisters.

"I'm so sorry, Mr. Leslie. I'm afraid I wasn't attending."

"I said I hoped that you were not angry with me because of this morning, or that if you were you would have the Christian charity to forgive me."

"Don't be so soft," Judy said impatiently. "If you didn't let the children see that they upset you they'd soon stop."

"I could not bear it if you were angry with me."

"For Heaven's sake, nobody is angry with you. Cicero is waiting for you to take some ham."

Hastily he served himself from Cicero's platter, but when he turned back to her she was busily engaged in conversation with Theo.

"And now, Cousin Theo, you must tell me all about yourself and your brothers. I think it so surprising that we have never met."

"What sort of thing do you want to know?"

"Everything."

"That's Jack across the way. He's the youngest. He is, they tell me, brilliant. He is certainly very impatient and bad-tempered on occasion. There is but one star in his firmament and that is our brother Dick—" he smiled—"the one you keep craning your neck to see."

"The fair-haired one."

"Quite so. Will you have a biscuit?"

"Thank you. Do go on."

"Where was I?"

"You were telling me about your brothers ... about Dick ... he is the eldest?"

"Ah yes, the first-born. Industrious and kind, gentle and forgiving, and quite filled to the brim with all the noblest virtues. Our brother Richard, the very model of what a young gentleman should be, and, since I can see that you are palpitating to know but afraid to ask, quite unattached to any young female."

"I can't think why you should believe that that would interest me."

"Really? Then you must be as exceptional as he is. Usually one glance from those blue eyes and girls quite swoon away. I expect the hedges will be littered with them from Williamsburg to Bizarre before we finish our journey."

"I think I should tell you that I am no great admirer of a sarcastic wit."

"Then perhaps we shall never get on, which I would regret very much. You see our brother Richard casts a great light. Jack basks in it. But a great light makes for a dark shadow, and there, my dear cousin, we find Theodoric, the wicked one. Indolent in his studies, low in his tastes, and generally considered to be well launched on a career of the utmost depravity. Do I frighten you? Please say that I do or I will be extraordinarily disappointed."

"Then I am afraid you must be disappointed. You are far too young for your pose."

"You think it a pose? Perhaps you are partly in the right, but surely one can never be too young to set one's course in life. I am sure that the angels sang hosannas round my brother's cradle."

"You will not convince me. I think you are unhappy and discontented and more than a little envious, but not wicked."

"But surely, discontent and envy are important first steps for me to have taken."

"Then you must pray to God and he will help you retrace them. True happiness lies in being content in whatever form or station in life God has placed you."

"That sounds very much like something from a particularly gloomy improving text."

"It's not at all gloomy. Mr. Leslie says there is nothing more joyous than—"

"Mr. Leslie," Theo interrupted, "being the very red young man you just snubbed so badly. And is he content with his station in life? He looks perfectly miserable to me."

"He's upset at the moment because Nancy and Harriet have been teasing him."

"Surely a station in life that leaves one open to the tormenting of your sisters must require a great deal of prayer to be content in."

"Mr. Leslie is a truly religious man."

"I should think he would have to be."

"I am sorry for you, Theo," Judy said gently.

"Splendid. That is the one thing I do really well, making people sorry for me. It's a poor talent but at least it's my own."

"Oh Lord," Judy said, "try it on with Nancy. She's just the sort for you. She'll think you're one of those pale young men with a secret sorrow in those trashy books she reads."

"You see your little moment of kindness passed very quickly, didn't it? Wasn't that quite wicked of me?"

"All right. I give in. You are quite, quite wicked, but what is worse you are not serious. And now I shall finish dinner with Mr. Leslie."

"I think you should. He's been pushing his food about his plate in a most dejected way. And, Judy," he said as she started to turn away, "don't worry. I shan't warn Dick. You'll be able to creep up on him quite unexpected."

"Mr. Leslie, my cousin has been telling me that he hopes to complete his studies in Edinburgh. It would be a real kindness if you would take him aside after dinner and tell him all about your home."

"I had hoped that we might walk in the garden a bit."

"I'm afraid it's far too hot for that. I think I will just read in the book you so kindly lent me and then later we can have a good long talk about it. And, oh yes, Mr. Leslie, my cousin is most interested in religion, most particularly the doctrine of Original Sin. He would truly enjoy your attention to him."

Dutifully Leslie sought out Theo after dinner and regaled that at first bewildered and then amused young man with a recital of Edinburgh's virtues, moral and intellectual, interspersed with good solid Calvinist doctrine. Theo and Leslie disposed of, Judy arranged herself in the hall where the light would fall most flatteringly, her book in her hand, one finger marking the page, the perfect picture of a serious young woman looking up from her book as some thought of great profundity struck her.

Unfortunately when Richard came out of the dining room he was deep in conversation with her father and Tom on the difficulty of bringing Bizarre back to some measure of prosperity with only twenty hands in the field, some of them, as he said, not prime. Her father insisted that he come now to talk to Mr. Rockford, who could be most helpful if Richard planned to act as his own overseer. He bowed, smiled, and was gone. A day wasted, and since she had now committed herself to reading a theology text, a day worse than wasted.

* 3 *

Judy had never shared Nancy's love for horses, thinking them just a means to get from one place to another and far from the most comfortable one. But next morning she was at the stables early, had Cato saddle her mare, and was riding slowly around the exercise ring when her father came down from the house with Richard. If her father was surprised when she said that it was such a beautiful morning she thought she might ride out with them, he said nothing; and Richard seemed gratifyingly pleased to see her. On the next day she rode out with them again, and again the day after. In the afternoons after dinner when Colonel Randolph just closed his eyes for a moment in his chair in the library, Judy kindly volunteered to show her cousin the kitchen gardens and the tobacco press and the wharf where the lighters tied up.

The cousins' visit, which was to have been a matter of two or three days, became a week and then ten days. Colonel Randolph's store of advice for the young planter was exhausted, but Richard and his brothers stayed on. By tacit agreement the other young people left Judy and Richard much to themselves. Even though they could all see what was happening, they found it difficult to believe. Theo and Jack assured Nancy and her brothers that they had never seen Dick in such a state. He had always seemed quite oblivious of the effect his looks and his manner had on young females. Mr. Leslie grew redder and gloomier by the day. To Nancy the whole affair was completely incredible—that her sister, serious Judy, reasonable Judy, prayerful Judy, could be struck by a *coup de foudre* was on the face of it impossible, and yet the evidence was there. The others were content to watch and speculate, but Nancy determined on a blunt attack and found her opportunity when she and Judy were dressing for dinner.

"Are you in love with him?"

"Can't you tell? How could I not be? Of course I love him. I'm going to marry him."

"Has he asked you?"

"Not yet, but he will. In six months I'll be sixteen."

"How do you know he'll ask you? Has he . . . ?"

"Because I couldn't feel this way about anyone without his feeling the same way," Judy interrupted. "Oh, Nancy, have you ever seen anything as beautiful as the way he holds his knife and fork?"

"It's rude to watch people eat."

"Not when they do it so beautifully."

Nancy sighed. "Judy be reasonable."

"Why should I?"

"Because that's who you are—the reasonable one, the careful one. Suppose he does love you?"

"He does, he does."

"Suppose he even thinks you eat beautifully, which is truly silly ... Mama and Papa would no more let you marry him than they would have let you marry Mr. Leslie."

Judy looked at her in surprise. "How does Mr. Leslie possibly come into this?"

"Because a week ago you were mooning about after him."

"I wasn't. I was simply being kind to him because the rest of you were so horrid."

"That's not what he thought was happening. Have you so much as looked at him in the past few days? He's half crazy."

Judy smiled with delight. "Really? Do you think other people have noticed?"

"If by other people you mean Dick, I don't see how he could help it. Mr. Leslie just sits and glares at him at every meal."

"How wonderful! Do you think I should wear the poplin with the blue pattern or the rose muslin? I wore the rose the first day."

"Whatever you like. It can't matter. If you are in love, it's done you a world of good. You look far prettier and much more amiable than you ever have. Everyone notices it."

"Truly?"

"Cross my heart, even Willie."

Judy studied herself with pleasure in the pier glass. "I must be kinder to Mr. Leslie. How could I have been unkind to anyone when the world is such a marvelous place?"

"Listen to me, Judy. I want to talk to you seriously."

"I'm listening, listening, listening," Judy sang.

"Then stand still. I can't talk to you when you're dancing about the room."

"I am standing still. I am listening to my darling little sister who is talking seriously about something besides horses which is a miracle in itself. Talk to me, little sister."

"They will not let you marry him. Not now and not in six months."

"Then I will wait . . . or we will run away . . . or I shall pine and droop and they will fear for my health and send for him."

"Judy, he doesn't have a penny."

"Who needs money?"

"You do, for one. Everybody does."

"He has Bizarre. He says it is very beautiful and that I will love it. He says there is a special tree whose roots grow out over the bank and make a throne and that if I were sitting there the whole meadow would become a palace hall."

"I would rather have some good solid chairs in the dining room and something to put on the table, and so would you if you'd only think about it."

"That's because you are talking about the old Judy. I'm a different person now and a much better one. I know the things that really matter. If two people love each other they can conquer all adversity."

Even at thirteen, Nancy rather doubted this. "Every servant he owns except Syphax is mortgaged in London."

"I know."

"If he gets Bizarre afloat again, then the money will have to go to Jack's place in Roanoke and Theo's downriver."

"I know."

"He can only do it all if he watches every cent. He can't afford a wife."

"Some wives would be a help to him."

"I can't see how."

"Making economies around the house. I could turn sheets sides to middle and see that the cook doesn't steal."

(53)

"Judy, for heaven's sake, he doesn't have a household where economies can be made. He has an empty house and more land than he can manage. Haven't you been listening when he talks to Papa?"

"Grandpa Cary would give me a wedding present."

"He would do no such thing. He has far too many granddaughters to begin doing that. You'd get a nice piece of silver from him and you'd have to polish it yourself."

"Nancy, you disappoint me. You're the one who's always talking about adventure and romance. I should have thought that you of all people would be on my side in this."

"I am on your side. I am just trying to explain to you that it isn't all going to turn out happily ever after like a children's story."

"Yes it will," Judy said confidently, "because I won't allow anything else. I want Dick Randolph and he wants me, and that's the whole of it."

"It isn't, you know. You may be ready to defy Mama and Papa, but he won't."

"If it's necessary, he will."

"He won't. He'll go quite properly to Papa and Papa will explain to him why you can't be married and Dick will be very honorable and agree and just go quietly away. I know what will happen. I've been talking to Theo and Jack."

"About me? How could you be so impertinent?"

"Not about you but about Dick. He feels his duties and responsibilities very strongly. He is determined not to be a burden to his stepfather any longer."

"Mr. Tucker doesn't consider Dick and the boys to be burdens. Dick says they are like his own sons to him."

"That's just the point. They aren't his own sons and Dick intends to repay him."

"You see, that's just what I'm saying. He's not only beautiful, he's a man of character and sensitivity. Oh, Nancy, I hope you may be as lucky as I am. Think if they hadn't met Papa in Richmond. Think if Papa hadn't invited them to visit. We might never have met . . . or he might not have noticed me. That first day I didn't think he had and I thought I would die."

"There's no point in even talking to you."

"Not if you are simply going on to make more difficulties . . . but stay with me anyway. Have you noticed his eyes? Have you ever seen more beautiful eyes?"

"Never," Nancy said resignedly.

"And his nose . . ."

"A nose above all others."

"And his mouth and his hands and his carriage. Do you know yesterday evening when he came in from riding out with Papa and the boys, he was standing against the mantelpiece with his crop in his hand, looking at me, and I had this peculiar feeling . . . I can't describe it. It was like a warm place in the bottom of my stomach that just spread all through me until I could scarcely see or move I was so lightheaded. Dear Nancy, can't you see, he is perfect in every way."

"Judy, has anything at all that I've been trying to say come through to you?"

"Of course it has and I think it's very dear of you to worry about me. But you mustn't, you know. Mama and Papa are not ogres. Have they ever denied us anything we really wanted?"

"No, but this isn't a new riding cloak or even a new mare. This is the whole rest of your life."

"I know. Isn't it a wonderful thought?"

"I give up." Nancy laughed. "Let's go on down to dinner. I'll walk and you float on that cloud of yours."

After dinner, the forgotten member of the triangle drew Nancy aside. "Miss Nancy, may I talk to you?"

"Surely you are talking to me, Mr. Leslie."

"Please, I know we haven't always gone on well together, but I've always felt there was real kindness in you, and I must speak to someone."

Nancy hesitated. "I think I know what you wish to talk about and I really can't."

"I beg you, just come out to the garden with me, and if anyone asks we can be talking about lessons."

"I am sorry, but I really don't think I can help."

"She thinks more of you than any of the others. She confides in you. I know that she does."

"And would you want me to break a confidence?"

"Of course not. Not in the normal way of things. But I must know. Has she said anything to you about me? Have I offended her some way? Is she angry with me? You can tell me that much. Because if there is some way I can make her see . . ."

Nancy thought and then spoke carefully. "I can tell you this, quite honestly, she hasn't spoken to me about you at all, but I am sure that she has the greatest respect and affection for you and always will."

"But what sort of affection? That could mean everything or nothing."

"What could there be, Mr. Leslie? We are still in the schoolroom, your schoolroom."

"You may be, but Judith is nearly a woman and I believed that she felt far more than respect and affection for me."

"She was, she still is quite fond of you."

"You can be fond of a puppy." He turned on the path to face her and Nancy saw to her dismay that there were tears in his eyes. "She has fallen in love with your cousin, hasn't she?"

"You know that I can't talk to you about it. You must ask her yourself."

"How can I? She's never away from him. She won't talk to me alone, and she must see how I am suffering."

"Poor Mr. Leslie, we Randolphs have been cruel to you. Would it do any good to tell you I'm sorry?"

"No, it would not. It's just unbelievable. Judith was the only one of you who seemed a serious, high-minded person, and now in a week's time she's changed, everything's changed."

"Perhaps she was always like she is now, and she just

seemed different to you because that was what you wanted and she wanted to please you."

"I don't believe that for an instant. The old Judith is the real Judith. This is just a passing thing, a fever. When they leave she'll settle down again."

"Mr. Leslie, I don't want to be unkind, but you mustn't place your hopes in Judith. It would never have come to anything."

"You can't know that. She might have come back with me to Edinburgh, or I might have been able to borrow to start a school here. We talked of it."

"Then it was very wrong of Judy. Because it would never have happened. Judy wasn't raised to make a wife for a schoolmaster."

"If she were taken away from this atmosphere of frivolity, Judith is, no matter what you say, Judith is not the same as the rest of you. There is a core of religious feeling in her that the rest of you can't even dream of."

They were sitting on a bench at the end of one of the garden paths, and Nancy put her hand, she hoped comfortingly, on his black sleeve. "Look, partly you are right. Judy isn't exactly like the rest of us. But don't you see, she is far more like us than she is different and much more like us than she is like you."

"None of you understand her," he burst out.

"Poor Mr. Leslie."

"Don't just sit there saying poor Mr. Leslie like a parrot. Even a child like you should be able to see that this is not simple flirtation for me. I love her. With me she could be the kind of woman that she was meant to be. I would value those things in her that the rest of you either can't see or laugh at."

"I believe you would," Nancy said thoughtfully.

"Then talk to her for me."

"Trust me, I would try, but there is nothing I could say that would help."

"Nothing at all?" he asked despairingly.

"Nothing."

He sat for a moment in silence and then stood and took her hand in his. "Then I would be most grateful if you would not tell Judith anything of our conversation. I do not want to distress her."

Nancy nodded.

"And thank you Nancy, for listening to me. You are light-minded, but you have a generous heart."

Light-minded indeed, Nancy thought. As far as I can see I'm the only one around with any practical sense at all. "Poor Mr. Leslie," she wrote that night in her journal. "It must be so boring to be a bore."

* 4 *

Like all the bedrooms at Tuckahoe, that of the senior Randolphs was dressed for summer. Mrs. Randolph watched Colonel Tom anxiously as he fumbled with the netting around their bed.

"Are you sober?"

Her husband was indignant. "What a question. Have you ever had me in your bed drunk?"

"Not drunk, of course, but sometimes a bit flown."

"Never been so insulted. Who am I supposed to have been drinking with? There's nobody but children down there."

"It's just that I must talk to you about something very important and I don't want you rolling over and falling asleep."

"Can't it wait for morning?"

"That's just it. It can't."

"Come, Ann, everything's better for a good night's sleep on it." He plumped his pillow and settled into it. "Besides, our young cousins will be leaving in the morning and then I'll have all the time you need."

"That's just why it can't wait. We must talk now and decide what to do."

"About what?"

"About Dick and Judith, of course."

"Splendid young man, Dick. What's he got to do with Judith?"

"Where are your eyes? Judith is in love with him, and, unless I misread all the signs, so is he with her."

"Nonsense. He's a very levelheaded, serious boy. He isn't entertaining any notions in that direction, not for Judy or any other girl. Can't afford it and knows he can't. As for Judy, she's known him short of a fortnight. He's a new face, that's all. You are seeing trouble where there isn't any and furthermore—" he turned over—"keeping me from sleep which I badly need."

"Don't you dare to close your eyes. You go to sleep and before you're half awake in the morning, Dick Randolph is going to ask to speak to you privately and we won't have decided what to say and you are likely to agree to anything just so there won't be trouble."

"All right, all right, I'm listening, but you are quite wrong. How old is she now? Fourteen? Fifteen?"

"Nearly sixteen."

"There you are, then, far too young for that sort of thing. Besides—" Colonel Tom had thought of a convincing argument—"not two weeks ago she was holding hands with young Leslie under the dinner table. Saw it myself," he said triumphantly.

"This is quite different."

"Ann, you've always been a worrier about your children. If—" he raised a finger—"and I say if, Judy has been having a harmless little flirtation with her cousin, why, I say good for her. It's better than dawdling about with that walking prayer book."

"This is not a harmless little flirtation."

"That's what I said. Now go to sleep."

"They want to be married."

"Don't be daft. Might as well talk of Willie or Nancy getting married."

"And when Dick comes to you in the morning is that what you are going to say?"

"If he comes to me in the morning, that is precisely what I shall say, in somewhat politer terms, and he'll be on his way to Bizarre and we'll forget all about it."

"And I will be left with a hysterical girl on my hands."

"Judy is never hysterical. Now, if it were Nancy . . ."

"That's just it. If we were talking of Nancy it would be different."

"When it's Nancy, we'll just have to check and make sure he isn't a centaur."

"Be serious."

"I am. Never known a girl as foolish about horses as she is. Pity she isn't Willie and the other way around. Willie's got no hands at all. Never trust a man who can't handle a horse."

"Are you saying that Willie isn't trustworthy?"

"He's my son and I love him, but there's something small and mean there."

"How can you talk that way?"

"When you have as many children as we do, Ann, you can afford to be realistic about them."

"Then be realistic about Judy. She isn't like Nancy, who'll fly in and out of love the way she flies in and out of her tempers. Judy won't forget so easily."

"For God's sake, she's only sixteen."

"That is precisely the point. At sixteen when you fall in love, you think your lover is the most perfect being on earth. You think that your whole life together will be a romantic dream and then, when it's too late . . . Oh, what's the use," she broke off. "You aren't paying any attention to me."

"On the contrary," her husband said slowly and propped himself up on his elbow to look at her. "I think you were about to say something very important and not about Judy."

"It's just that I want my children not to marry until they are old enough to know what they are doing. I don't want them to lead disappointed lives."

"As you have, Ann?"

"I did not say that."

"I think perhaps you did without knowing it. You were not much past your sixteenth birthday when we married. Have we truly rubbed along so badly?"

"Of course not. You know that's not what I meant. When we married I'd known you all my life. I loved you, but I wasn't dazzled by you. I knew what our life together would be like. The good things and most of the bad. We knew what we were doing. We could strike a bargain. I knew you liked a pretty face and that you always would and that sometimes I would have to turn a blind eye for my own peace. I didn't expect to be in the straw quite so often, but I expected to take pleasure and comfort in our children, and I have, even those we lost."

"If I hear what you are saying, the only reason you have for not being disappointed in me is that you never expected much to begin with."

"Please, Tom, don't pretend to hurt feelings you don't have. I didn't expect perfection in you. Did you in me?"

"To tell you the truth I always found your nose a shade too long and the rest of you a bit skinny."

His wife smiled. "The years have taken care of one of my flaws at least. But don't you see . . . Right now Judy and Dick think that their love for each other is the only important thing in the world. They haven't had a chance to discover that there are other things in life and other people, or to find the rough spots in each other's character. If they marry too young, it will be too late when they do find out."

"All right, all right, your point is taken. Assuming that you are right, though I hope you're not, what do you want me to say to them?"

"Give them permission to write to each other, but no more visits for at least six months. All we are asking for is a little time to consider."

"I think that what young Dick will find waiting for him at

Bizarre will leave him little enough time for writing, let alone coming to call."

"Promise me you'll stick to that. You won't let Judy talk you around."

"Haven't I said so? Do you really think I'm as soft as all that?"

"No, but you do give in sometimes just so they will stop plaguing you."

"And is that one of the things you've found disappointing?"

"Sometimes I think so. But on the whole I'd rather have you as too fond a parent than too strict. I grew up with one tyrant. I wasn't looking for another."

"Ann Cary, your father would have your head for calling him a tyrant. To hear him tell it, he's spent his life in fighting tyranny."

"Only outside Ampthill. Inside it was quite another thing."

"Until I came riding to your rescue, the parfait gentil knight."

"Well, nearly parfait."

"It's a most curious thing," Colonel Tom said. "As something of mine gets longer, that nose of yours gets shorter to my eye."

"Get away with you, you're a lecherous old man."

"Old man? Old man indeed. Does this belong to an old man?"

"Let me put out the candle."

"Leave it. I like to see you."

"I'm a fat old woman."

"Hush yourself. You're my beautiful Ann, whom I love more each year though she isn't above fishing for compliments, and sometimes talks too much ... like now ... and now. ..."

* * * * * * * * * *

Weddings

* * * * * * * * * *

* I * * * * * * * * *

Tuckahoe seethed with the frustrations of young lovers the next day. Right after breakfast Dick was closeted with Colonel Randolph while Judy hung about the closed door straining to hear. Then both Dick and Judy were alone with Ann Randolph and the colonel in their bedroom for nearly an hour while Nancy lingered on the stair landing and relayed the occasional passage she could hear to the brothers and cousins in the hall below.

Judy came to the dinner table with her nose and eyes flaming red. She gave an occasional small hiccuping sob as if she might burst into more tears at any moment. She managed her goodbyes to Theo and Jack quite properly, but she followed Dick down the steps to the drive and clung to his horse's bridle, sobbing, until he gently disengaged her hands and gave her his handkerchief.

Nancy, who had begun the day as an avid partisan of romance and had found the conferences and sobs and tears all very like something out of a book or a play, thought this final display a bit more than she could tolerate. It was somehow much more affecting when you read it or saw it on a stage. This was, when you thought about it, just Judy making a fool of herself in front of the servants. Curiosity overcame her distaste, however, and she followed her sister up the stairs when the Randolph cousins had finally ridden off.

Judy smoothed out the creases in Dick's handkerchief and tucked it inside her bodice. "I shall wear it always, in memory, next to my heart."

"As little as you have in front, it'll make you lopsided. Maybe he'll give you another one the next time he comes." It was the sort of remark accompanied by a sidelong glance in the mirror at her own more impressive endowment that would normally have enraged Judy. This time it just inspired fresh floods of tears.

"He won't be coming back. Not for six months. Mama made him promise. Nancy, I shall die if I don't see him for six months."

"I shouldn't think you would, you know. After all you lived for more than fifteen years without even knowing he existed."

"She's already writing a letter to him," Nancy told Willie later. "She says she's going to write a bit everyday and then if anyone comes through on the way to Cumberland County she'll have it all ready to send on to him."

"I expect in six months time he'll have forgotten all about her," Willie said. "Can't think what he sees in her anyway. Speaking of that, has anybody seen old Leslie?"

"He didn't come down for dinner," John said. "I suppose he's in his room praying."

"For the Appomattox to rise in flood . . ." Willie said.

"Just as Dick Randolph reaches the ford," Nancy continued.

Two weeks later Mr. Leslie sadly boarded a ship back to Edinburgh after one last fruitless talk with Judith. Tom and Willie went back to Williamsburg to the college and took John with them. Something would be found for him to do. Colonel Randolph traveled with them and made the trip an excuse to speak to St. George Tucker about his stepson.

"Tucker can't sing Dick's praises too highly," Colonel Randolph said to his wife when he returned home. "But he put paid to any notion that Dick might forget about Judy while they were separated. Among other good qualities he says he's no trifler. Tucker says he'll do what he can for them in a financial way, but I don't suppose that will be much. He's not a rich man, and Dick is far from being his only responsibility."

The prospect of becoming the wife of a relatively poor man did not bother Judy at all. She was quite certain that it was only a temporary state, and she read aloud to whoever would listen the parts of Dick's letters that spoke of his plans for the future of his plantation. Very boring indeed, Nancy thought them, but to her irritation those were the only bits that her sister would read aloud. Judy read the interesting parts silently, smiling. Dick never forgot to ask Judith to remember him kindly to her sisters. Nancy was not at all pleased to be lumped in with Hattie and the baby, but she would not say so because Judy was already far too satisfied with herself.

To Nancy's surprise she had a letter herself that October from Theo in New York. Her mother opened and read it before she gave it to her. "You may answer it, of course, but you are far too young to enter into a regular correspondence with any young man except your brothers."

"I don't know why he wants to write to me. He was very high-nosed when he was here and didn't say over three words to me. Spent most of the time with Willie."

Theo wrote that Columbia College was if anything even more boring than the college in New Jersey had been, but there were more opportunities for entertainment in New York. He asked Nancy to speak to her sister about a source of great unhappiness for him. His brother Richard had not written to him once since he had come up north though Jack had had several letters. "It's always the way with me. No one gives me any of the attention that I deserve as a measure of family or brotherly feeling. They never speak to me except to chastise."

"Nonsense," Judy said. "I dare say Dick writes to Jack meaning the letters for both of them. Theo just likes feeling sorry for himself and put upon. You saw how he was when they were here, positively boasting about how wicked his family thought him. I'll tell Dick because I believe in peace in the family, but I shall tell him that I don't take Theo's complaints seriously and neither should you."

"I never in my life heard of a Randolph family with peace in it," Nancy said.

"It will be different at Bizarre."

At first Nancy thought that she might not reply to Theo's letter at all. Writing letters was only fractionally more interesting than the lessons that had blessedly stopped with Mr. Leslie's departure. But there was something so irritating about Judy with Dick's letters, the sighs, the tears, the special lacquered box they were kept in, even the ribbon that bound them all together much creased from being constantly tied and retied. It wasn't that she was at all envious of her sister, Nancy told herself, but it would do no harm to demonstrate that it was possible for a young lady to have a correspondence with a gentleman without all that fuss.

So began a regular exchange, not of love letters—there was no hint of that—and in any case all of them went through her mother's hands before they were either delivered to Nancy or sent on to New York. There were only a few of them, and if they grew progressively slightly more personal in tone, Mrs. Randolph lacked the energy to worry about it. She was keeping more and more to her bed these days. She only rarely came down the stairs before dinnertime and sometimes not even then.

In February the six months of separation were over, and on the very day after Richard Randolph came back to Tuckahoe. He brought with him all the accounts and records from Bizarre, and immediately after a tearful and disappointingly public reunion with Judy he insisted that she leave him alone with her father to go over them.

"If he knew how much Papa hates to look at his own accounts, he might think twice about making him go over Bizarre's," Nancy said to her sister.

"That shows your ignorance in these matters. Dick is doing what any serious young man should do."

Nevertheless, her father seemed to Nancy distinctly out of sorts when he and Richard came to the dinner table. Looking at figures always fouled his mood. He was made even more dejected by the news that his wife did not feel well enough to come down but hoped that Dick would wait upon her later. Nancy would have thought it prudent to lead the conversation to something that would cheer her father up, but Judith was far too single-minded. "Papa, weren't you pleased with how well Dick is doing at Bizarre?"

"Yes, of course. Splendid, splendid."

"And you'll tell Mama so, so she'll know she needn't worry?"

"I'll tell her, certainly, but money is not what concerns her. You must know that no daughter of mine would ever want for anything. Your mother, and myself too naturally, we both feel that you are still much too young to be thinking of marriage."

"I'll be sixteen in a month."

"Sixteen in a month does not appear to be any great age to either your mother or to me. In any event we will not discuss it now."

"If not now, when? We agreed not to see each other for six months, and the time is over and we still feel the same way."

"For Christ's own sake, girl, let me have my dinner in peace."

Judith quieted temporarily, but after dinner she insisted that the lovers were entitled to a hearing. All pretense that the decision would be made by her father was abandoned. They all knew that Mrs. Randolph's would be the decisive voice. Nancy and her father both reminded Judith of Dr. Harvie's instruction that their mother not be disturbed or upset.

"He didn't mean in something important like this," Judy

protested. "He meant household matters. She'll worry more if I'm unhappy. And besides, she said that she wanted to see Dick."

"For an exchange of courtesies, not a great whopping family quarrel," her father said.

"It needn't come to that. It won't come to that."

"It will, you know," Nancy said. "It's bound to."

After a long discussion at her mother's bedside, a compromise was reached that Dick persuaded Judith to accept. They could consider themselves engaged but no one outside the family was to know of it, and they must wait a further year before they married. In agreeing to the delay, Judy won the right to have visits from Dick as often as he could get away.

"Although that won't be near often enough," she told Nancy tearfully that night. "I don't think I can bear it."

"I just hope you didn't make Mama sicker with your selfish carrying-on."

*   **2**   *

That February was the wettest, dreariest that Nancy could remember. Most mornings it seemed to rain too hard for her to ride with her father, and indoors there was no one to talk to but Judith, who sat surrounded by lists and hand-hemmed linens. She started to work on embroidering a petticoat for Judy's trousseau, but her fingers were too cold and baby Jenny got into her embroidery silks and her mother wasn't well enough to help her with the pattern.

Her mother never left her room now and seldom rose from bed. On a morning in March when Nancy and her father finally coaxed her into a chair by the window so that she could see how the garden was beginning to green up, Nancy knelt to put slippers on her feet and drew in her breath in shock. Her mother's feet and ankles were swollen to twice their size, the skin shiny as if about to burst.

"Just tuck a shawl around them, Nancy. Your father used

to say I had the prettiest turn of an ankle in all Virginia, but not any more. Old and dropsical."

"You're not old."

"Perhaps not. Dr. Harvie says that it's just that my heart is tired and needs to rest. It's funny, you hear of hearts being broken, but I never knew anyone to die of it. But mine's not broken, just tired." She turned her head as her husband hurriedly left the room. "Poor dear man, it's so hard for him. Are you looking after Jenny for me? I'm so afraid your father will just let her grow up wild and forget about her lessons."

"Mama, Jenny won't be ready for her lessons for ages. You'll be feeling stronger then and—"

"But if I'm not," her mother interrupted, "you'll watch over her."

"Of course I will."

"And your father too. You must keep him from being lonely. And Aggie, you must be especially kind to Aggie . . ."

"Mama, you're frightening me."

Ann Cary Randolph died early one morning in the middle of March. Her husband sent messengers to his sons in Williamsburg and to Molly's and Elizabeth's husbands and then shut himself up in his study with a brandy bottle. "We must pray to God to give us comfort," Judy said.

"What good will that do?" Nancy burst out. "I prayed and prayed to make her well and look what happened."

Without her the house seemed to have no center. Her husband's grief made him indifferent to nearly everything else, and, when Judy told him that she wished to marry Dick at the turn of the year even though the house would not be out of mourning, he gave his consent almost absent-mindedly.

"You really should be sharing the responsibility of directing the servants and running the house. When I've gone to Bizarre you'll have it all to do on your own."

"All the more reason not be bothered with it now."

The servants were universally unhappy under Judy's direction. It seemed clear to Nancy that they knew more about running the house than either of the girls did, and it would have been better just to let them have their way. Besides, quarreling with servants was undignified and, if truth were told, a waste of time. They would do just as they had always done anyway.

Judith did not agree. She saw her role at Tuckahoe as a rehearsal for being mistress of Bizarre and spent nearly every moment of the day doing what she described as "seeing to the household economy" and the servants called prying and poking about. Hattie had entered the first throes of twelve-year-old horse fever. Jenny was, after all, no matter how enchanting, only a baby, and Aggie, though sympathetic, was only a servant. Her father seemed to have entered into an alliance with a brandy bottle that nothing would pull him out of. Nancy was left all alone. She even welcomed the visits of Cousin Archie. He was a bore of bores and he had only just outgrown his spots, but he was at least a comfortable and friendly face.

"What I like about you, Nancy, is that you're the only girl I can really talk to. You aren't silly and you don't fuss me the way most of them do."

"Thank you, Archie."

"I mean I can talk to you just like you were Willie or Tom. I don't know why it is with most girls I can't think of anything to say and when I do it comes out all wrong, if you know what I mean. It's like you weren't a girl at all, only of course you are. There, you see? It always comes out wrong."

In April even the doubtful pleasure of Archie's company was denied her. Along with half the male population of Virginia, including her father and her brothers, he made the journey to New York to see General Washington inaugurated as President and to join the celebration of the new government.

"I do think it's unfair," Nancy said to Judy. "I never get to go anywhere."

"What would be the point of your going? You don't care anything at all about politicking."

"Neither do John or Willie. John's too stupid and Willie doesn't care about anything unless there's money in it. But they get to go just because they're boys."

"It will only be a lot of speeches. Just like having Grandfather Cary back again."

"And bands and parades and dances and fireworks . . ."

"You'd be too young to go to the balls anyway, even if you weren't in mourning."

"But I could hear the music and watch the carriages come and go and see the ladies' jewels and laces. It would be exciting."

"There are things far more important for a happy and contented life than excitement."

"I'm sure you're right. You always are. But I certainly hope I have a chance for a little excitement before I die."

Her brothers brought her a painted fan from New York that showed George Washington standing on a puffy white cloud while cherubs circled him, one of them blowing a little golden horn, the other carrying a laurel wreath. The General looked uncomfortable. They also brought a letter from Theo.

It was another litany of complaints, including the old one that Richard did not care for him as a brother should, that he had even written to Colonel Tom and young Tom when they were in New York as well as to Jack, and still Richard ignored him. At the very end of the letter was an afterthought. "I was sorry to learn of your mother's passing. My mother has been ill too or she would never let the others treat me so badly."

"And what does Theo have to say this time?" Judith asked.

"It's just a letter of condolence."

"Really? How unlike him. Dick says Theo never thinks of anyone but himself."

"Perhaps he wouldn't need to if anyone else ever gave him a thought."

"If you believe that whining twaddle of his, you're a bigger fool than I take you for."

Privately Nancy agreed, but there was a certain satisfaction to be had in Hattie's belief that Judy was not the only one with a lover's correspondence. It was the same desire to impress that led her to tie a ribbon round Theo's letters and keep them in a corner of her petticoat drawer. It was there that Aunt Polly Cary, now Polly Page since her marriage to Carter Page, found them and went puffed up with indignation to Colonel Randolph.

"Your Aunt Polly here tells me that you've been carrying on a secret correspondence with young Theodoric."

"There's nothing secret about it. You brought me one of the letters back from New York yourself. I don't see what concern it is of Polly's anyway and I'd like to know who gave her leave to go prowling and spying through my things."

"If it wasn't a secret why were they hidden away from me?" Polly asked.

"There's a deal of difference between keeping something secret and keeping something secret from you, Polly."

"That's just the sort of impertinence I'd expect from you. I'm only trying to do what my poor dear sister would have wanted me to do. To look after her girls as if they were my own, and look at the thanks I get for it. Do you think I like leaving my own home and my dear husband to come running to Tuckahoe? Nothing would bring me except the strong call of duty."

"I am sure we are all very grateful to you, Polly, but I don't think you need worry about this. Nancy's a good sensible girl . . ."

"Who's only just turned fourteen," Polly put in.

"Is that all you are?" Colonel Randolph looked at his daughter. "Thought you were older. Certainly look older. Doesn't she, Polly? And she has such a look of your sister about her. I expect that's why you are so particularly anxious about her."

Polly agreed and put her handkerchief to her eyes. Colonel Randolph patted her knee comfortingly with one hand and waved his daughter out of the room with the other. Later in the day when she was alone with him, however, her father passed on a warning. "You're right about your aunt being a damned nuisance and a busybody, but nevertheless she does live on closer terms with the Tucker family than we do and the word she has about Theo is not at all promising. So it might be better if you were to begin to discourage the correspondence."

"It makes no difference to me," Nancy said with a shrug. "His letters are really not very interesting at all, filled with nothing but complaining. I just don't like Polly telling me what to do, when Mama said it was all right for me to answer Theo. After all when Judy marries Dick, he'll be close family."

"Yes, well, I suppose . . . I trust you to do whatever you think best, but don't make a fuss about it with Polly. Can't stand these women's slanging matches."

* 3 *

The year that Judy and Dick had promised to wait was not yet over and the household of Tuckahoe was still in mourning for its mistress, but Judy had swept aside all her father's weak-spirited objections and planned her wedding for New Year's Day, 1790.

There would be no bride's party, only a family wedding breakfast. Richard's two brothers came down from New York and Judy's brothers from Williamsburg. The house seemed nearly full again. Half a dozen young men seemed like a troop of cavalry in the house, although you could fit twice as many girls softly giggling into one large bedroom and never know they were there in the rest of the house.

Nancy was a little shy about seeing Theo again. Unaccountably so, he was after all only a cousin, and if he found her sympathetic and chose to write her often, surely that was nothing to make their relationship at all strained. Both Jack and Theo were rail-thin. Theo looked as if weight had been burned away from him, leaving the hawk bone of his nose to jut out between the deep-set eyes. He looked far older than his eighteen years, and to Nancy he carried an air of romantic mystery. Jack's thinness was of a different nature. It was as if he had been constructed from bones much longer and more slender than other men's. His fingers when he took Nancy's hand in greeting were half again as long as hers. His face was still innocent of any trace of beard; his voice was still the clear sweet soprano of a young boy, but even at seventeen the power of his personality and convictions made one forget his strangeness after the initial shock. Twenty years later visitors to the Congress in Washington would wonder who the young boy tapping his riding crop against his boots could possibly be and, when he rose to speak, would be even more astonished as the treble voice came up to them and they realized that this was not a boy but Randolph of Virginia, the leader of his party and its most eloquent spokesman.

But at Tuckahoe in the last week of the first year of the newly constituted United States he was far from contemplating a career in its government. "You mark my words, Colonel. It will turn out to be the greatest mistake the men of Virginia have ever made. There's a rot there, clearly to be seen if you'll only look. It may not be the wish of the President himself. I don't pretend to know what he thinks any more than any other man, but the men around him are bent on establishing a court. They're vain men and ambitious and they long for titles and ceremony and privilege. In ten years' time we'll have to fight the Revolution all over again and this time against our own neighbors, and I shudder to think of the consequences. You have only to look at the fan your daughter is carrying. Cherubs crowning him with laurel wreaths. That was the whole spirit of the inauguration and it's been that way since. Do you know there are New York merchants who've put up placards saying 'By appointment to the President' with the Washington crest? If that isn't rampant monarchy, I don't know what is."

"Well now, Jack," Colonel Randolph put down his glass. "I suppose I'd be more likely to call it shrewd on the part of the shopkeepers and I wouldn't take my political warnings from a girl's gimcrackery fan."

"But that's where you're wrong, sir. Politics comes from opinion, and it's things like that of which popular opinion is made. You accustom the people to the idea of a court and a monarchy . . ."

"And I think you see conspiracy where none exists. I've known the General for a great many years and I can assure you that he has no interest in making himself king of the Americas. As for the men around him, I would remind you that one of them is our cousin Tom and he's as hot a Republican as you are."

Richard intervened with a warning look at his brother. "I think, sir, that you must forgive Jack. He didn't mean to offend you."

"And he didn't, not at all. But I would point out that General Washington has very little interest in hereditary honors. He has no child, nor likely to have one."

Jack flushed crimson and looked down at his plate. There was an awkward silence at the table that Nancy broke. "If anyone were to ask me . . ."

"Which they won't," Willie interrupted.

"If they were to ask me, I don't see what would be wrong with a court as long as it was American lords and ladies and duchesses. I thought it was only the English ones that the war was over."

"I think," Theo said, "that Nancy even rather fancies the notion."

"Why not? Papa would be at least a duke and I'd be Lady Nancy."

"Lady Nancy sounds like a horse," said Willie.

"Or a boat," John offered.

"Lady Ann, then." Theo raised his glass in salute. "Gentlemen and ladies, I give you Lady Ann Randolph of Tuckahoe."

"As for me," Judith said, "I shall be quite content when I am plain Mrs. Randolph."

Oh Lord, Nancy thought. Was there ever anyone so damping to a conversation as Judith? Richard smiled and lifted his love's hand to his lips. Only Theo caught Nancy's eye and seemed to share her thought.

Later they walked alone for a while in the garden, Theo snapping off a few lingering leaves with a swing of a dead cane from a berry bush. "Your sister isn't much given to fanciful flights, is she?"

Nancy laughed. "It isn't so much that she isn't given to them, she doesn't recognize them. She won't even read a novel and never enjoys a play, because they're all just lies after all. And you can hardly ever joke with her or tease her. For an instance, if I were to say to you, 'Kneel, Theodoric, and give me your sword.' There, you see?" she said as Theo promptly knelt in the path before her and presented the cane to her. She tapped him on both shoulders and offered him her hand to kiss. "You may rise, Sir Theo. Now Judy would say first of all 'What are you talking about? What sword?' and then she would exclaim over the muddiness of the path and the likelihood that you have permanently stained your suit, and finally she would give you a little superior sort of history lesson on the subject of kings and queens and knighthood, and everyone would be sorry they had ever started."

"Poor Dick."

Nancy was conscience-stricken. "Oh no, I didn't mean it like that. Judy is ever so much more sweet-tempered since she fell in love with Dick, and she's good, she really is and she'll be a perfect wife to him."

"As he will be a model husband." They walked in silence for a moment contemplating the serenely uneventful future happiness of their brother and sister. "It does sound a dreary prospect, doesn't it?"

"Oh Theo, can't you just see it? Mr. and Mrs. Perfect and all their perfect little children." Nancy laughed. "At least it's not a fate that's likely to befall me. Or you either from all that I hear of you."

Theo stopped short and swung her around to face him. "Who's been talking to you? You mustn't believe them. They all lie about me, you know." He was suddenly so angry that she stepped back a pace.

"No one. Not really. My aunt only said that she thought it would be unwise for me to write you, but Polly would think it unwise for me to enter into correspondence with an archbishop."

"No one's said anything to you about me?"

"No. Except that when you were here before, Judy said that you seemed to take a positive pride in your wickedness."

"If it's all you are celebrated for, you can do no better than to take pride in it. Every family's entitled to one black sheep and in my family it's I."

"And at Tuckahoe, it's Nancy."

Theo looked at her measuringly. "No, I don't think so. You may not be quite as woolly a little lamb as you look, but you are nowhere near reaching the place I have. Your family may carp and criticize and sigh over you, mine despair of me. I don't believe you even know what that means. To see my stepfather whom I love, a man competent in every other sphere of life, look at me with such grief and say, 'I despair of you, Theodoric' and know that he means it and there's no way that I can help him. If I knew what was to be done about me, I'd do it."

"I do know what you mean, Theo. It is sometimes very hard to be good."

"You haven't the faintest understanding of what I mean."

"I am trying."

"It's not just failing to be or do good. It's being dragged by a team of runaways in the opposite direction. Sometimes the things that happen don't seem to have anything to do with me at all."

"If you want to know what I think, I don't think you're wicked at all. I think that you just hold yourself to too high a standard."

"Richard."

"Perhaps, although I dare say even Richard isn't quite the

nonpareil that everyone thinks. It seems to me that the only real sins are those of cruelty and I don't believe you could ever be guilty of that."

"If you do have that much faith in me, it's more than anyone else does."

"Of course I do. I'm your friend, Theo. I thought that was agreed between us."

For the rest of that week between Christmas and New Year's, Theo and Nancy were much in each other's company. She saw no sign of the much heralded wickedness of the middle Randolph boy. It was true that there weren't too many opportunities for vice at Tuckahoe as compared to New York or Philadelphia or even Williamsburg, but if he did indulge in the one available and had too much to drink it was after the ladies of the household had gone to bed and only an occasional melancholy air in the morning would have revealed it to a more suspicious eye than Nancy's.

Every day she liked him more and more. He was not so handsome as Richard or as clever as Jack, but he had a nice turn of complimentary phrase and the wit to follow any of her fancies. He was tall and dark and sat a horse nearly as well as her father. Her sympathies were touched by what she saw as the injustices done him by his family, but her feeling for him went no deeper than that.

She was more than a little annoyed, therefore, when Judith, on the last night that they would be together in the room they had shared for so long, stopped her packing to give her one last warning. "Richard and I both hope that you are not growing too attached to Theo. He is a very great worry to all his family and we don't want you to be touched by it."

"I think you're most unfair. You've never heard a thing against him except that he sometimes drinks too much and he's been here a whole week and I haven't seen him the worse for wine once and neither have you. As for his being an inattentive scholar ... If that were a crime there would be a very great many Randolphs to be punished."

"There are other things as well. Things I can't discuss with you."

"I suppose you think I don't know what that means. So he goes with low women. He's not the first young man to do that either."

"Nancy, it's a matter of degree. Richard says he's like a wild man sometimes. He disappears from his rooms in New York for days at a time until Jack is frantic with worry about him, and only comes back when his money is gone and the people he was with have thrown him out in the street."

"And Jack, of course, hurries to carry the tale home."

"He's told Richard of it, certainly. It's too great a responsibility for him to try and carry it alone."

"All right . . . I'll grant you that Theo doesn't always behave well. He would be the first to say so himself. But try and think what it must be like to feel that everyone you know and care about is looking at you with the eyes of a censor instead of with love."

"Richard loves his brother very much, but he isn't blind."

"It's a fine kind of love I must say that tries to warn off the first good friend Theo has had in years. What Theo needs is just to feel that there is one person in the whole world who loves him completely, who isn't always standing by waiting for him to make some kind of mistake. If he had that to hold on to he wouldn't be forever getting into scrapes."

"Oh no, Nancy." Judith was appalled.

Nancy shook her head in reassurance. "Don't worry, I don't plan to be the one to reform Theo. And in any case I don't want to waste our last night together talking about him."

"It won't be our last time together. I'll be coming home for visits just like Molly and Elizabeth do, and you can come to visit me whenever you like. Dick says that you and Hattie and the baby are already just as dear to him as his own little sisters."

"But it won't ever be the same again. It's funny, it seems that I'm almost always cross with you and yet I'm going to miss you quite dreadfully when you've gone away."

"And I'll miss you. I know you don't want me to but I'll worry about you too. I can't help myself."

"I know you can't."

"I do love you, Nancy. Best of all my family, and I'll remember you in my prayers every single night."

I'm sure you will, Nancy thought and looked at her sister with affectionate impatience. Even tomorrow night.

Judy and Dick left Tuckahoe in a carriage decorated with ribbon rosettes and greenery behind horses similarly bedecked. By custom the men of the household would ride escort for them as far as the crossroads. Nancy watched uneasily as Theo mounted his horse. There had been a great many toasts at the wedding breakfast.

"Do you think he's all right to ride?" she asked Jack.

Jack was unconcerned. "It's a good horse. It's carried him before when he was worse off than this." It took all the concentration Theo could muster to stay in the saddle. There was nothing left for a special goodbye or even a smile.

The servants under Cicero's direction were busy clearing up the hall when she went back in the house. The loneliest room there is must be after a party when the guests have gone, Nancy thought.

"Did all the servants get some of Miss Judith's bride cake?" she asked.

"They did indeed and drank her very good health in the claret cup and Mister Richard's of course, too."

"Are you sure? There seems to be a great deal of cake left."

"Miss Nancy, you surely didn't mean for the field people to have cake?" Cicero was shocked.

"Well yes, I did. I mean they needn't come into the house, but we could send some out to them."

"Field people never eat from the house," Cicero said firmly. "Have you thought about what you would like for supper?"

"I'm not hungry, Cicero. I'll just take some of the cake and a plate of biscuits in my room."

(82)

"Your father and brothers will be riding back and the kitchen needs to know."

Nancy stopped short at the foot of the stairs and felt the whole weight of Tuckahoe settle on her shoulders. "Oh dear," she said. "I mean, I don't know. They may have stopped at Cox's Tavern."

Cicero helped her. "We could spread a cold supper tonight and just keep the fire up to boil a kettle for tea."

"That sounds splendid. Will you tell them in the kitchen for me? And, Cicero, thank them all again for me. Everything this morning was perfect."

She'll do, Cicero thought.

She settled into her role as mistress of Tuckahoe far more easily than anyone would have thought possible. She had profited from watching her mother and Judy more than she knew, and she had the great good sense to let Cicero run the house just as he always had. She even, although with some trepidation, did the doctoring when the annual spring sickening hit the servants. She dosed them all liberally from the bottle marked "Stomach Mixture" in her mother's hand and hoped for the best.

If anything, there was too little to do. Tom was away at Monticello, where he and Martha Jefferson would live after their marriage. The younger boys were in Williamsburg. She had treated Hattie all her life as no more than an audience; it was difficult to make a real friend of her now. She was lonely and she was bored and the winter seemed to stretch into a spring it drowned with rain.

The letters from Theo that once had been no more than a useful way to titillate Hattie now began to take on an importance of their own. He wrote her often and the letters arrived in bunches of three or four. In one group might be a witty and sprightly letter describing some freakish thing he had seen in New York and along with it a single sheet of paper much crumpled and spotted with only a few words scrawled across it in an almost illegible hand. He wrote that he was ill, that he wanted to come home. He asked her to speak to her father to see if he could influence his stepfather. She was frightened by the very look of the notes that she thought of as the "other letters." She put them on her bedroom fire and forgot them as quickly as possible. There was no question about asking her father to help Theo. Not only was she sure that such a request would get a cold reception, but there was never a proper opportunity. Her father was making more and more trips to Richmond, and sometimes he stayed for two or three days at a time. She had quite looked forward to keeping her father's house for him. She had wanted to show him how much better she understood his needs and comforts than Judy had. But there was no joy in running a house if no one seemed to notice.

*   4   *

Colonel Randolph rode home to Tuckahoe late on a Tuesday morning, flushed from the journey and with an air of exuberance that Nancy had not seen for a year. He had brought gifts for all three of his daughters, a china-headed doll for Jenny that Nancy promptly confiscated for safekeeping, a gathered silk parasol for Hattie, and a velvet hat with one side swept up and held by a cockade for Nancy.

"It's called an Espagnole," her father said. "All the ladies in Richmond are wearing them. See, you let one curl fall down the low side and then you wrap all the rest someway round your head and it comes down under the cockade. Very dashing, just right for you. Try it on."

Nancy stroked the folded ribbon of the cockade with one finger. "I'll put it on after dinner when I have time to do my hair properly."

"You don't like it," her father said with disappointment.

Nancy threw her arms around him. "It's a beautiful hat and here's a kiss to thank you. I was just thinking what a proper fool I'll look wearing it out to the vegetable garden and back."

He took her arms from around his neck and held her hands in his as he looked at her, his face suddenly serious, his voice gentle. "Poor Nancy, things have been dull for you, haven't they?"

"Not dull, exactly."

"It wasn't right to make a little girl like you have to take all the responsibility for this great house and your little sisters."

"Don't say that," Nancy protested. "I'm not a little girl and I love taking care of you. I only wish you were home more, the way you used to be, so you could see for yourself how well I go on."

Her father shook his head. "Thoughtless of me, not to see that you and Hattie must have been as lonely and lost as I've been. But there—" he smiled broadly and swung her hands— "that's all past now. Everything will change. I've a bigger surprise for you than a Spanish hat."

Nancy glanced at the gift. "Why, of course," she said with delight. "It's a city hat. We're going on a visit to New York . . . or Philadelphia."

"No, and there's no use guessing. I'll tell you all about it after dinner."

"Papa, that is so exasperating. Tell me now."

"After dinner," he said firmly, "and tell Cicero to open a bottle of the claret. We'll celebrate."

"How can I celebrate when I don't know what it is?"

"You can celebrate having a glass of my best. That doesn't happen very often."

"You bought a horse . . . two horses . . . two horses and carriage."

"Not till I've had my dinner. Have Cicero give me ten minutes, time for a wash and a brush." He started up the stairs and looked back. "Let Jenny come to the table. I want all three of my girls there."

"Jenny's too little to come to table yet."

"Have Cicero put her on some books and drape a cloth

around her. If she spills, she spills," he laughed, "nothing matters today." He went whistling up the stairs.

Jenny perched on two volumes of *The Spectator* and watched with interest as Cicero added a few drops of wine to her glass. "Pink water," she chuckled and slowly poured it on the cloth.

"Oh Jenny, shame," Nancy said reproachfully. "Papa, I told you."

"Never mind, there wasn't enough wine to stain. Sit down, Nancy, and don't fuss yourself. Let one of the girls take care of it." He leaned over and gave his youngest daughter a loud smacking kiss. "Jenny knows what to do with watered wine, doesn't she? She's her Papa's girl, right enough."

There was silence as their father addressed himself to the carving of the ham. "Now that," he said with satisfaction as he watched the delicate pink curl away from his knife, "that is a ham. You girls know why a Tuckahoe ham is the best in Virginia? Hattie? Nancy?" Both girls nodded. Their father's theory was one they had heard many times, but they knew they were about to hear it again.

"Freedom, that's what it is. Freedom. Put a hog in a pen and he just gets fat. But let him run free, and he's solid meat ... keeps the snakes down too, that brush by the river would be crawling if the pigs didn't eat them. Freedom makes good hams, good children, and a good country. That's my motto and I'll stand by it. Your Aunt Polly fears you girls are running wild here without your mother or—" he hesitated—"I told her no."

"Oh no," both girls groaned. "You haven't invited her to visit?"

"Is that the surprise?" Hattie said.

"Papa, how could you?" Nancy said.

"How could I indeed. You must be daft. Since when has a visit from your Aunt Polly been a cause for a celebration? Cicero, fill Miss Nancy's glass again."

"No thank you, Papa. It will just make me sleepy."

"Then you'll take a little nap. Nothing wrong with that. Like a little nap after dinner myself."

"But not today," Nancy objected. "You promised to tell after dinner."

"Quite right, so I did. Is there a fire in the library?"

"It's been laid," Nancy replied.

Her father told Cicero to send a boy to touch a light to it and to put the rest of the bottle on a tray with two glasses, in case Miss Nancy should change her mind, and put it by the fire.

"What's the sweet?" he asked.

Nancy and Hattie exchanged glances. "I'm afraid it's just a boiled custard, Papa," Nancy said. "I didn't know you would be at home."

"Boiled custard?" he said incredulously. "Boiled custard? One of you sick or something?"

"No, Papa, we have it quite often where there are no gentlemen."

"Never knew anybody in good health eat that muck." He called Cicero back and asked that a piece of brandy cake be added to the tray with the wine. He crumpled the damask napkin on the table by his plate and came around to draw Nancy's chair out. "Hattie, you move round by the baby and help her with the custard. A couple of well-aimed spoonfuls of that stuff could make hell's own damage in here. Nancy, you come with me into the library before curiosity makes you burst your petticoat strings."

Hattie looked up in indignation. "You mean you're going to tell Nancy and not me? I don't call that fair."

"It isn't," her father agreed, "but it's the way it's going to be done. You'll get your turn."

"Nancy's only two years older than I am, and she thinks she's the queen of the world."

"This is a happy day for me, Hattie. Don't spoil it by being quarrelsome. And, Hattie—" he turned as he reached the door—"don't come listening at keyholes."

"I never."

"Of course you don't. No lady would, but just don't do it this time."

The fire in the library had caught and was blazing, but its warmth had penetrated only a few feet into the room.

"Cold as a witch's, uh, nose in here."

"We don't light this fire when you're away," Nancy apologized.

"Why not? I thought you liked to stay in here."

"I do. It's my favorite place in the house, but Cicero says having a fire all the time is bad for the books, so I just come in and take what I want and read in the sitting room or my bedroom."

"From now on tell Cicero to let me worry about the bindings and you have a fire in here whenever you feel like it. Damp does more harm than heat anyway."

Colonel Randolph sat down in the broad high-backed leather chair by the fire, loosened his waistcoat and poured himself a glass of wine from the tray table at his side. "Is my Nancy too old to share this chair with me?"

"I'll never be too old for that."

"And I'll remind you of that when you're a great pouterpigeoned lady with children of your own and much too dignified to sit on your papa's lap."

"That's years and years and years away."

"Not too many. You're not one that's going to hang on the branch very long."

Inside his circling arm, Nancy put her head down on her father's shoulder and closed her eyes. The warmth of the fire, the faintest of leathery smells, the crisp linen of his stock against her cheek, she was for the first time in months totally content. With a little click her father put his glass on the tray and looked down at her. "I believe you're falling asleep on me. You'll have to learn to handle a glass of claret better than that."

"I'm not sleepy, truly. I just had my eyes closed trying to make them match."

"Make what match?"

"Remember when I was little," Nancy said dreamily, "you'd take me up on Shakespeare, and I'd sit across you with my head on your chest and I could your heart going thump thump thump, and I used to think if I could make my heart match perfectly, then we could just go on riding forever, but I never could because the harder I tried the faster mine would go . . . so then I stopped trying but I'd keep my eyes closed and I could always tell when we were coming to a fence. I could feel it and hear it even before you leaned forward."

"I never in my life took Shakespeare at a fence with you on board," her father said indignantly. "Do you think I'm crazy?"

"A hedge, then, or a ditch."

"It would have to have been a very little ditch."

"We're coming to a fence now, aren't we, Papa?"

"What makes you say that?"

"Thumpity, thumpity, thump . . . I can hear it coming."

He wound one of her straw-colored curls around his finger. "Your hair smells just like your Mama's did. It was the strangest thing, even on the worst day of winter, your mother's hair smelled like sunshine, as if she stored it up."

"Is that why you named me for her?"

Her father laughed. "When we named you, you were bald as a hen's egg, but still—" he paused—"even then you did have a certain look about you that was like her. I see it more now that you're older. You have her eyes and her nose. Your mama always thought that I thought her nose was too long. I used to tease her about it, but I thought it perfect."

"Did you never tell her, about her nose and her hair?"

"Probably not, but she knew nevertheless."

"I think a lot about the things I would have said to her and the times I made her unhappy . . . when if I'd known that . . ." Nancy's voice broke.

Her father kissed the top of her head. "Poor little duck, you still miss her very much, don't you?"

"Papa, you just don't know," Nancy burst out. "Sometimes it seems as if there were a great empty hole in the house and that Hattie and Jenny and the servants and I were just drifting around about it. It's not just Mama. I miss Judy and Tom, sometimes I even miss Willie."

"Come on now, surely not Willie. You'll be telling me next that you miss Mr. Leslie."

"No, not Mr. Leslie. But I miss you, Papa. I miss you very much."

"I'm right here."

"Today you are and probably tomorrow, but lately . . ."

"Lately, I've been neglecting you," he finished for her.

"I didn't say that," Nancy protested.

"It's true nonetheless, but from now on, I promise you, everything will be different. Tom Randolph of Tuckahoe will be here where he belongs."

"No more Richmond trips?"

"No more." He beamed at her. "Darling girl, you may not be too big to sit on my knee, but you're far too big to bounce on it like that. I'll be lame for a week. Besides, you haven't heard the best of it." With the teasing air of a conjurer about to manufacture a bouquet from the air, he said, "Someone else will be here, too. Someone who already loves you very much."

Puzzled, Nancy frowned. "Who?"

"My wife, Nancy."

"Your what?"

"My wife—that's the surprise. I'm getting married. Tuckahoe will have a mistress again."

Somehow the conjurer's hand had lost its cunning. The wand had waved over the empty vase, but nothing bloomed. Instead of the cries of delight he had expected he looked at a face as blank as a stone.

When she spoke her voice was small and tight. "Tuckahoe has a mistress now. We don't need anyone else."

"We do, Nancy. I do."

Nancy blinked and shook her head. "Why? Haven't I kept things the way you wanted them? I know I made some mistakes at first . . ."

"Dear child, you've done beautifully, far beyond what anyone could have expected from you."

"Then why are you bringing some stranger in?"

"The Harvies are not strangers."

"The Harvies? Miss Harvie?" Nancy laughed with relief. "Oh, Papa, you're a worse tease than the boys. Miss Harvie is a hundred and ten and she has a mustache, just like her brother's. I can just see you married to her."

"It's Gabrielle Harvie I'm marrying," her father said. "Not her aunt."

In the silence of the room, a log burned through, scattering sparks. Nancy slipped from her father's knee and bent over the fire, brushing the embers back. When she stood up to face him again, she kept her hands clasped firmly in front of her, holding on.

"Gabrielle Harvie is your son Tom's age."

"I'm quite aware of the difference in our ages."

"Is she?"

"She could hardly not be. We've talked about it frankly and it is not a matter which bothers either of us."

"Why should anything bother her?" Nancy said angrily. "It's quite a step up for her from living over her father's surgery to coming here as your wife."

"Nancy, that is both unjust and unkind."

Nancy ignored the warning note in his voice. "It's also perfectly true, and you know it."

"That is insulting to me as well as to Gabrielle. You disappoint me."

"I disappoint you?" Nancy cried. "Just what did you expect? That I'd fall over in a fit of rapture because you think you can put a pushy slip of a girl in Mama's place? I think it's disgusting."

"I expected that you would be happy for me, and pleased

(91)

for yourself for that matter, to have a close friend and companion so near your own age."

"Did you really?" Nancy said scornfully. "If you thought I would be so damn well pleased, why have you never said one word about this before? All those lies about business in Richmond, when all the time you were sneaking off . . ."

Her father got up from his chair and came toward her, and for a moment the look on his face was frightening. "That's quite enough, Nancy. There is a limit to what I will allow even you to say."

"And just what do you think everyone else will be saying? Everyone in Virginia will talk about what a perfect fool you've made of yourself."

"Those I care about will be happy that I'm not to spend the rest of my life alone."

"You wouldn't be alone," Nancy wailed. "You'd have me. I would never never leave you."

Her father sighed. "Nancy, love, try to calm yourself. I can see I've made a mistake."

She seized on the word eagerly and threw her arms about him. "It's not too late to undo it," she said quickly. "You can go to Dr. Harvie. It's not been public yet. You can tell Dr. Harvie, tell him that you've thought it over and that Gabrielle is too young to be tied to an old man. That it would be unfair to her. He couldn't be offended by that."

Gently he disengaged her. "You misunderstand me. I only meant that I was wrong to tell you so suddenly. I should have given you more time to get used to the idea. Taken you with me to Richmond to visit so that you would get to know her better."

Nancy stood stiffly where he had placed her. "I already know her quite well enough, thank you."

"You can't know her at all or you wouldn't say the things you have."

"It's no more than anyone else would tell you if they were honest."

"Now there you are mistaken completely. I rode out to visit Molly and Elizabeth, and they are both very well pleased for me."

"It doesn't matter to them what you do. They haven't lived here for years, they are hardly even part of the family."

"They are my daughters just as much as you are, and at the moment they seem to me to be far more loving ones."

Nancy stonily refused to acknowledge the rebuke. "What about the boys?"

"Willie likes Gabrielle very much and has sent a letter of congratulations."

"If he thinks she's such a marvel, why doesn't he marry her? They'd make a proper couple."

"Nancy, stop a moment, you are saying things you'll regret later."

"Not half as long as you'll regret what you're bent on doing," and then at last came the tears. "Papa, how could you?" she sobbed. "I thought you loved me."

"For God's sake, Nancy, I do love you ... the one has nothing to do with the other, and if you'd stop this hysterical ranting you'd see that it doesn't."

"I am not hysterical," she said indignantly.

"You are. If I thought for a moment you were not your conduct would be unforgivable."

She drew herself up icily. "I wouldn't dream of begging your forgiveness for telling you the simple truth."

Her father's patience was finally at an end. "No more, Nancy, no more. I will not let the mean-spirited jealousy of a little girl ruin what was to be a happy day for us all."

"I am not hysterical or mean-spirited or jealous, and some day you'll be sorry that you wouldn't listen to me about this dreadful mistake you're determined to make."

"The only mistake I've made," he shouted, "is to let you get so above yourself that you think I will tolerate this sort of talk from you." Nancy stood and looked at him coolly, her eyes dry, then she brushed her palms down, smoothing her overskirt, and turned toward the door. "Where do you think you're going?"

"To my room, with your permission, of course." She bowed her head in a parody of meekness.

"Not before you hear me out. Now listen carefully. In two weeks' time I am going to marry Gabrielle Harvie. Nothing is going to change that. In three weeks I will be bringing her back to this house, where I expect her to be met with every courtesy due my wife."

"I have never been discourteous to a guest or—" she paused—"a hostess."

"Gabrielle will not be a guest in this house."

"I know, Papa," Nancy smiled, "but from now on, I will be."

Outside the door to the library she found Hattie, as she had expected, her eyes wide with excitement. From the bench in the hall she grabbed up her father's gift to her and thrust it into her startled sister's hands. "Here, tell him I gave you his damned Spanish hat. You can wear it to the wedding, because I'm not going."

On the night before his marriage to Gabrielle, Nancy's father came to her room to try once more to persuade her to come into Richmond with him in the morning. "I think Gabrielle will find it very strange when Hattie is there and you choose not to come."

Nancy didn't give a dud penny for what Gabrielle might think. "If it worries you, just tell her that Jenny was unwell and I thought it best to stay with her."

"And what excuse shall I make to myself? I'll miss my favorite daughter very much."

"It's a bit late to be thinking of that, isn't it?"

Colonel Randolph got up and went to the door. "Gabrielle and I will be back here to our home in a week's time. I hope that we will find you with a warmer heart."

* 5 *

Cicero had posted the fastest boy on the place at the turn into the drive, so that by the time the carriage stopped at the front door the welcoming committee was in place. Hattie and Jenny stood on the steps clutching bouquets of flowers, Cicero behind them, ready to swing the door open with a flourish.

"Welcome to Tuckahoe, Mrs. Randolph," he said. "Welcome home, Colonel Tom."

Nancy watched from the top of the stairs as Cicero presented each of the house servants to their new mistress, who repeated their names with a smile as each of them bobbed his head in greeting. Quite a triumphal procession, Nancy thought, and she struts like a little pony with her damned flowers. Not until the line of servants had broken up under Cicero's orders and Nancy could see her father's eye casting about for her did she come slowly down the stairs. Her father started toward her eagerly, but she held him off with a low curtsy—"Father—" and an even deeper one to Gabrielle. "Mrs. Randolph."

Her father stood stock-still, but Gabrielle moved swiftly across to her. "Please, dear Nancy, there must be no formality between us. I am still Gabrielle to you, just as always."

"As you wish, madam." She turned to her father. "I have had a fire lit in your bedroom. It should be quite comfortable if your wife would like to rest from the journey. I am sure she must have found it fatiguing."

Her father shot her a look that should have made her tremble, but she returned it coolly. Gabrielle denied that she was at all tired, and then, looking at her husband and his daughter, flushed and said hurriedly that she would rather like to go up and supervise the unpacking of her things. Hattie took Jenny by the hand and announced that they would come and watch. Cupboard love, thought Nancy. They think she has gifts tucked away for them. Two men were already humping a trunk up the stairs, and behind them a line formed carrying dress boxes and hat boxes, and to Nancy's displeasure even Aggie joined them swinging a reticule in one hand.

"Cicero," Colonel Randolph ordered, "bring me a toddy in the library. And, Nancy, you come with me."

"Now then," he said as he closed the library door behind them, "I should have Cicero bring me a switch for you. I thought by now you'd be over your tantrums and ready to behave yourself. What sort of a greeting was that for Gabrielle? Do you think she has no feelings at all?"

"I treated your wife with perfect politeness."

"And perfect coldness."

"You can't expect me to pretend to feelings I don't have."

"And does that include any affection for me?"

"You know that's not so."

"Then your performance was very deceptive. I had a warmer greeting from the servants than I had from you."

"The servants are children." Nancy shrugged. "Anything new is an excitement for them."

"If you mean that you are not behaving like a child, you are very much mistaken . . . and like a badly spoiled one at that."

Nancy drew in her breath to reply, but a tap on the door announced Cicero with the toddy fixings, and as he bent over the tray she started toward the door. Her father stretched out his hand and caught her firmly by the sleeve and held her there while Cicero mixed his toddy, was complimented on his skill and bowed himself out.

"And where did you think you were going?"

"I thought I would go look in on your wife and make sure she has everything she needs and give her Mama's keys."

"The keys can wait. I'm not finished with you yet. In the first place you are not to call Gabrielle 'your wife' in that unpleasant tone."

"What should I call her? Stepmama? I can hardly think she'd want me to call her Mother."

"She asked you to call her Gabrielle, just as you always have."

"If you wish. I thought you might find it disrespectful of her position in this house."

"It's not a question of respect or position," her father exploded. "It's one of understanding and sympathy, not ceremony. This is a family, goddammit, not a court. And incidentally, Gabrielle has shown considerably more sympathy for you than you have earned. She most particularly reminded me that I must show you special consideration. She understands you might be uneasy with her at first."

"How extremely generous of her," Nancy murmured.

Her father sighed. "Nancy, try and understand. I'm not a man who was meant to live unmarried. I needed someone . . ." He held up his hand to stop her protest. "And the most loving of daughters is not the same thing. But you must know that my marrying could not possibly mean any less affection for you."

"But if it came to a choice between us?"

"That's what I am trying to tell you. It will never come to a choice unless you force it."

"Or Gabrielle does."

"She won't. Gabrielle knows you've always been my very special girl. She wants to be your friend and companion. She wants me to be happy and she knows I couldn't be if I quarreled with my Nancy." He put his glass down and cupped her face in his hands. "Come now, be my pretty Nancy and smile for your papa."

"Papa, I truly hate being angry with you. It makes my stomach hurt. But I tried so hard to help you after Mama died and Judy went away and you kept running off to Richmond and you didn't even care whether I was miserable or not, and I miss Mama so much."

"Poor little girl." He pushed her curls back from her face. "Of course you miss your mother. We all do. We always will, but . . ." He thought better of what he had been about to say and pulled his handkerchief from his sleeve. "Here take this."

"I'm not crying."

"Well, dry your eyes anyway. Come on, Nancy, you're still your papa's pet. Give us a proper welcome-home kiss and a hug and after dinner we'll ride out together to see how things have been coming on while I've been gone."

"Alone? Just the two of us?"

"Just the two of us."

* 6 *

Gabrielle Randolph settled easily into her new role at Tuckahoe in a few weeks. Her husband visibly doted on her, the younger children and the servants were captivated by her; only Nancy was obdurate.

"Nancy hates me," Gabrielle said to her husband as he sat watching her at her dressing table preparing for bed.

"You exaggerate. Bit jealous, perhaps. Put yourself in her place, if your father had brought home a beautiful young wife."

"I have. That's how I know she hates me."

Her husband frowned. "Has she been rude to you?"

"No, not at all. She treats me with perfect correctness."

"There you are, then. She's coming round. Nancy has tantrums but she doesn't bear grudges."

Gabrielle put her brush down and swung about on the bench so that she could look at her husband directly instead of in the mirror. "This tantrum, as you call it, has gone on for weeks now. I've tried very hard to be friends with her, but she won't have it. I give her a present and she thanks me very sweetly and puts it away and never wears it. Surely you've noticed that she is never down in the hall with us."

"Try to be patient a little longer, Gabby. She's a warmhearted girl. She'll come around."

"She doesn't give me a chance to show her that I mean her no harm. Except for meals she's shut up in her room with Aggie all day . . . and that's another thing," she went on. "It sets a bad example for the other servants for Aggie to be made such a pet of, besides spoiling her for any other work."

To her surprise her husband looked away from her and spoke uneasily. "As to Aggie, Gabrielle, I'd tread very cautiously there." He cleared his throat. "The girl does belong to Nancy and stands in a certain, I don't know quite how to put it, stands in a rather particular relationship with her."

Nothing Gabrielle could do was right in Nancy's eyes. If she smiled and courted her, Nancy thought it hypocrisy. If she tried to ignore her thorny stepdaughter, Nancy took it as an attempt to drive her away from Tuckahoe with coldness. In July with John and Willie at home, Dick and Judy came to visit bringing Theo with them, and Gabrielle had the first flicker of hope that there might be a happy solution for the problem not too far away.

She gave a dancing party in the hall and watched with pleasure the way Archie Randolph's eyes followed Nancy all through the sets even when he wasn't partnering her. He was an eminently suitable young man and quite handsome now that he was not so spotty; and even though he was far from being the cleverest man in Virginia his obvious infatuation with Nancy could not help but make him attractive company for her.

"Archie dear," Gabrielle said. "It's warm in here and poor Nancy is looking quite flushed. Why don't you take her for a little walk in the garden?"

"But she's dancing now, Mrs. Randolph. Nancy won't ever stop as long as the music's playing."

When the music stopped Nancy had vanished, gone into the garden with her cousin Theo. Archie consoled himself with another glass of punch and a very pleasant thought. It was good to know that Nancy's stepmama favored him. Very encouraging.

The morning after the dancing party when the gentlemen had ridden out for the day, Nancy and Judy had time to be alone together. Nancy curled up on the bed and watched as Judy sewed back some lace that had come adrift from one of Dick's shirts. She laughed at her sister giving the linen the same loving little pats that she was in the habit of giving its wearer.

"There's no need to ask if you're happy. You bounce around the house hugging and kissing people as if you were Jenny's age."

"It's strange. Loving Dick and being married to him makes me love everybody twice as much too. I never knew it would be that way."

"I don't think it is, usually," Nancy said.

"It's as if I were a completely different new person. Back there was the old Judith who was so serious and sometimes so cross, and over here is Judy who laughs all the time, even when there isn't anything at all amusing. Nancy, darling Nancy, you must fall in love immediately. You can't think what you're missing."

"Who with? Since you've already skimmed off the cream."

Judy shrugged. "Anybody. There are dozens of young men about if you look. Fall in love with Archie, why not? You've always liked Archie, haven't you?"

Nancy giggled. "I like my brothers too, at least some of them, but can you imagine me running around the house hugging Gabrielle because of Archie Randolph?"

"Isn't there anyone you fancy, even a little?"

"Afraid not. I might marry Archie in a year or two, but I'm not likely to fall in love with him."

"Oh, no, dear Nancy." Judy was suddenly grave. She sat down beside her sister on the bed and took her hands. "You must never think of marrying someone that you have no feeling for. Mama would tell you if she were still here. There are some things in marriage that would be very uncomfortable if you didn't love . . ."

"You mean in bed," Nancy interrupted. "You don't have to talk around it with me. It always seemed to me that you could just shut your eyes and think of something else. Besides, mares don't seem to mind it much and sometimes they never even saw him before, let alone falling in love."

"It's not the same thing at all."

"Isn't it?" Nancy replied. "You forget that I live with a newlywed pair. You haven't seen your father following that woman up the stairs with his thing making such a bulge in his trousers that he can hardly walk. It doesn't look too much different from Shakespeare to me."

"Nancy!" Judith gasped.

"Now that sounded like the old Judith. I've shocked you proper, haven't I?"

"You shouldn't even know about such things, and you especially shouldn't take notice of them."

"You can't very well help what you notice. I mean, things are just there or they aren't there, you can't pretend not to see them."

"That's as may be, but it's a very unbecoming way to talk about Papa, even to me."

"Unbecoming?" Nancy laughed. "As if anything I might say would be as unbecoming as what he's done."

"Nancy, don't. I can't bear to see you making yourself miserable over something that's done, that you can't do anything about."

"I suppose you think it's the match of the century."

"I'd be better pleased if Papa had chosen someone nearer to him in age, but he's content or would be if he wasn't worrying over you."

Nancy scoffed at the very notion of her father worrying over her when his head was filled with nothing but Gabrielle. When Judy offered as evidence of his concern for her happiness a suggestion he had made to her that she invite Nancy to visit at Bizarre, Nancy could only see it as part of a plot by Gabrielle to get her out of the house.

"Don't be foolish. Gabrielle had nothing to do with this. It was just Papa and I talking. He doesn't like to see you moping about when you were always so lively. And· it would give me and Dick so much pleasure to have you, and it would be good for Theo too, to have someone new to talk to. He is sometimes very low in his mind."

"Splendid," Nancy said. "It would be good for Theo, and company for you, and God knows it would be a blessing for Gabrielle. Isn't anyone thinking about me? If she once gets me out of this house, I'll never see my father again."

"Don't be ridiculous. This would just be for a visit. You could come home anytime you wanted to."

"And then be shipped off for a nice visit at Presqu'ile with Molly and David and then over to Elizabeth's and when I've run out of sisters maybe Aunt Polly would like to have me as long as I don't bring Aggie along."

"Nancy," Judy pleaded, "things aren't the way you think they are. Do it for me. I miss you."

"If you miss me so much, why didn't you think of inviting me without Papa and Gabrielle prompting you?"

"I told you Gabrielle had nothing to do with it."

"That shows how little you know. He doesn't do or say anything that she wouldn't like or hasn't told him to do. But sooner or later he'll come to his senses and then I want to be here with him. To take care of him the way I used to."

Judy looked at her sister and shook her head slowly. "Nancy, listen to me," she said in the slow, reasonable voice that she had always used when her patience was about to run out and which Nancy had always found particularly irritating. "Gabrielle is Papa's wife. Nothing is going to change that. If you are unhappy here with her, then come away with Dick and me."

"I wish you wouldn't speak to me in that babying way. I'm not a child, you know. I'm fifteen. When you were fifteen you were already planning your wedding to Dick."

"If you don't want to be treated like a child, then stop behaving like one."

"Thank you very much indeed," Nancy said stiffly and slipped off the bed and flounced over to the window.

Judy sighed. "Nancy, don't let us quarrel. Dick and I both love you and want you to be happy. Promise me you'll at least think about coming to Bizarre."

"Oh, I'll think about it, but I won't change my mind, and as for loving me . . . I thought Papa loved me and look what he did. You and Dick are so in love with each other right now that you think you love the whole world, but you forget that we didn't always rub together all that well, and things might soon be the same again if I came to you. The truth is nobody has really loved me since Mama died, except Jenny," she paused gloomily, "and she'll probably outgrow it."

To Nancy's annoyance, her sister laughed at her. "If you weren't so ridiculous, you'd be truly exasperating. Moaning around about nobody loving you. You sound just like poor Theo."

"The truth of the matter," Theo said, "is that there is nowhere in the whole world where I can be sure of a welcome."

"I know just how you feel," Nancy said. "Ever since Papa married Gabrielle I've been made to feel a stranger . . ."

"Ever since my mother died," Theo interrupted. "I mark that as the time when even my stepfather turned against me. I was supposed to go to Edinburgh three months ago and he says that if I was too ill to go to the lectures in New York, I am too ill to cross the ocean."

"I don't suppose you'd find Edinburgh much to your liking anyway. Not if our old tutor is anything to go on."

"That's not the point. He doesn't think I was really ill in New York. He believes the tales they told about why I left Columbia. So does Dick and besides Bizarre is his home now and not mine."

"Judy and Dick want me to come to Bizarre, but I . . ."

"My own place isn't habitable and there's no money to make it so. There won't be for years. Not until Dick gets Bizarre on its way. I blame my father . . . laying it down in his will that the money was to be spent on education. What's the good of an education for a gentleman if there isn't any money?"

"Well, at least you're a man and get away. Think what it's like to be a girl and forced to stay somewhere where they have no regard for your feelings at all."

"People expect too much, that's all. It's not my fault that I'm not as clever as Dick and Jack."

"The worst thing about Gabrielle is the way she has everyone else fooled."

"They keep on and on at me about wasting my youth. I never pretended to be a saint . . ."

If she had been asked what she and Theo found to talk about, Nancy would have said that they told each other their troubles. But there was something curiously unsatisfying about their conversations.

"Are you in love with Theo?" Hattie asked. "Willie says you are."

"What would Willie know about love?"

"Willie says you'd better stick to Cousin Archie, that Theo hasn't a penny and doesn't have the stuff to ever make any."

"It would be a very good thing if Willie could learn to mind his own business."

"He says that it would be a pity if you were to marry into a poor family as well as Judith because the more Papa is out of pocket for you two the less there'll be for the rest of us."

"I hope that Willie marries a squint-eyed heiress with a mustache and a terrible temper."

"I expect if she's rich enough he wouldn't care."

Theo went back to Bizarre with Dick and Judy and left Nancy quite uncertain about her feeling for him. She knew that she probably felt more sympathy for him than anyone else outside his immediate family, but she knew better than to believe him when he said that she was the only person in the world who cared anything at all about what happened to him. Still, it was flattering to feel that there was someone to whom you were very important, perhaps the most important, especially when your own family seemed determined to ignore your feelings.

They had not spoken of love, but she felt the same little shiver of pleasure when his hand brushed hers as she did when she let her mind drift to those low women in New York. She had lied when she told her sister that she thought half the things that were said about him were untrue. She thought it quite probable that he had behaved as badly as everyone seemed to think. If anything, it was that side of him that intrigued her, set him apart from the other men and boys she knew.

She was fifteen years old and as ignorant of the world as it was possible to be, though she thought herself very knowing. She did not think herself in love, but she thought Theodoric a most romantic name, much better than plain Theodore. She remembered that she had always thought dark men better-looking than fair ones.

The letters from Theo at Bizarre were wild and miserable. When she replied to them it seemed no great harm to make her professions of sympathy a bit warmer than they had been, and sometimes a particularly telling phrase that she had read in one of her books would find its way out of her pen almost without her willing it.

She was at an age when girls are known to fall into a romantic daydream that lasts for weeks over one glimpse of a stranger riding by. It is only a rehearsal for love, but it is easy to mistake for a performance, sometimes even by the actors.

Theo came again to Tuckahoe in the fall, alone and unannounced.

"I'm of two minds about letting you see him at all," Nancy's father said to her. "He looks half crazy and he's ridden his horse nearly into the ground. If I hadn't taken pity on the beast I'd have turned him away."

"Oh Papa, you couldn't."

"I not only could, I probably should have. But it's too late now. He's waiting in my study."

Theo stood with his back to the door, hunched over the fire in the grate. When he turned toward her and she took his hands in hers she could feel the tremors that shook him all through her own body. "You're freezing, Theo. Let me have Cicero mix you a toddy."

"No, no, nothing to drink. I mustn't have anything to drink. I have to tell him, don't I, that I've had nothing to drink? Fire will put me right."

"I don't understand. Did you come out without your cloak? It's quite a mild day really. How did you get so cold?"

"It's in my bones. First the cold and then the burning. A little taste of what's to come for me."

He was on his way to Williamsburg to appeal one more time to his stepfather. This time not to be sent back to any college or to Edinburgh but just to be allowed to read for the law under him. "He takes in half the young men in the state to read privately with him. He can't say that he doesn't have time for me."

"No, of course not. But isn't he like to think that it's just a fancy of yours? Are you sure it isn't? I never heard you say that you wanted to go for a lawyer before."

"Do you think I couldn't do it? You're going to be just like everyone else and think that I can't do anything properly."

"Theo dear, don't be angry with me. I think you can do anything that you really want to do. I'm just surprised, that's all."

"What else is there for me? It'll be ten years' time before Dick has the mortgages paid off on the people at Bizarre, and until he does there'll be nothing for me downriver. Even with the church the state it's in these days I don't think they'd welcome me into orders. I haven't the stomach to be a medical man. It's the law or nothing. If Father Tucker won't take me in . . . if I must go back to living the way I have . . . Nancy, I'm frightened. I won't survive it."

"Don't talk like that. You know that it's always a mistake to put all your hopes on one chance. If something doesn't go quite right . . ."

"It isn't just one chance, Nancy. It's the only one I have and the last one."

"Then I'm sure that your stepfather will see it your way. Because he does love you, Theo, I know he does, just the way Dick and Jack and Judy do, no matter what you think."

"He did once . . . and even if it weren't for that, there are the promises he made my mother. But even love gets out of patience. Still, when I come to him sober, and I will, I haven't had so much as a glass of wine with my dinner for a week, just to show that I could."

"I'm sure that will please him."

"And I come to him this time not just telling him that I have resolved to change my ways, but with a reason to be believed, to be taken seriously. It will make all the difference to him."

"Do you think he will truly believe that you are all that dedicated to the law?"

"Perhaps not. But when I tell him that I fixed my interest in you and that you have given me your promise . . ."

Nancy pulled her hands from his and clasped them firmly behind her back. "But I haven't," she whispered. "At least I never meant . . ."

"Please don't say anything without hearing me out. This isn't just a summer night's flirtation. This is my very existence. Would you stand on shore and watch a man drown?"

I would if I couldn't swim. The thought came all unbidden to Nancy's mind and she pushed it firmly away.

"I know that you love me. Admit it. It's not just for the sake of persuading Father Tucker. I need you. I have to have the knowledge of your love to hold on to. I can feel myself slipping away, and then I think of you and your gaiety and sweetness and affection."

Nancy seized the word. "Affection . . . certainly I feel the greatest possible affection for you, Theo . . . and sympathy, that too. But I . . ."

Theo's thin, strong fingers bit into her upper arms as he pulled her roughly toward him. His mouth on hers, her head bent back, his tongue darting between her lips, and her body with a will of its own molded itself to his. She had had a premonition of this feeling before, sometimes when she was reading and again when he had taken her arm as they walked, but it had been only a pale shadow of what she felt now. It was a discovery. So that's what it's like, she thought. It's certainly nothing to do with my heart, no matter what they say.

Theo released her abruptly. "There. Now tell me that what you feel for me is no more than affectionate sympathy."

"I don't think I have the breath to tell you anything."

There were more kisses, more caresses, each of them adding something to Nancy's new knowledge of herself. Who would have guessed that Theo's fingers trailing across the back of her neck could have such devastating effect? It was all beyond her experience and nearly beyond her imagination. In the end she scarcely knew what she had promised, but whatever she agreed to, she did gain one concession from Theo. He was to say nothing of any of this to anyone except his stepfather, particularly not to her father. It was a promise he was more than willing to make.

He stayed through dinner. Colonel Randolph invited him grudgingly and only, as he muttered, because he felt some pity for Theo's horse. It seemed to Nancy unbelievable that no one noticed the difference about her. She felt a current running between them that must be visible to everyone, but the conversation ran on politics and horses just as it always did.

Even Hattie, lingering in the hall as Nancy said goodbye to

Theo, was only perfunctorily curious. "What were you and Theo talking about so long this morning?"

"Nothing that has anything to do with you."

"You needn't be rude about it. I couldn't possibly care less. Besides I know a bigger secret than you can possibly have."

There was never any need to pump secrets from Hattie; she always relinquished them as fast as they were told to her. Nancy simply shrugged and waited.

"Gabrielle's going to have a baby."

Nancy stopped frozen on the staircase. She took hold of the banister and lowered herself slowly down onto the step. "I don't believe you."

"It doesn't matter whether you do or not. A thing doesn't need you to believe it to make it true."

"But then she'll never leave Tuckahoe."

"Nobody but you ever thought she would."

By Christmastime it was abundantly clear that Hattie had been right about Gabrielle's condition. She had only the most delicate swelling at the waist, but she walked leaning back, belly high in the triumphant manner of all mothers carrying for the first time. To Nancy's disgust her husband fussed over her as if no one had ever carried a child before, ordering hassocks brought for her feet and pillows for her back.

"She's strong as a horse," Nancy said to Judy when she came with her husband for Christmas week. "I never saw him carry on that way over Mama and she was really unwell. He doesn't have time or attention for anything or anybody else."

"I should think there were some things that you'd be just as happy not to have his attention on at the moment."

"I don't know what you mean."

"Yes you do. There can't be any pretense between us. Theo spoke to Dick in Williamsburg."

It was a relief to Nancy to have someone close to her know her secret. Now all the questions that she had been bursting to ask came flooding out. "How did he look? Were his studies going well? Was Mr. Tucker pleased with him? Did he talk much about me?"

"Of course he talks about you. He has an insatiable curiosity about you. He wants to know what books you read and what music you like and what you were like as a child."

"And what did you tell him?"

"The truth. That you were the wickedest child ever born at Tuckahoe, but no one ever had the heart to punish you when you smiled at them."

"You didn't say that."

"Yes I did. And he said that he could easily believe it because he felt that he could bring the world to its knees when you smiled at him."

"Dear Theo. How is he getting on with Mr. Tucker?"

Judy hesitated before she spoke. "Well, you know Mr. Tucker has always been the most loving of fathers to all three of his stepsons. And he still is."

"Is he pleased with the progress that Theo is making in his studies?"

"When we were there Theo wasn't actually still reading law with his father."

"He hasn't written to me about changing his plans."

"Perhaps it was only temporary, just when he was ill and he didn't want to worry you about it."

"It worries me a good bit more to find out that he's been keeping something from me. Something as important as his being ill. He hasn't said one word about it in any of his letters. What's wrong with him?"

"I don't really know, Nancy. It seems to be some sort of congestion of the chest, but then his health was never good. I think myself that he would be much improved if he would drink less."

"But he isn't drinking anymore."

"Whatever made you think that?"

"He told me so. He promised me."

Judy looked away from her sister. "Well then, perhaps I'm mistaken." She frowned, started to speak, took a breath, thought again and finally, her mind made up, spoke in a rush. "Nancy, what promises have you made to Theo? Dick and I are both anxious that you not be hurt by anything that happens with him."

"There's no need to be concerned. The only way Theo could cause me unhappiness is for him to be unhappy himself."

"You haven't said any of this to Papa, have you?"

"Of course not. Not that he'd care if I did. He'd probably just say that's good and run get another pillow for dear Gabrielle."

"I wouldn't be so sure of that. It's my guess that he'll go right through the ceiling, and I'd think a long time before I even mentioned it to him. Besides, the fewer people who know about it, the simpler it will be if anything . . ."

"Nothing will go wrong," Nancy interrupted.

"I hope not. But still I think it would be wise not to tell anyone, especially Papa."

"The problem is," Judy said to her husband later, "that Nancy is so stubborn. If she once commits herself to something in public, she'd never pull back from it even if she wanted to."

In January of the new year on a day when her father had made what she considered a sickening display over his wife, Nancy made her decision. She would soon be sixteen. She considered that it was time she took the direction of her life into her own hands.

* 8 *

Over Cicero's protests Nancy took the tray away from him at the study door. Anybody can mix a toddy, she told him. Her father sat before the fire, his feet up on the fender, his eyes closed, the Tuckahoe stud book open on his knee. "Best reading in the world," he often said.

"Wake up, Papa."

"Not asleep," he murmured, "just resting my eyes." When he realized whose voice it was he sat bolt upright. It had been months since Nancy had been in to see him. He watched her with a smile as she fixed his drink and, when she would have chosen a chair across from him, reached out with one foot and hooked a stool over toward him so that she could sit with her head at his knee.

"It's been a long time since I've had my Nancy in here with me. Too long."

For a moment Nancy almost relented. Then in a rush of words, knowing that unless she did it quickly she would never be able to do it at all, she told him. In a week's time she was leaving Tuckahoe for Bizarre and as soon after that as possible she would marry Theo Randolph. She had given it a great deal of thought, she said, and was willing to wait the six months until she reached sixteen, but she would wait them out at Bizarre where she and Theo could be together.

Her father came to his feet so abruptly that her head fell back against his chair with a crack that brought tears to her eyes.

"If this is your idea of a joke, it's a damned unfunny one."

"I was never more serious in my life."

"Then I can only assume that you've taken leave of your senses entirely. Marry Theo indeed. If it weren't for the family connection he'd never have seen the inside of this house twice. And this is how he repays my kindness, sneaking behind my back to get at you."

"He didn't sneak behind your back," Nancy said indignantly. "He would have spoken to you himself, except that I had not made up my mind when he was last here."

"And because he damned well knew that I'd have pitched him out ass over ears if he'd said one word to me about you. Nancy, do you have any notion what life with a man like that would be like?"

Nancy lifted her chin defiantly. "I know we would be poor at first, like Judy and Dick, but I could . . ."

"Poor?" her father roared. "Poor indeed. I wouldn't let you marry him if he were the richest man in the Tidewater. When have you ever known me to judge a man by the weight of his pocket? Theo Randolph is a drunkard and a womanizer and half dead from it. You saw it yourself, puking in the garden at your sister's wedding. Never known him to go to bed sober and can't climb out of bed in the morning without an eye-opener."

"You have no right to talk about him that way. You like your toddies and flips as well as anyone, and so does every other gentleman I've ever known except Mr. Leslie, and he didn't seem to any of us any the better for never touching it."

"You've never seen me or any other gentleman you know more than a little merry. Theo Randolph is a sot and a danger to himself and everyone around him."

"I won't permit you to talk that way about him."

"You won't permit me?" Her father stared at a Nancy quite unlike any he had ever seen before. "You won't permit me. Since when have I had to have permission from an empty-headed girl to speak the simple truth?" He waved away Nancy's protest. "It is the truth, you know. I've seen it myself. His own father has told me of it. His brothers despair of him."

"I'm not a fool," Nancy said. "I know that sometimes when Theo is unhappy he misjudges his capacity."

"That's a very pretty way to talk about a very ugly thing," her father interrupted.

"But it's only because he feels so alone in the world," Nancy went on. "If he had me with him as a center to his life . . ."

"He would forget the bottle." Her father shook his head in pity. "There speaks a very sweet and very inexperienced girl. Nancy love, men like Theo don't change, whatever romantic fancies you might have of rescuing him."

"You're just like everyone else. No one but me is willing to give him a chance to show that he—"

"To show that he can do what? Tucker has spent more time worrying over him than all the rest of his brood put together. He's been shifted from school to school and city to city and it's been the same story every time."

"That's only because he's never had anyone he felt cared for him."

"And you've elected yourself for the role? Why, Nancy? Why you?"

"Because I love him and I intend to marry him."

"And suppose you work a miracle and wean him from the bottle, do you think for one moment that I'd let a daughter of mine go to a bed that's been dirtied by every drab in New York and Philadelphia?"

Nancy gasped. "That's an unforgivable and unbecoming thing for you to say to me."

"You'll find it a damn sight more unbecoming when you get the pox."

The word hung in the air between them. Nancy's hands flew to her flaming cheeks. Her father looked away from her and mumbled an apology. "Shouldn't have said that. Forgot for a moment that you were too young for plain speaking."

In the past, whenever her father had lost his temper and said more than he intended, Nancy had been able to use his remorse to get her way. But this time none of her stratagems, not pleading, nor tears, nor threats would move him. She would not go to Bizarre or anywhere else Theo might be found. Theo would be turned away if he dared, which her father doubted, to come to Tuckahoe. She would not write him and any letters from him would be returned. Try as she might she could not gain any concession from her father.

"Then I'm to be a prisoner in your house?"

"If it suits your sense of melodrama to think of it that way, yes."

"For how long?"

"For as long as it takes to make you see reason."

If she was to be a prisoner, Nancy determined to play the role fully and refused to leave her room, not even to join the family below for her meals. The first week she almost enjoyed, sitting by her window in a pensive pose, her cheek on one hand, reading and rereading Theo's old letters now that there were to be no more of them. The second week was a bit dull. Her father had given up pleading with her and left her alone. Aggie was there and very biddable as always, but no matter how privileged she was still a servant and not really company. Jenny was a joy, but she was also still a baby and her only other visitor was Hattie, who seemed to take a perverse joy in ignoring Nancy's situation and speaking of nothing but the coming baby. "Papa is sure it's going to be a boy. He said Providence could not be so unfeeling as to plague him with any more daughters."

By the end of the third week boredom sat on her like an illness of the spirit. She listened to the laughter of her family at dinnertime and alternated between imagining that they laughed at her and deciding that they had forgotten her existence. She had very nearly decided that she would end her exile, that she had clearly demonstrated her seriousness in the matter and could now try other forms of persuasion, when Polly Cary Page came to visit. Aunt Polly said that she had never heard of anything so nonsensical and that Nancy must come down from her room at once and begin behaving like a sensible, dutiful girl. If Nancy could have borne to be honest with herself she would have admitted that there was nothing she was more eager to do. But it was a matter of honor never to do what hateful Polly wanted, and she stayed on in her room.

In the end it was Gabrielle who freed her. As the time for the birth of her first child came nearer, a time when she felt she had every right to the full attention of her husband, the presence of Nancy alternately sulking and crying in her room began to seem more and more that of the bad fairy come early to the christening. She quite agreed with her hubsand about Theo and would not have argued the point if she hadn't, but she considered herself in some ways wiser about the working of a young girl's fancy than he was and suggested that, given Nancy's stubbornness, perhaps a somewhat looser rein would serve better. "She'll be a long time forgetting about him sitting there in her room with nothing else to brood over. If she were to be somewhere else, meeting different people . . ." Bizarre, of course, would be out of the question. Dick could hardly be asked to bar the door to his own brother, but there were other places still within the family.

On a fresh green day in March, with Aggie beside her in the carriage and her brother Willie riding escort, Nancy Randolph left Tuckahoe.

* * * * * * * * * *

Bizarre

* * * * * * * * * *

She went first to Monticello, where her brother Tom, newly married to Martha Jefferson, acted as head of the house while his father-in-law served President Washington as Secretary of State. She thought it a very prettily situated house on its hill but an awkward and inconvenient one, especially when parts of it were more or less constantly being torn down and rebuilt as Mr. Jefferson had another new idea to be put in effect.

The sound of the carpenters' hammers punctuated the conversations of Martha and Nancy as they sat over their sewing in the long afternoons. Nancy had looked forward to becoming better acquainted with her sister-in-law, to listening to someone who had been to all the places that she longed to see, London and Paris, even Italy. But she was sadly disappointed. Of the days that she had spent as the daughter of America's Ambassador to France, Martha seemed to remember only that some places were dirtier than others and there were a great many more statues than in American cities. "My father doesn't care for statues," Martha said. Most of what Nancy learned of the capitals of Europe came secondhand from Aggie, repeating the stories that Martha's companion on her travels, a servant named Sally, told her. It was a bit like seeing only the underside of everything.

It was not just on the subject of statues that Martha thought her father infallible. She quoted him on everything. Nancy was used to deferring to the opinions of men on politics or business, but Martha's father had strong opinions on domestic matters as well, on music and cooking and the architecture of gardens and other matters that touched Nancy's life even more closely.

With time on her hands she had begun again with Aggie's education and Martha heartily approved. "Except that instead of teaching her so much from your books, it would be better if you helped to make her more skilled in a trade, as a seamstress, perhaps."

"She already sews quite well enough, beyond anything I could teach her."

"But if she were only a little bit better, she would be able to earn her living at it and then you could let her go free. My father says that it is a misplaced kindness to free a servant who isn't able to make his own way in the world."

"I'm sure your father is perfectly correct, but the problem is unlikely to arise. The way things are for me at Tuckahoe now, Aggie is probably the only servant I'll ever have who doesn't come to me as a stranger, and I certainly don't intend to let her go."

Martha was shocked. "Surely you don't mean that, Nancy. My father says that the only hope for any of us of escaping this dreadful institution is by holding to the ideal of freedom."

Really, Nancy thought, and how many of your blacks have you freed so far, Cousin Tom? She smiled and kept silent and ripped out the last row of stitches she had made rather more savagely than necessary. Aggie would fix it.

Half of Nancy's pleasure when an invitation came from sister Molly to a family party at Presqu'ile was at the prospect of seeing Jenny and Judy and Dick again, but the other half was joy at escaping from the relentless barrage of the opinions of Thomas Jefferson.

Judy and Dick had come by way of Tuckahoe and brought Jenny with them. She clung to Nancy like a limpet, crying all the while and saying that Nancy must never, never leave her again.

"Hattie and Gabrielle say you spoiled her," Judy reported. "That it's time she stopped being such a baby."

"If they think it's time she stopped being a baby, it's a wonder to me that they didn't notice that she's grown out of all her clothes. She looks like a waif."

"Never mind, one of Molly's girls will have something to fit her now, and Aggie will have all summer to make new things for her. Papa has given his permission for you both to come to Bizarre."

* 2 *

There was a special pleasure for Nancy that summer at Bizarre. Dick held firmly to his father-in-law's ban on any communication between Nancy and Theo, but she nevertheless felt closer to him than at any time since she had left Tuckahoe. He haunted the house for her. When she took down a book from the shelves she imagined that his hands were the last to have turned the pages. She sat at the window in his room and imagined that he sat beside her. And there was Dick. Nancy felt that she had never in her life known a man gentler, more considerate. He knew without being told when she was feeling unhappy and lonely and would single her out for special attention. He talked to her of Theo as a baby; he rode with her to the places where he and his brothers had played as boys. He said that he loved her as if she were his own sister, but her brothers had never been so attentive, not Tom or John and most certainly not Willie.

She thought Judy the luckiest woman in the world and was distressed to see her seem to be engaged in an all-out effort to test her husband's patience. First, Judy complained that the house at Bizarre was built too close to the river and the mosquitoes were devouring her. It was certainly true that the mosquitoes of the Appomattox, called gallinippers because of their fondness for French blood, were a fiercer breed than those at home and found the dark-haired Judy far tastier than either her sister or her husband. Furthermore, Bizarre did not yet have the icehouse that Dick had promised to build for her. She spoke so long and so often on this subject that even Jenny was overheard to say with a theatrical sigh, "If I don't have a little sliver of ice for my tongue, I shall die."

For the mosquitoes Dick could only apologize and agree that they were far worse this summer than ever before. As for the ice, she had his faithful promise that she would not spend another summer without it, but she must be reasonable. If he built the finest cold house in Virginia there would be no ice for it in August. Even the ships from the north didn't carry it as ballast in midsummer. Nevertheless the subject of ice seemed to arise again and again at the dinner table, and by perhaps the twentieth occasion Nancy saw the faintest of frowns on her brother-in-law's forehead as he turned back to his plate without comment.

"Don't you think," Nancy said to her sister when they were alone, "that you might give Dick a rest over the icehouse? Even the sweetest-tempered men have their limits."

"I can't see that it's any concern of yours."

"It isn't, except that I would be sorry to see you quarrel over something so silly. I think when a man sits down to his dinner table he wants good food and plenty of it and smiling faces and pleasant conversation. He doesn't want to hear complaints and whining."

"I never whine."

"You come very near to it. And there's another thing, men don't like to be drawn into quarrels with the servants, and they don't like niggardliness and cheese-paring."

"You think you're very clever, lecturing me on how to be a good wife from your great store of experience."

"Dearest Judy, I don't mean to lecture. It's just that I would be sorry to see anything spoil your happiness. I think we would all be the better for it you didn't fuss so over everything and weren't quite so strict in your domestic economies."

"There's gratitude for you. I do everything I can to save so that Dick's brothers can have a proper start in their own places, and all I get for it is criticism from the person who owes me most."

"I'm grateful for everything you've done. But, Judy, surely you don't think that denying your husband a little honey for his biscuits is going to make that much difference? Or making the servants run to you for every little thing because you've put those damn big locks all over?"

"Now there is where you're quite wrong. Even Mama always said that it was better to keep things safe, because it was so ugly when something went missing."

"She never put a lock on the woodshed, for heaven's sake. The lightest fingered black in Virginia isn't going to bother stealing a few sticks from you. And if they do and it comes out of my bride's portion, they are welcome to it."

"You will never understand," Judy said flatly. The Randolph sisters stood one on either side of the unbridgeable gap between those who can only live comfortably in a world under their control and those who are willing to chance living in blissful chaos. Since Judy would not take advice directly, Nancy was more than ever determined to show her by example. Dick would always find at least one smiling face at his table.

They heard very little from Tuckahoe, but they were not completely isolated. Willie came to take Jenny away, grumbling that he had been dragooned into permanent escort duty, and brought Nancy two very welcome pieces of evidence that her father had not forgotten her, her mare, Lady, and a letter. Her father wrote that he wished very much to have all his daughters at home with him and underscored the "all" several times. In the days that followed Judy spoke several times of how pleasant it always was at Tuckahoe in the fall and wondered aloud that

Nancy hadn't seen by the tone of her father's letter that he wanted her home again.

"He may want me at home," Nancy said, "or thinks that he does, but it's plain he didn't expect me to come or he wouldn't have sent Lady and all her tack here. In any case, I never think of Tuckahoe at all any more. It's just as you and Dick said it would be. I already think of Bizarre as my real home."

But it's not your home, it's mine, Judy said to herself and was instantly ashamed. It was an ungenerous and unsisterly thought. She would ask God's forgiveness for it.

Now that she was properly mounted on her own horse, Nancy enjoyed her excursions over the Bizarre lands with her brother-in-law even more. On one soft Indian-summer morning Dick declared a holiday for all of them and ordered dinner packed in a basket for a ride upriver. He had his own rod and had found Jack's and Theo's for the ladies; they would fish for their supper.

"I've never been fishing," Nancy said. "The boys went all the time but they would never take me."

"They probably didn't want to give away one of the great male secrets. Fishing isn't for fish. It's just the best possible excuse for spending a lazy day half asleep in the sun."

Judy could not be persuaded to go. She had too much to do in the house and didn't feel well. Riding all that way and sitting in the sun would make her head worse, she was sure. Besides, she wouldn't know what to do with a fish if she did catch one. "Nasty, wet, slimy things they are."

"Then leave your rod at home and bring a book and sit in the shade. I'll even undertake to keep a pipe alight the whole time to keep the nippers off you."

"As if the smell of a pipe wouldn't make nearly as ill as the sun would. I can't go and that's an end to it. I'm not a child who wants coaxing."

"Then we'll put it off for a day when you do feel well enough to go," Nancy said reluctantly.

Judy said that she wouldn't think of spoiling their pleasure. They must go without her. As if, Nancy thought, she hasn't already gone a long way toward making sure we'll spend half our time worrying over her. Still, it would be easier to forget for a part of the time a Judy languishing at home than to ignore a Judy on hand complaining of the heat and the flies and the muddy ground. It took very little urging from Judy before Nancy agreed to go.

She recognized the spot where Dick took her immediately, a tree by the riverbank with its roots undercut by years of spring flooding so that they hung out over the river like the broad arms of a throne, the seat that Dick had promised to Judy in their first days of courting.

"I know this place." Nancy settled down on the green velvet cushion of moss and leaned back against the trunk. "When you and Judy were first in love you told her you would bring her here and make her queen of everything she could see."

"You are laughing at me."

"No, I'm not. I didn't even laugh about it at the time, and I thought all talk about love ridiculous in those days. Did she ever come here with you?"

"Of course. A year ago in the spring. The first spring we had together. We came here and I even made a crown for her of meadow flowers though she said it wasn't practical, that they wilt almost before you can pick them. But she was pleased with it all the same." Dick smiled, remembering, and then sighed. "Poor Judy. I'm afraid she doesn't feel much like a queen these days."

"You mustn't take Judy's little crotchets too seriously. No matter how cross she gets I know she loves you very much."

Dick was startled. "Of course she does. I never doubted it for a moment. Dr. Meade says that it is quite in the nature of things for her to be out of sorts now but that she'll be her old self again when she's a month or two further along."

Nancy blinked her surprise. "Do you mean what I think you mean?"

He thought it very strange that Judy hadn't told her. "I would have thought she'd tell you almost before she told me. I thought that was one reason she so particularly wanted you here with us at Bizarre. Though in no way the only reason. She's often told me that she feels a stronger affection for you than for any other member of her family. Now that I have come to know you better, I can quite see why. It's meant more to me than I can say having you here with us, always so bright and cheerful."

A conversation begun with a compliment can never be anything but pleasing. They ate their dinner, they talked about every variety of thing from serious matters to the most trivial. She discovered that Dick's interest in politics was almost as small as hers, unlike most of the gentlemen of Virginia, and that his knowledge of bloodlines and the great English studs almost as great, though he had to acknowledge that his brother Jack was far more knowing than he was on both topics. Nancy almost absent-mindedly caught two nigger-knockers and a flatback, and Dick threw them back as too small and bony even to bother carting home for the servants' dinner. The hours went by in a golden haze. Neither of them thought of the time until the shadows had grown dangerously long. Nancy scurried about packing up the remains of their meal, and Dick cupped his hands under her foot to help her mount. She gentled Lady, who was eager to be off, and put out one hand to touch Dick's hair. "Thank you for today. I can't think when I've been so happy."

"I'm glad." He smiled back at her. "And now we're going to have to ride as if the Devil were chasing us if we're not to be late for supper."

They took the home fence side by side like two birds flying wing to wing and went together into the house, their eyes shining with the excitement of the ride, their faces flushed, their hair blown by the wind. Judy was already seated at the supper table and Nancy rushed over and threw her arms about her. "Darling Judy, you should have come with us. We had the most splendid time . . . and I sat on your throne and Dick told me your great news and I am so happy I think I might burst with it."

Judy looked over her sister's head at her husband. "I didn't know that's where you would take her." Something in her tone or a sudden stiffness felt within her encircling arms made Nancy look up at her sister questioningly, but Judy's face betrayed nothing. "I am delighted that you enjoyed yourselves so, but perhaps another time you would remember how cross it makes servants when meals have to be put back."

Judy wrote to her father at Tuckahoe the next day. She pointed out that it was most unfair to expect Dick to bar the door to his younger brother and that if he continued to insist that Nancy and Theo be kept apart, then some other arrangement should be made for Nancy. She had a reply almost immediately. She suspected that her father was hastened on by a Gabrielle worried by visions of Nancy arriving once again upon her doorstep. Colonel Randolph wrote that of course he would not even consider the impertinence of telling Dick whom he might properly receive in his own home; he'd had enough of that sort of interference from his own father-in-law. He had never intended that Dick deny his home to Theo. As for Nancy, if she would give assurances to her sister that nothing untoward would pass between her and Theo, then she might stay on there. It was perhaps not quite the result that she wanted, but still the prospect of Theo and Nancy both at Bizarre was infinitely better than Nancy there on her own.

There remained only one obstacle: Dick himself. "I can't bring Theo here, Judy. I gave your father my assurance that I would do nothing to encourage anything between them. He has my word on it."

"But surely his letter releases you from any obligation, and I can tell from every letter we get that Theo is longing to be at home. Father Tucker would agree, I know. It seems a shame when Theo's been so ill for him not to be able to come home and be with his own things in his own room."

"I shouldn't call the house in Williamsburg unfamiliar surroundings. He's spent the greater part of his life there," Dick protested, but in the end he allowed himself to be persuaded by the combined forces of both sisters and took the carriage to Williamsburg to bring his brother home.

* 3 *

Three times that morning Nancy changed her dress. Aggie was sent from the room in tears with a hairbrush sailing after her because the curls that were supposed to droop down each side of her mistress's face persisted in turning wispy.

"For heaven's sake, Judy," Nancy burst out when her sister came into the room, "why can't this house have a proper mirror? One that I can see all of myself at once in. I can see the top and then I have to stand on a chair to see the bottom. How you tolerate it, I don't know."

"You look very pretty."

"I want a certain effect, you know what I mean. And I can't see how the back of the skirt hangs no matter how I twist about."

"It's fine," Judy said soothingly. "Just stop fussing over yourself. You'll have yourself in such a temper that it will spoil your looks completely."

"But what shall I do if he doesn't find me perfect?"

Judy laughed. "I should think you would be grateful. Then he won't be so disappointed later on."

"Please don't tease me," Nancy said and climbed down from the chair and pushed her face toward the mirror. "Look," she said in despair, "I'm getting a spot on my chin. I can feel it."

Judy assured her that the spot was either imaginary or quite invisible, that the dress she had chosen was most suitable and becoming, and that in any case there would be plenty of time to wear the others for Theo.

"Not that they will be fit to wear if you don't soothe Aggie down and get her in here to hang them up and brush them properly. What possessed you to throw them on the floor like that?"

"Oh poor Aggie. I was so unkind to her. Where is she?"

"She's sitting on the floor at the top of the landing, crying. You do spoil her, you know. She'll never be good for anything if she collapses in tears over every little thing."

"I threw my hairbrush at her," Nancy said.

"From the way she's carrying on one would think you'd given her a whipping."

"Take her down to the kitchen and give her a bit of cake, do, Judith, and tell her I said for you to. She's like a baby. Something sweet in her mouth always pacifies her."

"You really must decide whether she's a pet or a servant, you know. It just won't do."

"I know, I know, but not today. Can you believe it's really happening . . . after all these months . . . I've practically pinched myself black and blue. Do you know, Judy, I used to laugh at you when you and Dick were separated and you drooped so, but at least you had his letters. I haven't even had that. Do you wonder I'm so excited?"

"No," Judy said slowly, "I don't wonder at it, but I . . ."

"Why do you have your gloomy sermonizing face on? Smile, Judy, be happy for me." She was struck by a sudden alarming thought. "Unless you know something you haven't told me. He's met someone else, someone older and more experienced. If you've waited till now to tell me you've been very cruel."

"No, no, nothing like that. I'm sure his feeling for you hasn't changed at all. But, Nancy, you do know that Theo is very ill."

"Of course I do, but everyone says that country air is the most sovereign of remedies. We'll ride out every day and you will make him custards. Maybe you could even teach me to make him custards with my own hands. Do you think I could learn? I know you find me ham-fisted in the kitchen, but I could learn for Theo, I know I could, and we'll soon have him well and strong again."

"Nancy . . ." Her sister paused and searched for words. "Dick and I are both at fault for not preparing you better. You'll find Theo much changed, I'm afraid."

"Changed how?"

"He's been very ill and he's still very weak. His doctor in Williamsburg had to be much persuaded before he would even allow the journey here and then only if it was taken slowly. So you see, he won't be able to ride out with you or be fit for much of anything." She stopped short at the stricken look on her sister's face and relented. "At least not just at first."

Nancy looked down at her hands for a moment and caught her lower lip in her teeth and raised her head defiantly. "Well then," she said, "the two of us will nurse him until he is strong again."

"Oh my dear Nancy, of course we will. If all it took was energy and will you could raise Lazarus."

"And you are happy for me?"

"Of course I am."

"Then why are you crying?"

It was well past the dinner hour before they heard the jingle of the carriage coming up the drive. Nancy ran out on the porch with only one quick glance in the mirror in the hall, and Judy followed more slowly. It was a mild October day, the trees along the drive still holding their green, only a little yellow crisping their edges. Though the carriage door was unlocked by a hand only dimly seen, Theo did not appear, and Nancy, straining against the sun, could see only a blur inside until Richard reached the step of the carriage and offered his arm. As if to a woman, Nancy thought.

Wrapped in a riding cloak that seemed to have been made for a much larger man, Theo stood blinking in the sun, one thin hand clutching a shawl across his chest, the other gripping his brother's forearm. He walked slowly to the steps, and when he reached them Syphax hurried down and took his other arm.

Theo was supported between them, his feet barely brushing the bricks, half carried like a child between his parents.

Nancy had pictured herself dashing down the drive and throwing herself in his arms, but now she came forward slowly, took his hands in hers and carried them to her cheeks. "Dear Theo," she said.

"This is not quite how we thought we would meet, is it? Wrapped in a shawl like an old man."

Nancy managed a weak smile. "Never mind, I was beginning to fear we would both be old and gray before we saw each other again. You're here and we'll soon have you fit again, that's all that matters."

Theo bent over Judy's hand, paid her his compliments, and told her that she could not imagine how grateful he was to be in his home again. Judy assured him that he was always very welcome at Bizarre and hoped that he would find his room just as he left it.

Theo smiled. "I hope not. As I remember I left it in turmoil. But if you will excuse me and Syphax will give me a hand up the stairs I shall soon find out. Dick warns me that Dr. Meade will be descending on us, and it's been my sad experience that doctors like to find their patients safely tucked in bed. Besides, I—" he faltered and swayed—"Dick, help me, please. I'm afraid the sun has made me a bit lightheaded."

"Take my arm, Theo, and Syphax . . . the other . . ."

"Dear old Syphax," Theo said. "It won't be the first time you've put me to bed, will it?"

"Just lean on me, Mr. Theo. You don't weigh a penny more than you did when you a baby. Why, I've carried you up those stairs kicking and screaming in a temper and I could still do it if I had to."

"You won't have to this time. I'll go most willingly."

"It's a very fatiguing trip from Williamsburg," Nancy said to her sister.

Theo turned his head back to her and smiled. "Yes, yes,

don't worry yourself. It's just the journey. I shall be quite all right when I've rested."

"There isn't much we can do with these cases," Dr. Meade said when he came downstairs from examining Theo. "Rest, good food. If we can build his strength back, the fact that he's as young as he is may help him throw it off. He'll have fever most of the time. I'll leave you some powders for an infusion, but I wouldn't use them unless his fever goes so high as to make him excitable or confused in his mind. I'll show Syphax how to make them up before I go."

"Please, Dr. Meade," Nancy said. "Will you show me too?"

Dr. Meade looked at her appraisingly. "So you're to be Theo's nurse, are you? Splendid. I've always said that a pretty face is a far more effective medicine than anything I can brew. But you have a job ahead of you, young lady. Right now he's tired out from the journey and more than willing to keep to his bed. It's when he begins to feel a little stronger that your work will begin. When I say rest, that's just what I mean. I want him in bed and quiet and not fretting himself away. Think you can keep him cheerful?"

"I can if anyone can."

"Can't ask more than that, can I? I'll look in on him again in a day or so or send for me if you need me, but I shouldn't think that you will."

Dick and Dr. Meade stood together on the porch and waited for the doctor's horse to be brought around from the stable. "Tell me truthfully, Doctor, how much chance does Theo have?"

"Depends what you mean. If you're talking about a complete recovery with a long and active life before him ... barring a miracle, none at all. From the chest sounds I'd say that one lung is already scarred beyond use and the other severely damaged. I'd guess that there's some bone infection as well. On the other hand, if he follows orders and rests, takes care of himself, he might go on for quite a long time."

"But you don't think that's going to happen, do you?"

Dr. Meade was silent as the boy brought his horse and was given a penny for his trouble. "As a doctor I can't answer that."

"And as a friend?"

"As a friend I'd have to say, regretfully, that no, I don't expect it to happen. You talked to the doctors in Williamsburg, what did they say?"

"Six months."

The older man bowed his head and considered. "I shouldn't like to put so exact a term to it, but I'm afraid they are probably not too far off the mark."

"I suppose I knew that was what you'd say. I only asked because I think that Nancy should be warned of what to expect."

"No, no, you mustn't do that. The one slim chance that Theo has is his own ability to fight the disease off. If he once thinks it hopeless he'll give up the struggle."

"Nancy can be trusted not to tell him."

"It wouldn't be deliberate, of course, but, believe me, if she knows, he'll know. He'll see it in the way she talks or doesn't talk about the future. He'll read it in her eyes no matter how hard she tries to hide it. The sick always search our faces for clues to their fate."

"It seems a terrible burden to place on her, not knowing."

"Don't worry about Nancy Randolph. There isn't a doubt in my mind that she will recover from whatever life brings her."

* 4 *

Nancy's days now settled into a routine that revolved around the sickroom. Syphax would help Theo to shave and put on fresh linen while Nancy breakfasted with Judy and Dick. She accompanied Theo's breakfast tray upstairs; he seemed to eat more heartily if she was there. When he had finished Dick would come in. At first he talked to his brother about what he planned to do that day on the place, consulting him on every decision that had to be made.

"I don't know why you come in here pestering me with these damn questions every morning," Theo fretted.

"Sorry, I didn't mean to be pestering you. It's just that since you are here I value your opinion on the things that need doing."

"You don't mean that. The man who took my advice on how to run his plantation would be a bigger fool than I am. You're trying to distract me, to get me to think about something outside the walls of this room. You mean well but you're wrong. I only have this little amount of energy, of strength, and I need to put it all to use for myself. I don't care what happens to the river meadows. I care about the next breath I draw and the one after that and that's all I can afford to care about."

"I'm sorry, Theo."

"I know you are. Tell you what. If you really want to do something for me you'll get out the board and the chessmen. Nancy there coudn't give a decent game to an idiot."

"My father always used to say that there wasn't a woman on earth who could learn to play chess properly."

"There you are then. I knew there must be something that your father and I could agree on."

After that day the brothers played every morning that Theo felt up to it. Nancy used the time to walk up and down the graveled drive or around the garden, taking deep gulping breaths of the cold morning air as if she could store it up against the hours ahead in Theo's airless room. She never failed to visit Lady in the stable and watched with dismay the mare growing fatter every day with no one to take her out. Dick had tried to ride her once or twice, but she sulked under the extra weight. Just one time Nancy slipped from Theo's room in the afternoon when he had fallen asleep and taken Lady for a glorious gallop along the river road. It would have been difficult to tell whether horse or rider was the more exhilarated at being released from confinement. When she came back to the house Theo was burning with fever and refusing all of Syphax's ministrations. He would accept only the cold cloth that Nancy held to his forehead and sent a much offended servant out of the room. After that she seldom left him alone.

She sat in her chair by the window, talking whenever Theo seemed to want to talk and watchful the rest of the time to make sure that he had everything he needed for his comfort. In the beginning she brought whatever sewing she had in with her, until Theo said that if there was a more boring occupation than watching a woman turn a hem on a petticoat he would be pleased if someone would tell him what it was.

What he liked best was to lean back against the pillows with his eyes closed and listen while she read aloud to him. She suspected that he often drifted in and out of sleep, but she seldom caught him out. She would stop and after a moment he would say without opening his eyes, "Go on, I'm listening."

She read *Charlotte Temple* to him and that scandalous tale of Bostonian misdeeds, *The Power of Sympathy*. She read straight through volume after volume of the American Museum. He seemed as little intrigued by its description of curious scientific phenomena as by the cautionary tales addressed to young ladies on the evils of being slaves to fashion, and just as interested by the text of government documents as by a thrilling description of a disaster at sea. She was perhaps a quarter of an hour into Alexander Hamilton's "Report on Manufactures" when she rebelled. "Theo, you can't possibly want to hear this. Nobody could. It's nothing but rows and rows of figures."

"Is it?"

"Haven't you been listening?"

"Most of the time I pay no attention to what you're reading. I just like the sound of your voice, so clear and cool. It's like bright water in a pebbled stream."

"If that's the case I might just as well recite my times tables. It couldn't be more boring and it would rest my eyes."

From then on she chose what they would read, the lighter

bits from all the newspapers that came into the house, a bound volume of *The Spectator* from under the leg of a chair in the old nursery and a series of novels, one very much like the others, intended, or so the authors piously hoped, to warn young ladies of the evils abroad in the world for the unwary.

"The curious thing," Theo said, "is that they're all written by men. You wouldn't think they'd be so eager to warn young girls off."

"Perhaps they know the truth of it . . . that they don't frighten girls at all, just make them sort of, I don't know . . . interested. The girls who might listen to warnings never are allowed to read them. My Aunt Polly would have a fit if she knew I ever read any of these books, and as for reading them to you . . . she wouldn't believe it possible."

"Then aren't we fortunate that Polly isn't with us."

The days flowed one into the other without anything to mark them. After two months Nancy felt that she had spent the greater part of her life sitting in a chair reading aloud, wringing out towels in cold water and having her dinner off a tray. The only thing that made it bearable was that she was sure that she saws signs of improvement in Theo every day. It was true that he was still very thin, but she thought his skin a much healthier color and his eyes to have a more natural light. Dr. Meade said that he agreed with her, but when an invitation came for all the household to go to the Tuckers at Williamsburg for the holidays, he absolutely forbade the journey for Theo.

Dick relinquished the idea of going away quite willingly, but Judy found it impossible to conceal her disappointment. It was to have been her last chance to go about in society before her pregnancy became too obvious. Dick could have resisted his wife's injured sighs about an unrelieved winter at Bizarre, but he had no defense to the onslaught of both sisters. Nancy assured him that she could manage perfectly with Syphax's help, that there was no reason at all beyond the proprieties for Dick and Judy to stay at home, and surely Theo's circumstances put their situation beyond the disapproval of the most puritanical.

It somehow became a question of Dick depriving his wife of a great pleasure simply because he was too selfish to travel without his valet, since they were all agreed that Syphax was essential to Theo's care. Put like that, and with Nancy's fervent assurance that she wanted them to go, that Theo would be unhappy if they didn't go, and his own inclination to see old friends and family, Dick gave in.

They left for Williamsburg the week before Christmas. Dick had a private talk with Dr. Meade, and Judy handed over her heavy ring of keys to Nancy, along with detailed instructions on the running of the house.

Nancy stepped into her new role before the carriage was out of sight down the drive. She thrust the keys into her apron pocket and went straight to the kitchen. She would oversee the making of Theo's broth herself. It might be only for a few weeks, but for that time she would imagine that she was in her own house, that her husband lay upstairs with only a temporary indisposition, that these were her servants to guide and care for. She knew it was only play-acting, but in her heart she could nearly make it true.

* 5 *

"Such a busy housewife," Theo said. "It must be a great relief to you to have something to do with yourself instead of being cooped up in here with me all day." He waved away her protests. "Not that I blame you. I know it's very boring, but I didn't ask to be ill, you know."

"I know you didn't, darling Theo," Nancy soothed. "And you're getting better every day."

"Of course I am. Dr. Nancy says so and she has so much experience in these things. I'm never going to be well and if you weren't just an ignorant girl you could see it for yourself."

Nancy bit her lip. "One thing I do know. Whenever I was ill as a child, or any of my brothers or sisters, we were always crossest when we were feeling better. When you're really sick you don't think about how tiresome it is."

"And if crossness is the test I should be able to ride twenty miles before breakfast tomorrow."

"Forty," Nancy corrected.

"That bad am I?" He shook her hand and put a kiss gently in her palm. "Forgive me?"

"There's nothing to forgive. I know it isn't me you're in a temper with."

"Never you." He nipped with his sharp white teeth at the end of her little finger. "Have I told you I love you?"

"Not today."

"Today and every day." He tugged gently on her wrist and she fell across him on the bed. "My own pretty Nancy, pretty eyes, pretty ears, pretty nose, pretty lips." He christened each of them with a touch of his dry hot lips. "Pretty . . ."

"Theo, please. Someone might come in."

Even though Theo pointed out with some asperity that her sister's servants were far too well trained to enter a bedchamber without tapping on the door, Nancy gently disengaged herself and stood up, adjusting her bodice which had somehow come adrift.

Theo watched her sulkily. The answer to all her suggestions was no. He did not want to play at draughts, or naughts and crosses, or categories, or to teach her chess, or most particularly to hear what instructions she had given Syphax for the house. Only when she suggested that they might return to their reading of *Tristram Shandy*—"Such an amusing book," Nancy said; "I would never have thought a clergyman would be so freakish"— did he show any interest.

"But then," he objected, "half the wit is in the way he's had the printer place the words on the page, and with you sitting over there I can't see."

Nancy offered to move her chair closer, but Theo was struck by an even better idea. "Come sit here beside me on the bed." Nancy perched on the edge. "Not like that. Really beside me with your feet up ... and I shall put my arm about you ... like this ... and then we can both see the page most conveniently."

"Theo ..."

"Are you comfortable, my love?"

The hand that was on her shoulder had drifted down, and Nancy drew in her breath with something between a sigh and a shudder. "To be honest with you I am, and yet I am not, both at once."

"Perhaps you are laced too tightly."

"I never lace."

"Yes, I can feel that you don't. How sensible of you."

"I do not feel very sensible right now," Nancy breathed.

"Perhaps it's as well. Being sensible can be very boring."

"But sometimes very necessary ... oh, please, Theo."

"Darling girl, don't be frightened. It's just that I have such a need to touch you, that's all. To have the knowledge of you in my fingers and not just what my eyes can see and be tantalized by. To see if these two beauties will really fit so roundly to my hands as I thought they would."

"Theo ..."

"So beautiful ... and see how the little pink buds spring up to meet my thumb. You see your lips obey you and say no, but these know better. They say kiss me. They want to feel the tip of my tongue slowly circling them ... like this ... and this ..."

"Theo, you must stop. If you don't I shall, I shall ..."

"Scream?"

"Of course not, but I shall be very disappointed in you."

"Oh, I can promise you, you won't be." Theo smiled.

"Behave yourself." She pushed his hands away. "You'll make me believe you're as big a reprobate as they say you are."

"There's no question about it. But isn't that part of what you find attractive in me?"

"Certainly not."

"Not even a little bit?"

"No."

Theo abruptly let go of her and pushed himself back against his pillows. "In that case, Miss Randolph, I suggest that you arrange your clothing. I shouldn't like to share that delightful sight with the admirable Dr. Sterne. Where is our book?"

"I think it must have fallen to the floor."

"What a pity, particularly since as I recall the next thirty pages or so are in Latin."

"I don't believe you."

"See for yourself. The book can't have gone far." He made a steeple of his hands in front of his mouth. "I can't wait to resume our reading and perhaps afterwards we might chat about some of the niceties of classical grammar. In between my bouts I managed to acquire some knowledge, and I dare say Mr. Leslie must have pounded some into you."

"Theo, are you terribly angry with me?"

"Should I be? Have you done some dreadful thing that I know nothing about?"

"You know why . . . because I couldn't . . ."

"Or wouldn't."

"I do love you, more than anything in the world, you know that."

"My darling, of course I know it . . . and I am the most patient of men. See me now sitting here meekly with my hands in my lap waiting for you to find that damned book."

"Theo," she whispered, "that's *my* lap."

"So it is," he replied in exaggerated surprise. "But if you'll notice my own has become rather seriously encumbered."

"Oh."

"I hope that was a sigh of appreciation. As the rest of me wastes away this seems to be rather more ambitious than usual."

"Theo, I . . ."

"Tell me, darling, I've always wanted to know. When you blush like that does it start at your toes and work its way up, or at your forehead and go down?"

"I don't know, my toes certainly feel rather . . ."

(140)

"Atingle?"

"Yes, but then my head seems to be swimming a bit as well."

"Perhaps it would be of scientific interest to investigate further."

"Perhaps, I don't know."

"You're not sure? I really don't think the experiment can be conducted without a certain willingness on your part."

"Theo," Nancy said in the smallest of voices, "Theo, am I being seduced?"

He looked up smiling from the knot in her waist strings that he was working at. "I certainly hope so."

"Then why am I enjoying it so?"

"Because if you didn't it would be rape, and you are much too generous to want me to have that on my conscience."

"And will I be abandoned to my fate," Nancy quoted dreamily, "left to wander, with a weary heart, shunned by all who know her, until at last in the sinks of some strange city . . ."

"Do hush, Nancy, and help me disentangle you from these petticoats. There seem to be dozens of them."

"I'm freezing."

"Then get under the cover and I'll soon warm you."

"Theo, darling Theo," Nancy said as she searched for the hairpins lost in his bed, "now we are truly husband and wife, aren't we? Not just pretending any more. I want to celebrate, to let everyone know."

"Good God, Nancy," he said in alarm.

"I know I mustn't tell anyone," Nancy hastened to assure him, "not even Dick or Judy."

"Especially not Dick or Judy."

"You know what it was like?" She knelt on the bed and sat back on her heels. "It was like riding Lady up to a fence. It starts slowly and then faster and faster till you reach the hedge and then you're soaring. Is it like that for you, too?"

Theo closed his eyes. "I've never ridden Lady."

"Don't tease. You know what I mean. Was it the most wonderful thing that's ever happened to you?"

"Of course."

"Is it always like this or is it just because it's the first time?" She reached down and shook his shoulder. "Why do I do all the talking after when you did all the talking before?"

"I don't know," Theo mumbled.

For a moment Nancy was silent, studying him, and when she spoke it was hesitantly. "Theo, I know you have . . . after all you're a man and young men are expected . . . and I don't want to know who they were, but how many girls have . . . ?"

Theo pulled her down on the bed beside him and put his hand firmly over her mouth. He told her that if he knew the answer to her question he still wouldn't answer it, and curiosity was a damned dangerous trait. Nancy would not be discouraged and returned to the attack the moment he released her. Surely he must remember the first time, she insisted. No one could forget that.

"It's not just curiosity. I want to know everything about you so I can share what you feel."

Theo gave her what she always thought of as his black look that presaged an explosion of rage. "Very well," he said abruptly, "here's a memory for you to share. The first was a whore and I was so drunk my friends had to roll me on her and afterwards I sicked up my dinner and a good bit of rum."

"Poor Theo, how dreadful for you. Not at all romantic." She paused. "Was it in New York or Philadelphia?"

"What possible difference does it make?"

"None at all. I only wondered."

"If you must know, it was in Princeton."

To his surprise, Nancy laughed. "You're teasing me. Everybody knows they're all Methodists in Princeton."

Theo's frown vanished. "Promise you'll never stop surprising me."

"Good, I've finally made you smile. I dare say," she went on thoughtfully, "if you hadn't been so drunk, she would have given you a tract."

"Compared to what she did give me, a tract would have been a positive delight." Try as she would, Nancy could not coax another smile from him.

She knew that what had happened was wrong or would seem so to everyone in her world. She resolved that it would never happen again. When her resolution failed to last until morning, she tried to tell herself that it was only pity for Theo that took her, barefoot in her shift, down the hall as soon as Aggie was asleep. It would have been a greater sin to deny him such pleasure.

In his arms, in his bed she was joyously unencumbered with guilt. She was Theo's wife in her heart. That was all that mattered. She found in herself an inventiveness in pleasure that delighted and astonished her. They did not have much time before them, and in that short time every avenue of desire must be explored. The only words of caution were Theo's. "Aren't you at all afraid? What if Aggie tells someone?"

"Aggie doesn't know."

"Of course she does."

"If she did she wouldn't tell anyone. She thinks she's too good for the people in the kitchen. She'd never gossip with them."

"And what if you started a baby?"

"I don't imagine I will. Look at Judy. She was married for over a year before, and besides, that might solve all our problems. Papa would certainly rather see me married to you than have a grandchild on the wrong side of the blanket."

Only one thing worried her. Theo could never see enough of her body. His eyes and hands and lips worshipped every part of her, but he would never let her see him naked. She knew why. Her hands told her, clasped over his buttocks as he pumped into her, stroking his chest under the night shirt wet with sweat. There was not an ounce of flesh left on him. He was burned down to the thinnest of skin stretched over bone.

She had discovered an appetite that grew stronger the more it was satisfied. She would come to him in the morning only hours after she had left his bed and try as she might she could not make herself stay demurely in her chair across the room. She was not just drawn to his side, to his kisses; she was compelled there.

It did cross her mind fleetingly that this was not the bed rest prescribed for Theo. But Dr. Meade called and gave her his usual vague assurances and seemed to find nothing more amiss with Theo than he had on his last visit. Besides, as Theo pointed out to her, she had particularly been instructed that he be kept "easy in his mind," and he would worry himself into a fever at the thought of her lying all alone in her spinster's bed down the hall.

On the night before Dick and Judy were due back home, their last night together alone, Nancy did not leave when Theo fell into an exhausted sleep. She stayed beside him propped up on one elbow, watching him until nearly first light, and then fell asleep with her head on the pillow beside him. She was roused by a tapping on the door.

It was Aggie, shivering in the hall, holding her mistress's dressing gown in front of her. "You'd better slip this on and come back to your room, Miss Nancy. I can hear them stirring around downstairs. Syphax will be coming up any minute now."

Nancy watched Aggie light the fire in her room and cleared her throat. "By the way, Aggie, it might be just as well if you didn't mention anything about this morning to Miss Judy."

"When did you ever know me to carry tales to your sister?"

"It's just that she might not understand."

Aggie thought that very funny. "She'd understand right enough. She'd have you down on your knees praying to God from sunup to sundown. But if you want to give Mr. Theo a warming before he dies, it's nothing to do with me and nothing to do with Miss Judy."

"Theo is not going to die, Aggie. I don't want you ever to say anything like that again."

"Everybody dies, Miss Nancy."

Dick and Judy came home at suppertime, bringing late Christmas presents from the Tuckers. Nancy had a pair of French enamel ear bobs, pretty in themselves, but especially valued because they meant to her that the Tuckers, at least, had accepted her as Theo's bride. Theo had a dressing gown of red velvet with corded lapels and cuffs. It had been made to his old measure at his tailor, Theo looked at it only briefly and handed it to Syphax.

"I could take the seams in," Nancy offered.

"It would be a waste of effort. In another month or so I'll fit right into it. I'm picking up all the time. All the time. Am I not, Richard? And Judy? You haven't said anything at all about how well you find me, how much improved since you've been gone."

"We are certainly delighted to see you in such high spirits."

"And why shouldn't I be? I'm feeling fitter every day. I shall soon be quite my old self again. Perhaps even a better self. You know what I think? I think we should have a party to celebrate your return and my recovery. Syphax, put a cloth on that table and bring it over here and we'll need another chair. It won't hurt the kitchen to bring everyone's supper up here this one night. And bring a bottle of claret, or two bottles even better."

"Do you think that's wise?" Dick asked.

Theo gave his brother a long level look. "Do you really think it matters?"

The party was not a notable success. Judy was so tired from the journey that she could scarcely keep her eyes open and begged to be excused. Theo's initial forced enthusiasm took on a frantic ugly edge. "It's not much of a party, is it? More like the times when we were boys and banished to the nursery for our dinner because Father Tucker had important legal matters to discuss with his guests. Only then we didn't have a pretty lady to share it with us. There was always Jack though. Mama kept him in skirts an unconscionable long time. Do you suppose that's what's the matter with him? Or did she guess something even then?"

With a quick glance at Nancy, Dick told his brother to hush.

"Why? Bless you, Dick, Nancy is not so maidenly as not to have noticed that there is something a little odd about our brother."

"What you are implying is false and you know it."

"Was I implying something? I only meant that there was no need for drastic measures to find a soprano for our family choir."

"That is more than enough of that, Theo."

"More than enough. More than enough of everything for Theo. Except wine." He raised his empty glass. "Never enough wine."

Dick took the glass gently from his brother's hand. "I think that's even enough wine for tonight, Theo. Nancy and I will leave you to Syphax. If you don't sleep now, you'll be sorry for it tomorrow."

All the spirit seemed to have gone out of Theo. He meekly agreed to let Syphax make him ready for the night but would not allow Nancy to leave until she promised to look in on him later to say good night.

"When you see someone every day it's hard to tell how much change there's been," Nancy said to Dick. "But it must be quite startling to you."

"It is."

"Of course he's still dreadfully thin and has his bouts with the fever. But he's in much better spirits. You could see that tonight, couldn't you? At least at first. You must understand, Dick, when Theo's tired he sometimes says things he doesn't really mean. But you do think he's getting better, don't you?" He sat beside her before the fire in the drawing room as her eyes begged him for confirmation.

The silence stretched ominously long. "He certainly seemed happier in himself, I suppose." Dick paused. "Nancy, I think that we have not treated you quite fairly. I could put the blame at Dr. Meade's door, but I am as wrong in this as . . ."

Nancy put her finger to her lips and shook her head. "Shh, don't say it, Dick. I know. And I know he isn't really better, but don't say it, and don't blame yourself on my account. I knew all along as much as I wanted to know. Besides, I still believe that everything's going to be all right. Perhaps when winter's over." Dick took her hand and kissed it and then continued holding it, companionably, comfortingly. Nancy took a deep breath and made her voice bright and brisk. "So then, tell me all the Williamsburg news. Did Judy enjoy herself?"

"I think she did. We took dinner with old friends most days and we went to the New Year's Assembly. She would only dance once or twice, but she seemed happy for the most part. It's strange how carrying a child seems to have made Judy so solemn. She laughed all the time when we first came here."

Dick stretched his legs out and propped his feet on the fender. He had taken off his boots and put on silver-buckled low shoes, but he still wore his close-cut riding trousers. It was impossible for Nancy, looking at the long smooth muscles straining against the fabric, not to think of the poor wasted limbs upstairs. To her horror, something inside her said, If you were to put your hand there, right there at the top of his leg, would he respond to it the way Theo does? Her cheeks grew hot, and she snatched her hand out of his grasp as if he might be able to read her thoughts through her fingers. It had come unbidden, but once out of its cage the idea would not be lured back. What kind of a person must I be to think like that about Dick, who has always been so kind and generous and understanding? And handsome and strong, added the other voice.

"Is something the matter, Nancy?"

"No, not at all." She made an elaborate display of yawning. "But it's been a long day. I'm off to bed myself."

She was in her bed with the candle out when she remembered that she had forgotten to say good night to Theo. But it's so late now, she told herself. I should only be disturbing him.

It was next to impossible to return to the old routine of reading aloud and playing at draughts and cards when they had been used to spending their days in quite a different fashion. But they made love only once in the days after Dick and Judy's return, and then it was hasty and furtive, so tuned to the sound of Judy's step in the hall, that it was only faintly more satisfactory than continence had been.

Two days later when Syphax was lifting him from bed to change his linens, something seemed to break inside Theo. He took one long gasping breath, coughed, and great gouts of blood came pouring forth. "So much blood," Syphax kept murmuring. "So much blood." Dr. Meade was sent for and forbade the room to everyone but Dick and Syphax. Nancy was only permitted to stand in the doorway for a moment. In the harsh white light reflected from the snow outside, his eyes were like holes burned by a poker, and when, after one brief glance at her, he closed them, he looked to be his own effigy, the bed a catafalque.

She did not know how long she lay sobbing on her bed when Dick came in to her. He sat on the edge of the bed and gathered her wordlessly into his arms. He held her across his lap, against his chest, and rocked slowly back and forth as he would have comforted a child, saying only "Hush, Nancy, hush now." Slowly her tears stopped and the pain in her chest and throat eased. She drew a long shuddering breath and pressed her face even closer into the lace of his shirt front. He put her down gently on the bed and pulled the comforter up over her. He brushed her hair back off her forehead, and, with his hand still on her head in a gesture of benediction, he bent over and gently kissed her swollen eyelids shut.

On the coldest day of a cold winter, early in February of 1792, a few months short of his twenty-first birthday, Theodoric Randolph died.

Dr. Meade would not permit Judy to leave the house for the funeral, and Nancy seized the opportunity to stay with her. She could not bear to hear the service for the dead read over Theo in the church where she had hoped to hear a more joyful service for the two of them. She watched the cortege down the drive from the broad windowsill of the room that had been Theo's, wrapped in the red velvet dressing gown that he had never worn. First came the cart with the coffin and then the Bizarre carriage with Dick and Jack, then Randolph and Mary Harrison from Glenlyrvar, and Aunt Polly and her husband, Carter Page. Nancy sat with her knees drawn up, her arms wrapped around her lower legs, her cheek pressed to the cold glass of the window, just as Dick had found her earlier.

"You won't change your mind and come with us to the church?"

She shook her head.

"Sometimes it helps, you know." He stood uncertainly in the middle of the room and looked about him. "Is there anything here of Theo's that you would like to have?"

"Just this." She stroked the sleeve of the robe. "It's the only thing that keeps me warm."

"Nancy, if there is anything, anything at all that I can do to help you, you have only to ask."

"I know, and knowing it is all the help I need."

The Harrisons went back to Glenlyrvar, but Jack and the Pages stayed on. Polly had planned on coming to Bizarre for Judy's lying-in. It seemed foolish to leave now when she might be summoned again at any moment.

Nancy did not come down to join the others for dinner until two or three days after the funeral, and when she did she had cause to regret it. Judy stayed in her room all through the day now as she waited for her baby. Polly went up to see if she had all she wanted as soon as the pudding was cleared away, leaving Nancy alone at the table with the gentlemen.

Nancy would probably have had no great fondness for anyone that Polly married, but she particularly disliked Carter Page. He had a habit of sniffing as a punctuation for every sentence he spoke, as if there was a perpetual drop on the end of his nose. He said very little when Polly was around, but when she left the room he felt free to offer his advice to the younger men.

"Have you two given any thought to what to do with that land of Theo's downriver? Does it have much of an encumbrance on it?" Nancy was surprised that he didn't know; she had thought that everyone in Virginia knew the size of the Randolph mortgages down to the penny. "If you ask me, I'd tell you to sell it off. It's a tidy little piece, you should get a good amount over what's owed in London. You could use the cash here, or down at your place, Jack, at Roanoke."

Nancy felt the tears gathering at the back of her throat. Dick gave Carter a warning glance that Carter ignored. "Of course it's a great shame, Theo going so young, but from all I hear about him he wouldn't have made much of the place in any event. If you're interested I might consider making an offer myself."

Nancy fled sobbing from the table and Dick followed her into the hall. Behind them Carter looked at Jack in bewilderment. "What? What'd I say?"

"That monstrous little man," Nancy cried. "He was all but saying that it was a good thing Theo's gone."

Dick held her close, patting her shoulder with one hand, cradling her head against his chest with the other and murmuring soothing nonsense. Then he released her abruptly, and when Nancy turned to follow his gaze she saw Polly glaring at them from the staircase. "If you've quite finished your dinner, Dick, I think your wife would be happy for a visit from you." The look she gave Nancy said as clearly as words: I'll deal with you later.

Nancy grasped the nettle. "Go on up to Judy, Dick. My Aunt Polly wishes to speak to me privately."

It was difficult for Polly to wait even as long as it took Dick to be out of earshot. "Just what do you think you are up to now, young lady? Do I have to remind you that he's your own sister's husband? Are you lost to shame completely?"

"I am hardly likely to forget in what relationship he stands to me when he's the only one who gives me the least sympathy in my trouble."

"What I just saw was only an offering of sympathy?"

"What else could it be? You know that Dick would never do anything in the least dishonorable."

"Which is more than I know about you. I suppose I should be grateful that you don't think me such a fool as to believe that."

"I don't think you're a fool, Polly, not at all. I think you're a meddler and a busybody and a gossip, and I think I should warn you that if you carry tales to Judy that upset her now when she needs her peace, you'll get a mighty cold welcome the next time you want to come to Bizarre."

"I don't come to Bizarre for my own pleasure. I come because my sister's children need me."

"We don't, you know. We'd all manage perfectly without you."

Nancy seldom wasted her time on regrets, but she wished that she had not given that particuuar weapon to her aunt a few days later when Judy was delivered of a fine large boy with only Polly's help while Nancy cowered in her room, pressing a pillow over her ears.

"Dr. Meade said that I did a splendid job of it," Polly preened herself, "that he couldn't have done better if he had been here himself. I expect if it had been a girl Judy might even have named her for me."

"I am sure that we are all very grateful to you, Polly." Nancy said.

"And wasn't it fortunate that I was here? What with the doctor being called away that way and you having no stomach for it."

"Very fortunate, Polly."

"So you see, I do have some uses after all, don't I?"

"For heaven's sake, Polly, I've said that we all thank you and I've no desire to contest with you in midwifery. I'm happy that Judy is well and the baby healthy and for whatever part you played in that I thank you again."

"My, we are touchy, aren't we? I suspect that someone is a little jealous of all the attention being paid to someone else." Nancy could think of nothing to say to that, especially since there was a grain of truth in it. With a new life in the house, everyone else seemed to have forgotten that Theo ever existed and Nancy was relegated to the peripheral role of aunt.

Polly and Carter stayed on for the chistening of young St. George Tucker Randolph. Nancy thought it likely that they planned to spend the whole of the spring and summer. Aside from her own feeling about her aunt, she had the problem of Aggie, who was afraid to venture into the hall when she thought Polly might be around. No matter how many assurances Nancy gave her that she was now beyond the reach of anything Polly might do to her, that there was no danger of being whisked away to Ampthill again, Aggie remained unconvinced. Nancy had thought the girl's fears foolish until Aggie showed her the marks still visible on her back where Polly had taken a crop to her just before Grandfather Cary had sent her to Tuckahoe. Nancy thought the whole thing very strange. She didn't like her aunt, but showing cruelty to a servant, especially one who was no more than a child at the time, was in neither Polly's character nor her upbringing. There must have been some special circumstance, but when she asked Aggie the girl shook her head and would not say more than "She just purely hates me, that's all."

It was therefore for a variety of reasons that she was pleased to hear that Polly was leaving. She had nothing whatever to hide from her aunt, but it would be more comfortable not to have to live under her ferret eyes.

On the last day of her visit, Polly sat with Judy while the new mother nursed her baby. She suggested that there was likely to be someone in the quarters with an infant who could relieve Judy of the responsibility.

"Perhaps later, Polly. Not right now. You can't believe what a marvelous feeling it is."

"You might at least let Psyche have more care of him. Clio trained her at Tuckahoe, she'll know how to handle him, even as young as she is."

"I dare say she would. He's such a good baby. Never frets or cries at all except to say that he's hungry. He doesn't need Psyche, do you, baby? He's doing just fine with me."

Polly sighed and tried again. "I'm sure that the baby does very well with you, but he's not the whole of your responsibility, you know."

"I'd never admit it before, but Syphax can run this house without more than five minutes a day from me, just the way Cicero ran Mama's house for her. I used to think it careless of her, but now that I have a darling baby of my own I can see the wisdom of it."

"My sister never in her life shut herself up in a room with a baby and left the rest of the household to their own devices. What about Richard and Nancy?"

"It's really a blessing they get on so well. He's been such a comfort to her over Theo. She misses him dreadfully."

"You surely don't believe that childish nonsense of Nancy's about Theo?"

"Oh I do, and so would you if you had seen them together. And of course Nancy is pleasant company for Dick as well."

There are none so blind, Polly thought grimly, and launched a direct attack. "Judy, how long do you plan to keep your husband in exile in that room down the hall? He was there when we came two weeks before the baby was born and he's still there with the baby rising six weeks."

"Dick moved there so that he could go to Theo in the night without disturbing me and then afterwards I had grown so large and slept so uncomfortably . . . And anyway I don't see that it concerns anyone but ourselves."

"Judy, I know I'm only a few years older than you are, but I sometimes think I'm a lifetime ahead of you in experience of the world. If a man wants to do something or the other, he'll always be able to find an excuse for it. But there's no point in simply handing it to him."

"I'm sure I don't know what you mean."

"And I'm equally sure that you will if you'll give it a little thought."

Polly's going seemed to bring the spring to Bizarre. As if to make up for the harsh winter, warm weather came almost overnight without the usual month of mud and misery. Nancy had always counted the years from one springtime to the next instead of by the calendar, and now at the beginning of the new year she looked back at the old one with disbelief. The girl who had begun the year seemed to have only the faintest family resemblance to the woman she now felt herself to be. She had lost her father, perhaps not irretrievably, but she could no longer persuade herself that Gabrielle was only a momentary aberration. Even if she made her peace with him it could never be on the same terms as before. She had discovered within herself a capacity for the most complete and perfect pleasure, far greater and far different from anything she had ever expected to know, and she had had it snatched away from her. She mourned Theo not just as a lover but as a wasted life; but it was the loss of passion that left her dry-eyed and tormented lying in bed at night on a rack of longing. It was all the more difficult to bear because no one knew but Aggie, and this was not a matter for the sympathy of a servant. Judy could not be told; she would see the nights in Theo's bed only as occasions of sin. Nancy wasn't even quite sure why she wanted someone else to know; she only knew that it would in some way comfort her and ease the hopeless yearning.

She thought that Dick might understand, but there was no time or circumstance that seemed appropriate for telling him. With the coming of warm weather they had resumed their rides together, and on one of those rare days when the very air seemed as soft and sweet as a caress they rode upriver to the throne tree.

"Theo and I used to talk about coming here as soon as the days were warmer and he was feeling better. I don't think he knew that he wouldn't get well until quite near the end. I mean, he used to say that he wasn't going to get well . . . but he didn't believe it. And now my life's over as well."

"I know that it's difficult for you to believe now, but you're very young and very beautiful. There'll be someone else, perhaps even quite soon. Even if you had been married and left a widow, your life . . ."

"But you don't understand. You don't know." Nancy interrupted him and her secret was out. Theo had been her husband in every way except that of the law and the church. When he looked at her unbelieving, she spoke more bluntly. "We thought of ourselves as man and wife. I came to his bed every night when you and Judy were away, and he loved me as a husband does. I was his wife, and now I'm his widow and I cannot bear to be treated as if it were just some passing romantic fancy."

"We should never have left you here alone with him. I knew, or at least I should have guessed, what Theo was capable of."

"I won't have you blaming him. I don't . . . I don't regret

one moment that I spent with him except that I was sorry to be deceiving you, and now that I've told you I don't have that to worry me any more."

"I didn't think that even Theo would do such a thing. To take advantage of your position in the house."

"He didn't take advantage of me. I wanted it every bit as much as he did, and God help me, I still do. I can't go back to being the way I was. Not now, not any more." She was sobbing, and he took her in his arms as he had so many times before, murmuring, "Poor Nancy, dear Nancy." But from the beginning there was a difference in this embrace; the new understanding between them had subtly changed it. It was as impossible to tell which of them first made the move that wholly transformed them from brother and sister to man and woman as it was to pinpoint the precise point when it was too late to turn back. Without either of them intending it, it happened. Against their conscious will, unrestrained by any thought of Judith, they fell on each other like two starving people brought to a banquet board.

* 6 *

Summer came as precipitately as spring had. The seasons that year all made their entrances on stage jostling the one before them and determined to do their turn at its highest pitch. It had been the coldest winter she could remember, the brightest spring, and now it seemed bound to be the hottest summer.

She blamed the heat for the way she felt. Judy's cold house had been built into the side of the low hill outside the kitchen door, and the cart had come from Richmond with the slabs of pond ice covered by sacking and sawdust. There were days when a few slivers of ice to melt her tongue were all she took. The very thought of food and drink sickened her.

The house was filled with visitors those months, and all of them except young Jenny noticed the change in Nancy. She seemed heavier in both body and spirit. Archie came and found her abstracted and snappish when he told her at length of the plans for his new stable, not at all like the Nancy of old. Even Jack, who rarely looked closely at any of his family, asked Dick what was wrong with Nancy. "She looks like a piece of old mutton fat."

"Some sort of woman's trouble, I would imagine."

Polly was the most persistent of those who were interested in Nancy's state of health. She asked so many questions, and hinted so broadly that she would like to do more than ask them, that Nancy took to staying in her room for the greater part of her aunt's visits, waiting almost as anxiously as Aggie for the sound of Polly's door closing before she ventured out in the hall.

Her brother Tom and Martha came briefly from Monticello. Nancy half hoped that they would invite her to return with them; she felt that she would be better off away from Bizarre. The invitation did not come, although Martha was concerned enough about her sister-in-law to send back a mixture that she had found very effective against a costive bowel. Almost as an afterthought in the note that accompanied the bottle she warned that the dose should be used with caution by anyone who was carrying a child. It had been known to cause a miscarriage.

The invitation that did come was for the whole family to spend the first week of October with the Harrisons at Glen-lyrvar. Nancy tried to beg off, saying that she would really rather stay behind with Jenny. "I don't think that's fair," Jenny said. "I've never been to the Harrisons. I don't see why I should have to stay away just because you don't want to go."

"Do come with us, Nancy," Judy urged. "Mary particularly wants you, and Archie is coming and Jack."

"I really don't feel up to matching wits with Jack or listening to Archie drone on."

"Nevertheless, it will be just what you need, a good shaking up. It's more than time for you to stop moping about here and begin to go into society again."

The trip to the Harrisons at Glenlyrvar was indeed a shaking-up. The roads were never good in any season, and by fall the stones that had been used to fill the potholes of spring now stood up as bone-jarring as the dips they had repaired. None of the party was very concerned or surprised when Nancy asked to be excused from the supper table, pleading illness. Mary Harrison showed her straight upstairs. She was far more interested in showing off her new baby to the other young mother in the party than she was in an unmarried female guest. Glenlyrvar was still not finished and the stairs were makeshift, opening straight into the large room that Dick and Judy were to share. To one side of the bedchamber a door led to the only other room on the second floor, one that could not be entered or left without passing through the first. It was a point that would be made much of later. Nancy's bed and a cot for Jenny were already made up, and, at Nancy's request, a pallet was brought in for Aggie and put down on the floor by the double fireplace. When Jenny came trailing sleepily in Nancy got up and helped her make ready for bed, listened to her prayers, and saw with some relief that this would not be one of her little sister's nights to fight sleep. Jenny was sleeping soundly by the time the party downstairs broke up and the others prepared for bed. When Judy and Dick came up the stairs they were met by a frightened Aggie, who insisted that a reluctant Judy come into the other room. She found her sister whimpering and sweating but cool to the touch, told her to take a dose of the medicine Martha had sent from Monticello, and closed the door between the rooms firmly behind her. She told her husband that in her opinion Nancy was suffering from nothing more than the gripes and an exaggerated notion of calling attention to herself. "If no one makes a fuss over her, she'll soon get tired of all that moaning and groaning and go to sleep."

But there would be very little sleep at Glenlyrvar that night. Judy by her own account never closed her eyes, sitting up in bed with her book. Downstairs, the Harrisons, their sleep already broken by the demands of a teething baby, listened with dismay to the increasing volume of sound from over their heads. They were awake when Aggie tapped on their door to ask for some laudanum for her mistress, and Mary Harrison herself took the squat brown bottle up the stairs. She found Judy sitting up alone in bed, the door of the inner room half ajar but lit only by a lamp on the floor. She could not see Nancy, but Dick came out of his sister-in-law's room and thanked her for the medicine. She offered her help, but both Dick and Judy told her not to worry, that they were quite used to dealing with Nancy's spells. Back downstairs in her own bed she tried to interest her own husband in the curious fact that Dick seemed to have taken on the nursing chores, but he only mumbled and rolled over and went back to sleep. Sometime later in the night both of them thought that they heard footsteps on the stairs, but they were in that state between waking and sleep when they could never be sure of what was dream and what was real. It might have been Dick going for a doctor, it might have been a servant, it might have been nothing at all.

Only Jack and Archie Randolph slept undisturbed in the bachelor house and heard nothing of Nancy's illness until they were told at breakfast. Archie was alarmed and wanted to send for a doctor, but Judy assured him that it wasn't necessary, that Nancy was very much better although she would keep to her bed for the day. With what Archie considered a chilly lack of feeling, Jack said that he supposed it was just another of Nancy's hysterical fits, and Dick said that it was something of the sort.

Randolph Harrison was eager to show the men the changes about the place, and after breakfast Archie and Jack rode off with him. Dick was dragooned as an escort for the ladies of the house on a trip to the store at the crossroads. Mary had it on good authority that he had new ribbons in.

Before they left, Mary went up to make sure that a fire had been properly made in the invalid's room and found Nancy looking very pale and tired with the blankets drawn up tight under her chin. Nancy promised her that she would be quite all right alone with Aggie, that she would in fact prefer to have no company since she had had so little rest the night before.

At midmorning the silence of the house was broken by the unmistakable bark of old Mrs. Harrison. "Pompey, where are you, you lazy old hound? Take my cape and give me an arm up these infernal stairs. I've come to see Miss Nancy."

"Aggie, for God's sake don't let her in, tell her I'm asleep."

But Aggie was helpless. With a final push against the balustrade Mrs. Harrison was in the upper room. She looked through the connecting doorway to where Nancy huddled under the covers, sniffed once or twice, and sent Pompey away.

"Well, Missy," she puffed, "what's this I hear?" She bustled by Aggie, untying her bonnet strings, slipping off her black lace half-mittens, talking all the while. "Your sister and young Mary came by my place and Mary said you had been very ill in the night, though Judy seemed to think it amounted to nothing. Still, you young people don't know everything, and I thought I'd just come and see for myself."

Although Nancy protested that she was perfectly recovered and just drowsy from the laudanum she had dropped and Mrs. Harrison shouldn't bother herself, the old woman would have none of it.

"Nonsense, it's my duty. You're my son's guest and I know what's due you if my daughter-in-law doesn't."

"You mustn't blame Mary. I made her go."

Mrs. Harrison nodded briskly. "Just as well it's only the two of us at that." With a backward tilt of her head she indicated Aggie. "That girl hanging about out there? She yours or belong to the house?"

"Aggie's mine."

"Fond of you, is she?"

"I think so, very fond."

"Know how to keep her mouth shut? Doesn't gossip in the kitchen?"

Nancy pulled the cover up closer under her chin. "I don't know what you mean."

"Now, Nancy love, I think you do. Just trust your old Auntie Harrison. First thing is to get these windows open and get some of the stink out of here. It's a dead giveaway." She threw the windows open and came back to the bed. "Now don't start crying, it's far too late for that." She sat on the edge of the bed and gave Nancy's hands a few brisk pats. "You're no more than a baby yourself. What are you now? Sixteen?"

"Seventeen," Nancy sniffled.

"Poor little mite and no mama when you need her." Mrs. Harrison touched her handkerchief to her own eyes before she gave it to Nancy and then she was all business. "Now then, tell Aggie to bring in the bath from next door and put it in front of the fire and bring up some water and get you a clean shift. We'll tidy you up a bit and then I want to look at you."

"Please no, Mrs. Harrison."

"Don't worry. I won't hurt you, but I have to make sure you aren't torn, though you look big enough."

Later, Mrs. Harrison herself panted down the stairs to her daughter-in-law's clothespress and came back with a roll of linen bands over her arm. "Mary won't be needing these. She's still got my grandchild at the breast. Now, you are going to bleed for a few days longer than your monthlies but not a lot heavier after today. You're not hemorrhaging, which is a blessing, but if you do start bleeding heavy again, don't hold onto your pride but have someone come for me. That comforter's clean, wrap yourself up in that and sit quiet in the chair and Aggie and I will see what we can do about a clean bed for you."

Under Mrs. Harrison's directions Aggie fetched pails of cold water. The sheets were put to soak, and Mrs. Harrison herself scrubbed at the mattress. "The feathers will have to come out of this to really clean it, but we'll just turn it over for now and then you can get back in and stay there."

"Mrs. Harrison, I want to explain . . ."

"There's no need," Mrs. Harrison hushed her. "What's done is done, and I don't judge others and I don't carry tales, so you rest and Aggie and I will get these sheets up by the fire and by the time the rest of them get home here you'll be tucked up all cozy and none the worse for your illness last night."

"That's a good girl," she said later when Aggie had left the room. "She come with you from Tuckahoe?"

Nancy nodded. "But before that she was at Ampthill. Grandfather Cary gave her to me."

"Old Archie," Mrs. Harrison laughed. "I thought she had the Cary nose."

Nancy looked at her in alarm. "She'll hear you," she whispered.

"She knows who she is," Mrs. Harrison said calmly. "They always do."

"I can't believe she does," Nancy said. "It's not possible."

"Well, perhaps I'm mistaken," Mrs. Harrison agreed. "I only meant she's a bright biddable girl and you should take good care of her." She pulled the chair over to the bedside and settled her bulk carefully down in it. "I'm going to sit right here and rest myself a bit now we've got you comfortable again, and I want you to close your eyes and try to sleep."

"Mrs. Harrison?"

"Yes, Nancy."

"I love you."

"And why not?" Mrs. Harrison smiled. "They say I've a rough tongue, but I'm a good old soul for all that."

For five more days the party stayed on at Glenlyrvar. For the first two of them Nancy kept to her room, attended by Aggie and visited by all the members of the household. On the fourth day she came down for dinner but tired quickly and turned a little lightheaded and had to be helped back up the stairs. Nothing was said about her illness, except that Judy expressed the hope that Nancy would be strong enough to travel on the day set for their return; she was beginning to worry about St. George left at home.

For the journey back to Bizarre, the sisters were joined in their carriage by Jack, who would later recall nothing of interest in the trip except that both Nancy and Judy were quieter than usual. This was for him an unexamined blessing; he had always preferred women as audience rather than participants. Back at Bizarre, he exclaimed appropriately at the growing beauty of his nephew and rode off the next morning to Roanoke, leaving behind the happiest of families, father, mother, lusty baby, and loving aunt.

*   7   *

When they had been back at Bizarre for a week, Nancy felt so well that she could scarcely believe that she had ever been ill. Willie came to take Jenny back to Tuckahoe, and Nancy parted with her reluctantly. Jenny did not protest at going home this time but went quite willingly, to everyone's surprise. But then, Nancy thought, she's growing up, not so much my little pet any more; she'd even been a little broody, like a tiny old woman, ever since they returned from Glenlyrvar.

The Harrisons came on a return visit, and the five young people made the round of calls and dinner parties at all the neighbors within an easy carriage drive. Once or twice Nancy caught Mary Harrison looking at her speculatively, as if there was something she wanted to say but couldn't quite manage.

Early in November a traveler brought both Judy and Nancy letters from their sister Molly at Presqu'ile. Judy read hers through twice, frowning. "What a very curious thing. Molly says I am to come to Presqu'ile whenever I choose and bring St. George and stay for as long as I like. I can't imagine what she could be thinking of. What does she say in yours?"

Nancy crumpled her letter up and threw it on the fire. "Nothing, nothing at all. Just pleasantries." It was very strange. It had been arranged months earlier that Nancy would spend Christmas at Presqu'ile, and now Molly wrote that she begged Nancy to excuse her but her husband's relations were all coming and it would be inconvenient for Nancy to be with them. It was an odd sort of house that had room for one sister and not the other. Still, there was probably a very simple explanation, she decided, and she would not let herself be offended. It was worrying, none the less.

A few days later an even stranger letter came from Jack. He was in Richmond, he scrawled across the page; he was ill but would soon be better. They were not to worry about him, and above all they were none of them to leave Bizarre until he had spoken to them. It was a matter of the greatest seriousness and he would come as soon as he possibly could.

Jack came in a hired carriage, still feverish and too weak to sit a horse. Judy and Nancy both tried to persuade him into bed, but he said that he had no time to rest, that he hadn't risen from a sickbed and bounced himself in a carriage with a wobbly wheel just to climb into another bed. He looked frightening, chalk-white. He gave Nancy so fierce a look that she shrank back against the stair. Surely he couldn't be that angry with her. He was just impatient to see Dick, she told herself. That was all.

The two brothers closeted themselves in the small back room that Dick used as an estate office. Nancy and Judy stayed in the hall, unashamedly straining to hear, but the clear, thin voice of Jack, which would usually cut through the heaviest door, was today so thickened by rage or fever that they could make nothing intelligible out of what little they heard until Dick put his head out the door. "Judy, have Syphax bring the brandy in, would you please, and then I think you and Nancy had better both join us." His voice was steady, but there was something in his manner that was more frightening than Jack's disturbance had been. He was preternaturally calm, as if he thought that he must hold himself firmly in control or the world would collapse around him.

"I want you to tell the girls what you've just told me."

"Do you mean it?" Jack was doubtful. "Don't you think they'd best sit down?"

Nancy sat in the high-backed chair by the window, but Judy walked over to her husband and stood by his side, her hand on his sleeve.

"About two weeks ago, before I fell ill," Jack began, "I was leaving Prior's place in Richmond and I heard someone in a group of men standing by the gates to the garden say something about Bizarre and brother and heard someone laugh, but I've been trying not to be so quick to take an insult, and besides I thought it was just an echo of something of Theo's doing."

"I should think you would be ashamed to speak of poor Theo that way now."

"Hush, Nancy," Dick said. "Let Jack get on with it."

"I would have thought no more about it, particularly since I came down with the fever the next day and didn't have the strength to think of anything else. I'd nearly forgotten it when a friend came to see me and told me a tale that was all over Richmond and Cumberland County for a certainty and well on its way to being all over Virginia." Jack stopped and appealed again to his brother. "Are you sure that Nancy and Judy should hear this from me?"

"Go on."

"I don't suppose it's any kinder to make a long story of it. In short, what they're saying is that Nancy was delivered of a child at Glenlyrvar and that Dick murdered it at birth."

Both women looked at Dick, but it was Judy who spoke. "That's a lie, a monstrous, monstrous lie."

"Of course it's a lie. I didn't need telling that by you or Dick. There is another version. Some people hold that the child was born dead and Dick is only guilty of concealing the body."

"And that's as great a lie as the other," Nancy cried. "Who dared tell you such a thing?"

"It was Rob Banister who came to me with it, but there's no call to be angry with him. He's denied the story wherever he's heard it, as have other friends of ours. He only came to me because his denials seemed to have no effect, and he thought it was time that we took some sort of action."

Judy had gone as white as the kerchief at her throat, and now she began to tremble violently. Dick forced her into a chair and held the brandy glass to her lips. Jack took hold of her hands and chafed them between his. I could fall to the floor in a swoon, Nancy thought, and not one of the three of them would notice.

"If it wasn't Banister, then who did start it? He must know where he heard it."

"He tried to track it down before he came to me, but he says it's like battling smoke. It seems clear enough that it started at Glenlyrvar."

"That's not possible," Dick said. "Randolph and Mary were here as our guests two weeks after we all left Glenlyrvar. They couldn't possibly be spreading tales about us."

"Not the Harrisons themselves. Apparently it began with some servants' gossip, something one of their people fancied they saw or heard the night that Nancy was so ill. Nobody knows when it made the leap from the kitchens to the drawing rooms, but it was brought back to the Harrisons straightaway. His neighbors kept pressing him until he allowed them to make a search of the grounds. They found a pile of shingles with what might be bloodstains on it, just where the blacks had said it would be."

"I never heard anything so lily-livered in my whole life," Nancy burst out. "Randolph Harrison should have sent his neighbors packing and taught his servants to keep a closer rein on their tongues, with a whip, if need be."

"There's no value in being angry at Harrison," Dick said.

"I'm sure he did the best he could. But there's something here I can't understand. Harrison may not be as firm a man as we would wish, but he is certainly known to be an honest one. So is Rob Banister. I can't see how a rumor like this can gain currency when it pits kitchen gossip against the word of reputable people.

"In the ordinary way, their word would be enough. Even allowing for the pleasure people get from a scandal about those higher placed than they are. In fact, Rob said that at one point he was sure that the whole thing had been scotched completely, but then some friends of ours went to Tuckahoe." He spoke directly to Nancy. "They thought Willie should be told so that he could come to your defense."

"They can't have known Willie very well if they thought that. Willie wouldn't lift a finger to help anyone unless he thought there was money in it."

"He was certainly unhelpful in this instance. At first he would only say that he knew nothing about it, that it was nothing to do with him, but then he went on to say that the family had always disapproved of Dick and Judy's marriage."

"But that had nothing to do with Dick's character," Judy protested. "It was only that Mama thought we were too young."

"We know that, others don't. Willie is also saying that Nancy was turned out of Tuckahoe because of her attachment for Theo and that the family has expected for some time that she would turn out badly. Rob believes he goes even further in private conversation with his cronies and tells them the story is true. He says it's Tuckahoe that is giving the story credence against all his denials."

"Loathsome Willie," Nancy said. "He should have been drowned as a pup."

"I quite agree," Jack said. "But it's too late for that. The question is, what do we do now?" Jack leaned back against the edge of the writing table and looked at the others, Nancy with her hands tight-clasping her elbows as if she were bone-chilled,

Dick kneeling at the side of his wife's chair still holding the glass of brandy she had pushed away. "Something has to be done and soon."

"But not tonight," Dick said. "We'll sleep on it. Perhaps by morning we'll be able to think a little more clearly."

There was very little sleep for Nancy that night and no more for the rest of the family by the look of the them in the morning. There was also no agreement at all what the proper course of action should be. Jack wanted to ride straight back to Richmond and challenge anyone he could find who was repeating the story. Dick would have none of that.

"It's my quarrel, not yours. If there are duels to be fought, I will fight them."

"Anything that touches your honor touches mine."

Judy, whose red swollen eyes spoke of a night of tears, began to cry again. "I can't bear to hear you talk of even one duel, let alone God knows how many."

"There wouldn't be many. Once you've pinked one or two the rest will run to cover."

"But what if they don't? What will become of me if anything happens to you? And to St. George?"

"What you ought to do," Nancy cut in, "is challenge Willie. Willie couldn't hit the backside of a barn with a pistol, and he was so clumsy with Papa's sword that Papa forbade him to touch it." Both men looked at her with shocked expressions and told her that Dick could not possibly challenge her brother. "Why not? From what Jack says he's easily half of our trouble."

"In the first place it would be highly improper for me to challenge my wife's brother and more importantly everybody shares your opinion of Willie's skills and they'd think I was choosing the easiest target."

"My God, I do think that men's honor is the most unpractical thing there is. If women could fight duels I'd fight him in a minute and there wouldn't be any of this damned gentleman's nonsense of firing in the air either."

It was far from the proper moment to try to explain the gentleman's code of honor in these matters to Nancy. The words would have fallen on stony ground. Jack interrupted his brother before he had spoken more than a few words. "You know, there might be a way to handle Willie. Suppose we were to put him in a position where he had to challenge you."

"Do you mean to tell me that it's all right for Willie to challenge you but not the other way around?" Nancy was incredulous. "That's the most ridiculous thing yet. Besides, Willie never would. He's just as cowardly as he is mean. Even if you caught him when he was so sozzled that he agreed to fight, he'd find a way to crawl out of it next day."

"That's more or less my point," Jack said to his brother. "If you were to call Willie a liar publicly, accuse him of cowardly and slanderous statements, attack his character, then he would have to challenge you or lose all credit with anyone. It would be taken as an admission that he lied."

Dick thought it as likely a plan as anything else they could think of. The problem remained of how and when to stage the confrontation with Willie. The surest way to attract the necessary widespread attention was through the newspaper publication of a letter. Judith objected to this, saying that it would only give the tale greater currency, and after more talk the three of them—Jack, Dick, and Judy—decided that it would be possible to write a letter phrased so that only those who already knew the story would understand.

"There's another thing," Jack said. "We shouldn't take any steps at all without consulting Father Tucker."

"I'm sure he knows nothing about this," Dick said. "We would have heard from him. One of us will have to go to Williamsburg. It would kill him to hear it from someone else."

Judy, still miserable at the thought of a duel, even one as unlikely as a challenge from Willie, welcomed the idea of consulting Mr. Tucker. "Perhaps he'll be able to think of some other course. Surely there must be grounds for a lawsuit, libel or slander or whatever they call it."

Nancy had sat mute since her first outburst at the mention of a duel with Willie, growing steadily angrier. "What about me? Does no one have anything to say about what's to become of me? I hear all this talk about Jack's honor and Dick's honor and sparing Father Tucker's feelings and not worrying Judy with any talk of duels and not one word for me. It doesn't matter what you all do. I'll still be marked as a Jezebel. Am I supposed to put my hair in a cap and spend the rest of my life in a closet when I'm only seventeen years old?"

Her sister turned on her in a fury. "You wicked, ungrateful girl. I suppose you like the idea of Dick getting himself killed to protect your precious reputation."

"Of course I don't. I don't want anyone to be hurt any more than you do. Besides, I can't see that that would do me any good at all. Everyone would think Dick very noble, but it wouldn't alter how they feel about me if he fought every man in the Dominion."

"Please, Judy and Nancy," Dick said. "We are altogether lost if we once begin to quarrel among ourselves. Nancy, you must know that we are all aware of your importance in this. We'll listen most willingly to whatever you want to say or do."

Nancy drew herself up. "Well then, if you want to know what I think, I think we are forgetting who we are. We're all Randolphs, and since when has anyone in our family cowered in a corner plotting away against some nasty gossip by people who wouldn't dare speak to us if they passed us in the street. I think Judy and I should pack our best things and have the carriage brought around and go into Richmond with our heads high and call on everyone we know. Then everybody could see how little these jealous lies mean to us."

Judy was horrified. "I couldn't possibly. What if we discovered that some of our friends were not at home to us?"

"Then we should know fast enough who were really our friends and who weren't."

"It would seem so brazen. I couldn't stand the humiliation."

"I don't see how you can call it brazen when we have

nothing to be ashamed of. If you're afraid to go, say so. I'll go by myself."

"You must not permit it," Jack said quickly to his brother. "If she were insulted in the street our hand would be forced."

"Don't worry about it. Nancy won't leave the protection of this house until the whole thing is over and done with."

Nancy argued the point but without much hope of changing her brother-in-law's mind. Her arguments did not carry great conviction in any case. She had spoken on a brave impulse and frightened herself nearly as much as she had frightened her sister.

Just as they had all four been brought together by their trouble, now, in the next few days, it seemed that the same troubles were forcing them apart. They none of them wanted to have to think or talk about it, and yet when they were together it was impossible to speak naturally of anything else. Except for the meals that were eaten in gloomy silence, they went their own ways. Dick found a multitude of things that had to be done before he could leave for Williamsburg. Judy shut herself up with St. George again. Jack buried himself in his lawbooks. Nancy tried to read but she found she couldn't concentrate on the simplest things. She would take up a piece of sewing, work at it a bit, and then hand it to Aggie to do properly. "Do you know about the trouble in this house?" she finally asked her maid.

"We all know there's some kind of trouble. We don't know what it is."

"There are some wicked people saying that Mr. Richard murdered a baby that they say I had at Glenlyrvar. You know that's not true, don't you, Aggie?"

"White people are saying that?"

"White and black, but you know it's a lie, don't you?"

"Oh yes, Miss Nancy. I know that very well."

"And if anyone should ask you, you'll tell them so, won't you?"

"Oh yes, Miss Nancy, I surely will. Mr. Richard never murdered any baby at Glenlyrvar."

"Good. You're a good girl, Aggie. I don't know what I'd do without you."

When Dick left for Williamsburg to see his stepfather, Jack went with him and the sisters were alone in the house, uneasily circling each other. They were not to be left undisturbed. On the second day Nancy saw Polly's carriage coming up the drive and hurried upstairs to her room with Aggie. "I knew she'd come. I could feel her hovering over us like a scavenger bird waiting to swoop down on some juicy tidbit."

"Who you talking about?"

"Aunt Polly, you idiot, who'd you think?"

"Miss Nancy, don't you let her come up here. You mustn't let her get at me."

"She's not after you, she's after me." Nancy opened her door a crack and listened to Judy greet her aunt.

"Poor, dear Judy. You don't look at all well. But of course you wouldn't. It must be a terrible, terrible strain for you."

"I'm really quite all right, Polly."

"But of course you're not. How could you be? I knew I was right to come. Carter didn't want me to, touching pitch and all that. But I said to him, 'They're my own dear sister's girls and I know where my duty lies.' "

It's enough to make a cat sick, Nancy said to herself and closed the door. Half an hour later Judy was whispering frantically through the keyhole. "You must come down. She won't go until she's seen you."

"Tell her I'm ill and can't see anyone."

"She'd never believe me. She keeps on asking questions and I don't know what to tell her."

"Tell her to go on back to Carter where she belongs and leave us alone."

"Shh, she'll hear you. Besides, she says she wants to help, and she is family, after all."

"So is Willie family and look what a great help he's been."

"If you don't come down she'll think you're frightened of her."

Polly's voice came up the stairs. "Tell your sister that if she doesn't come down those stairs straightaway, I'm coming up them."

"Go on, Miss Nancy." Aggie said. "Don't let her come at me. She can turn me around till I don't know what I might say. You don't want that."

"Dear Polly," Nancy trilled as she entered the drawing room. "How good it is to see you. And looking so well. How is Carter?"

"Don't pretend to me that you care anything at all about Carter."

"But Auntie, I do. I care at least as much about his well-being as I do about yours."

"Don't try that impertinence on with me, miss. I know you far too well. I've come all the way here in miserable weather, against my husband's wishes, to help you in your trouble, and I don't have to put up with your snippity-snappity ways."

"And what trouble is that?"

Polly gave the airy disclaimer just as much attention as it deserved. "People come to me every day as a near relation and a frequent visitor here at Bizarre to ask me the truth of it. What am I supposed to say?"

"If you're wise you'll say exactly what we should say if anyone had the boldness to come directly to us. That the whole thing is a farrago of lies and servant's tittle-tattle and malicious gossip and to say anything else whould be downright dangerous, because both Dick and Jack are ready to call out anyone who says different."

"They can scarcely call out the whole state of Virginia."

"They can make a good start on it. And on the husbands of gossips as well."

"Naturally I always deny everything, but I could be so

much more convincing if you would tell me the whole truth of it."

"The truth of it is is that there was no baby and Dick did not murder it."

"Will you take the Book in your hand and swear to that?"

"No, I won't. My word is good enough for my friends and should be more than good enough for yours. If someone thinks me guilty of murder they're scarcely likely to think I'd hesitate to swear false."

Polly had one more shot to fire. "There is one way that you could stop all the talk you know."

Nancy was skeptical. "Is there really? I'm sure we would all be glad to hear it."

"If I were to go back to town from here and say that I had examined you and found no sign of your ever having any connection with a man, then I could . . ."

She was not permitted to finish the sentence. "That is the most disgusting thing I ever heard in my whole life."

"It would take only a moment," Polly protested, "and I am your aunt, after all."

"I don't care who you are. Did you think for one second that I'd permit anyone to poke me about like a black at a Georgia auction?"

"Yes, I would, if you were as innocent as you pretend to be. And before you refuse me perhaps you had better think how it will look if you turn me away without satisfying me."

"You'd be better employed thinking about what people will think about a malicious, jealous, spitfeul woman who would spread ugly tales about her own sister's daughter."

"I'm warning you, Nancy. I came here as a friend, you don't want to send me away as an enemy."

"Why not? I've despised you all my life, your silly airs about Grandfather Cary, and ordering people about and prying into things that have nothing to do with you, and the way your eyes are set so close together that they're nearly on top of each other. And I'll tell you something else, Mama never liked you much either. She only had you to Tuckahoe because she thought nobody would ever marry you and you'd have to spend your whole life with your father and she felt sorry for that. But she laughed at you when you were gone, just the way everyone else does." Nancy did not wait to hear any reply that her spluttering aunt might make, but ran up the stairs and slammed and barred her bedroom door behind her.

Judy tried to persuade her to come down and apologize. "You wouldn't believe how she's carrying on. You've made everything much worse."

Nancy dug in her heels stubbornly. She didn't see how things could be much worse than they were already, and it had been too great a pleasure to vent some of the rage that had built up in her over the past days to back away from it.

It was left to Judy to try unsuccessfully to mollify Polly. If there had ever been any hope of help from the Carter Pages, there was no chance of it now. "I shall pray for us all," Judy said later to her sister.

"If you knew what to pray for you'd ask for a bolt of lightning to strike Polly down dead, and Willie and Gabrielle too while He's at it."

In Williamsburg, St. George Tucker read the letter that his stepsons hoped would force Willie to a confrontation and gave it his reluctant approval. His own inclination, as a man of the law, was to find some way to make the courts work for them. He did not feel that an action for slander was quite as hopeless a possibility as they and he asked that Dick delay any action until Tucker and his friends could determine whether or not the story could be traced surely enough to few enough sources to warrant a lawsuit.

"Give me until after the first of the year and then, if we can't make a case against anyone, publish your letter. Also, I think you and Judy, and Nancy as well, of course, should plan to stay here with us from the time you publish until the matter's settled. We'll show the world that your family is supporting you completely since Judy and Nancy's seem to be worse than useless."

Judy ordered a special dinner, and Dick opened a bottle of his best claret on New Year's Day, but none of the family had much appetite. The men decided that the weather was too threatening for them to ride out and make their New Year's calls on the neighbors. Only Dr. Meade called on the ladies of Bizarre, waiting in the drawing room. "Roads are in a shocking state," Dr. Meade said as he looked about the empty room. "I only got through myself because I'm used to being called out in all sorts of weather." No one was deceived. It was clear to all of them that the Randolphs were being shunned. It made the trip to Williamsburg all the more welcome.

Richard's letter, not naming Willie but unmistakably aimed at him, was published in mid-January and was greeted by total silence from Tuckahoe. After a week's time Rob Banister and two other friends rode out to see Willie and reported back. Willie said that he heard about the letter but had not read it himself and was in fact very curious to know at whom it was directed, since he knew nothing of the matters he understood the letter to contain.

"We know he's a liar, of course," Banister said to Richard. "But I'm afraid he's foxed us. There's really no way of accusing someone of backing away from a quarrel when he insists that he never heard of one."

"What would happen if I were to go to Tuckahoe and confront him directly? Make it impossible for him to ignore the charges I make?"

"My feeling is that Willie being Willie, he might very well just smile and say he forgives you. But it's worth trying, I suppose."

"It's just that I want to be sure that I've made every possible effort to draw Willie out, because if this doesn't work we may be forced to go with a plan that my father has that could only succeed because it is such a very desperate gamble."

"May I know what . . ."

"Not yet, I hope not ever. Though I'm afraid you'll hear of it soon enough."

* 8 *

Richard Randolph came back to his stepfather's home in Williamsburg early in March, having failed completely at Tuckahoe.

"The simple fact of the matter is that Willie will not be winkled out," he reported to his father and Nancy and Judy. "I carried with me a cutting from the paper with my letter and thrust it on him when he finally made his appearance, and he just waved it off, refused to touch it, said it had nothing to do with him. If he could have, he would have refused to see me altogether, but I told Gabrielle that I would wait in the hall until I had at least the satisfaction of confronting him myself. She said he was much disposed not to see me at all, and I waited upwards of four hours before he came out all smiling and said the servants had neglected to tell him I was there."

"Oh, he can smile and smile and lie and lie," Nancy burst out. "Why didn't you just pick him up and shake the truth out of him. That's what Papa would have done."

"Hush," Judy said. "You don't understand how these things are done."

"Maybe not, but I understand Willie and none of the rest of you seem to. He's a coward to the bone, and if he thought you were going to thrash him, he'd crumble away."

"And then he'd go about saying that Richard had beaten him into recanting and we'd be no better off than before."

"All right, all right," Nancy said impatiently. "Never mind about Willie. I never thought that nonsense about Willie challenging anyone would work anyway. What about Papa? What did he say? If you can't manage Willie, he can."

"I'm afraid we can't hope for any help from that quarter, Nancy," Dick said gently. "I asked first of all to see Colonel Tom, but your stepmother said that he was most unwell and that it would be wisest not to disturb him, that she had been warned to protect him from any disturbance."

"And you believed her? How could you be such a fool?" Nancy was indignant. "She's as big a liar as Willie—bigger."

"That's as may be, but in this instance she was telling the truth. She finally consented to letting me talk to him on my pledge that I try not to excite him in any way."

"He could hardly fail to be excited by what you had to say."

"Nancy, he couldn't even begin to understand what I had to say. He thought at first that I was Molly's husband and then that I had come from your brother Tom at Monticello. I don't believe that he was ever quite sure in his mind about who I was, to say nothing of our troubles."

"Are you sure he wasn't just a drop too much . . ."

"Nancy, how can you talk so?" Judy protested.

"Because this is no time to be dainty. You know as well as I do that Papa sometimes takes a bit heavy."

Mr. Tucker intervened. He had talked to Dr. Harvie in Richmond, and it was clear that Colonel Randolph had had an apoplectic stroke. Harvie was bleeding him and doing his best but had told Mr. Tucker that he didn't foresee much chance of recovery. Nancy heard him out dry-eyed and then turned to Richard.

"Dick, I will beg the loan of your carriage and go to him myself."

"I can't let you do that, Nancy. It would do no good for either of you."

"You can't keep me away from my own father," Nancy appealed to Mr. Tucker. "Please, tell Dick he must let me go."

"It would do no good, my dear. Your father is past helping you now."

(178)

"I don't care anything about that. If he's ill I want to be with him. Judy may be willing to trust him to Gabrielle, but I'm not. She'd like to see him in his grave, she would, and then couldn't she flash herself around Tuckahoe."

Dick and Judy looked at each other in dismay. The last thing they wanted this night of all others was for Nancy to whip herself into one of her hysterias.

"Nancy, you heard what Dick said. Papa might not even know you."

"Of course he would. Just because he was a little confused in his mind over Dick doesn't mean anything. He'd know me, I was always his pet. You know that even if you won't admit it. He'd know me and I could nurse him properly and make him well again. Please, Mr. Tucker, think if it was you and one of your girls wanted to see you, wouldn't you want someone to help her to you?" When Mr. Tucker agreed that he would indeed, she went on. "Well then, please help me. I must see him. I don't care about all this other nonsense. I just want to see Papa. If Richard won't help me, then you will. I know you are the kindest of men. Everyone has always said so."

"My dear child, if it were possible to help you in this I would, but neither his medical men or his wife would permit it."

"His wife indeed. How can you call that sly-faced witch his wife?" Nancy stormed. "She's the one to blame for everything. He was perfectly well before he married her, and we were all happy there together, and then she came along and now look at us. It's all her fault. All of it."

Judy reached out a restraining hand. "Nancy, calm yourself. You don't help anyone by getting into one of your states. We must pray for dear Papa."

"Pray, pray, pray—Judy's remedy for everything. You were the one who said we must pray for Mama to get well and you saw how much good that did. You'd be better off praying for Gabrielle and Willie to drop down dead in the street. If God knew what He was about they'd never have been born."

"That's blasphemous, Ann Cary Randolph, and you know it very well."

"I don't care if it is, it's the truth. It's not fair to me, first Mama and then Theo and now Papa, and all those people saying wicked things about me, when I never did anything to hurt anyone my whole life long, at least I never meant to. I tried to be good, Judy . . . Dick . . . you know I try."

"Nancy, hush yourself. They'll hear you howling in the street."

"I don't care if they do."

"You may not, but I do, and I'm sure Mr. Tucker does. Try and remember that we are guests in this house." Nancy's sobs went undiminished, and Judy looked up helplessly at her husband.

"We'll just have to let her cry it out," Dick said, "but then try and get her settled down. Father and I must talk to her about the other matter without any more delay."

"I'll try. But you know she doesn't hear a word anyone says when she's like this."

No amount of cozening and soothing could stop Nancy's sobs, and the others agreed that it would serve no purpose to discuss Mr. Tucker's plans with her that evening. Morning would have to be time enough.

Mr. Tucker watched with a worried frown as Judy helped Nancy up the stairs to the bed. "Is she often like this?"

"Not often, but very thoroughly," Dick said.

"Strange, Judy is such a steady young woman, and this one . . ."

"I know. Judy's like a well-banked fire and Nancy's like a Catherine wheel throwing off sparks."

"I'll tell you frankly that it worries me. If she were to go off like a firework in a courtroom, it could be very destructive. Perhaps we should reconsider."

"No, no, Father, you've convinced me that we must go ahead with it and the sooner the better. She'll cut up some tomorrow when we tell her of it, but once she's persuaded she'll behave sensibly. She's an intelligent girl, but her father babied and spoiled her and gave in to her."

"And then left her adrift."

"Exactly. She wasn't ready for it, and she is in some ways still very young."

"She's seventeen," Mr. Tucker said shortly. "Quite old enough to understand the seriousness of her situation, and yet, barring this outburst tonight which does nothing to reassure me, I have seen no evidence that she does."

"She understands very well, Father. She only tries to appear indifferent out of pride, bravado, call it what you will."

"I hope I won't have to call it damned foolishness. If my plan's to succeed it will need steadiness from us all."

"You'll have it," Dick assured him, "not at first, but you will have it."

Nancy rose in the morning dizzy and lightheaded and ravenously hungry, as she always was after one of her bouts. She was attacking a breakfast of ham and spoon bread with enthusiasm when Dick came to escort her to his father. Outside the door to his father's study, Dick stopped and turned Nancy to face him.

"Nancy, my father wants to talk to you about a plan he has to end our predicament. I warn you that you will probably not take kindly to the idea at first—I didn't myself—but I am now persuaded that it is the only possible course left to us."

"What is it?" Nancy was wary.

"I'd rather he told you himself. He can explain it far better than I could. But I am trusting you to listen to him calmly, to hear him out before you make up your mind, to show him that you really are the brave young woman I have promised you would be."

"I hate it when people tell you to be brave ahead of time. It means that they are going to tell you something dreadful."

Mr. Tucker seemed nearly as reluctant to tell Nancy about his plan as she was beginning to be frightened of hearing it. He fussed over the comfort of her chair, offered her another cushion for her back, a footstool, asked if she had breakfasted, if she would like another cup of tea. Only when Nancy folded her hands firmly in her lap and looked up at him expectantly, her china eyes blinking, did he begin.

"I've been afraid these past few days that you were perhaps not fully aware of the seriousness of your situation, but Dick assures me that you are. Is he correct?" Nancy nodded dumbly. "And you realize that action which may seem rather drastic to you might be necessary?"

"Yes," Nancy said with some hesitation.

"I don't suppose Dick told you anything of what we had in mind?"

"Just that he had agreed to it and that I must be brave."

"I am sure you will be," Mr. Tucker said hastily. "Very well then. I have given the whole unfortunate matter a good bit of thought in these past weeks, particularly since it began to seem obvious that Dick would get no satisfaction from your brother."

"I could have told him that. In fact I did tell him. Willie's a nasty cowardly piece of work and always has been."

Mr. Tucker cleared his throat and rearranged the row of quills lying ready on his desk. "Well, be that as it may, he certainly will not be drawn in this instance. Failing that, it seemed to me and to the others I consulted, men in whose judgment I have the greatest confidence, that the best way out of this affair would be a full airing of the matter in a court of law, putting an end to rumor with established fact."

"Oh, I do agree, Mr. Tucker," Nancy interrupted. "I said so right from the beginning. I said it at Bizarre and Dick and Jack and Judy will remember that I did. I said either ignore the whole thing and pretend not even to know about it or sue them all for slander or libel, whichever it is; I've never got them straight. You hit Willie or Gabrielle in the pocket and they will really sing for mercy—and Polly, too, although I don't think she's too much of her own. She'd have to get Carter to pay up, and wouldn't he sniff; he's very close-fisted, Carter is."

"Wait, wait, hold on, my dear." Tucker held up a hand to stem the flood. "You misunderstand me. A suit for slander won't answer here. However much certain members of your family may have contributed to your difficulties either by what they have said or failed to say, and I agree that they have behaved deplorably, nothing they have done is actionable. The tale did not originate with them. A slander case would only be effective for our purposes if we could find a single source of the libel, and the story seems to have been so widespread from the beginning that that would be impossible. Aside from that it seems to have its original impetus from the quarters, and a slave is not only not answerable to a civil cause, he isn't even competent to testify in any court."

"I wasn't proposing that we sue servants," Nancy said. "Can't their masters be held to account?"

Mr. Tucker looked to his stepson for help and Dick intervened. "Father has a different sort of court action in mind, Nancy, one that will require your help and all your courage."

"I told you that telling me to be brave only frightens me."

"Dick only meant that we want you to stay calm so that we can be sure that you really understand what we are saying before you have to make up your mind whether you will join us in our action. Now, Nancy, I want you to remember that I have not only thought about this a good deal, but I have also talked it all over with my friend John Marshall in Richmond, not just a friend but a most distinguished lawyer, and we agree that there is some precedent for what we propose. Not at all a frequent occurrence, but not altogether unknown either." Mr. Tucker paused and shot Nancy a wary glance, fearful of another eruption. "In short, what we suggest, my dear, is that you and Dick offer yourselves to the authorities of Cumberland County as defendants in a case of infanticide." Mr. Tucker ignored the half-stifled cry of protest from Nancy and hurried on, but Dick leaned over and took her hand. "The subsequent trial would be the most public and most clearly defined way possible to establish your innocence for all the world to see. It would be someone very foolhardy who would try to revive the story once it has been proven false in a court of law." He met Nancy's eyes for a moment and turned away. "I won't say that your troubles will be entirely over. You will no doubt always be a bit wary of gossip, but the root cause of all the speculation would vanish."

Nancy was silent for a long moment while both men looked at her anxiously. When she did speak it was slowly, wonderingly, as if she could not quite believe what she was saying. "You want Dick and me to go on trial for murder?"

"In essence that is correct, although as a practical matter it would probably be so arranged that Dick would be tried first and with his acquittal the case against you would be abandoned."

"But they hang people for murder."

Mr. Tucker gave her the half-pitying, half-soothing smile that lawyers reserve for an ignorant and alarmed client. "Only if you are convicted, and there is no chance of that. Mr. Marshall and I are agreed that there is so little evidence that if we were not in fact so eager to go to trial, the case would be thrown out of court. In fact, the commonwealth, left alone, would never bring it to trial. There is no risk whatever of either of you being found guilty."

"That's all very well for you to say, but it's not your neck or Mr. Marshall's that's being stuck in the noose."

Dick quickly hushed her, but Mr. Tucker said that he was not offended, that Nancy was quite understandably disturbed. Being on trial for murder was not a pleasant thing to contemplate, even when the outcome was assured.

"Not a pleasant thing to contemplate, indeed." Nancy was scornful. "It chills me right down to my bones, that's what it does."

"I can see that it would," Mr. Tucker sympathized, "and I think none the less of you for being frightened."

"I would have to be a perfect fool not to be."

"Perhaps," he agreed, "or at least one without too much experience of the vagaries of the law. Trust me, Nancy there is no possible way they can find you guilty. It will not even be a question of guilt or innocence, in fact. Instead it will be the destruction of the flimsy structure behind the whispers. Like lancing a boil, not a pleasant experience either, but a great relief when it's over."

Nancy sat and thought. Both men gave her encouraging smiles, and Dick patted the hand he held with approval for her calm.

"Must I give you my answer right away?"

Mr. Tucker shook his head. "Of course not. I wouldn't want you to agree to anything like this without thinking it over. But you should take into your considerations the fact that Dick has already made up his mind to this."

"So if I refuse?" The unspoken question hung in the air.

"Dick will still go to trial. It would be better since the whole procedure is only for appearance's sake that you join him, but if you decide not to, we will go ahead without you."

"And think the less of me."

"Not at all, not at all. We realize you are just a girl. You cannot be expected to face something like this with the same degree of boldness that Dick can summon up."

Stung, Nancy sat up indignantly. "I have been accused of a great many things, God knows, but a lack of boldness was never one of them. Quite the contrary, you have only to ask my Aunt Polly." She wavered a moment and then plunged in. "All right, if Dick trusts you and thinks this is the right thing to do, then so must I. I'll do whatever you say." She bit her lip and looked appealingly at both of them. "Only one thing, though. They won't put me in jail, will they? I don't think I'd like that at all."

Many times in the next week or so Nancy would regret her decision, but there seemed no way to retreat from it without damaging her self-esteem and, perhaps more importantly, suffering some loss in Dick's and his father's approval. It became even more difficult for her to sustain her courage when they moved to Richmond to begin the actual preparation of the case.

Engrossed in fine points of the law, discussing strategy, neither of the men had time for more than an occasional absent-minded smile or a brief pat on her hand. Not until she complained to Dick about being shut out of what did after all concern her very closely was she included in the planning sessions with John Marshall, and then only as a spectator, not as a participant.

She soon discovered that although they listened to any suggestion she had with grave politeness, when she was through the discussion would continue as if she hadn't spoken. She dimly remembered meeting John Marshall years before at Tuckahoe, but he was not a man who would long engage a young girl's curiosity. She still found him rather unprepossessing, but he had a kind face, and she was grateful to him for his unfailing patience with her, explaining every point of law that arose as clearly as he could, considering that his audience was one that had always found talk of law and lawsuits a bore.

Nancy was well aware, even without Dick constantly telling her, that if St. George Tucker was considered the most distinguished of the older Virginia men of law, then John Marshall was his equivalent in the younger generation. Mr. Tucker, she knew, would not take any part in the actual trial because of his relationship to the defendant, but she had thought that Marshall and his colleague, young Alexander Campbell, would handle it alone. She was therefore very surprised to hear John Marshall insist that a third lawyer be brought in. Particularly when it was someone whose name she remembered very well from the dinner-table conversations of her childhood, and never very respectfully.

"It's true he's no great bargain as a lawyer," John Marshall said, "but then that's not what we need him for. He can twist and turn a witness inside out and make a jury weep with a lift of his hand. We are agreed that we don't just want our young people acquitted of this crime; we want the world so convinced of their innocence that the very mention of their names in connection with any wrongdoing will bring shame on the speaker. He's a better man for that than either of us."

Mr. Tucker agreed. "The question is, will he do it? He's old and I hear he's not been well, and he's no particular fondness for any of us."

"He hasn't outlived his fondness for money," Marshall said. "Have young Richard ride out to Henrico and offer him two hundred and fifty guineas."

Dick came back to Richmond disappointed after his first trip out to Henrico Parish. The old man pleaded his age, the state of his health, said his constitution wouldn't stand the strain of a trial.

"Offer him five hundred," Marshall said. "A fee that big will tickle his vanity as well as his greed. And don't be ashamed to beg. There'll be a special little fillip for him in it if he thinks a Randolph is dependent on him."

Dick would always think it was the extra money that tipped the scales, but to Nancy it seemed clear that Patrick Henry had come to their defense not for the money, and certainly not because he felt any particular sympathy for them, but because the trial would offer him one more stage on which to perform, one more chance to prove that his power over men's minds was undiminished. He agreed with a great show of reluctance and only after extracting two more concessions: a snug, warm carriage was to be provided for him, and his fee would be paid cash down in advance.

On the twenty-fourth day of April 1793, Ann Cary Randolph and Richard Randolph were brought to the Cumberland County courthouse and there surrendered to the waiting prosecutor and to the judge currently assigned to that place, both men having been briefed beforehand by Marshall and Tucker. To maintain the appearance of a normal trial on a capital offense, Dick would be kept in custody until the trial began. Nancy was released in the charge of her attorneys. There were no accommodations suitable for her in the Cumberland County jail, and as Mr. Campbell pointed out, she was not likely to run away after having appeared voluntarily. The courtroom was cold and empty, but John Marshall said with some satisfaction that in a few days time it would be crowded to the doors. The trial would have the audience they wanted.

In the carriage on the way back to Richmond Nancy sat in silence remembering her last glimpse of Dick before the jailer escorted him out. Her lawyers discussed an interesting point of law that had arisen during the arraignment. I believe they are almost enjoying themselves, Nancy thought bitterly. They all seem to forget that there are real people concerned, and one of them is sitting in a cell.

The Trial

John Marshall's unhappy domestic situation would not permit a guest in the house, so Nancy was lodged at the Campbells' while she awaited the trial. But it was to the Marshalls' front parlor that she was brought for her interview with Patrick Henry.

Mr. Marshall met her at his door. "Mr. Henry is waiting for you and wishes to see you alone, but I wanted to warn you that he is sometimes a rather rough-spoken man. He may ask you questions that you won't want to answer and perhaps not quite in the manner you're accustomed to."

"If you mean he's not a gentleman, I already know that."

Marshall looked alarmed. "Try not to let him see that you feel that way. Even for his five hundred, he may still be a bit touchy." He hesitated as if there were something more he wanted to say but was not quite sure how to put it. "The important thing to remember is that he is here to help you, just like all the rest of us, and you mustn't be frightened."

Despite or perhaps because of Marshall's solicitude, Nancy was beginning to be afraid of what lay before her. She had a sudden panicky thought: If she was this frightened facing a lawyer who was serving her, how would she manage with those on the other side? For no matter how often Mr. Marshall and Mr. Tucker assured her that she would never have to stand in the box, that Dick would be acquitted and the charges against her dropped, she still was plagued with nightmares of being bullied and shouted at by a man in black with a face like Willie's, and she would wake hearing Polly's laugh.

Patrick Henry was leaning against the mantelpiece wrapped in a frayed camlet of a dusty brown that seemed to have been chosen unsuccessfully not to show travel dirt. What she could see of his linen could also have used the services of a laundress, but his boots were gleaming. He acknowledged Mr. Marshall's introduction and Nancy's curtsy with only a slight bob of his head and stood silent while Marshall excused himself and the clock in the corner of the room ticked off a full minute.

Nancy cleared her throat nervously. "Mr. Henry, I think you should know how very grateful we are that you have taken this case."

"Sit down, girl, here in the light where I can see you." He pushed a lyre-backed chair over by the window and drew another up so close that when he seated himself his knees were touching the edge of her petticoats. She was reminded of staring contests at the dinner table at Tuckahoe with her brothers; Patrick Henry's unblinking gaze would have beaten them all.

At last he sighed, took a copious load of snuff, sneezed, and pushed his old-style wig to one side and scratched vigorously behind his ear.

"I'm an old man with country ways. You mustn't mind them." He smiled. "But then, if I'm not mistaken, you've been acting in country ways yourself."

"If that's what you think, then why are you bothering?"

Patrick Henry shrugged. "You're charged with murder and you're not a murderess, that's one reason, and I'm not only an old man but a poor one as well, so there are five hundred other very good reasons. We don't have to love each other to work together, so let's get on with it. In the first place I haven't been hired to get you and your brother-in-law off on a murder charge; any first-year clerk could do that. Mr. Marshall and Mr. Tucker will already have told you that there isn't a chance in hell that you could be convicted, though they might have put it differently. Suffice it to say that you have no call to fear for that pretty neck of yours."

"I'm not afraid to die," Nancy said dramatically.

"That's a damn fool thing to say," the old man barked. "Do you often say idiot things about matters you know nothing about? Fancy you're being brave when you're just being stupid? Always take a fence when there's a gate right near? Read a lot of English trash, don't you, and fancy yourself some kind of noble heroine."

"You have no right to talk to me like that."

"I got the right to talk to you any way I please, when your brother-in-law rode out and disturbed an old man's rest and made me drive all the way in here when I could be sitting at my own fire instead of looking at a silly girl who got herself in trouble and is trying to wriggle her way out."

She was halfway to the door before she had her temper in check and stood trembling with her back to him.

"Swallow your tongue along with your pride, Missy, and come sit down. We don't have time for nonsense. We have a lot of work to do today."

Reluctantly Nancy came back, but she ostentatiously swept her skirts away from him before she sat down.

"That's better. Now don't interrupt me. Despite all the evidence to the contrary, I think you've got some brains under those curls, and I'm going to explain what I'm doing." He waved a hand toward the view out the window behind her. "Everyone in Richmond will be glad to tell you that I'm no great shakes as a legal man, not having had the advantages of some people in the way of schooling and all that, but I'm the devil himself in the courtroom. I can make the most mule-headed person in the Dominion think that black's white and the sun sets in the east and nigger-knockers are good eating. I already told you it's no trick to get you and young Richard acquitted. That's not my job. My job is to convince everybody that you and Dick are as innocent as newborn lambs, victimized by malice. That all the stories told about you are made up of nothing but moonbeams and slaves' chatter. And that anyone who says different is a vicious liar with some dark reason of his own. To do all that I need your help."

Henry picked up the pile of papers on the table beside him and began to riffle through them. "You Randolphs," he said, "for all your high-stepped, nobody else is good enough for you ways, you've about as much loyalty to each other as pigs in snake brush. All these witnesses, all relations, and the closer the kin the nastier the stories. Plain people like the Henrys find it downright disgusting. But never mind that. I'm going to find out from you everything you can tell me about those who will be called to testify. How you think they'll give their stories, how much they hate you, how far they'll go. Even whether they are good or bad liars."

"Why would any of them hate me? I've never done anything to any of them."

"How in God's name should I know why they hate you? But you can trust me that they do, some of them at least, or we wouldn't be sitting here like this. It would all have been swept under a very expensive carpet and you would have been sent away on a nice long visit with friends in the Carolinas until the next scandal came along. But don't you worry, young Nancy, I'm going to blow all your enemies out of the water at this trial, but you're going to have to give me the ammunition."

"But I don't know . . ."

"Yes you do. You just don't want to face it. Not everybody loves you, my dear. You've a pretty face and a bold eye, and I'll wager you have a sharp edge to your tongue from time to time. You don't fool me sitting there so meek now." He stopped and looked at her, struck by another thought. "By the way, you're not to come to court dressed the way you are now. Get that lace off your sleeves and find yourself a nice old-lady overskirt in gray or lavender."

"How about all white?"

He laughed until he choked and had to take another load

of snuff and sneeze heartily three times before he could recover himself. "You see, I said you had a sharp tongue in your head. But no white, we'll try for less obvious effects. Borrow something from your sister, she always looks as if she were in half-mourning. Speaking of Judy, I want you to sit together in court, leaning on each other's shoulders. It would be a pretty sight for the jury if you were to share a bottle of salts or something of that nature."

He consulted the papers in his hand. "Now the witnesses. First, the people who were at Glenlyrvar. Mr. and Mrs. Harrison, young people not much older than you are. Are they happy together?"

"What does that have to do with anything?"

"Just answer my questions. If they weren't important I wouldn't ask them, or at least I don't know whether they're important until I hear the answer. It's a simple enough question. Do Mary and Randolph Harrison love each other?"

"Of course they do, they're married."

"Don't make me lose patience with you, my girl," he said with some disgust. "Don't try and make me believe that you've lived nearly eighteen years without ever seeing a married couple who weren't in love. Is he affectionate toward her, considerate of her whims?"

"So much as I've seen, very much so."

Henry thought for a moment. "She had a new baby in the house, right?" Nancy nodded. "Randolph Harrison wasn't feeling a bit neglected, hadn't been putting his arm around a young visitor or being just a little familiar with a pretty girl like you?"

Nancy flushed. "Certainly not."

"No need to be so tetchy, it wouldn't be the first time it happened or the last."

"Nevertheless it did not happen with Randolph Harrison."

"So his wife has no reason, not even an imaginary one, to dislike you or be jealous of you?"

"Mary Harrison has never been anything but kind to me. She wouldn't even be testifying at the trial except that they say she must."

"Then you think she will be putting as good a face on things as possible?"

"She will tell the truth, if that's what you mean."

"As to that," Patrick Henry said, "there are a hundred different ways of telling the same truth, and I think you will probably learn about several of them before this week is gone." He dipped his quill in the inkwell on the table beside him and scribbled a note on his papers. "I don't think there'll be much to worry us in her husband's testimony either. I understand it took him over a week after the rumors reached him before he even bothered to look at the spot where the body was supposed to have been placed. Sounds to me like a man who will go a long way round to avoid any unpleasantness." He flipped the page he had been writing on over on its face and picked up the next. "That brings us to the other two guests. Archie Randolph, who's being called by the Commonwealth, and young Jack, whom we may call. What can you tell me about Archie?"

"He's my cousin. I've known him all my life."

"Nice young man?"

Nancy was not at all sure how she would describe her feelings about Archie. "I used to think so."

"But not now?"

"He's a miserable coward," Nancy burst out. "He said he loved me, he even asked me to marry him and I haven't seen or heard of him since last November."

Henry looked at her with some surprise. "You're surely not fancying that you're in love with him?"

"No, of course not, but . . ."

"Your vanity is hurt," Henry supplied. "He won't be the first young man to be scared off by a touch of scandal. Still he won't want to look like a fool. Did many people know that he was attached to you, was even thinking of marrying you?"

"Everyone who knew him I should think. He's not the kind of person who's very good at hiding what he feels."

"Then however he feels about you now he won't want you convicted," Henry said with satisfaction. "Makes him look like an idiot or worse. He will probably know nothing whatever about anything at all when he gets on the stand. We won't waste any time over him, can't think why they are bothering to call him. That just leaves Jack and I've already spoken to him."

"There's still Jenny and Aggie, they were there too."

"As far as the court is concerned they might both of them have been in Paris, France. One of them's a slave and the other's a child and neither of them is competent in the eyes of the law. So it seems to me that we haven't got anything to worry us about those who were on the scene that night. None of them is very eager to testify against you, and as far as possible they are going to be deaf, dumb and blind. Is that about the way you see it?"

"They don't need to be blind," Nancy protested. "There was nothing to hide. Nothing happened. How many times do I have to tell people that?"

"If you really want an answer to that and ain't just being heroic, I'll tell you. For the rest of your life, that's how long. But ..." He leaned forward and emphasized his words with sharp jabs of his bony finger against her knee. "Don't tell me about it. I'm defending you against a murder charge that I know is false, but don't tell me nothing happened. I don't care what it was but it wasn't nothing, so don't you play the innocent with me. It doesn't make any difference to me for one thing, and it gets in my way and wastes my time for another."

Nancy glared at him as he shuffled through his manuscript pages. The man had no feeling, no sensitivity, she thought angrily. It went far beyond just not being a gentleman, he was a monster. He looked up from the papers, gave her a fatherly smile and a pat on her knee. "Ready to go back to work with me now?" he asked. Nancy could only nod dumbly.

"As I see it our problem is going to lie with those we can call the outsiders, the ones who are going to testify to things that happened before and after Glenlyrvar. Martha Jefferson Randolph, for instance. I know she's Tom's daughter and your brother's wife, but I need to know about things only you can tell me. What's she like, how does she feel about you?"

"I don't know."

"You can do better than that." Mr. Henry was exasperated. "Do you mean you've never thought about it one way or the other? Or you've thought about it and can't figure it out?"

"Both, I guess. Mr. Henry, before this happened I never thought very much about how anyone felt about me. They were my family and my friends, and well, there was no reason to think anyone would want to do me harm. But since the trouble started everything's been turned upside down. Sometimes I think everybody hates me. I quarreled with Gabrielle, that's why I left home really, and Willie and I never got on, but I didn't think he hated me as much as he must, and my sister Molly won't speak to me either."

"I don't care a twopenny piece for your quarrels with your brother and your stepmama, they're not going to be in that courtroom. Tell me about Martha Jefferson."

"I've told you I don't know. I've never fought with her. She and Tom sided with me when I left home, because Tom didn't like Papa marrying again either. She's always been very pleasant, very polite." Nancy searched for words to describe her sister-in-law. "She doesn't laugh much."

"Let's go back, before the trouble, was she fond of you then?"

"She seemed to be, or at least . . ."

"Never mind," Henry interrupted. "She's Tom's daughter. Not one to demonstrate much feeling, but not much stomach for a fight either. Is she ambitious?"

"Ambitious for what?"

"Her father is probably going to be President in a few years' time, or at least make a damned hard run at it. Is she ambitious for her husband as well?"

"You mean politically?" Nancy dismissed the whole idea with a wave of her hand. "I never think about politics."

"I can promise you your sister-in-law does, and she'll be thinking about it on the stand. If she sees things going badly for you she may cut her losses and come down against you, if it looks like an even chance she may be helpful, she won't want a scandal hanging over her husband's career."

"Tom doesn't have a career, not the way you mean, he's just a planter like Papa."

"Don't worry. He'll soon get into politics if his wife has anything to say about it."

"How can you say that? You don't even know her."

"I don't have to know her. Her papa has hand-reared her and she'll be just like him. Clever with words, but cautious and no meat to him." He dipped his pen and put a question mark beside Martha Randolph's name on his list. "We'll have to gamble on her. But we'll treat her very, very tenderly."

Patrick Henry tilted back in his chair and rubbed his hands together. "Now," he said nearly gleefully, "tell me why your Aunt Polly hates you."

"How do you know she does?"

"Try not to be such a goose. It's as plain as the nose on your face. Whatever happened at Glenlyrvar, the Harrisons not only didn't want to spread it about, they didn't even want to know about it. It would all have been dismissed as slave tittle-tattle, without the work of your family, without your blessed Aunt Polly going around talking about how she suspected you and Dick months ago. She's going to testify to your immodest behavior, to seeking out an abortion producer, in short that she knew it all along. Now if she weren't a near relation maybe we could write it off as just the work of a natural busybody who wants to be first with bad news. But she's your own mother's sister, and even given the lack of family feeling you Randolphs seem to have, it still smells to me of a great personal malice. She hates you right enough, now you tell me why."

"She has no real reason."

"Real to whom? Maybe not to you or to me, but trust me, it's real to her. What did you do to her? Go back, you're almost of the same generation, she's closer in age to you than she was to your mother. Was she jealous of you?"

"I wouldn't give a dud shilling for Carter Page. He's the most boring man alive."

"There are other things beside gentlemen that cause jealousy, and there's a good chance you let her see your contempt for her husband a bit too clearly."

"She was lucky to get him, she was practically an old maid when they married."

Her lawyer smiled. "You know, it's a funny thing. You say she had no reason to hate you but it's clear you don't have any great fondness for her. Is that just since this affair or does that go back?"

"We never liked her."

"Who's we?"

"All of us, my brothers and sisters and Papa. She was always interfering, asking questions about what we were doing and then running to our mother. Whatever you really liked to do she disapproved of. She didn't like the clothes I wore, too bold. She didn't like the way I rode with the boys, like a hobbledehoy, she said. She thought I shouldn't read any of the books that Papa got from England unless they were what she called improving, which just means dull."

"She was a damned interfering nuisance, in other words." Nancy nodded. "And I suppose you let her know you felt that way about her?"

"I'm talking about years ago when I was still just a child, it isn't hard to tell whether a child likes you or not."

"And later, when you were older?"

"We used to make fun of her, she put on such airs. Whenever she met someone she made sure that they knew who she was, not just plain Miss Cary but Archibald Cary's daughter and if they weren't from Virginia she used to say 'when my father was Speaker' in about every other breath. Mama was Archibald Cary's daughter too, but she certainly never made a fuss about it. I don't think Mama even liked him very much. He gave her a headache."

"And how did you feel about your grandfather?"

"I liked him well enough. He talked too loud." Nancy smiled, remembering. "When I was little I thought that was why he was the Speaker, because he had the loudest voice."

"You were very nearly right," Patrick Henry murmured under his breath. "He ever show you any special favor, anything the Polly might have resented?"

"He sent Aggie to me," Nancy said slowly, "and then he left her to me in his will and Polly despises Aggie, but she felt that way before Aggie was sent to me, she cut her with a riding crop when Aggie was just a little girl at Ampthill. Sometimes I think that's why Grandfather gave her to me, he wanted her away from Polly."

Patrick Henry rubbed his hands together in satisfaction. "Now this is what we have here. We have a witness who can be very damaging to you. Is she a clever woman?"

"She thinks she is." Nancy shrugged. "She's not stupid."

"Then she'll know that she must appear to be testifying reluctantly, only doing her duty. A loving, sorrowful aunt. That's what she'll want the jury to see."

"She can do it, too," Nancy said glumly. "She can talk so sweet and pious, it'd turn your stomach."

"She can do it for a while," he agreed, "but I never knew a talking woman who couldn't be led into indiscretion. Sooner or later she'll give away her true feeling about you, and after that she's finished."

"You don't know her, she can go on for hours."

"Getting past her guard is one of the things I'm being paid for and nobody ever said I didn't give value for money." He smiled so broadly that Nancy could see the gaps where his teeth were missing. "Your grandpa threatened to stick a knife in me once, did you know that? Said if I were Caesar, he'd be my Brutus. Great one for Shakespeare, your grandfather was. But he didn't like me much. Your auntie ain't going to be overfond of me either." He squared the edges of his papers with his palms, rolled them up and tapped her with them. I think we've done a good day's work. You remember now, dress modest, very loving to your sister, and whenever anyone says anything you don't like try and look them straight in the eye. Makes 'em nervous. They don't any of them stammer, do they?"

"No."

"Too bad, very useful stammering sometimes, doesn't mean a damned thing but juries take it for lying."

* 2 *

Nancy rode to the trial in a carriage with Mr. Campbell and Mr. Marshall flanking her, so that they might demonstrate that they had kept their bond and ensured that she hadn't escaped the jurisdiction of the law of Cumberland County. She wondered where the law of Cumberland County might suppose she could have run to. She had followed Mr. Henry's instructions about her dress as nearly as she could, wearing a light-blue overdress with plain bands on the sleeves and a close-fitted, unadorned straw bonnet covering her curls. Nevertheless he had frowned when he inspected her that morning at the Campbell house, untied the bonnet strings from the bow under her ear, and retied it firmly under her chin. "You'll do," he said. He traveled alone to the courthouse, a little ahead of them, making time for him to confer with Dick. Only one lawyer at a time could be permitted in the cell.

It had been decided that Judy and Nancy were to enter the courtroom together for the benefit of any early arrivers. Mr. Tucker's carriage, bringing Judy, was delayed, and Nancy waited, wedged between her two black-clad lawyers, eagerly scanning each carriage as it pulled in. The courthouse yard was filling rapidly. They would have the crowd that Mr. Marshall had predicted. With each new arrival, Nancy's hopes rose, and each time she was disappointed. Her father's carriage did not arrive, and none of the grooms cooling off their masters' horses was a Tuckahoe man. She had known he wouldn't come, known that chances were he didn't even know about her troubles; still, it was hard not to feel abandoned among strangers.

Inside, the courthouse seemed to Nancy like a country church, a bit wider in the body, with the judge's bench where the altar should be and the empty jury box waiting for the choir. Mr. Campbell and Mr. Marshall seated the sisters on the first bench behind the railing and then took their places at the long oak table. Mr. Marshall's clerk brought him a silver inkstand, a stack of white paper, and a bundle of quills. Marshall ran his fingers along each quill, testing it, and handed some of them back to the waiting clerk before he unclipped the knife from his chain and began to trim his pens. He half turned to Nancy and smiled. "Like to do it myself," he said, "then I know it's done right." Papa used to let me make his pens, Nancy thought.

She could hear the murmur and rustle of the crowd coming in behind her. Each time the door opened, dust devils rolled back and forth on the floor in front of the bench. If Judy sees that she'll send for a broom, Nancy said to herself. But Judy's eyes were tight shut, her hands clasped in her lap, her lips moving.

Nancy sat rigid, willing herself not to turn around and face the eyes she could feel on her back. She jumped when she felt a hand on her shoulder, but it was only old Mrs. Harrison bending down to whisper something reassuring. The court usher hissed at her before she had more than a few words out, and she went back to her place, indignation in every creak of her old-fashioned crinoline. It wasn't often that anyone dared tell Mrs. Harrison what to do.

The room grew warmer as it filled with spectators. Nancy could hear a low buzz of conversation and even an occasional half-stifled laugh from the rows behind her. Then at some signal she could not see, the clerk banged his staff on the floor, sending the dust devils scurrying again, and prayed all rise for the judge.

Mr. Tucker and Mr. Marshall had tried to explain to both girls that morning what they could expect in the courtroom. They were to rise when the judge entered and to stay standing until told to be seated. They were not to speak out, no matter how offended they might be.

"One rises for the judge," Mr. Marshall had said, "not because of who he is in himself, for he may unfortunately be a very indifferent sort of fellow, but because he embodies in himself the majesty of the law."

"You mean like a wicked priest giving a sacrament," Nancy said.

Judy gave a shocked gasp, but Mr. Marshall smiled at Nancy. "Almost precisely," he said, "although a bad judge may be overset more easily. But it's true the two forces of law and religion come uniquely together in the law court. The witness places his hand on the Book and swears that his testimony is true. If he is a believer he knows that he risks his soul; if he is not he knows that he is in grave jeopardy with the law. Between the two, most witnesses are most uneasy when they stray from the truth."

Nancy thought of his words now as she looked at the judge, a small man with a wig too big for him. He should have been a comic figure, but somehow he was not.

"The Commonwealth of Virginia, in the court of Cumberland County, versus one Richard Randolph accused of feloniously murdering a child said to have been born of Nancy Randolph," the clerk intoned. Stop, Nancy thought. It's all a mistake, we shouldn't be doing this, it didn't sound at all the way it had when Mr. Tucker had first told her of it.

The judge cleared his throat. "The Court of Cumberland County, in the Commonwealth of Virginia, is now in session. Is the accused present?"

"He is in the court's custody, Your Honor."

"Bring him in."

The clerk opened the door at the side opposite the jury box just next to where Judy and Nancy sat. The jailer came first, a little mossy man with a jaw like a nutcracker. Patrick Henry ended the procession, dressed in black, shiny at the elbows and greenish at the edges, his wig askew, as if he had just enjoyed a good scratch, and between them walked Richard Randolph. Syphax had been allowed to attend to him and had outdone himself. Nothing about him said that he had just stepped from a jail cell, not a wrinkle or a smudge. Standing between the older men, he looked to Nancy like the young prince attended by gnomes. Judy half rose from her place, and her husband bent down and put his arms around her. Patrick Henry nodded approvingly and shot Nancy a warning glance. *Does he think I'm an idiot?* Nancy thought crossly and gave Dick the most formal acknowledgment of his bow, the slightest possible bob of her head.

"He looks so pale," Judy whispered, and Nancy reached over and took her hand. Patrick Henry beamed.

"Your name?"

"Richard Randolph."

"Residing at?"

"Bizarre in the County of Chesterfield."

"Occupation?"

"Planter."

"You are aware of the nature of the charge. May we waive the reading of the arraignment at this time?"

Dick looked at Mr. Marshall, who had risen to stand beside him. "The defense consents," Mr. Marshall said.

Nancy had been warned that the first part of the morning would just be the formalities and that the trial proper would not start until after the opening arguments, but it seemed to her interminable. First John Marshall introduced himself to the judge, then he identified Mr. Campbell and Mr. Henry as his colleagues. The prosecutors introduced themselves in turn. The fact that all of them had dined together at one time or the other in the hall of Marshall's Richmond house seemed not to enter in. All of them but Henry, and he needed introduction least of all. The clerk painfully scratched down all the names, stopping to inquire about the spelling. All but Marshall took their places at the counsel's table. Marshall stood at his client's side before the bench.

"How does the defendant plead?"

"Not guilty, Your Honor." There was a ripple of comment in the room and the judge banged down his gavel. What did they expect, Nancy thought, that we would go to these lengths so that Dick could stand up and say that, yes, he murdered Nancy Randolph's child?

"You may be seated, Mr. Randolph."

Dick took his seat at the defense table, looking as composed as if he were presiding at dinner at Bizarre. He was to sit there throughout the trial, never moving, never turning around. No further questions would be asked of him. It would begin to seem, in fact, that the trial had very little to do with him, that he was only there by chance.

"My client requests a trial by a jury of his peers, Your Honor."

"Very well, the clerk will call the veniremen."

The clerk rolled out each name as if he were the major-domo at the Governor's Ball, except that there was no "and his lady" tacked on. Nancy recognized the names, if not the faces, of most of the jurymen. They were in age from their twenties to their sixties, all planters except for one storekeeper who asked to be excused because his wife was attending the store and could not be trusted to do the "figgering." He was replaced to Nancy's mounting horror with the fourth Carrington to enter the box. She could not credit the blithe ignorance of Dick's lawyers. Everyone in Virginia knew that the Carringtons and the Bizarre Randolphs were enemies from so long ago that no one was even sure of the original cause. By the terms of his father's will Dick and his brothers had been forbidden to sell any of their land to any Carrington, and that had been by no means the first shot fired. And yet there sat four Carringtons ready to pass judgment on him, while his attorneys sat and looked on indifferently. She leaned forward and tugged on Mr. Campbell's sleeve, who sat nearest her. He moved his arm away, but she bent forward again and got a good grip on his lace, and he turned, frowning.

"The Carringtons mustn't be on the jury," she whispered. He nodded and put his finger to his lips.

"They hate the whole family," she persisted. Now Patrick Henry turned around and told her to hush, very crossly. She would have gone on, but in the silence she felt the judge's eye on her and sat back.

Mr. Campbell took a sheet of paper in front of him, wrote something on it, folded it up tightly, and passed it back to her. She unfolded it carefully in her lap, screening it from anyone curious who might be looking over her shoulder, but all she read was "Explain later." She didn't know whether that meant that she would have a chance to explain later or that he would have an explanation for her. In either case later would be too late, for John Marshall was saying that the defense found the jury acceptable and the prosecution agreed.

The jurymen rose to be sworn, looking excited and self-important, with one or at the most two of them seeming a bit embarrassed at the attention. It seemed to Nancy throughout the trial that the jury was thoroughly enjoying itself. There was, after all, room for only so many spectators in the court, and there were hostesses in Richmond and Petersburg and Williamsburg and on plantations up and down the James and Appomattox who would be more than eager for a firsthand account at their dinner tables. The appetite for scandal was insatiable, and this would be far better fare than some second-hand tale that filtered down from Philadelphia or New York.

"Is the Commonwealth prepared with its opening statement?"

"We are, Your Honor."

Nancy supposed later that if she had ever had to take the stand and face the prosecuting counsel directly they would have come alive for her, ceased to be faceless black gowns. One short, one a little taller, one wearing a full wig and the other a peruke with a thin black bow. Years later she would meet a man in Richmond who thanked her for her courtesy and generosity to him under the circumstances, and, when she looked bewildered, explained that he had been prosecutor at her trial. Even then she hadn't remembered him.

She listened in a daze as the taller one made his statement. He intended to prove that Richard Randolph had feloniously murdered the child born to Nancy Randolph in order to conceal the birth and their illicit relationship. He listed the witnesses he intended to call, one or two fresh names, but on the whole all people she had discussed with Mr. Henry.

"It is an unusual case, gentlemen, one which rests entirely on circumstantial evidence, but you must not be led to believe that because the evidence is circumstantial it is not valid. There were witnesses to the alleged deed, they are not, however, legally qualified to testify. I cannot ask you to believe that if they could testify they would without question be in support of the Commonwealth's case, but I also ask you not to draw the opposite conclusion."

At the defense table there was a short conference. Mr. Campbell wished to protest the mention of Jenny and Aggie, but Patrick Henry reminded him that they were agreed that they would make no objection to the prosecution's conduct of the case, do nothing that would seem to the spectators to be an attempt to conceal anything. Mr. Campbell nodded, but Nancy could see that he was not happy.

John Marshall's opening statement was a disappointment for the crowd. He spoke so low that those in the back could not hear him. One or two of them even cried out that he should speak up until the judge quelled them. "Gentlemen of the jury, you have been asked to serve your fellow citizens of Virginia in a most unusual case. Richard Randolph stands before you accused of murder, as innocent of the charge as you are, an innocence in fact so certain that my colleagues will not be presenting a full case in defense. We are confident that the prosecution's case will fall of itself, compounded as it is of tittle-tattle, speculation, and servants' gossip, and will be seen to fail by all fair-minded men, in which company I place each and every one of you. It is a fact that the prosecution cannot dispute that so weak is their case against my client that he would not have been brought to trial except at his own instigation. In defense of his name and his honor and that of his wife and her family, he has placed his life in your hands. I am confident that it is a safe resting place."

Marshall bowed to the jury and the judge and took his place at the table. He pulled the top sheets of the paper in front of him closer and selected a quill from the row at his right hand and with everyone else in the room waited expectantly.

"The Commonwealth calls Mr. Carter Page as its first witness."

The clerk repeated the name; the usher swung the doors at the rear of the courtroom open and bellowed "Mr. Carter Page" into the hallway. Carter stopped just inside the door and looked startled and alarmed as all heads swung toward him. Nancy would notice this momentary hesitation on the part of each witness as he entered. Some of them would stumble as if the impact of all those eyes was a physical barrier. Carter's hand flew to adjust his cravat, as if he read in the scrutiny some criticism of his appearance. He marched down the center aisle without looking to right or left, doing his best to give the impression of a man of affairs called away from important business, an impression that lost some of its credibility when he found it impossible to work the latch of the low wooden gate that separated the spectators' section from the courtroom proper. He stood fumbling with it, blushing, until one of the prosecutors leaned over and swung it open for him. He took the oath in a mumble and settled very uneasily into the high-backed witness chair.

The prosecution led him slowly through the opening questions: his name, his residence, how long he had known the defendant and under what circumstances. Mr. Henry had talked to Nancy about those first questions. "They are required for the record," he'd said, "so the jury can know who the witness is and whether he can reasonably be supposed to have the information that he will be testifying to. But to a good courtroom lawyer they serve an even more important purpose. All witnesses are frightened when they first step up on the stand. They are under oath to answer any questions, and most of the time they don't know what those questions are likely to be. The clearest conscience in the world has some little flaw in it, and most witnesses are convinced when they first begin their testimony that some way that little peccadillo is going to be wormed out of them. With a friendly witness, one whose testimony you want the jury to believe, you spread those easy questions out until he begins to relax and then you can lead him gently down the road. Sometimes you do it with an unfriendly witness too, but when I do you can be sure there's a thumping big pit in the road just around the bend."

By the time Carter Page had finished explaining the family connection—uncle-in-law to the defendant's wife—and establishing that he was a frequent visitor to Bizarre, he was quite at ease in the box and even seemed to be on the edge of enjoying himself.

"Now, Mr. Page, as a frequent visitor to Bizarre, you had many opportunities to observe the relationships between those resident there, is that true?"

Carter nodded and waited for the next question. The judge

leaned across and said, "You'll have to answer the questions aloud, Mr. Page. The clerk must have them for the record."

"I do apologize, Your Honor," Carter spluttered. "I'm not accustomed to this sort of thing." Spineless little worm, Nancy thought.

"And how would you describe those relationships?"

"Affectionate, amiable, nothing out of the ordinary way of things."

"Nothing out of the ordinary?" Counsel sounded very surprised.

Carter answered very slowly, "Well, perhaps it may have occurred to me that Richard was a little overfond of Nancy." Nancy wondered if this show of reluctance was something that Carter had thought of himself or if Polly had coached him. She somehow suspected Polly's hand. Carter hadn't the shrewdness himself.

"More specifically, Mr. Page, if you can."

"There was more kissing and embracing than I would think proper between a married man and his wife's sister."

"Quite so. Did you discuss this matter with anyone?"

"Only my wife."

"Now, during any of your visits to Bizarre, did you observe anything which led you to believe that Miss Nancy Randolph might be pregnant?"

"Yes, I did."

"And when was that?"

"Toward the end of May—last year that would be—I noticed an alteration in Nancy's figure which led me to believe that she might be in a certain condition."

"In other words, that she might be carrying a child?"

"That is correct, sir."

"And did you speculate about who the possible father of this child might be?"

"Certainly not." Carter drew himself up and gave a more than usually prolonged sniff. "I would not consider speculating about such matters." Look at him preening himself as if he were above such things, Nancy thought with disgust. He's a bigger gossip than his wife, for all he's a man.

"No further questions for this witness, Your Honor."

Patrick Henry came to his feet slowly and smiled seraphically at the witness. "I have just a few questions, Mr. Page. Just to clarify things in my own mind and for the jury, of course."

"Certainly." Carter was confident, at ease.

"This kissing and hugging you say you saw. It was not at all clandestine or surreptitious, was it?"

Carter frowned. "I don't think I understand."

"Forgive me and let me make my meaning clear. It was all done quite openly in front of you, is that correct? You weren't lurking behind a cupboard door and happened to see it, or opening doors suddenly to interrupt it, or anything of that nature."

"Certainly not." Carter expressed the appropriate indignation at the thought that he might have been spying.

"Then I put my question to you again. These embraces were neither clandestine nor surreptitious, at least not in so far as you were concerned, is that correct?"

"Yes."

"In fact, all quite open and innocent?"

"I don't know about that," Carter tried to recover. "It was more the amount of it that went on."

"Yes, yes, that improper amount." Henry turned away from the witness and seemed to be thinking. When he began the questioning again his voice was still low and sweetly reasonable, just seeming faintly puzzled. "I believe that your wife is not blessed with any living sisters, Mr. Page, is that true?"

"Yes."

"And in particular your wife does not have a younger sister, thrown into your care, who has recently suffered a great emotional loss?"

"No sir."

"You needn't call me sir," Patrick Henry barked. "I'm not

your schoolmaster. I am wondering, Mr. Page, and I think the jury must be too, whether or not you are really a very competent witness as to the proper amount of affection to be displayed in the circumstances I have described." He paused. "You needn't answer that if you prefer. It is sometimes difficult to judge one's own competence."

Carter looked helplessly at the judge. "I don't think I can answer. I'm not sure what the question is."

Henry waved the judge off before he could instruct him. "It's of no importance at all. I'll abandon the question." He walked back to the counsel's table and stood examining a blank sheet of paper with a great show of interest before returning to the attack.

"Mr. Page, leaving aside for the moment the question of the propriety of these friendly embraces that you say you witnessed, I ask you this." He paused. "Were you ever witness to criminal conversation between the defendant and Miss Nancy Randolph?"

"What?"

"Intercourse, man," Patrick Henry suddenly bellowed. "Intercourse."

"Certainly not." Carter Page nearly shouted his denial. If you raise your voice to a witness, Henry had told Nancy, he will almost certainly raise his in return. He was smiling slightly as he listened to the little buzz that ran around the courtroom. Carter, for the record, had only denied ever actually seeing Dick and Nancy in an overt sexual act, but the effect on the spectators as well as the jury was that of a denial that any such act had taken place.

"Now, Mr. Page, you've been patient in what I am sure is a painful duty for you, and I don't want any questions I ask you to lead you in any way to believe that I question your veracity. Your reputation as a gentleman of probity is well established."

Carter looked wary. "Thank you."

"Not at all," Mr. Henry bowed. "It is only that sometimes when one is necessarily trying to answer questions as economically as possible a slightly misleading effect may be produced. For example, you testified that last May you noticed an alteration in Miss Nancy Randolph's figure."

"Yes, yes . . . she was quite definitely thicker through the waist."

"Yes, Mr. Page. We have in mind what sort of alteration you meant, but that's not my point. You gave the impression to our minds that this was an independent observation. Was it in fact independent?"

"I don't take your meaning, sir."

"Just plain 'Mr. Henry' will do me very well. I'll make my question clearer. Did you in fact notice this supposed alteration yourself, or did someone—your wife perhaps—point it out to you first and then you made the observation?"

"I don't recall the sequence of events."

"But your wife did observe this same phenomenon?"

"Yes."

"It was not, I suppose, simultaneously," Henry smiled at the patent absurdity. "You did not suddenly turn to each other and both blurt out that you had noticed a change in Nancy's figure?"

"No."

"Then by all the rules of logic—" Henry was now sweetly reasonable again—"one of you must have observed it first. Am I correct, Mr. Page?"

"Yes."

"And which of you would it have been?"

"I suppose it would have been my wife," Carter said after a moment's hesitation.

"Are you sure?"

"Now that I think about it, it must have been. Ladies are much more likely to notice that sort of thing, you know."

"Quite so, Mr. Page, quite so. Then it would be reasonable to construct a sequence which went something like this. Your wife noticed a change in Nancy's figure, spoke of it to you, and shortly thereafter you made a closer than usual scrutiny of the waist in question and came to the same conclusion as your wife. Would that in substance seem accurate to you?"

"I would think that very likely."

"So would I, Mr. Page, so would we all. So, going back to my previous question. Despite the impression left in our minds by your answers to my friend the prosecutor's questions, your observation of the alleged alteration in Nancy's figure was in no way an independent uninfluenced one, was it? Was it, Mr. Page?"

"Yes, or rather no."

"We understand you very well, Mr. Page." Henry smiled at him. "Your Honor, I have no further questions for this witness."

"And your colleagues?"

"I believe I speak for them as well."

The prosecution waived their right to redirect, and Carter Page was dismissed with the court's thanks. He stepped down from the box looking faintly bewildered. The questions had been more or less what he had been told to expect, he had answered them as well as he could, and yet somehow, something seemed to have gone wrong. He felt obscurely foolish, and the benevolent smile that Patrick Henry now gave him did nothing to reassure him.

"The Commonwealth calls Mrs. Martha Jefferson Randolph."

Tom Randolph escorted his wife to the gate, and when he turned to hold it open for her he faced his sisters directly. He bowed and smiled in such a way that it was clear to the jurymen and the spectators that if it were not for the enforced decorum of the courtroom, he would have embraced them with great brotherly affection. Nancy did not know whether or not the gesture was planned, but she was grateful for it.

Martha Randolph appeared to feel that testifying in a murder trial was almost a normal social occasion, a bit trying perhaps but nothing that could not be handled gracefully. She turned back the glove on her right hand with a practiced manner before she placed her hand on the Book and repeated the oath in her firm, pleasant voice as if she were giving responses at a Sunday service. Nothing in her testimony would appear to affect her more than would a discussion of domestic arrangements at Monticello. Martha Randolph had always demonstrated a remarkable degree of composure in any circumstance, and Nancy alternated between envying her sister-in-law's control and disparaging her lack of feeling.

"Mrs. Randolph," the prosecutor began after the preliminary questions were disposed of, "would you be good enough to tell us the substance of a conversation with Judith Randolph in the presence of Nancy Randolph in early September of last year?"

"I would put it nearer to the middle of September, the twelfth, if I am not mistaken."

"I am corrected. The twelfth it is."

"Mrs. Randolph and I were discussing remedies for certain fairly common ailments. It isn't always possible to get a doctor in when someone is ill, and we both have done a good bit of nursing of our families and households. Nancy did not seem interested in the conversation and did not take part in it."

"I believe you spoke of a remedy known as—" the prosecutor paused to consult that paper in his hand—" gum guiacum."

"That is correct."

"And what was said about this substance?"

"I told Mrs. Randolph that I had found gum guiacum to be an excellent remedy for the cholic, if it be of the ordinary kind and not morbid. She was interested and said she would procure some, and I warned her that it should be used with caution if the person was female and possibly pregnant because it had in some instances induced miscarriage of the child."

"Did Miss Nancy Randolph express any interest at that time?"

"No, she did not," Martha said firmly.

"But I believe you received a request a few days later."

"Not directly from Nancy," Martha corrected him. "On my

return home around the sixteenth of the month, Mrs. Page sent to me for some guiacum for Nancy, who was suffering from cholic."

Nancy was startled. No one had ever mentioned to her that Polly had asked for the dose. It put a slightly different light on things, but she was not sure whether it made everything clearer or more obscure.

"Did you send it?" the prosecutor continued.

"Not immediately but within another few days."

"And to your knowledge did Nancy Randolph take this medicine?"

"I have no way of knowing whether Nancy ever received the medicine I sent and certainly no knowledge of whether she ever took any of it."

Martha Randolph was asked whether she had any further information on the matter before the court and stated very positively that she did not.

Patrick Henry had made the first witness sit and wait for him, but he was on his feet immediately when Martha Randolph was turned over to him.

"It is a very great pleasure to see you again, Mrs. Randolph, even under these very difficult circumstances. I shall be as brief with you as I can."

"Thank you."

"Gum guiacum is quite a useful medicine for a number of illnesses, is it not?

"I believe so, though in my own household we have used it only for the cholic."

"I can tell you from my own experience that, mixed with a salve, it's a sovereign remedy for the rheumatics."

"I have heard others say so," Martha agreed.

Henry paused, seeming to ponder this bit of medical lore. Get on with it, Nancy thought. Does he think they'll believe that I took it for my rheumatics?

"The delay in sending off the medicine interests me. Might we assume that you felt there was no great urgency? That since

Miss Nancy was subject to fairly frequent attacks of the cholic the medicine would serve for the next one if it failed to arrive in time for the current one?"

"Yes, that's true. Even if I had sent it immediately, it would not have arrived before the attack was over in the normal course of affairs."

"Would you consider the amount you sent to Bizarre a large amount or a small one?"

"Quite small."

"Only enough for one or two doses?"

"Yes."

"Would the amount you sent, if taken all at once by a woman expecting a child, would that have the unfortunate effect that you discussed with Mrs. Randolph?"

"It is difficult to say for sure."

"We would very much value your opinion as a person of some experience."

"Then, only as an opinion, I have known doses as large to have no ill effect whatsoever. It is by no means certain in its action."

"Thank you very much, Mrs. Randolph."

Patrick Henry returned to his place at the defense table, and Martha Randolph half rose to leave the witness stand. The prosecution, however, had thought of one more question.

"Mrs. Randolph, you have said that even though you knew Miss Nancy Randolph to be a chronic sufferer from the cholic, you sent her only a very small amount of the gum guiacum. Was this because you believed her to be pregnant?"

For the first time on the stand, Martha Randolph's composure was broken. "It's been some months. I cannot remember exactly, but it's possible that I sent a small dose because that is all I had in store at the time. Or it's equally possible that I sent only one or two doses as a trial, with the thought that I might send more later if it proved effective." A lesser woman would have been said to be chattering, and the prosecuting counsel cut her short.

"Mrs. Randolph, did you believe that Nancy Randolph was pregnant?"

Martha looked at her husband standing at the back of the room, at the judge on the bench, even, at last, appealingly at Patrick Henry, but there was no help to be found. Just as the prosecutor was leaning forward to repeat his question she answered in a voice so low as to be nearly inaudible. "Yes, I did."

"Thank you, Mrs. Randolph. I think you may be excused, unless counsel for the defense has any further questions."

Patrick Henry did not even bother to look up from the papers he was studying but waived his hand in dismissal, as if what had just been said was of no consequence whatever. Nancy could not believe that the gesture deceived anyone in the room; in fact the excited murmur she could hear behind her was ample evidence that the crowd was far from ready to dismiss Martha's statement so easily. Carter Page had been made to look a suggestible fool, but no such onus attached itself to Martha.

Nancy's dismay was compounded by the announcement of the next witness for the prosecution. Mrs. Carter Page was called. Aunt Polly herself, come into her glory.

She came down the aisle between the spectators nodding and smiling at those faces she knew. She might have been, from her manner, entering a crowded drawing room at a party given in her honor. From the witness chair she beamed at the judge and at the prosecuting counsel, gave the clerk a sweetly condescending smile as she gave back the Book, and even had a very faint forgiving smile for the defense table. Nancy had never hated her more fiercely.

"Mrs. Page, since you will be giving us a considerable body of testimony covering a period of some months, both before and after the alleged crime, it might perhaps be easiest if you were simply to tell us what you know of the case, and I will interrupt you only when I feel that there is something that needs clarification. It may make your narrative easier for all of us to follow."

This was a very satisfactory arrangement for Polly. She wanted only to know where he would like her to begin.

"You might start with your relationships with the principals in this case, and then tell us what you observed when you first became suspicious of any wrongdoing. If, indeed, you ever did entertain such suspicions."

Polly smiled, put her hand to her pearls, smoothed out her skirt, and leaned forward. "Before I married Mr. Page, I was Mary Cary, the daughter of Archibald Cary, the Speaker." She paused as Patrick Henry seemed overcome by a violent fit of coughing. "As I was saying, my late sister Ann Cary Randolph was the mother of Judith and Nancy. That's Mrs. Richard Randolph and Miss Nancy. I felt a certain responsibility as their mother's sister to watch over them as she would have done, although of course I am not very much their elder. I took it as my duty to her memory, especially since Nancy was estranged from her father, Colonel Thomas."

"Miss Nancy Randolph had in fact permanently left her father's household?"

"That was my understanding."

"She was then not just a visitor at Bizarre as you were but an established resident?"

"It was a natural arrangement since Judith and Nancy were the closest in age of my dear sister's daughters."

"Your husband has testified that you were a frequent visitor to Bizarre."

"Very frequent, until the last four or five months."

"Then we can assume that you were a close observer of the transactions of the house?"

"Oh yes indeed. I don't believe that there was much that escaped my notice, right from the very beginning. I told my husband at the time that there was trouble brewing there." Polly shook her head sadly. No one could escape the impression that if only the family at Bizarre had listened to their wise Aunt Polly they would not now be sitting in the court.

"Perhaps you would be good enough to tell us what you saw of the situation there."

"Well, at first it seemed one of perfect harmony. There was a natural concern over the health of Mr. Randolph's younger brother Theodoric and then grief when he passed away at such a very young age, but it was otherwise a wholly happy home, particularly with the expectation of the birth of Mr. and Mrs. Randolph's first child.

"When did this happy atmosphere seem to change?"

"Sometime in March or February it seemed to me that Nancy and Richard Randolph were becoming more closely attached than was at all proper as between a young girl and her sister's husband."

"Did you suspect an actual illicit relationship between them?"

"Perhaps not quite at that time. I believe my first thought was that it was simply carelessness of her sister's feelings on Nancy's part, allied with a natural tendency she has always had of being rather boldly flirtatious. Even earlier, however, I had a conversation with Judith which might have made me suspicious, except that I naturally was not eager to imagine any wrongdoing among those to whom I was closely attached by family ties."

"Could you tell us what you can of that conversation?"

"It must have been some time late in February. Richard and Nancy had ridden out together and I was with Judy in her bedchamber, she feeling quite unwell as a consequence of her pregnancy. Judy said to me then that Richard and Nancy were company only for each other. But she then went on to say that Nancy was chiefly in her own room and Richard busy about the plantation, so I did not see the importance of it at that time. Ladies having their first child sometimes feel a bit neglected and out of sorts and I put her complaint down to that. I have blamed myself bitterly for not having taken more heed and possibly averting the calamity that has overtaken us all." Polly took a handkerchief from her sleeve and dabbed the corners of her eyes.

The prosecutor was solicitous. "Do you feel able to continue? We would be happy to give you time to compose yourself."

"No no, it's quite all right," Polly rallied bravely. "I did make an attempt to put matters to right. I told Judith that it would perhaps be wise for her to resume her active role in the house despite her indisposition, but I did not feel I could speak more clearly without offense and it may already have been too late. I also tried to warn Nancy of the impropriety of her actions."

"And how did Miss Nancy Randolph respond to you?"

"She was excessively rude and heedless."

"Can you remember what she said?"

"Some taradiddle about Richard only trying to help her recover from her grief. She had fancied herself attached to Theo. She would not listen to my warning and took the occasion to make some very unpleasant remarks about me personally, which I have of course managed to forget."

"At some point you began to suspect that Miss Nancy Randolph might be pregnant. Can you tell us when that would have been?"

"Sometime in May. Nancy seemed quite melancholy and complained of feeling unwell with something other than the cholic, and I noticed a definite alteration in her figure, as did my husband."

"Did you question Miss Randolph about her indisposition?"

"I did, and her answers were far from satisfactory. Furthermore on several occasions she refused to allow me in the room where she was undressing and preparing for bed."

"Did you ever happen to see Miss Randolph in a state of undress during this period?"

"Quite by chance I did see Nancy in her room with her servant, preparing for bed."

"Was she aware that she was observed by you?"

"I don't believe so. The door to the hall was closed, but there was a crack in it. Nancy was in her shift, and her figure was quite definitely extended. There was no mistaking it."

"And did you hear anything on this occasion?"

"Nancy asked her servant if she didn't think she was getting smaller, and her girl said, 'No, Miss Nancy, you're getting bigger.' "

"Did you ever speak to Miss Randolph about what you had overheard, ever ask her for an explanation?"

"No, I did not. Around this time Nancy became more than usually unfriendly toward me and took my inquiries about her health in very bad part."

"Can you recall for us any other suspicious circumstances?"

"Oh yes indeed. I saw Nancy on one occasion, just as an example, I saw her look at her waist and then cast her eyes up to heaven in silent melancholy." Polly Page was clearly enjoying herself now. To illustrate her words she looked down at her hands folded in her lap and then rolled her eyes to the ceiling with a heavy sigh.

"Quite so, Mrs. Page, quite a vivid description. Was there anything else?"

"Oh yes, there were many similar occasions . . ."

Something in the relish with which she spoke seemed to warn the prosecutor and he interrupted her. "I'm sure that this must be most painful for you, recalling this. Perhaps it would be better if we passed directly to the events you witnessed subsequent to the alleged crime at Glenlyrvar."

"Well, when I heard the rumor that Nancy had been delivered of a child at Glenlyrvar, I was naturally eager to be in a position to deny it and stop the gossip immediately. So I approached Nancy and told her of this report that was being circulated, explained to her how prejudicial to her position it was. I told her that I should like to examine her so that I could deny the statements being made."

"And what did Miss Randolph reply to that?"

"She grew very angry and abusive. She refused to permit me

to examine her and said that if her own denial was not sufficient she would give no further satisfaction."

"You were not then able to examine her to see if a child had recently been born to her or not?"

"She was dead set against it. She wouldn't even remain in the same room with me. Naturally since she had rejected my offer to help with very little courtesy I did not feel bound to press the matter further."

"What you have told us represents the sum of your information on the matter before us?"

"Except for what I heard about what happened at the Harrisons' on the family's visit there."

"But of your own direct knowledge and observation, you have told us all you know?"

"As well as I can remember, yes."

"Thank you very much, Mrs. Page. You've been very helpful."

Patrick Henry sat slumped at the counsel table, his boots sticking out in the aisle. With his thumb and forefinger he pulled on his lower lip as he read the notes before him. He leaned over to confer with Mr. Marshall and Mr. Campbell and then returned to his study of his notes. While she waited for him Polly had at first sat back at ease smiling at her cronies in the spectators' section. As time passed she grew restless and began to tap with her fingers on the edge of the box. Not until the judge had cleared his throat in a meaningful way, and Polly had gathered her skirt in her hand as if about to take her leave, did Patrick Henry approach the witness box.

He came much closer to her than he had to the other witnesses, his elbow on the side of the box, his face thrust quite near hers. Polly drew back in her chair as far from him as she could. Nancy, remembering the distinctly musty smell that hung around her lawyer, could not blame her, but to those who had not experienced Mr. Henry's peculiar aura, the shrinking away could look very much like alarm.

"Mrs. Page, as an aunt to both Mrs. Richard Randolph and her sister Nancy, you must have known them both from birth?"

"Of course I was only a child myself when they were born."

Mr. Henry was gallant. "We can all readily see that you have only a few years' advantage of them. In fact, if I did not know otherwise, I should fancy from appearances only that you were quite of an age with them. My point, however, is that you are peculiarly in a position to know the real character of Nancy Randolph through long experience of her."

"I believe that to be true, at least as much as anyone can know her. She has always been very secretive."

"I will be calling on you for that special knowledge of Nancy in a few minutes. I gather that you were much together in your early days?"

"Oh yes."

"When you were all children I assume you saw Miss Nancy in a state of undress many times?"

"Certainly."

"Mrs. Page, you were a frequent visitor at Bizarre long before there was any suspicion in your mind concerning Nancy's conduct or condition, were you not?"

"Yes, I was."

"And during that period of time, bearing in mind that you are now a young married woman and Nancy is no longer a child, the easy freedom between you in matters of undress no longer existed, did it?"

"I suppose not."

"Can you in fact, Mrs. Page, recollect any time in all those visits to Bizarre that you ever saw Nancy Randolph in a state of undress, other than the time you have already described to us? I am speaking particularly of that period before you harbored any ill thought about her."

"I really can't remember."

"If I were to tell you that there was no such occasion you would be unable to contradict me. Isn't that true?"

"Possibly."

"Then if you had not seen Nancy in a state of undress in all those months before you began to suspect her pregnancy, there was nothing particularly remarkable about the circumstance that you did not see her so after your suspicions were aroused, was there?"

He waited for a reply, but Polly was silent. "I think I must require an answer, Mrs. Page. Was there anything remarkable in your not witnessing Nancy Randolph's preparations for bed in view of the fact that you had long been out of the habit of seeing her so?"

"If you put it that way, perhaps not. But as I told the other gentleman, the suspicious thing wasn't my not seeing her but that she refused to permit me to see her."

"Mrs. Page, did you ever consider the possibility that if Nancy was quite innocent of any wrongdoing she might think your request to see her in her shift a most extraordinary one?"

"Nonsense."

"Why do you say nonsense? You testified that it had been a very long time, since childhood in fact, since you had undressed together. In all those years had Nancy ever seen you in a state of undress?"

"Not that I know of."

"You were both accustomed to keeping the doors of your bedchambers closed when retiring?"

"Yes."

"Out of modesty, I assume."

"In my own case, certainly."

"And not in Nancy's?"

"I really couldn't say why Nancy does anything that she does."

"Of course not, and you, like your husband, are of too noble a character to speculate. Which leads me to some questions about Miss Nancy Randolph's character. I cannot help but feel that with the long years you have known her and the close family ties, you promise to be a most competent witness in this area. Would you say that Nancy Randolph has a full complement of the pride that seems to many of us lesser folk to run very high in her family?"

"Yes, I would."

"Some people might even call it in the extreme a certain arrogance."

"That is certainly true. Nancy was always very high-nosed."

"Even as a child?"

"Even then," Polly agreed.

"Would you also say that she was not always as prudent as she might be, not quite as conciliatory to her elders or as full of tactful courtesy as one would wish to see in a young girl?"

Polly nodded. "I could tell you things you wouldn't credit that I've heard her say."

"I'm sure you could, Mrs. Page, and I appreciate your willingness, but we should move on. After you heard the story about Nancy having given birth to a child, I understood you to say that you asked again to examine her, to determine the truth or falsity of it."

"And she refused again." Polly was righteously indignant. "She was very angry or pretended to be. She said that if her word was not enough she wished to have nothing more to do with me."

"She ordered you out of her room?"

"Certainly not. I don't take orders from Nancy Randolph. We were in her sister's drawing room and she flounced out upstairs to her own room and I didn't see her again for the rest of my visit."

"My apologies, Mrs. Page. Naturally you could not be ordered about by a young niece." Henry walked a few steps away from her and stood silently, apparently in thought. "Mrs. Page, bear with me for just a moment. Let us just suppose that a young girl has been wrongfully accused of something of which she is quite innocent, and let us further suppose that her denials have not been believed, and let us also suppose that she is approached by a near relative who wishes to examine her in order to have evidence to refute those charges. Is that a fair summation of what you stated were your actions in this matter after the story of Nancy's child-bearing reached you?"

"That's true. I was thinking only of her own best interests, the protection of her name."

"We are very conscious of your motives, Mrs. Page. What I wanted to ask you about this hypothetical case I just proposed: You would expect that a modest, prudent girl, anxious about her reputation, a naturally biddable girl, accustomed to doing as her elders asked, would have welcomed the opportunity to prove her innocence once and for all wouldn't you?"

"I most certainly would."

"So would all of us here present, Mrs. Page. But you see—" Patrick Henry frowned in puzzlement—"you see, you have described quite a different sort of girl to us. One proud to the point of arrogance. One accustomed since childhood to frequently ignoring her elders' advice, one who sometimes acted quite imprudently and against her own best interests. Might not a girl like that, a girl like Nancy, equally innocent, might she not have grown very angry that her word was not enough of a reassurance to someone who was a very near relation? Might she not have acted not in the wisest fashion but for her the most natural fashion? Thinking on it, it seems to me that the greater the anger of a girl like the Nancy Randolph you have described to us, the greater the presumption of innocence."

"To you, perhaps," Polly sniffed. "I certainly did not take it that way."

"Mrs. Page, there is something about your testimony that still puzzles me. You were quite convinced in May or sometime in the summer that Nancy Randolph was pregnant, is that correct?"

"Yes."

"Yet sometime in November you asked to examine her so that you would have evidence of her innocence. Are you sure that it was evidence of innocence that you were looking for?"

"I certainly hoped to find such evidence."

"Of course you did, otherwise your request would seem to some to be a rather merciless hounding of your dead sister's child."

"It was no such thing," Polly burst out.

"My dear Mrs. Page," Patrick Henry soothed her, "no one in this room, looking at you, could possibly believe that you acted from anything other than the best of motives. You hoped to prove your dear niece innocent, is that right?"

"Certainly."

"We can take it, then, that since you hoped to find evidence of her innocence and even the frailest of hopes must have some foundation, then there was some doubt in your mind that Nancy Randolph was pregnant the preceding summer? Your observation may have been faulty."

"Not at all."

"I don't really think we can let you have it both ways, Mrs. Page. Either you were not completely sure that Nancy was pregnant last summer, or you had no expectation whatever of finding her innocent when you asked to examine her in November."

"You don't understand."

"I readily confess that I don't."

Polly paused and chose her words carefully. "I believed Nancy to be pregnant last summer from the evidence of my own eyes and ears, but I hoped it was not so until she refused my offer in November and then I was convinced." She looked at Henry triumphantly and he nodded in acknowledgment.

"Thank you, Mrs. Page, that's admirably clear. We will remember then that your testimony regarding your suspicions of Nancy Randolph was based on belief and not conviction. I have a few questions about that testimony to ask you. First, concerning that night you happened to see Nancy Randolph in her shift and heard her speaking to her servant. You were by that evening already strongly suspicious about your niece's condition, were you not?"

"I was."

"And you heard her say to her servant—" Henry paused— "excuse me, I want to get this right." He picked up a page of notes from the table and read from them. "Miss Nancy said to her servant, 'Do you think I'm getting smaller?' and her servant replied, 'No, Miss Nancy, you're getting bigger.' Is that what you heard?"

"That's right, that's exactly what I heard them say."

"Now one would assume that if Nancy Randolph were far enough along with child so that it was visible, not to everyone but to someone with your keen powers of observation, she must have been herself aware of her condition."

"I would think so."

"Tell me, Mrs. Page, have you ever before heard of a woman who expected that she might grow smaller in the course of her pregnancy?"

"No, and neither did Nancy."

"But Nancy asked her servant if she were getting smaller. Surely this suggests that Nancy believed any alteration in her figure was from quite a different cause."

"It suggests no such thing."

"Doesn't it? Then must we assume that Nancy Randolph was a young woman of such lamentable ignorance that she expected the consequence of pregnancy to be a dwindling of the waist?"

"You can assume whatever you like. I only know what I heard."

"Of course, and no one doubts that you heard precisely what you have stated to the court. I am simply suggesting that for reasonable people there might possibly exist a difference in the interpretation of what you heard. But that does not concern you. I have never been fortunate enough to visit Bizarre. Is it a sound, well-constructed house?"

"Yes."

"Not falling into disrepair?"

"No." Polly looked at him doubtfully. She saw no point to his questions and was beginning to be wary of traps.

"No large cracks in paneling or doors, no hastily built parts of the house where unseasoned wood has warped?"

"No, it is generally considered a very fine house."

"There hadn't been any recent repairs to the door to Miss Nancy's bedroom, with a panel not yet replaced or anything of that nature?"

"No."

"My problem, Mrs. Page, and I hope you can help me with it, is that I am a bit curious about how you managed to see and describe for us so clearly what was going on behind a closed door. When one walks past a well-constructed door one can see, if there is a lamp or a candle in the room, a crack of light coming out from around or under the door, but, just passing by, one cannot see anything inside the room unless the door is very badly warped or damaged. Yet you seem to have walked by such a door and seen a great deal."

"I wasn't just passing by."

"Perhaps you had better describe the circumstances for us more completely."

"I would be happy to. Nancy had complained again of feeling unwell and had gone up to her room and a short time later I followed her up the stairs. As you say, there was a crack of light coming from between the door and frame, the door was not completely closed so that the latch was engaged. I knew from the light that she had not yet dismissed her servant and blown out her candle."

"But you had lingered long enough downstairs so that you felt confident she would have had time to remove her outer garments."

"Yes, but that was not my reason for coming upstairs," Polly added hastily.

"Perhaps you were also feeling unwell and had decided to retire early?" Henry suggested.

"Yes, that's right."

Patrick Henry was all solicitude. "You're quite recovered now, I trust."

"Quite, thank you."

Her questioner seemed struck by a sudden thought. "Your illness did not impair your vision in any way?"

Polly smiled with condescension. She was not to be drawn into such a blatant snare. "Certainly not. I saw everything very clearly."

"Go on, Mrs. Page."

"As I was saying, I noticed the light coming from between the door and the frame and I heard voices . . ."

"So naturally," Patrick Henry supplied, "you moved closer to the door than your normal path along the hall would have taken you."

"Yes."

"Quite close?"

"Yes. I found that by putting my eye right to the crack I could see a considerable part of the room, including that part where Nancy and her servant were standing."

"Your cheek would have been pressed tight to the door?"

"That's right, and I assure you I could see quite well indeed."

Patrick Henry nodded gravely. "Yes, I can see that an action like that would give you a much wider field of vision than that of a casual passerby."

"And what I saw and what I heard is exactly what I have said here today, several times."

"Let me see if I have the picture accurately. There was a very narrow crack between the door and the frame, but you were able, by putting your eye directly to this crack, to see all that was going on in the room?"

"That's correct."

"I assume you were moving quietly. Given Nancy's preference for privacy when she was undressed, I gather that you were reasonably cautious in your approach to the door. You would not have cared for her to discover you at that moment."

"There was no chance of that. She was much too concerned with watching herself in the pier glass."

"But of course you would not have known that until you were actually at the door, so you must have taken pains that she not hear you approaching?"

"I suppose so, yes."

"I think we can be sure of it," Patrick Henry said. "You understand that this is a most important bit of testimony. Let me go over the circumstances again so that they are clear to all of us." Henry walked away from her to the opposite side of the room. When he turned back, the consummate actor had transformed himself. In place of his usual old man's shuffle he had adopted Polly's mincing, bobbing walk, unmistakable to those who had just seen her progress down the aisle. "You are walking along the hall, feeling unwell, on your way to bed, when you happen to notice a light in your niece's room." He threw up his hands in a gracefully feminine mime of surprise. "You think to yourself what a splendid opportunity to either confirm my suspicions or allay my fears, and, moving very cautiously—" Henry moved toward the witness stand in an exaggerated tiptoe—"you come to the door and you put your eye right to the crack in the door." He leaned forward, one eye screwed shut, his head twisted to the side so that the open eye could be more closely applied to the crack in the door he had conjured up for the crowd. His nose seemed to twitch with eagerness. He looked the perfect caricature of a spy, sly and repellent. Nancy felt her skin crawl as if she were standing once more behind that crack in the door, naked, as something evil watched her. Patrick Henry held the pose for only a moment and then straightened up. He was standing quite close to Polly, and he turned to her and said in a quiet conversational tone that still carried to every corner of the hushed room, "Tell me, Mrs. Page, with which eye were you peeping?"

Polly looked bewildered, not quite sure what was happening to her. Patrick Henry turned his back on her and looked with a face of infinite sadness at the crowded courtroom. He spread his arms wide and raised his eyes heavenward. "God save us all from peeping Toms and eavesdroppers," he intoned.

There was a single long gasp from the spectators, a few calls of "Hear, hear," a muted burst of applause. Even one or two of the jurymen nodded with approval. Polly was standing in the witness box, sputtering that she would not stay to answer any more questions, would not be so insulted when she was only doing her duty.

The judge leaned over the bench. "Mr. Henry, have you completed your examination of this witness?"

"Very nearly."

"I must ask you to refrain from characterizing any of the testimony. You know quite well that the proper place for that is in your argument."

"I ask the court's pardon. I was somewhat carried away by the picture presented to us. It shan't happen again."

Polly appealed to the bench. "Must I answer any more of this creature's questions?"

"I'm afraid you must, madam."

Patrick Henry smiled innocently. "Mrs. Page, I seem to have inadvertently offended you. I know that this is a most trying experience for you as well as for your niece and your nephew-in-law. I have only one further question. You de-scribed—as a matter of fact, you demonstrated—for my col-league an occasion on which Nancy Randolph looked down at her waist and cast her eyes to heaven in silent melancholy. I am quoting you correctly, am I not?"

"Yes."

"You also said that she sighed heavily?"

"Yes, she did."

"Heavy sighs and eyes cast to heaven," Patrick Henry mused. "I gather that this was in the course of conversation with you?"

This time the glare of the judge and the banging of the clerk's staff on the floor could not stop the wave of laughter that came from the spectators. Henry looked around at his audience with an expression of bemused surprise as if he could not imagine what had caused this unseemly outburst. Polly Page looked quite prepared to kill him and, when he offered her his hand to assist her from the witness box, having announced that he had no further questions, she struck it away angrily. "Don't you touch me, you filthy little man."

Henry begged her pardon with an expression that declared his total innocence of any malice and a certain bewilderment. None of the byplay escaped the attention of the gentlemen magistrates in the jury box.

Henry stopped by the prosecution table and consulted them briefly. Mr. Willson rose to say that if it pleased the court counsel for both sides were agreeable to a recess before the afternoon session. The crowd filed out buzzing like theatergoers. They had come to see a performance by a master of courtroom dramatics and they were far from disappointed. Polly Page's progress through the courtroom could be charted by little pools of silence and a few embarrassed nods.

It had been arranged that Judy and Nancy and Dick would have their dinner away from prying eyes, in the jailer's house attached to the court. Patrick Henry was obviously torn. He could dine with Marshall and Campbell at the tavern and accept the plaudits that he was well aware he deserved, or he could join his clients in the jailhouse kitchen. In the end it was Nancy who decided for him, saying she must talk to him.

The jailer's wife had outdone herself. She served forth half a ham, cold chicken pies, beaten biscuit and a trifle made from the blackberries that grew rankly round the courthouse. The jailer took a particular pride in the berries. They grew wild all over Cumberland County, but nowhere did they flourish as they did in the courthouse yard. "They say it's because they are watered by the defendants' tears," he said and then added hastily, "not that you will have any need for tears, Mr.

Randolph." Dick insisted that the jailer and his wife join them at table and before long, to Nancy's amazement, the two married couples were deep in conversation as if they had come together in a normal social way. There was no mention of the trial, just talk about the weather and politics, the quality of fishing in that portion of the Appomattox that ran through Bizarre, while the ladies exchanged recipes and Judy told the jailer's wife how sorely she missed her son.

Patrick Henry was still too exhilarated to eat, or, at least, to sit at the table with the others. He paced the room talking excitedly, swooping down to pick up a sliver of ham or a biscuit and meticulously licking his fingers before he wiped them down the side of his coat.

"Did you hear how I handled her, Nancy Randolph? Did you see? If you didn't you're the only one in the room who didn't. Beautiful, beautiful, and all done by her own hand with just a little push from me. She showed the whole world that she's a malicious evil-minded busybody with a bad temper and no love for you at all. Convicted right out of her own mouth. Why do you look so glum? Your dear Aunt Polly will be ashamed to show her face for a year. Those who don't despise her will be laughing at her, her and that feeble excuse for a man she's married to. And I don't even get a smile or a thank-you from you? What's the matter with you anyway?"

"Why did you let them put so many Carringtons on the jury? You must know that the Randolphs and the Carringtons . . ."

"Have been feuding since about the time of the first landing? Of course I knew. Everybody knows."

"Then how could you even think of letting them judge Dick?"

"But that's the whole beauty of it. An acquittal by a jury packed with your friends, and your ill-wishers would all say that they expected nothing else, that they wouldn't convict one of their own circle. But an acquittal by a jury bulging with

Carringtons will be seen in quite a different and far more favorable light. If the Carringtons are all that's worrying you, you can give me your congratulations and drink to the successful destruction of your old enemy. Did you notice how, when she was getting a little suspicious, I gave her a glimpse of a trap I never intended springing, that question about her eyesight, and she stepped over that and sailed right on where I wanted her. Tell you the truth, Miss Nancy, I can't think when I've enjoyed myself so much."

Nancy acknowledged with a smile that there had been a certain amount of pleasure in the morning's work for her as well, especially in a look she'd had of her aunt's face as she pushed her way through the crowd after her examination, but still there was something that worried her.

"Well, speak up, girl. You'll never have a better chance to learn from me."

Nancy looked over shoulder at the others in the room. "Don't worry about them," Henry said. "They're not paying any attention to us."

Despite his reassurance, Nancy spoke in a whisper. "When Martha said that she thought I was pregnant, why didn't you ask her if she thought of it herself? I didn't know it was Polly who sent for that medicine. Couldn't Polly have said in her note—well, you know, the way you made it look with Carter?"

"Because Martha Jefferson Randolph has a mind of her own and Carter Page hasn't. I doubt if he's had a notion he could call his own since he married. I knew what his answer would be if I worked at him a bit. But you never, never ask a witness a question unless you are pretty well certain what the answer is going to be, particularly if it might be an answer you don't want to hear. As it stands now some of the members of the jury may think for themselves that Martha got the idea from Polly the way Carter did. But if I'd asked her about it, God only knows what sort of an answer we would have had and I wasn't about to tempt Him."

"You think I'm guilty, don't you?"

"Of murder? Certainly not. The thing is absurd on the face of it."

"Not of murder, of . . ."

Patrick Henry interrupted her. "Of being reckless, rash, imprudent, proud, and not sufficiently attentive to your elders? All of those things, and to make matters worse I don't see any sign of your mending your ways. Look at you trying to teach me how to try a case."

"That's not what I mean."

"I'll ask you a question instead. Why do you care what I think? I'm an old man and nobody listens to me any more. I'm not part of the Randolph world. Never was. Never will be. After tomorrow it's not likely you'll ever see me again."

"But I'll think of you, and I want you to think well of me."

"But I do, I do. I think you are nearly as brave as you are foolish, and that's the highest compliment I can pay a woman." He patted her hands briskly and stood up.

"All right, children. Finish up and wash your hands and faces. We are about to meet again on our chosen battlefield of truth. . . . I say that quite often, or was used to in my closing speeches . . . reminds them all of our glorious past . . . when I still mattered . . . but never mind, it's of no importance . . . I'll just have a wee sliver of that ham before you put it away."

Toddies, bimbo, flips, a warm afternoon and a heavy meal had visibly taken their toll of some of the jurymen. Even Mr. Henry seemed about to nod off once or twice, but he might have been feigning indifference.

Randolph Harrison, master of Glenlyrvar, was the first of the afternoon's witnesses. There was no mistaking his uneasiness as he took the oath and entered the box. This was not an occasion that anything in his background as a Virginia gentleman had prepared him for. Asked by Mr. Willson if he had ever noticed any familiarities between Richard and Nancy Randolph, he said that perhaps there had been a certain imprudence.

"Have you ever suspected them of criminal correspondence?"

"Certainly not. I have far too high an opinion of them both."

"Mr. Harrison, it is the understanding of the court that Mr. and Mrs. Richard Randolph and Miss Nancy Randolph were all guests in your house on the night of the thirtieth of September last year."

"And for some days after, about a week in all."

"Would you, as well as you can, recall for us the events of that visit?"

"They arrived on Monday, shortly before dinner. Judy and Nancy by carriage and Richard riding escort. I met them at the door and handed the ladies down from their carriage."

"Can you remember what Miss Nancy Randolph was wearing?"

"Some sort of greatcoat with a shoulder cape, blue, I think. It was closely buttoned at the waist." Good for you, Randolph, Nancy thought. You're cleverer than I would have thought you were.

"Did you note any signs of a possible pregnancy?"

"I did not. Not then or later."

"Would you tell us what happened after your guests arrived?"

"Nancy complained of feeling very unwell. We all thought it was simply from the motion in the carriage. Immediately upon coming into the house she lay on the couch. After dinner she still complained of being unwell and went up to her room. She stayed there for the whole of that afternoon and evening. After supper my wife went up with Judy to show her to bed, and I understand at that time she went into Nancy's room and found her very unwell but saying that she had taken the essence of peppermint or some such thing that she was accustomed to take for the cholic."

"I believe that the arrangement of rooms on the upper floor of Glenlyrvar is unusual. Would you be good enough to describe them for the benefit of the court and the gentlemen magistrates?"

"The upstairs of my house is not yet finished and is divided into only two rooms. The staircase, which is very narrow, leads directly into the room which we call the outer room, and from that a door opens into the inner room."

"Then it is impossible to go from the inner room to the stair without passing through the outer room?"

"That's right. Nancy was given the inner room and her sister and Mr. Randolph the outer."

"Was there a disturbance in your house that night? And if there was, what was its nature?"

"Late at night—I don't know what time it was, but I know that I had been quite soundly asleep—my wife and I were wakened by screams and groans from upstairs. We thought at first it was Judy Randolph, but when a servant was sent to us for some laudanum she told us it was Miss Nancy we heard."

"You didn't yourself take the laudanum upstairs?"

"I never went up the stairs that night. We sent the laudanum by Nancy's servant, and then a little later my wife went up to see if she could be of help. She stayed some time and when she came back said that Nancy was feeling easier."

"And did you hear anything else, later in the night?"

"I'm not sure. We went back to sleep and sometime later we were awakened by what we thought at the time might have been Richard coming down the stairs and then, after an interval, returning up them."

"What made you believe that it was Mr. Randolph on the stairs?"

"I wouldn't put it so strongly as to say I believed it was Richard," Harrison protested. "We only thought it might have been. It seemed a heavier footstep than that of the servants who had been up and down all night. We thought at the time that he might have come down to arrange for the doctor to be sent for."

"That is all you have to tell us about the happenings under your roof that night?"

"That is all I know," Randolph Harrison said firmly.

"In the morning was there any discussion about what had happened the previous night?"

"At breakfast someone said that they supposed Nancy had had another of her hysteric fits."

For the first time in the course of the trial the prosecutor turned and looked directly at Nancy. "Was she subject to hysteric fits?"

"So they said—in fact that she had had one only two or three days before."

"Nancy Randolph was not herself present at this discussion?"

"She remained in her bed for the whole of the day."

"Did you happen to see her that morning?"

"It was very cold that morning. The first strong frost of the year. I went up with Mr. Richard Randolph to see to the fire in her room before we all left."

"Were you able to observe her closely?"

"Not what you'd call closely, no."

"But you did speak to her and looked at her."

"Certainly. She seemed much as usual. She was quite pale."

"Did you notice anything at all unusual?"

Randolph Harrison seemed to be looking for the answer in the toe of his boot and his answer was barely audible. "There was a very disagreeable flavor in the room."

"This flavor, or odor, was it one that you associated with childbirth?"

"I put it down to quite contrary causes."

"You had no suspicion whatever of a birth at this time?"

"None."

"When did you suspect that a birth might have taken place?" Patrick Henry shook his head sadly at his opponent's maladroitness. "Clumsily done," Nancy heard him mutter.

Harrison raised his voice. "I never suspected anything of that nature."

"Really? It was my understanding that you were given information leading to that suspicion at a later time. Isn't that true?"

"It's true that a Negro women told me later that Miss Nancy had miscarried."

"One of your servants?"

"Yes."

"When was this?"

"I don't recall."

"Was it while the Randolphs were still under your roof?"

"It's possible. I don't remember."

"But you never inquired of any of the Randolphs concerning the possible truth of this information?"

"I had no need to. The story was absurd."

"Did you also receive from others of your servants an additional story?"

"There was a report among the servants that a birth had been put on a pile of shingles between two logs."

"Did you investigate the matter at that time?"

"No." Randolph Harrison's uneasiness was increasing with every question. His reluctance seemed to Nancy nearly as damaging as a direct accusation would have been. There was no one in the courtroom who could fail to see that Randolph Harrison's lack of curiosity was designed to protect his friends.

"Did you happen to see this pile of shingles at any time?"

"Perhaps six or seven weeks later I saw such a pile."

"And were these shingles stained with blood?"

"The topmost shingle was somewhat stained. I don't know that it was blood. But its appearance might have given rise to the story among servants predisposed to believe it."

"A considerable time had passed since you were first told of them. They had been exposed to weather, sun and rain?"

"I would suppose so."

"These shingles were at no great distance from your house, were they?"

"No."

"As part of material for the building of your house they were, I would think, placed quite convenient?"

"Yes."

"And yet six or seven weeks passed before you bothered to look at them. Wouldn't you agree that this showed a remarkable reluctance on your part to investigate so serious a charge?"

"I saw no need to investigate. I do not put credence in servants' gossip."

Mr. Willson seemed about to continue the questions and then changed his mind and indicated to the judge that the prosecution had finished with Randolph Harrison. To Nancy's surprise, Mr. Campbell rose for the defense after a whispered consultation with Marshall and Henry.

"Mr. Harrison, I believe that the Randolphs stayed on at your house for all of the first week in October?"

"Yes, until Friday or Saturday. I believe it was Saturday when they returned to Bizarre."

"Did you notice anything at all unusual in the behavior of the Randolph ladies in that time?"

"Nothing at all. On Tuesday Mr. and Mrs. Randolph and my wife rode to a store to make some purchases. Nancy was not out of her bed that day."

"And on Wednesday and Thursday?"

"Except that Nancy was recovering from her illness, everything was as usual. She was out of her bed on Wednesday but kept to her room, but by Thursday she came downstairs for part of the day and seemed very much better."

"And on Friday or Saturday they returned home?"

"It was on the Saturday, I believe."

"A short time later did you and your family pay a return visit to the Randolphs at Bizarre?"

"About three weeks later."

"Did you observe anything remarkable in the relationships or the atmosphere of their household at that time?"

"Not at all. Everything was just as usual. Richard Randolph

seemed a bit crusty, but there were problems with the estate that accounted well for that."

"You saw no signs of stress as between husband and wife?"

"None at all. There were none to be seen."

After he was excused, Randolph Harrison waited in the well of the court until the clerk had called his wife, so that he might escort her to the stand. For the first time one of the witnesses looked directly at Nancy and Judith and gave them a reassuring smile as she held the Bible in her hand. There was a brief conference between opposing counsel and the bench before the witness's identity was recorded. The witness now before them was Mrs. Randolph Harrison, Mary Harrison, but the prosecution anticipated a possible problem since their next witness, Mrs. Harrison's mother-in-law, was also a Mrs. Randolph Harrison with a Christian name of Mary. Why don't they just call them Mary and the old lady? Nancy thought impatiently. It's how everyone thinks of them. In effect that was what was eventually decided, with this witness to be known for the record as Mary Harrison and the next to be known as Mrs. Randolph Harrison, Senior. Whether or not it had been designed to do so, the minor contretemps had served the purpose of making Mary more comfortable in her position. She was far more at ease than her husband had been.

"Were you in the courtroom and able to hear your husband's testimony?"

"Yes, I was."

"Then in the interest of time can we assume that your testimony would be the same as his up until the time you were awakened by screams in the night?"

"Yes, except that he said that he might have noticed a certain imprudence in Dick's and Nancy's manner toward each other and I think he was mistaken. I never noticed any such thing and I had many more opportunities to do so than he did."

The prosecutor had no interest in exploring that statement. "We will note the exception," he said quickly. "Your husband told us that you thought the screams to be Judith's, Mrs. Richard Randolph's, and went upstairs. Is that correct?"

"Not immediately. First Nancy's servant came down and asked for the laudanum, so we knew that it was Nancy who was unwell, and then I waited for a time before I went up."

"Would you be good enough to tell us what happened when you went upstairs?"

"I went up the stairs and found Judy sitting up in her bed."

"Was the room dark?"

"I believe there was a candle burning in the room, and of course I carried one myself to light my way."

"And did you have a conversation with Mrs. Randolph at this time?"

"Yes, I did."

"Would you tell us about it?"

"I said what on earth is the matter with Nancy, she's screaming so, and Judy said she didn't know but she guessed she had the hysterics because she didn't think the cholic would make her scream so. She said that Nancy had taken her gum guiacum . . ." She broke off. "No, that's wrong, that was earlier."

"Earlier?"

"When I first went upstairs when Judy was going to bed. We both talked to Nancy then and either Nancy said she had taken the gum guiacum or Judy told her to take it. I'm sorry to be so confused."

"That's quite all right, Mrs. Harrison. We know it is difficult to remember exactly."

"Where was I?"

"You had just told us that Mrs. Randolph told you that she believed Miss Nancy to be having one of her hysteric fits."

"That's right, and she went on to say that Nancy had been subject to them recently, that she'd had a similar bout of screaming a few days before but not for so long or so loud."

"Did you at this time go into the inner room where Miss Nancy Randolph was?"

"I went to the door of Nancy's room and found it bolted."

"Did this surprise you?" the prosecutor asked eagerly.

"Not at all. The door had a spring catch which was broken and the only way the door would stay shut was to shoot the bolt. I knocked on the door and Richard opened it for me."

"Immediately?"

"Yes."

"And then?"

"Nancy and Richard both asked that I not bring the candle into her room because she was in great pain and had been taking the laudanum and the light from the candle hurt her eyes terribly."

"Did you blow out the candle?"

"No, I put it down on the top step outside the door before I went in."

"Then there was light entering the room through the door both from your candle and from Mrs. Randolph's in the outer room?"

"Yes, but not directly. It wasn't shining in her eyes."

"But there was light enough for you to see?"

"Yes, quite well."

"Who was in the inner room?"

"Nancy, of course, and Richard and Nancy's servant, who's about fifteen, and Virginia."

"How old is Miss Virginia?"

"Jenny is about six or seven. She was on the trundle and seemed to be asleep."

"Did you remain long in the room?"

"I'm not sure what you mean by long."

'An hour? Half of that?"

'Oh no, perhaps fifteen minutes. I talked to Nancy and she said that she was beginning to feel better, which I took to be the laudanum working, and I stayed talking to her and then I asked to be excused because I had a sick child downstairs, teething, and was afraid that she would not rest easily without me, and Nancy said that of course under those circumstances she wouldn't wish me to stay any longer and she thanked me for coming up to see her."

"After you returned to your bed, do you recall hearing the footsteps on the stairs that your husband has testified to?"

"Yes, but as my husband said, we were both half asleep and we only thought it might have been Richard on the stairs—we were never sure—and we realized later that we must have been mistaken. There had been a lot of confusion and noise in the night and we were just not very quick in our minds."

"I think we all understand your problem with this testimony very well, Mrs. Harrison." The prosecutor smiled. "On the following morning I imagine that you visited your guest to inquire after her health?"

"Of course."

"And how did she appear to you in the light of the morning?"

"She was very pale and she had the blankets drawn close around her. It was a bitter cold morning even with the fire in the room."

"Mrs. Harrison, did you see any stains that might have been blood on the bedclothing?"

Mary Harrison hesitated before she answered and her voice was low. "I couldn't see either sheets or the bed quilt, but there seemed to be some spots that might have been blood on the pillowcase."

"And did you find any stains elsewhere in the house?"

"There were some rusty brown spots on the staircase."

"Mrs. Harrison, when did you first suspect that Miss Nancy Randolph's indisposition might be other than cholic or hysteria?"

"I never suspected anything," she answered firmly. "I thought from the blood that she was probably unwell from quite a natural cause, and that might account for the hysterics. She's quite a young girl still and sometimes younger women get very disturbed at certain times."

"Were you ever told of any other possible explanation?"

She did not answer until he had repeated the question. "One of the servants told me later that Nancy had miscarried a child."

"One of the Randolph servants or one of yours?"

"One of mine."

"Was this before or after the Randolphs left your house?"

"I don't remember, probably after."

"Wasn't it in fact after they left when you and a servant were clearing out the room that Nancy Randolph had occupied?"

"I've already told you that I can't remember."

The prosecutor sighed. "Very well, but after your guests had left, you did examine the mattress on Nancy Randolph's bed, didn't you?"

"I didn't examine it, not the way you mean."

"But you did happen to see it?"

"Yes."

"And what was its appearance?"

"It looked as if someone had tried to wash it clean, but it was still stained. I had to take . . ." Her voice trailed off.

"I'm sorry, Mrs. Harrison, but I don't believe the jury can hear you."

"I had to take the feathers out before it could be washed properly."

"Thank you, Mrs. Harrison. I have no more questions for you at this time."

Mary Harrison seemed very near to tears. Her husband rose from his seat and started toward her, but Patrick Henry waved him back.

"Just one or two questions, Mrs. Harrison," Patrick Henry said gently, "and then this will all be over for you. This is not an easy experience for someone as gently bred as you are, I know. You've known all the Randolphs very well for a long time, haven't you?"

"All my life."

"And since you are about of an age, you would have known Mrs. Richard Randolph best of any of them, wouldn't you say?"

"Yes."

"And knowing her well, you would be able to see any sign of strangeness in her manner, wouldn't you?"

"I believe so. Judy and I have been very close friends."

"Then would you tell me, when you went upstairs with her at bedtime, and again when you went into her room in the middle of the night, was there any sign of alarm and confusion that might be expected if she supposed her sister to be in childbirth in the next room?"

"Oh no, not at all. She was naturally distressed because her sister was unwell, but she didn't think it was anything serious."

"And was there any sign of resentment she would naturally feel if she supposed her husband was the father of such a child?"

"Certainly not. She was worried about Nancy and about the disturbance for the others in the house, but that was all."

"You told my colleague about a few bloodstains on the bedding and the mattress. Was there anything that led you to believe that these came from anything other than a rather common natural feminine complaint?"

"No."

"And in fact that was what you attributed them to?"

"Yes."

"On your visit to Bizarre some three weeks later, what can you tell us about the relationship between Mr. and Mrs. Richard Randolph?"

"They were living together in perfect harmony, just as they always have."

"I am sure that you hope as I do that the next few days will see them restored to that state."

"With all my heart."

"And a very good heart it is, Mrs. Harrison." Patrick Henry gave her his arm as she stepped down from the stand and escorted her over to the gate where her husband stood waiting. She paused at the end of the bench where Judy and Nancy sat and bent down to give Judy a kiss and a hug and reached across to squeeze Nancy's hand. Judy was grateful for the demonstration, but Nancy was not at all sure. If she seems so friendly,

Nancy thought, they're like to think she's lying for us. She saw the faintest of frowns cross Patrick Henry's face and knew the old man agreed with her.

Now Mrs. Harrison, Senior, marched to the stand, glaring impartially at the judge, jury, both sets of counsel and the spectators. In her full mourning, she looked like a small black bomb ready to explode, and Mr. Willson approached her with the greatest caution.

"You are Mrs. Randolph Harrison, Senior, the mother of the Mr. Harrison who testified here earlier?"

"I am."

"And would you be kind enough to tell us what you know of this matter?"

"I most certainly will. It is nothing but a lot of old twaddle put about by people with nothing better to do. I'm an old lady and I've heard a great many tales, but I never heard such nonsense as this in my whole life."

The prosecuting counsel appealed to the judge, who leaned across the bench to address Mrs. Harrison. "Your conclusions about the case may be valuable, I'm sure, Mrs. Harrison, but they are not evidence that can be placed before the court."

"I don't know why not." The old lady bristled. "Polly Page certainly placed her opinions before this court and she wasn't even there at Glenlyrvar nor likely to be after today's work."

Someone in the courtroom laughed and Mrs. Harrison smiled triumphantly. At the prosecution's request the judge instructed the jury to forget the witness's answer but then told counsel that he might find he would not provoke improper answers if his questions were more specific. Mr. Willson acknowledged the rebuke.

"You yourself were not at Glenlyrvar on the night of Miss Nancy Randolph's illness, were you?"

"That would be on the Monday?"

"That's right."

"No, I was at my own home, which neighbors my son's.

But quite early next morning I heard that Nancy had been taken ill and I went over to see her."

"Who told you of her illness?"

"Either her sister or my daughter-in-law. They came by with Richard and the little girl—Jenny her name is—on the way to the store at the crossroads."

"Did they ask you to visit her?"

"Didn't need to ask me. I had my bonnet on as soon as they told me of it. It didn't sound to me as if anyone over there had the first idea what her trouble was, and they were all young people without much experience in nursing."

"What happened when you arrived at Glenlyrvar?"

"I went up to Nancy's room and asked her how she did. She told me she had been very sick in the night but was much better now. She was half asleep, poor child, what with being awake all night and then dosed with laudanum. I don't hold with laudanum myself, except a very little bit when a baby is cholicky. If you want my opinion it just makes the bowels more constricted in a grown person. Anyway, I could see for myself that she was better and that the best thing now was just to let her sleep, so I came away after just a few minutes."

"And when did you see her again?"

"I think it must have been the Friday. I had thought it was Saturday but Randolph says they all went on back to Bizarre on Saturday, so it couldn't have been. Friday it was, Friday in the morning."

"And on this occasion did you spend a longer period of time with her?"

"I sat with her most all of the morning. We had a real good talk about when her mother and I were girls. I've never seen Nancy more cheerful than she was that morning. She laughed when I told her about the things we used to get up to when we were young, and she was particularly pleased to talk to me about her mother. She misses her sorely yet, poor mite."

"But no mention was made of the matter before this court?"

"Why should there be?" Mrs. Harrison was indignant. "I told you before. It didn't happen. It's a story made up out of nothing at all and put about by some people who know who they are and ought to know better."

Mr. Willson retreated rapidly. "Thank you, Mrs. Harrison. I have no further questions."

Instead of the smile and the brief bob of his head that he had given the other witnesses, Patrick Henry gave Mrs. Harrison a sweeping courtly bow in the old style that was going out of fashion in Republican days. She acknowledged it with a half-mocking smile and offered him her hand. All they need is a fiddler, Nancy thought, and they can go into the dance.

"It is always a great pleasure to see you again, Mrs. Harrison, no matter how unpleasant the circumstances."

"Thank you, Mr. Henry. It's been far too long."

"I have only a few questions to trouble you with and then you may get well away from this farrago. The first one may seem rather obvious, but it's just to establish the background. You have several children yourself, do you not?"

"Four living, three I lost."

"And you have been present many times either during or shortly after childbirthing by other women?"

"Black and white, so many times I couldn't make a start at saying."

"So we can all assume that you would have no trouble recognizing the signs of a recent childbirth?"

"I should think not, indeed."

"Now, was there anything at all in Miss Nancy Randolph's condition on either of the days that you visited with her that would have given rise to the slightest suspicion that she had recently been delivered?"

Nancy held her breath. Patrick Henry had not asked her a single question about the old lady and seemed now to gamble everything.

"Absolutely not. There was no milk, no fever, nothing whatsoever." Mrs. Harrison's voice was firm and clear; her eyes never wavered. "The first day she was tired from a wakeful night and I left her to sleep, but the second time she was perfectly well and happy. And so may she be again if certain people will learn to curb their vicious tongues. Those are the ones who ought to be on trial here. It's the foolishest way of going about things I ever heard of. You'd think Virginia didn't have a law against slander. In olden days they used to cut their tongues right out, and a very good thing it would be to bring it back if anyone was to ask me."

"Your Honor, if you please," Mr. Willson said. "This is really improper."

"Mrs. Harrison is your witness, Counselor." Patrick Henry smiled. "I myself am very well pleased with her testimony and prepared to let her leave the stand at any time."

"Then the witness may be excused."

"With our gratitude," Henry added.

Mrs. Brett Randolph was called next, and Nancy saw with some satisfaction that she looked nervously at Mrs. Harrison, who had taken a seat in the courtroom and now sat glaring malevolently at the witness who had followed her into the box. Mrs. Randolph was frightened; her voice rarely rose above a whisper. She said that, yes, she was a frequent and unceremonious visitor at Bizarre and knew them all very well. No, she had never seen any marks of ill-will or discontent between Richard and Judith and nothing but amity between the sisters. Richard was quite attentive to his sister-in-law, and it was possible that some might think rather more than to his wife, but she understood that Nancy was grieving over the death of Mr. Randolph's younger brother and Richard's marks of affection were quite possibly on that cause.

"You were at Bizarre shortly before the party set off for Glenlyrvar, were you not?"

"Yes, I was."

"And how did Nancy Randolph appear to you then?"

"She seemed in a rather nervous state and not very well."

"How was she dressed?"

"She wore a close gown with no loose coverings, and there was a certain amount of change in her figure that might possibly have led some people to suspect that she was pregnant."

"You visited Bizarre again after the return from Glenlyrvar?"

"I did."

"And how did Nancy appear then?"

"She was somewhat diminished in size."

Alexander Campbell arose to question the witness after a few whispered words from Patrick Henry. "Mrs. Randolph, have you ever known a similar alteration in the figure to come from other than pregnancy?"

"Oh yes." Brett Randolph's wife seemed eager to disassociate herself from those who might have been suspicious. "Sometimes when there is an obstruction there can be a very similar change in shape."

"When Nancy Randolph returned from the Harrisons', did she seem to be in better health as well as diminished in size?"

"Yes indeed. In fact I put down the change in size to that very cause."

"And only when you heard other rumors did you begin to even think about pregnancy?"

"Yes, but I truly never believed it," she said hastily. "It was just that everybody seemed so sure it had happened that it made me think it might have."

"But it was never in your mind more than a possibility?"

"That's right."

The witness was excused and hurried down the aisle and out of the courtroom, looking neither to right nor left. Thank God for the old lady, Nancy thought; she frightened her off. I could see Mrs. Brett thinking about having her tongue cut out for slander. Cripple her for life it would, since all she's good for is talk.

Poor Archie, Nancy thought, as the Commonwealth called Archibald Randolph as its next witness. He must be the most miserable of all. He knows that some way he's been made a fool of, but he doesn't even know yet who did it to him. She even entertained a hope that Mr. Henry wouldn't be too hard on him, he would die of mortification and he wasn't truly wicked, just weak and more than a little stupid.

Before the prosecution could ask the first question, Archie was protesting that he really knew nothing whatever about the matter and couldn't for the life of him think why he had been called. It was true, he said, that at one time, maybe eighteen months ago, he had thought that perhaps Richard and Nancy were growing overfond of each other, but long before the night at Glenlyrvar he had decided that there was nothing in it.

"Is it true that you escorted the ladies to Glenlyrvar along with Richard Randolph?"

"Yes, but only because I was going there anyway." Feeble, Nancy thought. Everyone knows you were chasing after me, so what's the use of pretending otherwise?

"Did you notice any change in Nancy Randolph's figure?"

"Oh no, not at all, she seemed much the same."

"You were also a guest at the Harrisons' that night, I believe?"

"I was, and for some days after, but not in the same house. We were in the bachelor house, which is detached."

"So you didn't know about Miss Nancy's illness at the time. Didn't hear her screams in the night?"

"We all knew she wasn't well, she didn't come down for supper, and at breakfast the next morning there was talk about how ill she had been in the night."

"But you didn't visit her sickroom?"

"I didn't think it proper. I didn't see her again until the Thursday when she came down from her room."

"What happened on that Thursday?"

"Well, we talked a bit, you know, and I said how sorry we all were that she had been ill and that we had missed her and just the usual things one says. Then she decided to return to her room and she went to the stairs and she seemed very weak and asked that I please give her my arm. She rested on my arm for some little time before she went upstairs."

"Was there any particular thing that you noticed on this occasion?"

Archie turned the color of redbud in March and appealed to the judge. "Must I answer that, sir?"

"I'm afraid you must unless counsel withdraws the question."

Archie looked hopefully at the prosecutor, but Mr. Willson was examining the nail of his forefinger with great interest.

"I noticed a very disagreeable odor," Archie whispered.

"Was this disagreeable odor one that you associated with childbearing?"

"No, quite the contrary. I mean I never suspected anything about a pregnancy until Peyton Harrison told me some time after that Nancy had either had a child or miscarried."

The defense had no questions for Archie Randolph, and his relief as he stepped down from the box was so evident that even some of the jurors smiled. Nancy watched him go and wondered that she felt so little. Cousin Archie had been a part of her life for as long as she could remember. Many times in the past two or three years she had told herself that if all else failed, there was always Archie. He wasn't a great romantic hero, but he was kind and loving and predictable; she could have been safe and even perhaps content as his wife. Now he scurried down the aisle and out of her life without a backward glance and she felt only a mild pique, a wounded vanity.

There was a hurried consultation at the prosecution table, and Mr. Willson approached the bench. "Sir, the Commonwealth has a very few witnesses left to present. We think that even though the day is growing late we could manage to put in all their testimony in a short period of time, leaving the defense case until tomorrow morning. It seems the more orderly way to do it, if the defense agrees."

"How long is what you call a short period of time? I think we are all growing tired."

"Not more than half an hour, Your Honor."

"Very well, I was about to adjourn, but if you will make it brief I see the merit in your suggestion."

As it happened the prosecution's case was completed in less than the time allowed, for all that remained was the parade of the "Know-nothings" as Patrick Henry called them, men whose names had been given to the prosecutors for being most active in spreading the tale. Only the first of them, Peyton Harrison, spent more than two minutes on the stand. He testified that although he had no firsthand knowledge of the happenings at Glenlyrvar, he had observed for himself that Richard Randolph was indiscreetly overfond of his sister-in-law.

For this witness Patrick Henry made no attempt to conceal his contempt. He stood some distance away from the box, his voice cutting; there would be no gentle leading of Peyton Harrison but a direct assault.

"Mr. Archibald Randolph has testified that you were the one who told him that Nancy Randolph had had a child, is that correct?"

"Or miscarried."

"Or miscarried. May I ask where you acquired this information?"

"I was told by a servant."

"It was not your own observation?"

"No, I was not present at Glenlyrvar."

"Let me get this clear. With no direct knowledge of your own, on the word of a black unsupported by any evidence, you told Archibald Randolph that Nancy Randolph, a young girl you had known since childhood, in whose home you had been entertained many times, you told Archibald Randolph that this young girl who deserved your protection had had a child out of wedlock. Did you imagine that you were doing her a service?"

Peyton Harrison was distinctly uncomfortable. "No. But I thought I owed a greater duty to Archibald. I thought he should know."

"I am sure we are all curious to know your reason."

"I knew that at one time he had been very interested in Nancy Randolph and I did not know if his feelings were still the same and I told him."

"Because you thought it your duty as a friend?"

"Yes."

"It's become a very strange world, Mr. Harrison. In my youth we had a rather different meaning attached to the notion of duty. We thought we owed it first to the defenseless. But I'm an old man. I mustn't bore you about better days. I have no more questions for you."

Beverly Lloyd, William Bradley, John Kerr, one after the other they mounted the stand, took the oath, and swore that they knew nothing whatever about the matter before the court. They each looked warily at Patrick Henry sprawled at the defense table, but he waved them away without any questions. Toward the end the spectators began to leave. The bailiff had brought in a light and lit the tapers at the front of the room, but the back was in darkness when the last of the prosecution's witnesses was dismissed. The clerk of the court rapped his rod on the floor, and everyone rose except for one juryman who had to be nudged awake. The judge departed through the small side door at his back. The last spectators filed out slowly, looking back over their shoulders for one more glimpse of the three Randolphs and their attorneys. Mr. Tucker came forward from his place in the back of courtroom, embraced Judy and Nancy and congratulated Mr. Henry. "Worth the money, ain't I?" Patrick Henry laughed.

"Every penny of it," Mr. Tucker agreed.

"Glad to hear you say that, though to tell the truth I'm enjoying myself so much it doesn't seem quite right to take the fee."

Even John Marshall's long, gentle face seemed less sad than usual. He put an arm around each of the girls' shoulders in a gesture that seemed unnatural and clumsy for him. "You've been good brave girls, both of you. It's been a long, tiring day and a most unpleasant business, but it will all be over tomorrow."

(258)

"By dinnertime tomorrow, Richard, you'll be a free man," Henry called to him as the jailer led him out.

"And missing the jailer's wife's good cooking," Mr. Campbell added.

* 3 *

The second day of the trial was as bright and beautiful as the first had been dull. Even the crowd of spectators seemed in a lighter mood, perhaps because there were more of the ladies of the county present than there had been the day before. Those who had hung back out of shyness or a sense of impropriety had had their imaginations teased at supper the night before by the accounts brought home by the gentlemen of their households and had come for the final act themselves. It seemed to Nancy very like a theater audience settling into their seats, nodding to friends, or, if not quite the theater, something between that and Sunday morning in the parish church. She recognized acquaintances from all the neighboring counties. Every plantation in Cumberland County must have had its guest rooms bulging. But there was no one there from Tuckahoe and, now that Martha's testimony was over, no one from Monticello. I will know who my friends truly are after this, she thought, and none of them will be family. Polly and Carter Page were nowehere to be seen, which she took as a favorable sign. Surely if Polly expected a verdict of guilty she would have been around for it.

Alexander Campbell would handle the defense witnesses while Patrick Henry occupied himself with scribbling away on his sheets of foolscap. There was a murmur of disappointment in the crowd when Campbell arose; they had come to see the star, not his understudy.

Jack Randolph carried with him into the witness stand his own rather special air of elegance. His long thin fingers held the Bible delicately as if it were something fragile. His sweet boy's voice as he took the oath startled those in the courtroom who didn't know him. At first Nancy was puzzled. There was something about him that seemed very strange, but she could not place it until she realized that she had never before seen him without his crop in his hand except at the dinner table. Even in church, sitting beside him, she was used to hearing the gentle tapping of its tip against his boot.

Mr. Campbell needed to ask very few questions. Jack Randolph would testify without prompting.

"My name is John Randolph of Roanoke and Bizarre. Richard Randolph is my elder brother, my surviving elder brother."

"You are perhaps, of all the witnesses we have heard, the best qualified to testify to the relationships between the members of the household at Bizarre, being a part of it yourself."

"I would think that I was."

"Then would you give us the benefit of your impressions?"

"To go back some two years ago, when I was in Philadelphia I was told by my late brother Theodoric that he was informally engaged to marry Miss Nancy Randolph, the younger sister of my brother Richard's wife, Judith. It was at about that time that Nancy became a more or less permanent member of the household. After my brother's death when I returned to Bizarre, Richard and Judith both told me that Nancy was in extremely low spirits and asked me not to mention Theodoric's name in her presence."

"Did you have occasion to witness this for yourself?"

"Yes, unfortunately. I did inadvertently mention Theo's name in Nancy's presence when Richard and I were discussing family matters."

"And what happened?"

"Nancy burst into tears and seemed quite inconsolable, despite the attention of both Richard and her sister."

"You say that Mrs. Randolph attempted to console Miss Nancy. May we assume then that the relationship between the two sisters was an amicable one?"

"Always. I have often heard Judith say how much fonder she was of Nancy than of anyone else in her family, and that fondness seemed to increase in the period we are speaking about."

"There was no evidence of jealousy of her husband's attentions to her sister?"

"None at all. Richard and Judith lived in perfect harmony with each other. And they were both particularly attentive toward Nancy because she was not only very unhappy but seemed not at all well."

"Now we have heard testimony that there was a suspicious alteration in Nancy Randolph's figure, and you speak of her being in ill-health. Did you observe this supposed alteration, and did you at any time associate her ill-health with a possible pregnancy?"

"That seems to be two questions and the answer to both of them is no. Nancy was never accustomed to wear stays or to lace up, and she didn't change her style of dress. I often lounged on the bed with both Nancy and her sister and never had any reason to suspect that she might be pregnant. I thought myself from her appearance she was somewhat emaciated and from her complexion, a rather greenish-blue under the eyes, that she was laboring under an obstruction of some sort, which might account for the swelling some people imagined that they saw."

"Did you accompany the party to the Harrisons and remain there for the week?"

"I joined them there. I was visiting nearby on the night when all this is alleged to have happened and arrived at Glenlyrvar the next day."

"On your arrival I assume you were told of Nancy's illness. Did you yourself see Nancy and, if you did, what were your impressions?"

"I sat with her one day while we were all at the Harrisons, and I may have noticed the rather unpleasant odor that others have mentioned, but on the Saturday when we returned to

Bizarre I rode in the carriage with Nancy and Judith and there was no trace of it then."

"How did Miss Nancy appear to you?"

"Much the same except that her complexion seemed somewhat clearer. I thought myself that her illness at Glenlyrvar might have been a consequence of a breaking down of the obstruction to which I laid her previous ill-health. She was certainly in excellent health once we returned to Bizarre."

Splendid, Nancy thought. Half the men in the county have been told that I stink in my monthlies, and now Jack wants to discuss the state of my bowels with them.

The prosecution had no interest in cross-examination and no objection when Jack asked if he might sit with his brother at the defense table instead of returning to his place among the spectators. The judge summoned both counsel to the bench. "Could you tell me how long this part of the case will run? Do you think we could complete testimony and argument and put the matter before the panel by dinnertime?"

"The defense has only one more witness," Mr. Campbell told him. "We do not expect that it will take any time at all to complete the case."

Mr. Willson said that the prosecution's argument would be very brief, and Mr. Campbell said that the defense argument would be carried by Mr. Henry, and Mr. Henry was noted for the pertinence of his speeches, not their length.

"Good, good. It would be best for all of us if the jury could deliberate before their dinners rather than after. So let's proceed."

Brett Randolph was called to the stand to answer only two questions. He said that he had been a frequent and informal visitor at Bizarre and had never witnessed anything but perfect accord in the house. He had seen no evidence of pregnancy or of any improper conduct. He felt, in fact, that such conduct was inconceivable, given the character of the people involved.

John Marshall rose as Brett left the box. "Your Honor, that concludes the testimony for the defense."

"Mr. Willson, is the Commonwealth ready with its argument?"

"I should like a few minutes, Your Honor. I had anticipated a somewhat larger number of witnesses for the defense."

"How long?"

"Perhaps fifteen minutes."

"Very well, I will adjourn for that period of time. The clerk will maintain the privacy of the panel while court is not in session."

"There, what did I tell you?" Old Mrs. Harrison's voice carried through the room. "Whole thing is a farrago of nonsense. No wonder he can't make his argument straight off, bricks without straw, if you ask me."

"Shhh."

"Don't shush me, Mary Harrison. Judge's gone out and I can talk if I want to. If you'd shushed some of those blacks of yours we wouldn't be here today. Nobody would pay any mind to what Polly Page had to say. Talk about old women being meddlesome, she's not thirty yet and she's made as much trouble as a dozen her size. You notice she didn't dare to show her face here today."

"Mother please, people are listening."

"I'm delighted to know it, it's time they heard some sense."

With the nodded consent of his jailer, Dick had moved from the company of his lawyers to the bench beside Judy and Nancy. He put his arm about his wife and her head down on his shoulder. "May I send for something for you? A cup of tea? Some water?"

"Nothing, thank you."

"Just be easy. It will soon be over and then we can all go home. I miss St. George. Never thought I would miss something so insignificant as a baby, but I do."

"How dare you call St. George insignificant?"

Dick laughed and gave her shoulder a squeeze. "I thought that would rouse your spirits up."

Nancy moved slightly away from her sister and brother-in-law. She did not want to hear the conversation of husband and wife, not now, not here. She leaned forward and tapped Mr. Henry on the shoulder.

"What is it now, Nancy?" Henry was irritated at the interruption.

"What happens to me when they finish with Richard, will it all be done over again?"

"No, nobody will have the stomach for it. Just be patient, you'll be free to go home again this evening too."

The jurors closest to Nancy were discussing the relative merits of Henrico Parish over Goochland as hunting country.

"Henrico's getting too filled up, not enough wild land left. Fences everywhere you look."

"Young Jack's got good country for sport down at Roanoke."

"It's all it is good for, can't afford to put it under cultivation."

"Their father left those Randolph boys in debt to their ears. Know for a fact that Tucker was just beginning to get them back on their feet."

"This'll set them back some. Old Henry don't come cheap."

"Too much money spent on their education."

"It was spelled out in old Richard's will, education first, plantations second."

"Tucker would have done it that way, anyway."

"All that expensive learning didn't keep them out of some nasty messes."

"Yes, but it shouldn't have been Richard, Theo was the one you expected to have trouble."

"Did, too."

"Killed him, they say."

"Philadelphia liquor and New York girls."

"Think young Nancy would ever have married him?"

"Not if Colonel Tom had anything to say about it."

"Speaking of the Colonel . . ."

"Don't say it. Never showed his face. Never knew him to dodge a fight before."

"Married that Harvie girl, didn't he?"

"Nothing like a young wife to rule an old man."

"Tom Randolph's not so old. He was at school with my brother, must be about of an age with me."

"Ah, but you've got a wife with bones as old as yours, not so exhausting if you take my meaning."

Do they think I'm deaf? Nancy thought angrily. She was glaring at the broad back of the one whose brother had gone to school with her father when there was an anticipatory stir in the courtroom, a rustle of silk as the spectators stood. To the rapping of the clerk's rod, the judge took his place on the bench.

"Is the Commonwealth now ready to proceed?"

"We are, Your Honor."

"Then let's get on with it."

Mr. Willson began his address to the jurymen, slowly, almost apologetically. "Gentlemen magistrates of the county of Cumberland, we bring before you a case that is one of the most painful it has ever fallen to me to try. But difficult though it may be, the object of the court is to determine the truth, not to let any extraneous considerations of place or birth or old friendship interfere with the proper working of the law. I have no need to remind you of the serious nature of the charge. Murder is murder no matter what the age or condition of the victim.

"I would like to sum up for you the testimony given here yesterday, to refresh your recollections, with every confidence that you will return a proper verdict. We have first the testimony of many people that they noticed a degree of familiarity between the defendant and his sister-in-law, Miss Nancy Randolph, that seemed to most of them unusual and to some of them improper. We have evidence from Miss Nancy's own aunt that she noticed an alteration in her niece's figure last May. We may not be pleased with the manner in which the evidence was observed; nevertheless, it was observed, and I think none of us doubt that Mrs. Page was speaking the truth as to what she saw and heard. We have the evidence of Nancy's illness on the night of October first, and though there have been varying explanations of it, there has been no denial of it.

"We have had put to us reluctantly the evidence of the bloodstained bed, the blood on the stairs, the stain on the pile of shingles. Both Mr. and Mrs. Harrison remember the heavy footsteps on those stairs in the middle of the night. They believed them to be those of Mr. Randolph, and the defense has never seen fit to deny it. Remember, then, the heavy footsteps and ask yourselves: If Richard Randolph was not carrying down those stairs the best evidence of his crime, the victim of it, then what was his errand in those black hours? Mr. and Mrs. Harrison assumed that he was sending for a physician, but may I remind you that no physician was ever brought to attend Miss Nancy on that night or on subsequent days, although surely an illness which caused her such great distress would normally call for the services of a medical man. I would also suggest to you that the work of this court might well have been made easier if, out of a natural tenderness of feeling for old friends, Mr. Harrison had not failed to investigate the circumstances immediately upon hearing from his servants that something untoward had occurred.

"I will not pretend to you that the Commonwealth has a perfect case. The absence of the body of the victim may seem to you to be a problem, but, as the judge will instruct you, it is necessary in law only to prove that a victim existed, that a crime was committed. I submit to you that the Commonwealth has proved this, and the absence of the physical body is not in itself a bar to the verdict of guilty." Mr. Willson took out his handkerchief and blotted his forehead, although it did not seem to Nancy that the room was excessively hot. Quite the contrary, in fact, ever since he had begun his address she had grown increasingly chilled.

Mr. Willson came to the edge of the jury box and spoke softly, confidentially to the jurors. "I am well aware of the difficulties this case presents to you. I am not insensitive to your problems. The Commonwealth asks only that each of you think about the evidence placed before you, that you examine your own conscience and, without any thought of the consequences to a man who may well be a friend or acquaintance of long standing, render a just verdict in this case. For surely if Richard Randolph is guilty of this crime, as I believe the state has proved, then he has forfeited all right of consideration and mercy from his peers. I know you will do your best and I thank you for it." Mr. Willson was forced to pass directly before Richard at the defense table to get to his own place, and Nancy saw with satisfaction that his eyes slid away and he made a nearly hidden gesture of deprecation with his left hand.

Patrick Henry blew his nose copiously in a gray handkerchief with a ragged edge, examined the results, tucked the cloth back in his sleeve, glanced briefly at the papers before him on which he had been assiduously scribbling and then crumpled them up and tossed them down as he arose. The spectators gave a collective sigh; they had come for a performance and for the first time today the star had come upon the stage.

"Gentlemen magistrates, I find myself in a most peculiar circumstance. I rise to answer a case against my client, Richard Randolph, and I am at a loss for words for one of the very few times in my life. For the simple truth of the matter, gentlemen, is that there is no case to answer. Richard Randolph is accused of murder and the evidence consists of a few drops of blood on a staircase, which the witnesses are agreed could have come from another cause, and a shingle stained with what may have been blood. I submit to you that a discolored shingle is thin evidence on which to hang a man." He rolled the last phrase out in an ominous tone that conjured up the gallows for everyone in the room. One or two of the jurors fingered their cravats as they could feel the hemp.

"For make no mistake about it, not just the reputation but the life or death of Richard Randolph is in your hands." He walked back toward the defense table and waved at the crumpled paper. "I studied my notes; you saw me toss them away. One cannot reply in a rational, measured way, point by point, to a tissue of absurdities. It is a grappling with phantoms.

"The Commonwealth has advised you quite correctly that it is not necessary to produce the victim to legally bring a charge of murder. It is sufficient in the law to show that the crime occurred even though the victim's body never be recovered. If it were not so, a murder committed in full public view with the victim carried out to sea by a raging tide would go unpunished. Or a murder committed in a secret place with the body buried could go unpunished. Yes, it is true that the law does not require the body of the victim to prove a charge of murder, but, gentlemen, if we are not all to dwell in Cloud-Cuckoo-Land, there must have been a victim.

"Gentlemen, in the case before you now, the victim never existed except in the gossip of servants and the malicious and fevered imagination of a few who should have known better. The victim is a phantom and a phantom that it is our joint duty to exorcise forever.

"Richard Randolph is accused of murdering a child said to have been born to Nancy Randolph on the night of October first at the plantation of Glenlyrvar. So reads the charge, and if there were any truth in it I would agree with my colleague that Mr. Randolph has forfeited his right to mercy from you. A heinous crime, if it had been committed. But what evidence are we offered that it was committed?

"We have heard those who testified to a too great fondness between Richard Randolph and his sister-in-law. But when pressed they acknowledge that what they witnessed was in no way clandestine but quite open, affectionate gestures. Gentlemen, think about it. If every affectionate gesture produced a child the population of Virginia would be bursting its bounds. You may well smile—" he nodded at the jurors, who were doing just that—"it is but one absurdity among many.

"I ask you, as reasonable men, could not these gestures have been quite naturally inspired in a young man whose beloved wife's younger and favorite sister is grieving over the death of his own much-loved younger brother? I think they were, and I think the guilt in this matter lies in the cold heart of the witness, for there is really only one primary witness, rather than in the affectionate warmth in Richard Randolph's heart.

"Now we have been told that there was an alteration in Nancy Randolph's figure, which might have indicated that she was pregnant to some witnesses but, according to others, might equally be laid to another quite innocent cause. Even if we assume for a moment that it was a pregnancy, what a very peculiar pregnancy it was!"

Mr. Henry frowned, scratched his head and shook it wonderingly in a vivid dumb show of bewilderment. "It was visible in May to two witnesses and invisible to six others at the end of September. Gentlemen, if this pregnancy existed—and I am confident that you will agree with me it did not—if this pregnancy existed it defied not only all the laws of logic but that of nature itself.

"Nancy Randolph was described to you by her aunt as headstrong and imprudent, flaws in her character perhaps but neither sins nor crimes in the eyes of reasonable men. But even Mrs. Page, who has no love for her niece at all, never accused her of being stupid or lacking in ordinary mother-wit. So what are we to make of that overheard conversation so vividly described to us? I agree that we should not dwell on the manner in which it was overheard. No matter how distasteful to us that picture of a woman creeping up the stairs to spy on her young niece may be, Mrs. Page's evidence has as much standing under law as if it were acquired openly and honestly. So we can assume that Mrs. Page heard, as the Commonwealth has pointed out, exactly what she reported to us.

"But, gentlemen, I ask you, what was it that she heard?" Henry paused and the jurymen leaned forward. "She heard a young girl say to her maid, 'Do you think I am getting smaller?' and the maid replied, 'No, Miss Nancy, you're getting bigger.'

Henry smiled and shook his head. "Now does it seem at all reasonable to you gentlemen that a woman who knows or even suspects that she might be pregnant would have any expectation of getting smaller in her term? Nancy Randolph was alone with her maid, she knew nothing of the eavesdropper lurking in the passage, and she asked if she were getting smaller.

"Gentlemen, I not only accept Mrs. Page's testimony, I welcome it, for it proves to my entire satisfaction the reverse of its purpose. Whatever the cause of Miss Nancy's change of figure, the one cause it could not have had was pregnancy.

"So if there was no pregnancy—and I have every confidence in your common sense to tell you that there could not have been—then what do we make of the events of the night of October first? We have a bloodstained bed, a hysterical girl, and a disagreeable odor. Without being embarrassingly explicit, gentlemen, those of you who are married men will be able to find an explanation other than childbirth to account for them all. And if more positive evidence is needed to set beside it we have the word of that staunch Virginia lady, Mrs. Harrison, surely the best qualified of anyone on the scene, who told us that there was not the slightest doubt in her mind that no birth had taken place.

"I have told you that there is no crime to defend my client against. That there was no victim. I am confident that you find that argument to be true and that you will acquit Richard Randolph purely on the facts presented here, but I cannot let this case go to your consideration without a few more words."

Henry had been standing before the jury box, speaking in a calm, reasonable tone, but now he stepped back and slumped against the counsel table, one hand on the crumpled papers there, the other at his forehead. He seemed to be fighting for control over an overpowering emotion, and when he again began to speak his voice was choked.

"Gentlemen, it is true that the alleged victim in this case is a phantom, one that never existed. Nevertheless, there is a true victim in this matter, not just one but three and you see them sitting here before you—Richard Randolph, his beloved wife Judith, and her sister Nancy." He gestured toward Judy and Nancy and put his hand on Richard's shoulder. "Persecuted for months by idle tittle-tattlers and malicious scandalmongers, the peace and tranquility of their home laid waste, their faith in those they thought to be their friends most cruelly destroyed. Their reputations a matter of discussion in circles that would, in the ordinary course of affairs, not even aspire to mention their names. Sadly the hurt they have suffered can never be truly healed. Those months of pain and despair are gone, never to be replaced."

Henry half turned and addressed the wider audience. "The true criminals in this case are not on trial here. Except, and let them mark this, for they know who they are—" his voice rose— "except, I say, in the minds and hearts of the good people of Virginia who will this day condemn them as they so richly deserve." Henry stood with his arm upraised like an avenging angel and listened with satisfaction to the murmur of approbation from the crowd.

"Gentlemen, it is unfortunately not within your power to punish the truly guilty in this case. But by your verdict you can bring the suffering of these innocent victims to an end. I charge you with your responsibility as gentlemen magistrates of Virginia, but even graver I charge you with your responsibility as Christian gentlemen, to do what you have in your power to do. Free those you see before you of the cloud that has hung over them these last weary months. Let them go home again, to be again the loving, warm-spirited young family that they once were. Anything less would be a compounding of the crime that has been committed against them." Henry bowed his head and stretched his hands toward the jury like Isaac offering his first-born to the altar. "I place them in your hands. They trust you as I trust you, as the good people of Virginia trust you. I beg of you, do what is in your power to bring some measure of justice to them."

For a moment the courtroom was silent when Henry sat

down, and then there was a single long exhalation, a rustle of handkerchiefs, a sniffing up of tears.

"Mr. Willson, do you wish time for rebuttal?"

"No, Your Honor, the prosecution waives the privilege."

Only the occasional phrase reached Nancy as the judge began to read the law to the jury. "As Mr. Willson has told you it is not necessary in law to produce the victim's body in support of a murder charge. . . . On the other hand, as Mr. Henry so ably pointed out . . . gentlemen of the jury, the matter is in your hands. Each of you is to judge the evidence as to its truth on his own and is to arrive at his judgment independently. If you find that you are not in agreement, there must be a free and frank discussion among you until such time as you are in agreement or until you consider any agreement impossible of attaining. You must remove from your minds any consideration of the consequences of your verdict. Your task is simply the finding of fact, not the working of the law, which is reserved to the court. The clerk will escort you to a private place and you will communicate only with each other and with him until your verdict is ready." Most of the jurors turned and looked back as they filed out of the room. Conscious of their eyes, Nancy took Judy's hand and held it tightly.

John Marshall rolled up the papers in front of him and tied them about with tape. "Very fair charge to the jury, I thought," he said to his colleague.

Henry rubbed at the back of his neck. "I'd have liked it better if he'd left out that bit about not considering the consequences."

Marshall shrugged. "Doesn't matter. He's bound to say it and the jury is going to consider the consequences in a capital trial no matter what he says, and he didn't come down hard on it. I can't see how there can be any problem. You and Mr. Campbell ready to handle the other matter?"

"I'll talk to Willson now while the jury is out and see what he is willing to do," Campbell volunteered.

Patrick Henry's laugh sounded very loud in the room.

"He'll want to forget the whole thing. He never wanted any part of it."

"If you and Campbell will plead in Nancy's case and make the dismissal motion, there are things I should attend to in Richmond," Marshall said to Henry.

"It's all right with me. Speak to your clients."

Marshall stepped over to the Randolphs. "My dears, if you wish me to stay I shall do so most willingly, but I can't believe that there will be anything further that Mr. Campbell and Mr. Henry won't be able to handle with dispatch, and there are family matters in Richmond that really demand my presence."

Dick spoke for all three of them, thanking him for all that he had done. Marshall smiled. "I could not have done less for Tucker's children. But you know the best thing I did for you was have you ride out to Henrico for Mr. Henry here. If you'll forgive me now for leaving, we'll meet again in happier circumstances."

From the back of the room Marshall's servant came forward and took his notes from him and gathered up his quills and inkstand.

"My carriage here?"

"I had it brought round when the judge started in talking."

"George, I believe you're beginning to know the courtroom almost as well as I do."

"I've got the best teacher, sir."

As soon as Marshall left, Mr Henry pulled his turnip watch out of his pocket. "Well, Mr. Campbell, would you like to make a small wager on how long they'll be out? It's been about ten minutes, time to get settled in, light a pipe. I'd make it another half hour."

It's a capital case, Mr. Henry, they'll be longer than that."

"Ah, but you're forgetting it's dinnertime. They won't want to stay out one minute longer than they have to to make it look respectable."

"Mr. Henry," Judy protested, "how can you be so frivolous?"

"Now Mrs. R., if I thought there was any chance they'd

find against us I wouldn't be joking, now would I? You children just be easy with yourselves, it's almost over. If you go about looking so worried you'll put doubts back in people's minds and all the trouble I've gone to will be for nothing."

"There's Willson coming back in," Campbell interrupted him. "You want to talk to him or shall I?"

"You do it. Tell him we'll agree to accept the testimony in the previous case as part of the substance of this one. No need to swear another jury. He won't want to put any new witnesses on, and most of his old ones are home hiding under their beds. Tell him we have just one witness for the defense. Shouldn't take more than ten minutes or so and then he can ask for dismissal."

"What if he wants to ask for dismissal without further trial?"

"Tell him your client won't agree to that. He'll go along with whatever you say, hasn't any stomach for this job."

Campbell moved over to the other table and spoke in whispers to Mr. Willson, who nodded, then frowned and said, "Why? We're willing to dismiss right now. We could do it in chambers before the jury gets back."

"Mr. Henry's client doesn't want it that way."

"Mr. Henry's client?" Nancy asked in alarm. "Does that mean me?"

"That's right." Henry nodded calmly. "What we are going to do is stipulate that the previous testimony can be accepted as part of your trial."

"My trial?" Nancy was horrified. "But you promised me that I wouldn't have to go on trial. You all said so. You said Dick would be acquitted and that would be all there was."

Henry stroked his chin. "I think what I said was that probably we wouldn't bother to put you on trial, but I changed my mind."

"But why? If they are willing to forget all about it, why can't we just let it go?"

"Because we want to clear up every little loose end and I have a witness I want to present."

Nancy swallowed hard. "Who? Not me," she said quickly. "You can't make me go up there."

"I am going to testify, Nancy," Judy intervened. "Mr. Henry and I have already discussed it."

"Judy, you can't, you mustn't."

"I can and I will. Who knows better than I what happened that night? Unless of course you would like to speak up."

"Listen, Judy, you don't know what you're doing. All those people staring at you . . ."

Judy cut her sister off impatiently. "Just what do you think they've been doing for months? Staring at me and whispering behind my back. You and Dick seem to think that you are the only ones with anything at stake in this, and it's not so. It's my husband they're accusing, not yours."

"Judy, you must not do it. Mr. Henry, tell her she can't."

"Why should I tell her to keep silent? I was the one who suggested she speak up. Me and Mr. Tucker, that is."

"But you don't understand . . ." Nancy began.

"Hush, jury's coming back."

The jury filed back into the box, smiling and looking well pleased with themselves. The clerk summoned the judge from his chambers.

"Gentlemen, do you have a verdict?"

"We do."

"Would you give it to the clerk to read."

"We, gentlemen magistrates of the Commonwealth of Virginia, being duly sworn, do find the defendant, Richard Randolph of Bizarre in the County of Cumberland, not guilty of the charge laid against . . ." The rest of the clerk's words were lost as the spectators stood and cheered. They converged on Dick and Judy, slapping him on the back and embracing Judy, who for the first time since the trial began let the tears stream down her face. Nancy found herself in the musty, snuffy embrace of old Mrs. Harrison.

"You've been a good brave girl. Your mama would have been proud of you. And I'll give old Tom a piece of my mind when next I see him for not being here with you." Before Nancy could thank her, she was swept away by the crowd. Then came the Meades and the Creed Taylors, Brett Randolph and the young Harrisons, all the loyal friends, and at the outer rim St. George Tucker, staying back diffidently but beaming with pleasure.

In the noise and confusion, which the court officers had given up trying to control, Nancy lost sight of Patrick Henry. She searched the crowd desperately. She knew that she must talk to him before it was too late, must warn him of the danger he was courting so blithely. But he had vanished, and the Meades hurried her out to their carriage, where they had a hamper of food and wine waiting.

"Where's Judy? I must talk to Judy."

"I think I saw her with the Taylors."

"I must find her, I need to talk to her."

"There'll be plenty of time for that. Have a little of the chicken."

"I can't eat."

"It's the excitement, but you must eat, you know. Or at least have a glass of wine."

Nancy waved them away. "I must see Judy or Mr. Henry."

"Well then, you have your wish," Mr. Henry said at the carriage door. "Come along, Nancy. The court requires you."

Nancy took his arm and stepped down on the graveled yard. "Where did you go? You knew I wanted to talk to you."

"That's why you couldn't find me. Can't have your chatter rattling my poor old brains."

"Mr. Henry, please, it's not a matter for joking. You mustn't ask Judy to testify."

"She's quite willing."

"But don't you see, now that Dick's free, there's no need . . ."

"I think there is."

"Listen, Mr. Henry," Nancy said desperately, "there's something you don't understand about Judy. You mustn't let her get in the box."

Patrick Henry's grip on her arm tightened and he brought their progress to a halt. He bowed and smiled to the bystanders, but his voice was low and harsh. "In the first place, you are to stop looking so agitated and smile at me as if we were out for a Sunday stroll. That's better. In the second place, don't you tell me what I don't understand. My understanding was good enough to get us all this far. It will hold up for another half hour."

"But Judy . . ."

"Smile, damn it," he interrupted. "Don't worry about what Judy is going to say."

Nancy pulled her arm out of his grasp. "I won't permit it."

Henry beamed most amiably at her, but when he took her arm again his bony fingers dug into it. "You won't permit it?" he whispered. "My dear girl, there isn't one damn thing you can do to stop it, unless you would like to stand up there and plead guilty."

"You know I can't do that."

"Then trust your lawyer and hush up."

Once again the clerk rapped his staff. The gentlemen magistrates filed back in the box, one or two still wiping the last of dinner from his lips. Then it was Nancy's turn to stand before the bench, to murmur not guilty when Mr. Henry prompted her, to walk stiff-legged and stunned back to the defendant's chair at the long table. Mr. Campbell took her hand and held it while Mr. Willson and Patrick Henry conferred with the judge, who nodded agreement and turned to the jury.

"Gentlemen, since the evidence to be placed before you in this case would be substantially the same in every particular but one from that in the previous case, the attorney for the Commonwealth and the attorney for the defense have agreed to stipulate that the testimony you heard previously be accepted as part of the record of this case. I am sure that it is all fresh in your minds and you will not need it repeated in order to render an appropriate verdict." If one or two of the jurors looked a little disappointed or bewildered the judge chose to ignore it and turned back to the lawyers. "Mr. Willson?"

"The Commonwealth waives opening statement and will call no witnesses, Your Honor."

"Mr. Henry?"

"The defense calls Mrs. Richard Randolph to the stand."

As Randolph Harrison had, Dick escorted his wife to the witness box. To Nancy it seemed that he was half carrying her, so heavily did Judy lean on his arm.

"Your Honor, may I take the oath on my own Bible?"

"It's not usual, but I have no objection if counsel has none. Although perhaps I should point out that it is the spiritual substance of the oath that concerns us here, not the actual Book."

Judy took the oath in a barely audible voice. When she sat down she kept the book in her lap, both hands clasped firmly around it. The morning crowd of spectators had been enjoying their dinners, less than half of them had found their way back into the room when Judy began to answer the preliminary questions. From outside Nancy heard someone call, "Hurry up. Judy's on the stand." The judge looked up quickly, he had heard it too. He halted the questioning until those already pushing their way in had found seats and then ordered the doors closed and an officer of the court posted to keep any more late-comers out. Half the seats were still unfilled when Henry turned back to his witness. Years later, what Nancy would remember most vividly of her trial for murder was the sight of some of the most distinguished faces of Virginia society with their noses pressed flat against the glass of the window panes. Throughout the confusion Judy sat rock-still, looking, Nancy thought, like one of the martyrs in her book.

"Mrs. Randolph, you are a woman of strong religious convictions, are you not?"

"Yes, I am."

"And you understand very well the meaning of the oath you have taken in both its spiritual and temporal aspects?"

"I do."

"I ask you this only because those who do not know you well might suppose that self-interest could color your answers to some of my questions."

"I understand, and I assure you that . . ."

"There's no need to assure me, Mrs. Randolph. Your pledge has been made to God." He smiled reassuringly at her. "To shorten what must of necessity be a very difficult time for you, I will ask you only about the events on the night of October first. From the time you went up to bed until you rose in the morning. Were you awake all through the night?"

"Yes, I was."

"Where were you?"

"Part of the time I was in my sister Nancy's room and for the rest of the time I was in my own room outside her door."

"Would you tell us what happened?"

"I went to bed but I couldn't sleep because Nancy was so very ill, and I could hear her crying. Her servant was very frightened, so I went into her room and tried to make her more comfortable."

"And did you succeed?"

"No, I didn't. She seemed to grow much worse. She was screaming and I couldn't quiet her, and at last I was exhausted. I hadn't been well myself, so I went back into the outer room and asked my husband to please go in and drop some laudanum for her."

"And did he go?"

"Not at first. He said that Nancy was just hysterical and would soon hush if we left her alone, but just before Mrs. Harrison came upstairs he finally consented to go in and see what he could do. He took the laudanum with him and then Mary, Mrs. Harrison, came upstairs and after a bit Nancy was quieter and he came back to bed."

"There was no door from your sister's room except into your room, is that correct?"

"Yes."

"And you have told us that you were awake all night?"

"Yes."

"Would it have been possible for a child to have been born that night without your knowledge?"

"No."

"Could your husband have gone down the stairs that night without your knowledge?"

"No." Judy gave each of her responses firmly but without any expression, an automaton.

"And was, in fact, a child born to your sister, Nancy Randolph, on the night of October first at Glenlyrvar?"

"No. And my husband never left my side the whole night through except at my request that he help dose Nancy, which he did most reluctantly and only because he feared for my own health, as I was excessively fatigued."

Patrick Henry thanked and excused her. Clutching her Bible, Judy stepped down from the stand, her lips clamped in a straight line, her face as white as her linen cuffs. She will faint away waiting for the thunderbolt, Nancy thought.

Judge Murdoch cleared his throat. "The bench will entertain a motion from the Commonwealth's attorneys if they so desire."

"Yes. Your Honor, the Commonwealth has no interest in the continuation of this trial. We move to withdraw the charge on the ground that there is not sufficient evidence before us to sustain it."

"The motion is granted. All charges against Miss Nancy Randolph are dismissed with prejudice."

"Well, that's it, Nancy." Patrick Henry shrugged, stretched, and went into an orgy of scratching under his wig. "I've had my fee in the case, but you might give an old man a hug and a kiss for his troubles."

Nancy was bewildered. "You mean that's all? It's all over?"

"All over bar the shouting . . . and I guess that's over too. They shouted themselves out before dinner."

"What do we do now?"

"Nothing. You go on home and behave yourself and don't be so snippity with your elders, particularly aunts. Come on now," he said hurriedly as saw the tears starting in Nancy's eyes, "give us our hug and get out of here. Your sister's waiting."

With his arm about Judy, Dick was pushing his way through the crowd. A few of the jurymen, none of them Carringtons, had caught up with him and were offering their congratulations. Dick thanked them but begged to be excused. "My wife is really very tired. Would you forgive us if we leave now? She hasn't been well and these months have been difficult for her."

Nancy trailed behind them, alone until Jack came up and took her arm. He whispered sharply in her ear, "Keep your head up and smile, you look like a hound with a mouthful of chicken feathers."

From somewhere in the crowd a woman's voice came through clearly. "Nevertheless, something very strange happened, whatever the law says." Nancy stiffened and would have turned to find the speaker, but Jack tightened his grip on her arm.

"Let it alone, Nancy," Jack said. "Pretend you didn't hear it."

Out in the courthouse yard people raised a small cheer as Dick and Judy came out into the afternoon sun. The Bizarre carriage and Jack's horse were standing ready. Dick settled Judy in the carriage and Jack handed Nancy up. Automatically, she moved her skirts to make room for Dick beside her, but he turned to his brother. "Do me one great favor, Jack? Will you carry the girls on home and lend me your horse? I want to be in the air."

"Don't ride him too hard, he came up a little lame week before last."

"Did I ever spoil a horse?"

"No, but you never before had such a good reason for hard riding. Go on ahead. I'll be pleased to escort them."

They rode back in the carriage like three strangers, drawing apart quickly when a turn in the road threw them together, begging each other's pardon for every bump. Judy grew whiter with every passing mile, blotting away the thin film of sweat that kept forming on her upper lip. Finally she broke her silence. "Tell him to pull up, Jack. I must get out."

"What's the matter?"

"I'm puking sick. Tell him to stop, please. Here, anywhere. It doesn't matter."

She had the door open the minute the carriage came to a stop. Nancy moved to follow her out but Judy pushed her back on the seat. "For God's sake, leave me alone in this at least." She fell on her knees at the side of the road and bent over into the ditch. Inside the carriage they could hear her dry, hard retching.

"Hand me the water bottle," Nancy said. "It'll give her something to bring up."

"Let her be, Nancy. She doesn't want the help of anyone on earth right now. And have the pity not to watch her."

"She's my sister. I've seen her puke before."

"And doubtless will again. But let her be now."

I shall be sick myself, Nancy thought, if she doesn't stop. She never gets carriage sickness. What ails her?

Just when Nancy thought that she could bear it no longer, Judy sat back on her heels exhausted and then came back to the carriage door.

"Are you all right?"

Judy nodded. "I'm fine, but I want to be out in the air a bit longer. Would you hand me my Bible, please?"

"Whatever do you want that for?"

"Please, Nancy, don't argue. Just hand it to me. I'm going to walk over as far as that knoll for a while."

"Watch out for snakes," Nancy warned.

Judy laughed, a single harsh bark. "That's very funny. It was like Paradise and a snake came in there, too."

Jack and Nancy watched her walking away through the grass, ignoring the nettles that caught at her skirts. When she reached the little hummock she sat down on the ground, the Book in her lap.

"She'll ruin her dress and slippers," Nancy said. "They weren't made for country walking."

"The last thing your sister gives a damn about at the moment is her dress. I very much doubt that she will ever want to wear that dress again."

"Whyever not? It's nearly new. She had it made up while we were at the Tuckers', she can't have worn it more than two or three times."

"You really don't know your sister very well, do you?"

"Of course I do. I know her better than anyone else on earth, and she won't be half sick when she sees she's torn out the hem of her dress and probably ruined her stockings as well."

Jack looked at her with bemused wonder. "Sometimes I think you must be deaf and blind to everything around you. I'm not even at all all sure that you understand yourself very well." He paused and then burst out. "Tell me the truth, Nancy. Did you really think you were in love with Theo?"

Nancy's hand flew to her throat. "How can you ask such a question?"

"Why does one ask any question? Because I'm puzzled by the problem. I was his brother and I pitied him, because I remembered him as a child before everything began to go bad. I was sorry to see him throw away everything that should have mattered to him. But it simply wasn't possible there at the end for anyone to love him, especially a young girl like you."

"But I did."

"I can't believe you. Nancy, he stank, not just from his illness but from the rot inside him."

"I won't listen to you talk like that. I loved him more than my life itself and I shall never never stop grieving for him."

"Nonsense. You're just being fanciful."

She crossed her hands on her chest in the attitude of a dedicated saint. "I shall never marry," she breathed.

Jack shrugged. "That may very well be, but it won't be because you're in mourning for Theo."

Nancy dropped her air of tragedy and turned to him sharply. "What are you talking about?"

"You surely don't think you are the most marriageable girl in Virginia, do you? And if Gabrielle has her way you won't even be carrying much of a dowry. You're far too vain to marry much beneath you, and I don't see young Archie or any of your other beaux flocking about lately."

"If that's true, you certainly weren't much help." Nancy was annoyed. "First all those people saying right out in court that I stink in my monthlies, and then you had to get up and talk about an obstruction in my bowels and my face being green and all that."

Jack shook his head with a half smile of incredulity. "Nancy, you amaze me. Half of Virginia thinks you're guilty of incest or infanticide, or both, and you're afraid they'll think you're a little less than dainty."

"Well, nobody likes those things talked about in front of strangers. If you were a girl you'd know."

"Who do you think you are? One of the heroines in those trashy books you read?" He stopped and stared at her. "I believe that's it. Of course it is. You don't mind being thought some great romantic sinner. Maybe you even enjoy it a little. I don't think you know even yet what has happened to you, except in some storybook way."

"That's not true. No one can possibly know what I have suffered this past year. Just because I don't make a display of myself . . ."

"Not make a display of yourself?" Jack repeated. "I never in my life heard anyone carry on the way you do. That's not what I'm talking about. What I mean is that you seem to be living your life without any thought about the consequences of your actions to yourself or others. Without giving one thought to tomorrow. For instance, have you considered what is going to happen to you next? Where are you going to go? You can't go back to your father even if he would permit it."

Nancy was indignant. "I can't see what business it is of yours and, besides, my father would always welcome me back. He loves me, he always loved me best of all. It's only Gabrielle who doesn't want me."

"It's Gabrielle who's in charge at Tuckahoe."

"That's just for now. Tom said I could come to Monticello."

"For a visit. Do you really think Martha is waiting for you with open arms? It's her house, you know."

"No it isn't. It's her father's and Cousin Tom has always been very kind to me."

"Being kind to someone and having them as a more or less permanent lodger are not quite the same."

"I absolutely refuse to worry about it now," Nancy said airily. "Right now I'm going home to Bizarre with Dick and my sister, and then we'll see what happens." She stuck her head out the carriage window. "What on earth is Judy doing up there all this time? If she doesn't hurry back here, it'll be black dark before we get home."

"I believe she's praying."

"Don't be silly. Praying in the middle of the day? On a weekday? She can pray all she pleases when we are to home. Tell her to stop."

"I wouldn't think of interrupting her. It wouldn't hurt you to offer up a little prayer of thanks, you know."

"Please don't you turn all religious on me. Judy is bad enough. I thanked Mr. Henry and Mr. Marshall and Mr. Campbell and Dick thanked the jurymen. They had a lot more to do with it than God did."

"Then you might pray for the strength to see you through the times ahead. It may not be as easy as you seem to think it will be."

"I never said it would be easy. I'm not a complete fool no

matter what you think of me. But my father will come around when he's feeling better and the new wears off Gabrielle and Willie gets out of his house. Willie is a really mean little coward, you know, not just lightheaded. He must be half sick now that he did all that talking. I hope somebody tells him how that crowd of people cheered for Richard. He never could learn to keep anything to himself. But he's not the worst. It's Gabrielle that's the trouble. She was jealous of me from the moment she set foot in the house. You have no idea what I had to suffer from her. Did you know she wanted to put Aggie to kitchen work, and Aggie is my very own from my grandfather. It was right in the will, all legal. And I know he never wanted Aggie to be a regular house servant, that's why he sent her to me in the first place. She's a proper lady's maid."

"It's too bad she doesn't have a proper lady."

"It's easy for you to make jokes, Jack Randolph, but you don't know what it was like to be made to feel like a stranger in your very own house."

"And will you be happier as an indefinite guest in your sister's house?" He looked at her speculatively. "That's supposing that Judy is willing to let you stay."

"Why shouldn't she be?" Nancy asked, but Jack thought it wiser not to answer. "Judy would never turn me out. She'd think it a sin and so it would be. It's probably even in the Bible someplace."

"Just after the prodigal son, no doubt."

Nancy giggled and then broke off quickly. "Here she comes, don't fun about the Bible where she can hear you. Hurry up, Judy," she called. "You're ruining your dress and God only knows what time we'll be getting home."

Still pale but looking far more composed, Judy settled into the carriage. "Thank you for stopping, Jack. I'm all right now, but I don't know when I've felt so ill."

"Jack said you were praying."

"So I was."

"Whatever for?"

"I prayed for the ease of all our souls and for his forgiveness of our sins and for those that sinned against us."

Nancy sniffed. "I wouldn't have prayed one little bit for them. I hope Polly is absolutely totally miserable for days and days and months and years, and I hope that Carter will prop himself up and give her the rough edge of his tongue for dragging him into it. He didn't look half sick in court. Mr. Henry made him look a perfect fool, which is what he is letting Polly lead him around by the nose. And did you hear how they laughed when he said, 'Tell me, madam, with which eye were you peeping?' The story must be halfway across Virginia by now. Serves her good and proper, too."

"Nancy, please, please hush. I shall be ill again."

"Oh very well. But you know, Judy, you'd be much better off if you tried to see the funny side of things."

Judy drew in her breath, struggled for control, and lost. "And you'd be better off, we all would be, if you could realize for even one minute that you weren't placed here on earth for your own selfish pleasure. Selfish, selfish. You still don't even know or care what you've done."

"Now, Judy, don't carry on so. It's all over now. You heard what Mr. Henry and the others said. We can just put it behind us."

"It will never be over. Never as long as we all live."

* * * * * * * * * *

Family Matters

* * * * * * * * * *

* I * * * * * * * * *

"For heaven's sake, Aggie, stop that caterwauling. You can see I'm perfectly all right."

"But, Miss Nancy, I thought you were a dead one for sure. They all said you were going to get hanged by the neck and your face would turn blue and your tongue drop out and then what would become of me?"

"What would become of you, indeed. Is that all you care about? If my face turned blue and my tongue dropped out, how could I care what became of you? You'd have to go do a proper day's work in the kitchen like the other servants instead of lazing around up here."

"I was so scared."

"Serves you right for listening to all that tittletattle. You should have had the sense to know they were just trying to overset you. I told you before we went to Mr. Tucker's that everything was going to be all right."

"But, Miss Nancy, sometimes you're wrong."

"Don't be pert, Aggie. Do you mean to say that I ever told you anything that wasn't perfectly true?"

"Not exactly. It's just sometimes you more cheerful about things than they turns out. Like you said when we left your papa's place that it was just for a little bit of a while and it's gone past two Christmases now."

"That's not my fault, so just don't you pull such a long face on me. I can't abide people around me who can't be happy."

(291)

"Yes, Miss. Nancy."

"And besides, you're happy enough here, aren't you? Isn't it better being here with me than with someone who'd take a switch to you at the least little thing?"

"Yes'm."

"Well then. Go wash your face and hands. You're all sticky. And then come back and start unpacking my things. Everything I own needs a good turnout. Maybe we'll even find something I can't wear any more for you to have. You'd like that, wouldn't you?"

"Oh, yes'm, I'd like that right enough." Aggie smiled but made no move to leave.

"We'll then, shoo, get on with you."

"I got something else I gotta tell you."

"Not now, Aggie. I'm purely exhausted."

"I gotta tell you anyhow. Psyche she said I gotta tell you and then you can tell what to do."

"What on earth has Psyche got to do with me?"

"It's not to do with you exactly."

"Then what does it have to do with?" Nancy was impatient. "I've told you and told you I don't want to hear about your quarrels with the other servants. You just are going to have to learn to get along with them and not let them think you're getting above yourself."

"I don't quarrel with Psyche ever. It's the kitchen people I don't get on with. And anyway that's not it. While you all were away Psyche she let me help her nurse the baby and we seen things . . ." Aggie broke off.

"Go on."

Aggie began to cry. "Oh, Mrs. Nancy, there's something terrible wrong with Miss Judy's baby."

"St. George? You mean St. George is sick or hurt somehow? What's the matter with you stupid girls? Why didn't you send for Dr. Meade?"

"He's not sick and he's not hurt neither. Psyche and I we

take good care of him. He's just as strong and as healthy as can be and getting bigger every day."

"Then what are you going on about?"

"Miss Nancy, I can't tell you. I don't know about these things, but Psyche, she's nursed other babies before and she knows and she says for you to wait until Miss Judith puts the baby down and then come along to see because Psyche is frightened of telling Miss Judith because she going to go just crazy when she knows."

"You're imagining things, the pair of you. I've never known a better baby than St. George. Sleeps like a little lamb, he does. Never a bit fussy."

"Yes'm, that all true. But you come along and talk to Psyche and you tell her how to do."

"Good evening, Psyche," Nancy whispered. "I've come to pay a call on my nephew. Look at him. Did you ever see a prettier baby in all your days?"

"No, Miss Nancy, I never. He's mighty pretty right enough."

"And good as gold. Look at him sleep."

"Yes'm. Miss Nancy, did Aggie talk to you?"

"About St. George? She told me some nonsense about there being something wrong with the baby, but I can tell by looking at him that you've been making things up to scare yourselves."

"I pray to God that was so, Miss Nancy. But it ain't. That's why I gotta talk to you."

"Not now, Psyche. We'll wake him up and you've only just got him down."

"He ain't gonna wake up and there's no call for you to whisper and tippytoe about. That baby wouldn't wake up if the Angel Gabriel walked in here with his horn blowing."

"Such a good little baby."

"He surely is a good baby and I loves him and takes good care of him, but, Miss Nancy, that baby can't hear nothing."

"What are you talking about?" Nancy was puzzled and beginning to be alarmed.

"I mean that baby has something gone wrong with his ears. He can't hear nothing." Psyche began to cry. "Somebody has gotta tell his mother and I just can't. She thinks Master St. George is the most perfect thing God ever made."

"I don't believe it. He's always been a very strong sleeper, not fussy and touchy like some."

"Yes'm, that's what I used to think and I was mightily pleased about it, but while you all were away I was cleaning up and I dropped that old china washbasin—my hands were soapy like—and it fell right on the floor next to his bed and made a crash that would wake the dead. Aggie came down the hall to see if the roof had fallen in and Master St. George, he never moved a finger, just went right on sleeping . . . and then I guess I had some notion in the back of my head before that, because I right away knew what was wrong and I told Aggie, and we brought up Miss Judith's bell from the dining room and rang that right by his head and we yelled at him and he still never moved. Except if you shout right up close he sort of feels your breath coming at him and moves his head a little. He sleeps straight on till he's wet through or hungry, won't nothing bother him. And I been so frightened of telling Miss Judith, but somebody has got to before she finds out for herself."

"Why didn't you send for Dr. Meade?"

"Ain't nothing a doctor can do for this trouble, Miss Nancy."

"How would you know, you ignorant girl? Miss Judith left strict instructions that you were to send for the doctor right away if the baby got sick."

"He's not sick." Psyche was stubborn. "He just can't hear nothing."

"But he could have a sickness that makes him not be able to hear," Nancy protested.

She shook her head. "No ma'am, he been this way since the day he was born. I seen another baby born this way and so have you only maybe you didn't know."

"What other baby?"

"He's not a baby no more, but you remember the boy helps out Cato in the stableyard at your daddy's place? He born like this one."

"Don't be stupid, Psyche. That boy isn't right in his head. He can't even talk."

"Oh no, he talks. He just can't talk right 'cause he never heard any talking, but Cato understands him well enough and so does his mam. And anyway, the way I know a doctor was no good for this was your daddy had the doctor out to see that boy when he was just a little run-around, and the doctor say nothing to do."

"I don't believe you."

"Miss Nancy, it don't matter none whether you believes me or not. That doesn't make it a lie and somebody got to tell your sister and I tell her she's goin' to blame me and and I swear to God, Miss Nancy, it weren't any of my fault. Nobody every tended a baby better than I do, not even Clio at your mama's. Miss Judith is like to go crazy and have me whipped when I done the best I know how."

"Oh hush, Psyche, stop that bawling. We don't whip servants in our house and you know it perfectly well. But you must give me time to think how to go. Do the other servants know?"

"No, Miss, just me and Aggie and now you."

"Well, that's something, I guess. Don't you tell them either. I'll talk to Mr. Randolph and he'll know what to do."

It was midafternoon of the next day before Nancy could snatch a moment alone with Dick. Judy was napping and Dick was curiously reluctant, to Nancy's view, to come with her up to the nursery. Psyche scuttled out when they came in and it was left to Nancy to tell Dick about his son. At first he refused to believe it as Nancy had and insisted on testing for himself, calling softly to start with and then louder, clapping his hands. Only when he gave the high-pitched whistle that he used to call his hounds did St. George stir, and then just rolled over, smiled and put his thumb in his mouth. Dick put his hand gently on his son's head and walked over to the window, his back to Nancy.

Nancy was suddenly acutely conscious of all the sounds of the house and yard. Sounds that were always there but never noticed. She wondered if Dick was listening to them as well. "Somebody has to tell Judy," she said.

"Oh my God, Nancy, I can't tell her now. St. George is the only thing she takes any comfort in. St. George and her prayers. She's so fine-drawn now that something like this might tip her right over the edge."

"We have to tell her. She was in here this morning trying to get that poor baby to say 'Mama' for her. She'll know herself that something's wrong soon."

Dick seized on her words eagerly. "Perhaps we should wait and let her discover slowly, when she's stronger and less unsettled in her mind from all our troubles."

Nancy stared at him with astonishment. "That would be both cruel and cowardly, and you know as well as I do that you could never be either."

In the end they agreed to wait until Dr. Meade could be brought to examine St. George. Perhaps after all Psyche could be wrong and it was just a temporary affliction. Perhaps the baby had had a cold that had gone to his ear and his nurse didn't want to admit it. Nancy had had a night and most of a day to consider these possibilities and to reject them, but she let Dick go on hoping. One more day of peace could do no harm, and it would be best to tell Judy only when they were completely sure of the truth.

Dr. Meade was as helpful as he could be, given the circumstances. St. George was deaf and had been born deaf; there was no sign of any infection. He told Dick and Nancy that there was nothing medicine could do for the child but that he could send them to other medical men if it would ease Judith's mind. "Would you like me to talk to Judith?"

"Thank you, no." Dick said. "We'll choose our time and tell her."

"Richard, you must remember for your own comfort and your wife's ... you're both young and strong. You have the pleasure of many healthy children before you."

"That doesn't help my son much, does it, Dr. Meade?"

At first Nancy thought that her sister had not understood what they were trying to tell her. She had been sitting at her dressing table, making herself ready for bed, a hairbrush in her hand. As she listened to them explaining what Dr. Meade had told them she kept on brushing her hair, staring at herself in the mirror as if she watched a stranger.

"Judy," Nancy said tentatively, "Dr. Meade says that if you like we might consult other doctors."

Judith put the hairbrush down and looked at her sister without expression. "It isn't a matter for doctors." She turned back to the mirror and seemed to address her image in a soft, flat voice. Some of it Richard and Nancy could not hear and much of it they could not understand, but all of it was frightening. "I knew that I'd be punished. I knew it would be soon. But I never never thought that He would be so cruel as to punish poor St. George for my sin. I should have known. The sins of the fathers. He warns us right there in the Book. The sins of the fathers. My son punished for my sin."

"Judy, please, don't talk like that. We've brought you dreadful news and you're upset." Dick looked at his wife helplessly. "You can't blame yourself."

"There's no one in the world with less to reproach herself for," Nancy said.

Judy looked directly at her sister. "What would you know of good and evil? You only know what pleases you. I gave the Prince of Lies dominion over my soul because I put earthly love above my love of God, and now I pay the penalty." She began to cry. "But it was such a little lie. I only closed my eyes for a moment."

Dick knelt beside her and put his arms around her, trying to comfort her, telling her again that she must not blame herself.

"I used to pity those who didn't share my faith," Judith said, "but now I envy them. You can grieve for St. George without guilt, but I know better, and I'll carry the burden of it all my life." She turned to her sister. "And you, Nancy, you remember it well. God is just like every other man. He only punishes those who love Him."

"She's mad." Nancy said flatly to Richard when Judith had sent them both away so that she could be alone at her prayers.

"Don't say that. It's just the shock. Any mother would be distraught."

Nancy was unconvinced.

The three of them lived together uneasily. Judith would accept no comfort from either her husband or her sister and spent her days on her knees begging her God to relent, to spare St. George, to punish her in some other fashion. Nancy drifted from one room to another, unable to settle to anything, inexplicably in tears at every unguarded moment. Richard, bombarded by prayers from one woman and tears from the other, fled the house as often as he could, inventing errands, things that must be seen to on the far side of Bizarre.

* 2 *

In October a letter came to Richard from Gabrielle at Tuckahoe.

> My dear husband and your father-in-law left this earth early in the evening of last Thursday. He had, as you know from your visit to us last spring, been in ill health for some time and his departure, while distressing in the extreme, was far from unexpected. He had not been conscious of his surroundings for some few weeks but seemed in no pain or even any great discomfort.

Services have been read for him at our church, but I know that Judith will want to remember him in her prayers as well.

Nancy was inconsolable when Richard brought her the news. "How could she be so cruel not to let us know? she wailed. "How would it have hurt her to let me see him one more time?"

"It would have been pointless, Nancy. He wouldn't have known you. I told you when I was there in the spring he had the greatest difficulty in remembering who I was, and he's growing steadily worse."

"He would have remembered me. He loved me. He was the last person left who loved me, first Mama and then Theo and now my darling Papa and I'm all alone."

"You're not alone." Dick was patient. Nancy's tears no longer frightened him.

"Yes I am, and I'm the most miserable creature on earth and nobody cares for me."

"You have us and your brothers and sisters."

"What brothers and sisters?" Nancy was scornful. "I don't even know where John is, and Willie and Molly have shown clearly enough how little love they have for me. Jenny's just a baby and Gabrielle will never let her come to me now. In a year she'll have forgotten all about me. And Tom? Tom tries to be kind, but I'm just an embarrassment to him and his wife, who thinks so much of herself. And you can see for yourself how Judy acts."

Dick frowned. "Judy loves you above all her brothers and sisters. She often used to say so, and she still prays for the ease of your soul every night."

"Praying for my soul may help Judy but it does damn little for me. She does nothing but pray. She's gone God-crazy again like she was as a girl."

"There's nothing wrong with prayer if Judy finds comfort in it."

(299)

"That's like saying scratching a chigger bite comforts it. Judy's praying has always made things worse. She likes to be miserable and she wants everyone around her to be miserable too. She reads her damned religious books and comes up with a sermon for every occasion. Don't you see that as long as Papa was alive there was always a chance that I could go home again, and now I have nowhere to go and no one to take care of me and love me. No one at all."

"Nancy, hush yourself. You know very well that Judy and I both think of Bizarre as your home now, and your sister would be much distressed if she were to hear you talking this way."

"Of course she would. But she could add another line to her prayers tonight, asking God to forgive my ingratitude. I don't want to have to be grateful to Judith."

Dick was at the end of his patience. "Then at least have some consideration for others. If you go on this way you'll make yourself sick again and Judy has more to do than worry over you."

"And now I've made you angry with me."

"Never angry, but disappointed."

"Please, don't ever be angry with me, dear love. I couldn't bear it if you were."

"I am not angry with you, far from it. But I am at a loss to know what I can say to you."

"There was a time when you would have known. A time when only you could comfort me. You can't have forgotten any more than I have."

"Nancy, don't."

He stood with his arms stiffly at his sides as she embraced him. "Please just hold me for a moment. I need someone's arms about me. Please, Dick, I'm so cold and lonely."

"Nancy, don't do this. You'll shame yourself and me."

Nancy had said to herself so often that she was all alone in the world with no one to love her and set off the easy tears that it came as a great surprise to her that night as she lay dry-eyed in bed to discover that now that it was truer than ever before she felt more anger than sorrow. "How could he be so cruel to me?"

* 3 *

The months passed, the seasons changed. Time did not heal, but it cast a dull film over all that they felt and did. The brightest days were those that Jack spent with them. He brought back all the *on dits* of the world outside Bizarre, scandal and fashion from Richmond and Williamsburg, political news from New York and Philadelphia. He could make them all laugh, even Judith, seemingly without effort, although the effort must have been very great indeed.

Some nights Jack would stay on in the dining room long after supper sinking a bottle of brandy, and Nancy would wake in her room to hear Syphax helping him on the stairs. At other times he would spend the evening with them and seem to be at his most relaxed and amiable best, playing chess or arguing politics with Richard, gossiping with the sisters and then, near midnight, when the rest of the house was asleep, he would go down the stairs and out to the stables, saddle his horse and ride the night away. He carried his dueling pistols in the pocket of his greatcoat, and he would fire them in the air as he rode and scream like a woman or a meadow creature in the grasp of a night hunter. He would come home just before dawn, firing his pistols back over his shoulder at the phantoms that pursued him.

"Don't you think," Judith said to her husband, "that you could speak to Jack about it? It frightens the servants and who knows what the neighbors make of it."

"No, I couldn't. Jack suffers torments that no woman could ever possibly understand, and if it eases him to ride all night every night of the year, I'll saddle his horse and load his pistols for him."

On one morning after a night excursion Jack watched impatiently as Nancy sat in the drawing room, a book in her hand, the pages unturned, alternately sighing and sniffing up tears. "You know, Nancy, to some men at some times tears are an incentive to love, but in excess they can go far toward drowning a friendship."

"I can't help it."

"Of course you can, if you want to. Try to wear a more cheerful face, God knows someone in this house has to."

"How can I? I'm the most miserable creature on earth."

"You needn't be so proud of the title. They don't give prizes for it, and if they did, I shouldn't wonder if I wouldn't take the trophy myself."

"Would any of us have thought that we'd ever be sitting here arguing over which of us was the most deserving of pity?"

"At least I've finally made you smile."

"You often do. You're good for us, Jack. I wish there was something we could do for you."

"The best thing you can do for me is to make life easier for Richard. It seems to me that your sister is much gentler with him than she was on my last visit, you might encourage her to go on in that fashion."

"I don't think Judy would want to hear anything from me on the subject."

Jack looked at her sharply. "Perhaps not. Then all you can do is not to make such a parade of your own trouble. I think that Dick and Judy are on the way to being happy together again, and we may have to find our only satisfaction in that."

Although Nancy dismissed as an impossibility any thought that she might find her happiness in Richard's and Judith's, Jack's words did make her observant of them. It certainly appeared that Judith was spending less time on her knees beside her bed and more time with her husband, and there was a certain difference in the look he gave her as he handed her out of her carriage, a gentle solicitude in his smile when he kissed her good morning and inquired after her health.

Only a wicked person could fail to be pleased, Nancy told herself firmly. Still, it was curiously hard to bear.

Judith's and Richard's second son was born in April 1795 and christened Tudor, after a much treasured Randolph family fancy about their ancestry. "You might just as well have called him Tudor Powhatan," Jack said. "At least we know for sure that's a king he's descended from, and God knows he looks and howls like a red Indian." It was true that Tudor was a particularly fussy, cranky baby. The lightest step on a creaky floorboard was enough to set him off, to the great unexpressed relief of everyone in the household.

Tudor's birth seemed to signal the beginning of new and better times at Bizarre. Having given her husband a healthy child, Judith was far less oppressed with guilt, and the lightening of her spirit was reflected in all the house. Even little St. George seemed to feel the difference in atmosphere and was less frequently racked by the paroxyms of rage that overtook him when he could not make himself understood.

Judith and Richard began again to entertain their friends and discovered there were more of them than they had dared to hope. Gradually Bizarre once more became a hospitable house, a warm and pleasant place to stop for travelers.

One of these visitors early in the summer of 1796 was an Englishman, Benjamin Latrobe, an artist and architect on his way to call on Jefferson at Monticello. Richard had been ill for several days with the gripes and Judith insisted on nursing him herself, so Nancy was left to look after the traveler. It was far from being an onerous task. A man of great personal charm, Latrobe needed only his own sketchbook for entertainment. He found himself a spot on a low hill to work on water colors of the hands in the field below. Nancy thought it a curious choice of subject. "There are some very pretty scenes farther up the river. Would you like me to take you there?"

"Thank you, Miss Randolph. But I have exactly what I want. You see, we don't have blacks working the fields in England."

It never ceased to amuse and surprise Nancy that Englishmen and Frenchmen alike thought all Americans wholly ignorant of their countries. She thought it probable that it was simply a reflection of their own ignorance about America, expecting a savage behind every bush. She thought Mr. Latrobe's sketches very handsome despite their subject. She would not mind at all if he should happen to ask her to sit for him. She arranged herself in what she knew was a becoming pose in the drawing room after dinner, but he begged her to excuse him; there was a trick of the afternoon light on the river that he wished to try and capture. Still, she told herself, there's supper and the rest of the evening ahead of us.

* 4 *

The evening began very well for Nancy. Judy had not come down from the sickroom for supper, and Nancy had been alone with their guest, who seemed to enjoy her company quite as much as she did his. It was a rare pleasure for her to be with someone who knew nothing of her troubles, who could laugh and chat with her as if she were any pretty and amusing girl and not one with whom he must be guarded. She even listened patiently to his rhapsodies on the republican form of government, though he made her think of poor Mr. Leslie, freezing away in Edinburgh, she supposed. She thought, not for the first time, how strange it was that these newcomers to America were always far more excited by its politics than Americans themselves were. From all that Nancy heard at her sister's dinner table, Virginia gentlemen were as discontented under the new government as they had been under old George the Third. She even listened with appropriate smiles and comment to his eager anticipation of his meeting with the "great Jefferson," although she longed to tell him that her grandfather had sold Peter Jefferson his western land for a bowl of arrack, being a bit foxed at the time and feeling generous toward the poor young man who had married into the Randolphs. She had always thought it a trifle mean of Martha's grandfather to have taken advantage of a gentleman in his cups, though dear Papa was far too generous ever to have mentioned it. There was one awkward moment when her guest spoke of having been entertained on his way from Richmond by other Randolphs at a house called Tuckahoe. But she merely agreed with him that it was indeed a very fine house and they passed to other matters.

Syphax had brought the tea tray into the hall and Nancy was about to pour when Judy came down the stairs, filled with apology for her neglect of her guest and her husband's regret that he had not been well enough to entertain him properly.

"I am sorry not to have had more of your company, but your sister has been a charming substitute, and I hope that your husband may be sufficiently improved in the morning so that I may pay my respects to him before I leave."

"I should think he would be much improved by then. These summer fluxes are miserable, but they are not usually too long-lived. Do you take milk or sugar, Mr. Latrobe?" Judy had taken Nancy's place at the tea tray, as was her right. "Or perhaps you would prefer a little rum? Syphax can easily bring it, and I know some gentlemen do like their tea warmed a little." Judy's hands shook so that the spoon clattered in the saucer and she put the heavy silver pot down on the tray with a thump, as if she lacked the strength to hold it. It seemed to Nancy that she had never seen her sister look so tired, not even in the days at Williamsburg before the trial. She can't have slept for days, Nancy thought with alarm. He must be much worse than she lets on.

"I understand that you are going to Monticello from here. You'll find it a very interesting house for an architect. Mr. Jefferson is full of innovations."

"I'm looking forward to it with a great deal of pleasure, although I must confess it's the political man and not his house that most intrigues me. I have had such a stimulating conversation with your sister this evening. Tell me, Mrs. Randolph, are you as concerned and knowledgeable about public matters as your sister is?"

Judy looked surprised, as well she might. "I think it would be fair to say that I am easily as concerned as Nancy. As for knowledgeable . . ." She left the sentence unfinished and gave Nancy a skeptical look.

Nancy answered her sister silently with a shrug and a lifted eyebrow. If Judy didn't know how simple it was to convince a man of your intelligent interest with smiles and murmured agreements, this was not the time to enlighten her.

Nancy had never found her sister oversubtle, and now she confirmed that judgment. "Will your wife be joining you over here, Mr. Latrobe?" Judy asked. "Or perhaps you are still unmarried?"

"No, no, Mrs. Randolph. I'm very much a married man and only waiting to see what my prospects might be in this country before uprooting my family."

"Very wise." Judy smiled. "Although I am sure that a man of your talents will find much to occupy him here."

Nancy moved brightly into the silence that fell. It would not do at all for anyone to think that she cared a particle whether Mr. Latrobe had one wife or a dozen, though she did think he might have mentioned it. "I'm afraid that once you have tasted the intellectual delights of Monticello you will quite forget us here at Bizarre."

"I assure you that would be quite impossible." Benjamin Latrobe rose gallantly to the bait. "Even if your company were not so memorable I would have my sketchbook to remind me of the delightful days here with you."

"How very kind of you," Nancy said demurely. "Perhaps we shall have the pleasure of seeing you again on your return journey."

Before their guest could reply, Judy intervened. "Mr.

Latrobe, would you excuse me and my sister for just a moment? There are some household matters I wish to discuss with her."

"Surely they could wait for morning," Nancy protested.

Judy insisted that they could not, ushered her sister out of the room, and closed the door firmly behind them.

"Why have you suddenly decided you need to discuss the household with me, just when I finally have someone new to talk to?" Nancy pouted.

"Talk to indeed. I never saw anything as brazen as you are. You heard him say he was a married man. I can't think what stories he'll carry away of your flirting."

"I wasn't flirting with him. I was merely making polite conversation, something you have nearly forgotten how to do."

"Is that what you call it? 'I'm sure you will quite forget us here at Bizarre once you have tasted the delights of Monticello,' " Judy quoted with a mocking simper.

"Judy, for heaven's sake, he'll be gone in the morning. What harm can a few compliments do?"

"He may be gone in the morning, but you can't deny you were angling for his return. And what right do you have to extend an invitation to Bizarre, anyway? This is still my house, however free you make yourself in it."

Nancy sighed. "It's Dick's house too, and I didn't invite him, at least not really. I only thought that if he were to stop here on his way back, Dick could meet him, as I know he would like to."

"Dear sweet Nancy," Judy hissed, "always so unselfish, always thinking of others. Nothing on your mind but Dick's happiness, while I work like a black nursing him."

"That's more than unfair and you know it. I would be glad to help care for him, but you guard his door like a dragon. Anyone would think you wanted to make yourself sick as well. You can wear yourself out from pride and then you blame me."

"I'm no dragon guarding his door," Judy retorted. "If you think it'll give you pleasure to hold the basin for him to sick

(307)

up, you go right ahead. You take over tonight and Syphax and I can get some sleep."

Put that way, the prospect was uninviting. Nancy's own nursing skills were of the gentle hand on the forehead and rearrangement of pillows order, but Judy had challenged her and she couldn't back down. She swallowed hard. "All right, I'll just go in and say good night to our guest."

Her sister said that she would make her apologies to Mr. Latrobe. It would be best if Nancy went up to the sickroom straightaway before she was distracted. Nancy had one reluctant foot on the bottom stair when Judy called her back. She turned around, half hoping for a change of heart, but Judy was only fumbling in the pocket of her underskirt for a squat brown bottle. "Here, take this. You can give him a dose now if he's awake. Two dessert spoons in a glass of claret."

"And if he's asleep?"

"Then give it to him when he does wake."

Nancy took the bottle and held it out away from her dress. She could see the stain it had made on Judy's pocket. The bottle was not nearly as heavy as it looked. There could not be more than a little left in it. "Just the one dose?"

"None at all unless he wakes. If you're lucky he'll sleep through and won't be needing it."

The candles in their sconces downstairs lit the upper hall fitfully, but their light did not extend to Dick and Judy's room. All Nancy could see when she pushed open the door was the black shadow of Syphax sitting patiently by the window.

"Miss Judith?" he whispered.

"No, it's Miss Nancy, Syphax. How is he?"

Syphax knelt and lit a candle at the low fire and fitted it into the shaded holder on Judy's dressing table before he spoke. "Miss Nancy, you're not supposed to be in here. Your sister said just her and me so Mr. Richard could rest."

"It's all right. She said for me to sit with him tonight, and you're to go down and see if our guest wants for anything before bed and then go on to bed yourself."

"You sure?"

"Yes, Syphax, don't fuss."

"What about his medicine dose? Miss Judith don't like nobody to give him that except for herself."

Nancy showed him the bottle in her hand. "She gave it to me to give him if he wakes. Now hush yourself and get out of here before we wake him up."

"He's been godalmighty sick, Miss Nancy."

"Yes, I know."

"I never seen anybody sick up so in my life and he hardly have the strength to lift his head to the basin."

"Yes, Syphax."

"If he get sick like that again while you here, you just leave the basin on the floor side the bed and he can lean over cause I don't believe you strong enough in the arms to lift him up."

"Syphax, will you for God's sake get out of here?"

"I got some fresh clean towels over on the table and there's plenty of water in the jug. He's filled right up with fever, so you just wring out a towel ... and there's a bowl of ice I cracked for him, but it's mostly melted down now."

"Yes, Syphax, I know, I know." Nancy was impatient.

Syphax sniffed with wounded dignity. "You don't want to go talking cross to me, Miss Nancy. I was tending Mr. Richard before you were born."

"I'm not cross with you. This whole house knows how much you've done for us. I just don't want you to fuss yourself so. I can take care of Mr. Richard tonight perfectly all right."

"I've been half worried to death, and no doctor coming."

"I know you have, we all have," Nancy soothed, "but he's sleeping quiet now. You'll see by morning he'll be much better and up and around in a day or two."

Syphax was mollified but still unwilling to leave. "That fire's getting low. I'll just send up one of the boys with some sticks for it."

"Please don't. It's far too hot in here as it is."

"Then I have one of the boys sleep here in the hall and if you need me in the night you have him come and get me."

"Dear Syphax, please just go. I won't need you half as much as you need your sleep. Why, what would we all do if you got sick?"

He nodded gloomily at the idea. "I'm an old man. I'm not going to be here forever. It's time this house got itself ready to do without me."

"But we can't think about that now, can we? Truly, you had better go now or Miss Judith will think you've forgotten all about our guest."

"I'm going, I'm going. Did I tell you about the towels?"

"Yes, you did. They're on the table with the water and the ice."

He stood in the doorway, looking around the room for another excuse to stay, but Nancy put the medicine bottle down on the dressing table and pushed him gently into the hall. She leaned back against the closed door and took a deep breath, which she instantly regretted. With a glance at where Dick lay unmoving on the bed she hurried across the room to her sister's chest and began a frantic search in the corners of the drawers.

A slurred, breathy whisper startled her. "What are you looking for?"

"You're awake?"

"I'm asleep and dreaming that someone has crept in with designs on my wife's petticoats. What are you after?"

"Nothing." She closed the drawer and clasped her hands behind her. "Nothing important. I just thought that I remembered that Judy kept a pomander ball."

Dick rolled his head on the pillows. "I expect the room must stink to the heavens, but I can't smell it any more."

"No, no, of course not," Nancy protested.

"You needn't be delicate of my feelings, and you'll find what you're looking for on the candlestand by Judy's chair. She thought I didn't see her, but it was getting too strong in here for her as well."

Nancy came over to the bed and took his hand between both of hers. It seemed to throb with heat. "Never mind that. How are you feeling?"

He didn't answer her and closed his eyes. She thought that he had fallen asleep again, but after a moment his eyes flickered open and he spoke as if no time had passed. "Hush, please hush, Nancy. If she hears us she'll know I'm awake and she'll come at me with that dose again. And I just can't . . . I can't . . ."

Obediently Nancy lowered her voice. "But whispering will do you no good. I have it by me and firm instruction from Judy to give it to you the moment you woke."

"I'm asleep."

"I think you must be much improved or you wouldn't be joking."

"I think I am. It's hard to tell." He spoke slowly, as if he had to search for the simplest words, and so softly that she had to lean forward over the bed to hear him. "At least the pain is gone. Such a pain in my gut. I couldn't stand the weight of this . . . What do you call this?" he said fretfully.

"Coverlet," Nancy prompted.

"That's right, coverlet." He picked at its edge with his fingers. "Groaning and moaning like a woman . . . But now it just feels hot, very hot . . . like a fire inside. Went away all at once . . . like something burst open . . . but hot, very hot . . . much better now though, much much better." He opened his eyes as Nancy moved away from the bed. "What are you doing?"

"I'm just looking for the spoon for your dose."

The words seemed to give him strength, and his voice rose as he pushed himself back against the pillows and tried to reach out and catch hold of her skirt. "Please don't, Nancy. I mean it. I can't take any more of it. I beg you. It only makes me sicker."

Nancy had found the spoon and was about to measure the

medicine into the claret glass. "But you just said you were feeling better."

"But I'll be worse again directly I take it."

"It does smell something frightful," Nancy said doubtfully. "What it is?"

"God knows. Some hell's brew from Judy's receipt book."

"It's probably just a purge."

Dick waved his hand weakly in front of his face. "There you are then. I promise you I'm as empty as a Rhode Islander's promise already. There's nothing left to purge."

"I really do have to give it to you, you know. Judy will know if I don't and she'll be very angry."

Dick frowned. "Judy. Where is Judy? She was here a minute ago."

"She's in the hall. We have a guest."

"Yes, yes, I remember. Some Frenchman."

"English," Nancy corrected, "but with a French name. You'd like him. He's an artist, made a sketch of the sycamore." While she talked to distract him she poured the medicine into his glass and brought it over to the bed.

"Nancy, I beg you, take that vile stuff away."

"You must take it."

He shook his head. "It will kill me."

"Don't be such a great baby. See how much better it's made you already."

"I mean it. I'll take no more of it. If Judy asks you tell her I didn't wake."

"She'll know better."

"Then pour it in the slops and tell her I had it, or, better yet, crack the window open and throw it out. Better the hedges die than I."

Nancy hesitated. "Judy will know. She nearly always knows when I'm not telling the truth."

"What can she do but give you the rough edge of her tongue? You've had that before."

Nancy held the glass in her hand standing midway between

the bed and the window. His lips formed the one word more of entreaty and she turned about, opened the casement. One drop glistened on the sill and she wiped it away with a towel.

"Thank you," he breathed and fell back against the pillow. "Leave the window open. I'm burning up." He had summoned the last of his strength for the argument over the medicine and he slept, exhausted, for nearly an hour.

She sat beside the bed, holding his hand in hers, listening to his rapid shallow breathing, loud in the room. Once she heard a laugh from the quarters and realized that it must be earlier than she had thought. She had a long night before her. She slipped her shoes off and tucked her legs up under her. With one elbow on the chair arm she propped her head on her hand.

She woke with a startled jerk with no notion of how much time had passed. She might have slept for an hour from the cramp in her legs, but the candle flickered only a little shorter. Dick was staring past her at the open window. "Mustn't tell Judy," he muttered.

"Never fear," Nancy whispered. "I won't."

"Who're you? You're not Judy."

"It's Nancy, Dick. You remember I was here before."

"Nancy," he murmured, "that's right, Nancy." He turned his head on the pillow and looked straight at her. "You must be careful of Theo, Nancy. He's not well."

She wrung out a towel in the bowl where a few chips of ice still floated and held it to his forehead. In minutes the towel was warm to her hand. He would be quiet and she would permit herself to hope that he was a little cooler, but then he would stir restlessly and begin to talk again. She could never be sure whether he was awake and confused in his mind or asleep and talking out of a dream. Sometimes he seemed to know who she was and where he was, sometimes he thought she was Judy. Once he called her Jack and asked for the stud book. She told herself that it was only a fever, that it would break by morning, but she grew more and more frightened. She thought with something approaching panic of the medicine thrown out the window and tilted the bottle over the glass, but only two or three fat drops rolled over its lip. When she bent over him with a fresh cold towel she could feel the heat rising from his body before she touched him. An hour went by. Two. Time stopped. He opened his eyes and smiled very sweetly. "You must be gentler with your sister," he said clearly, "so much trouble for the poor dear girl." She trembled so violently that she had to hold onto the chairback to steady herself. One of the kitchen boys was curled up against the balustrade in the hall at the top of the stairs. She sent him for Syphax and knocked on the door where Judy was sleeping. She did not know whether his words had been to her or to Judy. She never would know.

Nancy brought Dr. Meade the medicine bottle when he asked for it. He uncorked it, sniffed at it, ran his finger along the edge and tasted it.

"Did he have the whole bottle?"

"I don't know. There was only the one dose left in it when Judy gave it to me last night." She was afraid to ask the next question but knew that she must. "Dr. Meade, would it have helped Dick if he'd had more of the medicine?"

"Good God, no. It was more like to have speeded him along." He mistook the release from guilt on Nancy's face for something else. "But don't you say a word of that to your sister. It would only make things worse for her, and I dare say I would have given him much the same thing if I'd been here when he first fell ill."

Judith sat beside her husband's bed, sunk in a stupor of grief, refusing to allow the servants even to clear away the basin and towels. She roused herself only once when Nancy came in and tried to persuade her away. "You are not to wear mourning for my husband, do you understand me? I won't have you wear mourning for him."

* 5 *

Like many young men, Richard Randolph had written a will without any real sense that he might actually die, that lofty idealism might have to be translated into cold, hard cash. It was an expression of love and great humanity, a spiritual testament of immeasurable value to his memory, a comfort and an exhortation to his heirs. It was also, in Nancy's eyes, a financial disaster.

"It's the most foolish thing Dick ever did," she said to Jack.

Jack was offended. "It was a matter of conscience. One that I should be proud to emulate."

"That's all very well for you, but you don't leave a wife and two babies. How is she to live? What will happen to Bizarre? You know as well as I do that the place is worthless without the people to work it. If you want my advice you'll throw it in the fire and pretend you never found it."

"Putting aside the fact that what you suggest is illegal, it's also impossible. Father drew up the will for him and his clerk witnessed it. There will be a copy of it in Williamsburg."

"The law, the law, I'm sick of the law. It does nothing but make trouble. Surely Mr. Tucker would realize that Dick didn't intend for his children to starve for his conscience's sake."

"The children aren't going to starve, and neither Father nor I nor Judy would think of trying to overset Dick's wish. You're the only scofflaw in the house and it's of least concern to you."

"It seems to me that I'm the only one in the house with any common sense."

"It's not common sense to go flying off without any knowledge of the facts. In the first place, slaves under mortgage can't be manumitted, and nearly a third of the field people are still encumbered in London."

"The most worthless third, I don't doubt. Still—" Nancy brightened—"I suppose that's better than nothing. Who would think I would ever praise God for debt?"

"Who indeed would expect you to praise God for anything?"

The will of Richard Randolph was not offered for probate until December 1796. It was a document that would be much admired by those who shared his feeling about what he had come to consider the "curse of the dread institution." All male and female servants not encumbered by debt were set free, and the part of Bizarre known as Israel Hill was to be given freely to his former bondsmen so that they might become independent. Judy was made executor with many expressions of her husband's full trust and confidence and only a word of caution that she not be excessive in her maternal love. The rest of it, Nancy thought privately, was nothing more than pious claptrap. Dick might have been better suited to Judy than she had known. It was pleasant though to hear Dick's praises so generally sung once again.

Syphax simply refused to accept the judgment of the court. He pointed out that he had never been a field hand and he wasn't about to go off to Israel Hill at his age and become one. He had never expected to live longer than Mr. Richard, and he was certain that Mr. Richard had never intended to turn him out of doors when he was an old, old man. Most of the house servants followed his lead, lining up before Jack and Judy to receive their documents of freedom and then giving them back to Jack for safekeeping.

Nancy thought them all fools and said as much to Aggie. "But you needn't think that means I'm going to give you your papers," she added hastily.

"I didn't expect you would, Miss Nancy. I'm about the only thing you got left." The truth of this struck Nancy coldly, and she snatched the hairbrush angrily out of Aggie's hand and began to dress her own hair. Aggie went on unperturbed. "They know what free means as well as anybody. Those papers make their children freemen too. That's why they give them to Mr. Jack to keep safe. They don't want to leave this house and this kitchen to go live at Israel Hill and eat what they can scratch out of the dirt, but they'll save up what pennies they can and they'll send their children off with enough for a start.

The field people don't care. They'd just as soon work at Israel Hill as work here. They'll all go and we'll see who's a bigger fool."

By the spring of 1797 it was clear that Aggie was right. All the free field hands except for a few who had family ties to the house servants left, though not all of them took up the land Dick had left them. Jack made up for their loss by again postponing the work at Roanoke and bringing some of his people to Bizarre. From then on he was the master of the house, the responsible head of the household.

* * * * * * * * * * *

Sisters

* * * * * * * * * * *

"In our new circumstances you'll have no need of a personal servant," Judith said. "I've decided that Aggie would be better employed in the kitchen."

"Aggie was not trained up for kitchen work."

"Then it's time she was. She's needed there to replace the girls who went off to Israel Hill. Jack's people from Roanoke are only fit for the fields or the stables."

"She already does most of the sewing for the whole house, not just for me. Who's going to do that if you put her in the kitchen?"

Judith smiled. "Naturally I had hoped that you would offer to bear part of the burden. The expense of keeping you weighs no more with me than it did with Richard, but even so . . ."

"I despise sewing and you know it."

"We must all do many things we don't like."

And Dick freed his servants to make a slave out of me, Nancy said to herself.

Without an escort Nancy could no longer ride Lady any farther than the boundaries of Bizarre, and her new household duties gave her little time even for that; but riding was still her greatest pleasure, and she managed it often enough to keep both mare and mistress from growing fat and lazy. It sometimes seemed to Nancy that the only time she felt alive these days was when she was on board her horse.

(321)

From the window of her room she saw a groom leading Lady down the drive, put down her sewing and raced out of the house after him. "Where are you going with her? Is something the matter?"

"No, Miss. Lady's fine and frisky. Miss Judith sent down word for me to take her over to Cawthorne's this morning because I can get a ride on the farm cart coming back."

"But there's some mistake. She meant one of the other horses." The groom stood mute. He was old enough to know better than to involve himself in white folks' quarrels. "You stand right here and don't move an inch until I get the straight of it from my sister."

"The fact is," Judith said, "that the grooms have enough on their hands with the carriage and working horses without having to bother with a fat old mare eating her head off."

"You know damn well that if it's expense you're worrying about, I'd rather starve myself than part with Lady."

"I do hope not. Because she's been sold to Cawthorne, and that's the end of it."

"Then you're no better than a common horse thief even if you are my sister."

"I shouldn't be so quick to speak of thieving if I were you. I have the money right here by me, in a paper with your name on it. You should be grateful that there's someone around to look after your interests. You'd have hung onto that horse until there was no price to be had."

"I don't want the money. Send it back."

"You know I can't do that. A bargain has been made. It would be dishonorable to back out of it now."

"Dishonorable is a curious word for you to use in the circumstances," Nancy sputtered. She argued, she pleaded with her sister, she cried, but the only victory she won was a small one. She refused to speak to the groom herself and had some satisfaction from making Judith go down the drive and repeat her order, and from the thought of the tale that would be told at Cawthorne's about the goings-on at Bizarre.

Since he was three, St. George had stood beside Nancy when she played the spinet in the drawing room, watching her fingers, his own hand against the case of the instrument, his face wreathed in smiles. She called him the best audience a girl ever had and sometimes abandoned any real tune and just played the strumming bass that he particularly liked. It was admittedly no pleasure to a hearing ear, but still Nancy was surprised when Judith swept St. George up and closed the keyboard firmly, pleading a headache made intolerable by the noise. On the next day Nancy found the keyboard locked and the key mysteriously missing. Both Psyche and Syphax swore ignorance about it.

The period of formal mourning drew near its end and there was a small dinner party at Bizarre, with family connections Lucy and Ryland Randolph up from Richmond. Ryland had a number of stories about the new people trying to force their way into Tidewater society, and he told them with a very creditable imitation of the back-country accent. Nancy found him very amusing, but Judith said that she thought it wrong to "mock those who haven't had our advantages." Ryland looked momentarily affronted, but then turned to Jack with a serious discussion of political matters. The change in tone came too late for Nancy and Lucy, however. They found themselves in that helpless state common to young girls the world over. No matter how hard they tried to keep a sober face, anything, or even nothing at all, would set them to laughing again. One of them would manage a straight face and then make the fatal mistake of looking at the other and their mouths would twitch and they would be off again. If they were questioned they would not have had the faintest notion of what they found so amusing; they simply could not help themselves.

"I was shocked by the extravagance of your behavior at table yesterday and so were our guests, I'm sure. In future I will have to ask you to refuse both wine and coffee. I'm afraid they are far too stimulating for a person of your temperament." The guests' carriage had scarcely cleared the drive before Judith had come to her sister's room.

(323)

"What you really want is for me to keep to my room with my face to the wall for the rest of my life."

Judith shrugged. "As to that you may suit yourself. I did think of requiring you to have your meals privately when we had guests but decided it was unnecessarily harsh, besides being another burden for the servants. However, it would be best if you could manage not to enter into any conversation at the table."

"We'll both look proper fools if I must sit mute."

"Of course you may reply if you are spoken to, but I think it would be far more becoming in you if you did not put yourself forward. That way we can avoid any further exhibitions."

On the day that Judith ordered two of the servants to bring some crates to her sister's room to box up the books there, Jack was in the house, and a desperate Nancy appealed to him for the first time.

"She's taken away my maid and my horse and my music, she's forbidden me the comfort of wine or coffee, she won't even allow me the free conversation of friends. If she takes my books away as well I shall go as mad as she is."

"Come, Nancy, I think you exaggerate. Judy is perhaps a bit more economy-minded than she need be, but that's not a bad trait in a housewife."

"That may have been her excuse before, but my books don't cost her a penny. She says they fill my head with pernicious nonsense and recommends that I read those damned tracts of hers. As if I needed advice to a young girl setting out in the world, when I am neither very young any more or very like to set out."

Jack's intervention saved her books for her, and he even managed to pry the key to the spinet from Judith when he was in residence, but further than that he would not, or could not, go. "I saw poor Dick chewed up between the two of you," he told Nancy. "I'm not about to put myself in his position. Your quarrel with your sister has nothing to do with me."

"If you would only once, just once, admit that you are punishing me," Nancy burst out one day to her sister.

"I am only thinking of your welfare. You would be much happier if you did not chafe so under life's restrictions."

"Why must you pretend that I live, have lived for years, under some immutable law of nature when they are only rules that you've laid down?"

"Do try and calm yourself, Nancy. Your temper tantrums only make you ill, and I have quite enough to do without nursing you."

At first she managed to escape once or twice a year on visits to the houses that were still open to her, or to her brother Tom at Monticello. But then quite often Judith could not spare the carriage for the trip, or Martha would write postponing the visit because her father would be arriving with guests. For the most part she was well settled into a routine that, as she wrote to a friend, "makes me no different from the other slaves of this house except in the color of my skin."

Long after Aggie had become one of the house servants there remained a special relationship between Nancy and her maid. When Aggie's work was done in the kitchen she still came up to help Nancy prepare for bed.

"I'm going to have a baby, Miss Nancy."

"I thought you might be. I suppose it's Billy Ellis's. Syphax thinks he's the best of the young ones and I dare say he's right."

"There's something else I need to ask you. You know Joseph in the stable, the one who came up from Roanoke? He's a preaching man and Billy and I want to be married all proper."

Nancy was startled. "I don't know, Aggie. I don't think I ever heard of servants getting married. I don't think any of the

Tuckahoe people were. Still," she went on as Aggie's face fell, "still, I don't see what harm it could do. But maybe you'd better not say anything about it to Miss Judith."

There was something else worrying Aggie. "Billy and I don't ever want to be apart. But I belong to you and he belongs to Miss Judith and if ever . . ."

"Don't worry about it. The way things are I may never leave Bizarre, and if I do I'll find a way to keep you together. Papa didn't believe in separating families and neither do I."

The century ended, another century began. Mr. Adams succeeded General Washington as President with Cousin Tom as his Vice President, and the federal government moved to the new town of Washington City. "And a damned raw, uncomfortable place it is," Jack wrote back to Bizarre as he started his second term in Congress, the brilliant leader of the Jeffersonian faction. He was Nancy's window on the world and, although his letters were seldom more than hasty scrawls folded around newspaper accounts of his triumphs on the floor of the House, still she treasured them as she did his visits home.

The strongest passion can be worn away by the monotony of daily living, as most marriages will bear witness. It is as true for rage as it is for love, though far less common.

The sisters now lived in a state of truce. Sometimes, when they joined in nursing Tudor through one of his frequent bouts of fever, or watched St. George's pencil racing across his pad, they almost felt a faint echo of their old affection. But the restrictions on Nancy's life were never relaxed, and a day never passed that Judith did not plead with her God to forgive her sins and bring her sister to repentance.

One night at the beginning of her thirtieth year Nancy opened her bedroom door and thought she saw her mother coming toward her with a candle in her hand. She nearly spoke to her before she realized that she was looking into her pier glass, left at an angle to the door by one of the servants. "It's having my hair up in a cap and looking so tired," she told herself. She supposed that half the houses in Virginia held someone like her, the unwanted female relation growing dry and dusty in an upstairs room. It was a common enough thing. "But who would ever have thought it could happen to me?"

* 2 *

In the spring of 1805, Judith reluctantly let Nancy have the carriage for a trip to Williamsburg, only because St. George Tucker wrote to her in terms as close to an order as that gentle man could ever use to a lady. The weeks that she spent with the Tucker family were the happiest she had known for years. Looking in the mirror with the smiling faces of the Tucker girls framing hers, she could almost believe that she was once again as young as they were. Certainly she was nearly as lighthearted. Together they contrived a new dress for her, not quite in the latest mode but far more in the fashion than anything she had brought from Bizarre, cut rather dashingly low in the neck and falling free from the pink ribbon inserts of the high waist. She went with them on their rounds of calls, met old friends, dined in good company every night and found that she had not, after all, forgotten how to make conversation on frivolous matters, to laugh or even, very discreetly, to flirt. There was one young man in particular, a law student of Tucker's, not at all suitable, but still the once familiar refrain "I think he quite fancies me" appeared again in her journal. She stayed three weeks beyond the time set for her visit and would have been quite content to stay forever, if Judy had not sent a querulous note summoning her and the carriage home to Bizarre.

Aggie looked doubtfully at the dress spread out across the bed. "You wearing that down to supper?"

"It's new. Don't you like it?"

Aggie shrugged. "What I like doesn't matter. Your sister been in such a temper while you're gone you wouldn't believe it. Even Syphax says he's never been spoken to so in all his life. She's some better since Mr. Jack came but she still have that fierce look she get."

Nancy leaned toward the mirror, wetting her fingers to get the curls in front of her ears just the way they had been much admired at the Tuckers'. "If I dressed to please Miss Judith I'd never wear anything but sackcloth and ashes. Be a good girl and find my new slippers for me. They should be in the small bag."

Aggie obeyed but she was still grumbling when she held the door for Nancy to sweep out. "The trouble with you, Miss Nancy, is that you don't never hear what people is trying to tell you."

Nancy smiled at her. "And the trouble with you is that you're getting above yourself again."

Jack and Judy were already at the table when Nancy came into the dining room. "You're late," Judy said. "You know very well that it upsets the whole house when meals aren't on time. Now the soup's gone cold and they'll have to put it back on the fire for you."

"I'm sorry, Judy, but I had to change from the journey. I was all over dust. They needn't heat anything up for me. I won't have the soup."

"You'd better have it. There's nothing but cold mutton to come." Judy looked her up and down. "Although I would suppose from the way you're done up that you have a taste for fancier things."

"Please don't be cross with me tonight, Judy. I've only just come home."

Jack stepped in hastily. "And very welcome you are. You're looking blooming, I must say. Something about the air in Williamsburg seems most agreeable to you."

"I think near everything in Williamsburg is agreeable to

me. Your sisters must be the kindest girls on earth. I couldn't love them more if they were my own."

"It would scarcely be possible for you to love them less." Judy's voice was ice.

Nancy's face mirrored her despair. "Dear Judy, that is both untrue and unfair. You know I only meant . . ."

"For a loving sister you've shown yourself in no hurry to come home," Judy interrupted.

"Surely you don't begrudge me a few weeks away?"

"Begrudge?" Judy examined the word as if she were somehow unsure of its meaning. "Why, what right would I have to begrudge you anything? One would think you were a prisoner here. It's nothing to me whether you go or stay, I'm sure."

Nancy closed her lips firmly over the retort that sprung to them. Then why did you call me back? she thought. Surely not because you missed my company.

All three of them were silent as Syphax carved and served the second-day joint. Nancy sat and looked glumly at the white fat rimming her portion, quite sure that she would be sick if she ate as much as one bite.

"You're not eating, Nancy. Perhaps the kitchen here is not up to your taste any more."

"I'm sure it's very good," Nancy said quickly.

"Excellent, excellent," Jack said. "I've told everyone in Washington that my sister-in-law Judith Randolph sets the finest table in America."

"But not fine enough for her sister, obviously."

"I'm just not very hungry."

"The roads around here are enough to unsettle anyone," Jack said. "Have a glass of the claret. It'll give you back your appetite."

Judy stretched out her hand as he was about to pour. "You know quite well that my sister does not take wine or spirits."

He raised an eyebrow. "Surely an exception could be made? The rigors of the journey?"

Nancy shook her head. "Please, Jack, I really don't want any."

A shrug of his shoulders said plainly that he felt he had done his best. "Whatever pleases you," he said.

They finished the meal in silence. Nancy cut the smallest possible slivers of meat and chewed them over and over, feeling Judy's eye on her with every bite. When Syphax at last cleared the plates she rose with relief, but Jack called her back. "Don't go, Nancy. I want to hear what Williamsburg is saying about things in Washington."

"I think Judy would prefer that you excused me this evening."

"Sit down, Nancy," Judy ordered. "I'm sure your observations will be most valuable to Jack, and as for me, I am more than curious to know what you found so enticing in Williamsburg that you could not come home until you were summoned."

"Then I am afraid you will both be disappointed." Nancy managed a smile. She told her sister that her visit had been quite the usual thing, making and receiving calls, going to the shops, an evening at the theater. As for Jack's question, "You know I have no head for politics. You've told me often enough. But there was one young man, a student of your father's, who told me that in his opinion you were quite the best of all the Virginia men in the Congress. In fact he never stopped singing your praises." It was only a slight overstatement of the truth, but Nancy was rewarded. Jack wanted to know more about this obviously astute young man and in answering him she could almost pretend that her sister was not glowering at her.

Judy would not be denied her quarrel for long. "Did you go about Williamsburg prinked out in that ridiculous fashion?"

"I don't know what you mean by ridiculous."

"Oh, yes you do. That dress and those absurd curls. Where is your cap?"

"My caps are folded away in a bottom drawer and I mean them to stay there. I hate them."

"What an extremely childish thing to say."

"I don't care if it is. Lucy Randolph says that I am far too young to put my hair up in a cap, and she showed me how to dress my hair this way and everyone in Williamsburg thought it very pretty and so do I."

"Then they were too well mannered to tell you the truth. Lucy was an extremely silly girl, and she's a foolish and vain woman with nothing better to do than to make a circus of you. I should think you'd be ashamed to go about looking like that."

Nancy was still defiant. "Well, I am not. And I find it most discourteous of you to talk about my friends in that way."

"Lucy is not your friend. She was simply amusing herself with you."

"That's not true. And if it were, what of it? Certainly I find her amusing. She loves to laugh and play games and she knows all the latest scandals."

"Does she indeed? It doesn't surprise me that you think a proper goal in life is amusement."

Nancy was close to tears, too angry to consider her words. "If my goal in life is amusement, God knows I've had precious little success in reaching it, no small thanks to you."

"How dare you speak to me in that way? You owe me everything."

"You take my point precisely, madam."

The two sisters stared at each other across the table, Nancy flushed and breathless, her eyes filled with angry tears. As always, Judy seemed nourished by her anger. She sat very still, but she seemed to the others to loom over them.

Jack looked wearily at the two of them. "Ladies, dear sisters, please, no more. Nothing curdles our digestion like angry words. You know you don't mean half of what you say."

"I cannot see that digestion matters to Nancy. She didn't find the food from my kitchen palatable after the pleasures of town. I'm sure that everything is done much better at the Tuckers', although I do my best with no thanks at all."

This was a familiar theme and Jack's reply to it had become habit. "Now, Judy, we are all most grateful to you for all the ways you care for us. But you know," he unwisely added, "you know, you must not diminish yourself so by this quarrelsomeness."

"I can hardly be said to diminish myself when I am already a cipher in my own house. My authority is ignored, my wishes flouted."

Jack was bewildered. "For the love of God, now what are you going on about?"

"Nancy knows quite well, or should."

The offending curls bounced as Nancy shook her head. "I don't. I haven't the least notion."

"I'm sure if you search your mind. Or your conscience, if you should chance to have one still, you'll know what I mean."

"If it's my dress, I could not know that it would upset you so. It harms no one."

Her sister was scornful. "It's nothing to me if you choose to look a fool, going about as mutton dressed like lamb. I am speaking of a far more serious trespass, but I can see Jack is growing uneasy. He does not care to be troubled by domestic matters."

"You're quite right," Jack agreed. "If there is one thing on earth I find intolerable it's women's argle-bargle."

Judy put her napkin down on the table and carefully smoothed out the creases she had made. It was Jack's turn to feel her displeasure. "Then I will ask you to excuse me for the evening. I very much fear that you would not find me at all amusing." She stood up and waved off Jack's assistance. "There is ample brandy on the sideboard to soothe any disturbance that I may have caused you. Not that you need direction to it." At the door she turned back and spoke again to Nancy. "I should like to see you in my room tonight before you sleep. In fact, I must insist on it." She closed the door behind her with an extra firmness that fell just short of a slam.

"Well, my girl, you've really done it this time. Can't think when I've seen her more angry."

"I know." Nancy sighed. "I suppose the best thing would be to go upstairs to her now and get it over with."

"If you'll take counsel from me, you'll give her some time. Wait until she's in her praying manner instead of a rage."

"Given a choice—" Nancy shrugged—"I think I'd rather be raged at than prayed over, but it's most likely I'll get a heavy dose of both."

Jack went over to the sideboard, poured a glass of brandy, tossed it down and poured another. "Don't think me unsympathetic," he said over his shoulder, "but what possessed you to come to table dressed for the Governor's Ball? You might have known it would set her off."

"It didn't matter. If it hadn't been my clothes or my hair it would have been something else. Probably my keeping the carriage beyond the time she lent it. She didn't want me to go at all, you know." Nancy twisted one of her curls around her finger. "Besides, I really intend to stop wearing a cap whatever she says, and I thought I might as well start as I mean to go on."

Jack brought his glass and the bottle back to the table and looked at her appraisingly. "I must say I do think it very becoming, but since you rarely see anyone but Judy, surely it would be wiser not to annoy her unnecessarily."

"Probably, but one does get so tired of being wise and discreet and being afraid to squeak for fear Judy will pounce."

"Alas, poor Nancy," Jacked mocked, "just back from weeks of heady society and already moaning about her dreary life."

"You may quiz me about it all you like, but I shall pay ten times over for every minute of pleasure I had at your family's. In any event it was not quite the whirl you think it was. I can't go about as if . . ." She broke off, looking for the words. "If things had been different for me."

Jack's eyes softened as he put his hand gently over hers. "Dear Nancy," he said, "what's past is past."

"Except it isn't you know. It's only the good things that don't last. Like being young."

"What a gloomy philosopher you've become." He lifted the bottle in invitation. "Have a drop of the brandy. It'll cheer you up."

"I couldn't. She'd smell it on me for sure."

"You talk about her as if she were an ogre." Jack frowned. "She's your sister, after all. There's still love between you. She has her tempers, God knows I've seen them myself, even when Dick was alive. Had him so distraught he even spoke to me once about going north to Connecticut and having the marriage dissolved."

Nancy leaned toward him eagerly. "Did he really? When was this?"

"Don't remember. Not too long before he took sick." He looked at her warningly. "Don't you say anything about it to Judy. He didn't mean it. He never could have done it. I only meant to say that you know what she's like. Why can't you try to be a little less prickly?"

Nancy rubbed her arms. The fire was guttering and the room was colder. "Do me a favor, Jack, and don't talk to me about things you know nothing about. It's not just her tempers as you call them. She means to make sure that I never draw another happy breath as long as I live."

"But surely that is not in her power. One makes one's own happiness."

"That's all very well for you to say. You are perfectly free to come and go, to do as you please. Why shouldn't you be happy?"

"Why not indeed?" His fluting voice was acid. "You might get on better, Nancy Randolph, if you could manage to remember that not all the trouble in the world has to do with you."

"Forgive me, Jack. I don't mean to be thoughtless."

"There's nothing to forgive you for. I should be grateful that you can forget. Most people are hard-pressed to keep their minds from my peculiarity when they are with me. They have only to look at me or hear me speak."

"I never think of it," she corrected herself hastily, "of you, in any way except as my dear nearly brother."

"What are you saying?" he jeered. "You never think about it, never speculate about what it must be like to be a man and yet not a man? A eunuch?" He saw Nancy's wince and smiled bitterly. "I see you know the word. I wonder why, since you say you never think of it." He tilted his glass, found it empty and filled it again. It's the brandy talking, Nancy thought. He'd never speak about it if he weren't drunk. She could only hope that he would drink enough to forget this evening. If he remembered, his pride would never let him forgive her. He was staring into his glass and seemed oblivious to her. She pushed her chair back quietly and tiptoed to the door. She had her hand on the knob when his voice cut through to her. "You say you never think of it. If that were true you'd be a far more remarkable being than anyone has ever taken you for. And I don't think you are at all remarkable, Nancy Randolph, not at all. I think you are the most ordinary of creatures, a woman whining with self-pity."

She half turned away from the door to come back to him, but he waved her away. "Go on. Leave me alone. Save your tears for your sister. They give me no pleasure. No more than anything else about you."

Nancy hung her new dress in the clothespress. One of the ribbons caught in the latch of the door and she heard it tear. There would be no hurry to mend it. God alone knew when she would ever wear it again. She put on a wrapper over her shift, reluctantly tucked her hair up into a cap, and went along the hall to her sister's room.

Outside Judy's door she hesitated, hearing the murmur from inside. But if one waited for Judy to rise from her prayers one might wait a very long time indeed, so she knocked softly and heard first silence and then the rustle of Judy's skirts before she was asked to come in.

Her sister was still fully clothed. She stood by the hearth, a crumpled piece of writing paper in her hand as if she were about to add it to the fire.

"You have interrupted my prayers."

"I'm sorry, but you did say that you had to see me before I slept, and I'm most tired from the journey."

"My prayers were for you."

Nancy's hands flew up in a gesture of hopelessness. "I never know what I should say when you tell me that. Do you want my thanks? I never asked for your prayers."

"You have always had them nonetheless."

"At least I can be grateful that you were praying for me and not over me. It's a deal less tiresome." She regretted the words the moment she spoke them, but Judy was remarkably calm.

"I'm afraid that my sister is incurably frivolous."

"I may be. But if there is a cure I'm sure you'll find the proper dose. I'm tired, Judy. Just tell me what you wish. If it's about the dress, I shan't wear it again if it displeases you so, but I should like not to wear the cap, at least not for a while and not all the time."

"I have already told you it is of no consequence to me what raggle-taggle way you get yourself up. I have a far more serious matter to speak to you about. Here." She handed the much creased and somewhat dirty piece of paper she held to Nancy. "Can you tell me what this is?"

Nancy glanced at it and shrugged. "It's a note to Billy Ellis."

"And in whose hand?"

"Mine."

"Then perhaps you can tell me what it means?"

"It means just what it says. It asks him to clean the grate in the dining-room fireplace."

Judy began to tremble. Her voice was ragged with anger. "And for how long have you been giving orders, written orders to my servants behind my back?"

Nancy looked at her sister with disbelief. She had been prepared to be railed at but not on this ground. "Judy, for as long as I have lived in this house, I have occasionally seen something that needed doing and told a servant to take care of it. Never in contradiction to your orders and certainly not behind your back. Not in your presence perhaps, but that's scarcely the same thing."

"A very casual occurrence of no significance whatever."

"And since you are such a watchful housekeeper, a very rare one."

"Do you mean to tell me that you think a written note signed in your hand to be a casual matter?"

"Yes I do, and so would you if you would allow yourself to think sensibly about it. Aggie is teaching Billy to read and she told me how much he wished for something addressed to him. He'd never had a letter nor is he likely to."

"But you couldn't be bothered to consult me."

"Why should I disturb you over something of so little importance?"

Her sister seized on the word. "Then you knew it would disturb me."

"Of course I didn't. It would never have entered the mind of any reasonable person. Aggie spoke to me when I inquired about the lessons, and I sat down right then and wrote the note. What harm could you possibly find in it? To give pleasure to two very faithful servants."

"Faithful to you, perhaps. Don't think I haven't always known about your precious Aggie, trained to spy since the day she came to you. Listening at keyholes and running to you with her servant's tittle-tattle so that you could turn my household against me."

"Judy, you're going beyond all reason. You must know that none of that is true. You mustn't permit yourself to fall into these humors."

"One thing I know is true. I know my servants laugh at me behind my back."

"I can assure you that that isn't so. They are far from laughing. They go in terror of you. Or at least in terror of these rages that come over you."

Judy was triumphant. "You see, you admit it. You admit that they come to you with their complaints of me and you encourage them in their disrespect."

"I admit nothing of the sort. If they come to me it's in the hope that I might intercede for them because they cannot realize that my position in this house is little better than theirs. Perhaps even worse since I was never born to slavery."

"You ungrateful trollop. You're a slave to nothing and no one but your own low appetites. God knows how I've labored to free you from them. You owe me everything. The food in your stomach. The roof over your head."

"I earn my food and shelter just like every other servant in this house, and I suffer your tyranny just as they do."

"It's little enough you pay. You owe me your life."

"And how long must I pay for something that grows more and more worthless to me with every passing day?"

"If your life is worthless, you made it so. The price I paid for it was dear enough."

"I don't know what you're talking about. I can't believe that you do."

"Don't you? Then let me remind you, dear sister, of the price I paid, am still paying, for you. One son shut off forever from the world and one so sickly that I fear for every breath he takes, my dear husband taken from me, my soul in torment that you have not the moral capacity to imagine, and all for a life that you call worthless. And you dare to dance in and out, treating this house as if it were a tavern, coming and going as you please, ordering my servants about and plotting with them against me."

She had lived with her sister's rage for years. She could not begin to count the times that they had quarreled, sometimes bitterly and over the most trivial of causes, but there was nothing familiar in the Judy who faced her now and the strangeness was terrifying. She steadied herself against the onslaught with her hand on the bedpost. Her voice was as soft and conciliatory as she could make it. "Judy, when you are yourself you'll know that I do none of these things. And you must know even in your state that I have always had the greatest sympathy for your troubles, but you can't let them overset your reason."

"It's not your sympathy I want or need. Day and night I've prayed for your penitence, just one sign, one word of acknowledgment of what you've cost me, and never a word, nothing but sullen looks and rebelliousness."

"You tell me what you wish me to say. Whatever you ask, I'll do it if I can, only please stop this raving."

"It's God's forgiveness you should ask for. But He won't hear you. He doesn't punish you because He has cast you out entirely. He scourges me out of His precious love, but someday he will forgive me. I cling to that. It's the only hope I have. I thought I could hasten the day when I would be welcomed back into His Grace, if I could bring you penitent to Him, but I have only to look at you to know that you are beyond redemption. Too small a soul to weigh in the balance against my sin."

Judy had been standing in the middle of the room, her hands clenched at her sides, dry eyes staring at the wall behind her sister. Now, suddenly, she crumpled to her knees. Her hands caught hold of Nancy's robe; tears streamed down her face. "Nancy, please tell me," she sobbed and her voice was a little girl's, "why won't God forgive me?"

Nancy sat down on the bed and put her arm around her sister's shoulders and held her close, rocking her gently. "Hush, Judy. Hush now," she murmured. If her sister was less threatening in her tears than her fury, she was no less frightening. She thought of sending for Jack, but he was not like to be fit for much this evening. She longed to escape to her own room but dared not leave. Judy's sobs grew less frequent and she began to shake with a hard chill. Nancy pulled her to her feet and led her, unresisting, to the chair by the fire. She knelt beside her and took her hands between her own and chafed them.

"Try to listen to me, Judy." She chose her words carefully.

"I'm sorry for any part I played in upsetting you so." Judy looked away from her. "And I don't want to say anything more that would disturb you, but you must listen to this. If you go on torturing yourself this way, you'll be unfit for anything. Think of your boys. Think of all the people who depend on you to be strong." Judy closed her eyes and nodded her head slowly. Nancy, encouraged, went on. "God is not punishing you, Judy. No more than I and the servants are plotting against you. If you let some imagined failing in the past rule your life . . ."

Judy snatched her hands from her sister's grasp. "Imagined failing," she repeated. "I have the weight of mortal sin to carry, and in your mouth it becomes nothing, a peccadillo. For such a petty soul I damned myself. And it began as such as little thing," she said, wondering. She seemed now not to know that Nancy was with her; she spoke to herself or to an unseen listener. "I could have said no to Father Tucker when he asked me. And then everyone talked and talked to me. And Mr. Henry said that I must do it. But I blame no one else. I knew what I was doing was wrong. I took the Book in my hand and it was heavy. So heavy." She looked down at her hands as if she felt the weight still. "I swore before my God to tell the truth, and in full consciousness of the sin I committed, I lied and my punishment will not end."

"The trial," Nancy breathed. "You lied at the trial?"

Judy looked at her sister as if she were surprised to find her there. "You above everyone know that I did. I knew that He would punish me. I thought I could bear it. But I didn't know that He would strike at me through my child. That poor innocent St. George would suffer all his life for my sin. He can never hear his mother's voice, because it is the voice of one who bore false witness."

"Judy, listen to me. St. George was deaf from the day he was born. Long before the trial, long before we went to Glenlyrvar."

Judy went on as if her sister had not spoken. "I came back

to my house, prepared for any atonement that He might demand of me. But He had come before me and my child was stricken."

"Dr. Meade told you, he told us all."

"Dr. Meade knows no more of the ways of God than you do. He called it an accident of nature, but what is that but God's will?"

"I don't pretend to any special knowledge of God's will, but one thing I do know. Not even your God could be so unreasonable as to punish St. George because you said that you hadn't slept. You couldn't even have been sure yourself whether or not you fell into a doze."

"But that wasn't a lie," Judy said quite calmly. "I didn't sleep that night, not for a moment."

For Nancy the world was turned upside down. Everything she thought she knew about her sister was proved wrong. She stood up and backed away a few steps, staring at Judy. "I don't believe you."

"You thought I lied when I said I hadn't slept. Those were the only true words I spoke."

"I didn't think you lied. I thought you were mistaken. Dick said you were sitting up in bed with your book open on your lap and that you had dozed off, the way people do, never knowing whether they were awake or sleeping. Even when you were so distressed and talked this way before, when we first told you about St. George, we thought that it was only because you had some doubts about whether you had fallen asleep."

"I was awake."

"You couldn't have been. You came into my room the next morning and said nothing except to ask if I were feeling better. You asked me if there was some errand you could do for me at the shop. You sent old Mrs. Harrison to me."

"Perhaps I was beginning to learn deceit from you even then."

"It isn't possible."

"Oh, but it is." Judy was chillingly composed. She might

have been telling an anecdote about someone else. "No one could have slept in that room that night. Even after you were quiet at last, I waited. I heard Dick unbar the door and when he opened it the light from the candle on the floor of your room streamed out. I couldn't see his face—I've always been glad of that—but I could see what he held in his hands. The pillow slip fell away when he pushed the door open and I saw it . . . stinking and red . . . I saw it clearly. The Devil's spawn. Then he covered it over again and I closed my eyes, and I heard him come toward the bed and his footsteps stopped and I knew he was looking at me. I could not have willed my eyes to open, but I knew what I had seen. It had a hand like a little red frog. Did you know that, Nancy?" she asked conversationally. "Your baby wasn't a proper one at all. But then, it hadn't had time to be. What a deal of counting on their fingers there would have been if anyone had seen that thing you birthed. I've often thought what a mercy it was that Harrison's hounds found it on that shingle. Do you suppose that's why Dick left it there?"

"They didn't," Nancy cried in horror. "Dick didn't. He only left it on the shingles while he looked for a place . . ."

"A grave?" Judy interrupted. "Strange, no one ever said that they saw a grave. So many people about the place all the time, and there wasn't time for him to go too far from the house. Still, I don't suppose we will ever know, will we?"

"You're monstrous."

"Am I? Someone here is, certainly."

"All these years you've known," Nancy said, still not able to believe it. "All these years and not one word to me, or to Dick while he lived."

Judy's face was once again distorted by fury. "What passed between me and my husband is no concern of yours. As for you, I've waited twelve years for you to come to me. To ask forgiveness not of me but of your God, for he is your God even though you scorn him. And in twelve years' time not one word, not one sign of penitence. You go about as blithe as you please, plotting and scheming and complaining of me. Hours spent before your mirror and not one minute on your knees."

"How you must have hated me."

"I don't hate you." Her look gave the words the lie. "How could anyone hate Nancy? Nancy's the pretty sister, the gay one. I pitied you and I loved you. Out of love I saved your life. I betrayed my God to keep your neck from the rope."

"That's not true. Mr. Henry and Mr. Marshall, everyone said I would never be convicted."

"And did you believe them? You've forgotten how frightened you were. You were less hardened, less indifferent to your guilt then. I saved your life and you mock me by calling it worthless."

"It wasn't done out of love for me, Judith. If you believe that you deceive yourself. If you saw what you say you did at Glenlyrvar, then the truth would have acquitted me. You didn't lie to save me from the hangman; you lied to save your house from scandal."

"I did it for you."

Nancy shook her head. "No, you didn't. You did it for yourself, because you're just like everyone else, not better. Because you care more about what people think of you than you do for the truth." Nancy stepped away from the mantelpiece and leaned over her sister's chair. "And there was another reason, wasn't there? You did it to keep Dick bound to you. Because the truth would have freed us, not just from the law but from you. I know why you never told him the truth. You let him go on thinking that you had been asleep, that you knew nothing, so that he would stay with you and protect you even when you knew that he had no love left for you."

"That's a wicked lie. I needed nothing to bind him to me. He loved me, only me, until the day he died."

"Did he indeed? And did he never speak to Jack about going to Connecticut for a divorce because you made his life unbearable with your rage and your sermonizing?"

"I won't listen to you. Get out . . . I want you out."

"I'll go gladly, but if you don't believe me, send for Jack. He won't tell you the truth, but he's too drunk to tell you a skillful lie." She looked without any pity at her sister cowering in her chair, started toward the door, stopped and came back. "Or maybe, just maybe you already know that's true. Maybe what's troubling your conscience isn't something that happened long ago in the Cumberland Courthouse but something that happened in this room a few years later." It had been a random shot; surprise was mixed with her horror when she saw it find its mark.

Judy rose stiffly from her chair and came toward her. The light from the fire distorted her features, but there was no mistaking her expression. Her words came in a strangled croak. "I never want to see you again. Or hear you. Not even your footstep in the passage." Nancy backed toward the door, one hand stretched out defensively in front of her, the other groping behind her for the handle. She wants me dead, Nancy thought. More than that, she wants to kill me.

She ran the length of the hall to her room. She slammed the door behind her and threw the bolt and turned to face Aggie. Aggie's face reflected her own fright.

"What's the matter? What's happening?"

Nancy drew a long shuddering breath. "Nothing's the matter, Aggie. Nothing that need concern you."

"You look like you seen a spirit."

She had a sudden wild impulse to laugh. More than one, she thought, more than one. She controlled her voice with difficulty as she told Aggie again that there was nothing wrong.

"You're shaking like a leaf."

"It's freezing cold in here. Slip downstairs and bring me some wood for this fire."

"You know you ain't allowed any extra wood."

"For God's sake, Aggie, don't argue with me. It doesn't matter any more what I'm allowed or not allowed."

Aggie didn't move. "The woodbox locked and Miss Judith

have the key. It's not so cold in here. You just feeling a chill because you went across your sister when I told you she was in one of her fits." She turned back the coverlet on the bed. "Get in here. You'll soon warm up."

"I don't want to go to bed. I can't. I have to think." She wrapped her dressing gown around her more closely and huddled in the chair by the fire.

Aggie hovered over her. "Everybody in the kitchen was talking about how pretty you looked at supper," she offered tentatively. Her mistress gave no sign that she had heard her. "You want me to stay in here with you tonight?"

"What?" Nancy looked up. "No, no, thank you. But there's something you can do for me."

Aggie folded her hands over her apron and waited.

"Go down and see if Mr. Jack is still in the dining room and ask him to come to me. Tell him it's important."

Aggie looked doubtful. "You sure you want him up here, Miss Nancy? He's taken a lot aboard tonight."

"If he can walk and talk I want to see him."

Aggie was carrying a few sticks in her apron when she returned. "Took them out of the box in the dining room. She'll think Mr. Jack used them."

"Is he coming?"

"Syphax and Psyche both with him. Syphax's trying to make him go up to bed and Psyche saying he must go to Miss Judith. Psyche's crying."

"Did you tell him I wanted him to come to me?"

"He says he's coming to you after he sees Miss Judith, but Syphax says he ain't. The way he is, you'd be better off if Syphax gets his way."

Aggie would not leave until Nancy promised to send for her if she was needed. When she was gone, Nancy stripped the quilt from her bed and put it around her shoulders. There was a crumpled piece of paper in her hand. She threw it on the fire and watched it blaze up brightly. She turned her chair to face the door and waited for Jack.

He came into the room with the rigid dignity that overtakes men who have drunk too much and are now called upon to conceal it as best they can. He refused her offer of a chair and stood in front of her, swaying only a little. "It would seem, Nancy, that your long stay at Bizarre is to come to an end. It is your sister's wish and mine as well that you leave here as soon as you are able."

"Did she tell you why?"

"Says you treat the house like a tavern, coming and going as you please. Can't say I've noticed that. And there was something about one of the servants—Billy. Letters or some such thing." He shook his head and made an effort to concentrate. "Fact of the matter is, Nancy, that it doesn't matter a damn what her reason is, if she has one. It's clear enough that there's never going to be any peace in this house with the both of you in it. If you continue on here I fear for her sanity. She's near to raving now."

"She isn't just near it, she *is* raving. I think she has been for a long time."

"There you are, then," Jack said. "Just what I said. Owe it to poor Dick's boys. Must keep Bizarre for them. Owe Judith something too. I'll say good night then, Nancy."

* * * * * * * * *

Travels

* * * * * * * * *

It was soon made plain to Nancy that a house that would once have welcomed her for a short visit was not quite as eager to see her when she arrived with all her belongings on the roof of the carriage and no date set for her leaving. For nearly a year she drifted from house to house, growing ever more worried about her future. She had hoped that Tom and Martha might find room for her, but now that Martha's father was President there were more demands than ever on the time and space at Monticello. The house must be kept ready for Jefferson and the guests he brought home with him from Washington. There was no room there for Nancy. In any event, Tom seemed to have no real grasp of her situation; he appeared to think that she had left Bizarre of her own choice and was only traveling to enjoy herself. Nevertheless, he did agree that some more regular provision for her support must be made and began to send her an allowance instead of the occasional bank draft for pin money.

It was not any great amount, but it was enough to cover the cost of the small bedroom up under the eaves at Pryors' in Richmond. The Pryors were both delighted to have her. Mrs. Pryor thought it a coup to have a Randolph under her roof, even a rather tarnished one. As secretary to the Jockey Club, Mr. Pryor had admired Nancy's father long ago and now had reason to admire her as well. "She's as good a knowledge of bloodlines as anyone I've ever known, and a very fetching girl to boot."

The Pryors' house was at the back of their property; the front, stretching toward the James, was called the Pleasure Garden and held a structure that was half tavern and half theater. The tavern was beneath her notice, but she had loved the theater since she was a child. Now for the first time she was able to see it close to, to dine every day with the visiting company of players, to share their lives vicariously, and even to daydream a little about going even further.

She thought Mr. Therkell, the company's manager and leading actor, quite a handsome man and a very amusing one. From her open window she watched as he supervised the building of a temporary stage. The company's scheduled Grand Spectacular, The Storming of Constantinople, with its horses jumping through flaming Saracen arches, could not be housed indoors.

Therkell caught sight of her and assumed a Shakespearean pose. "But soft what light from yonder window breaks. It is the east and Juliet is the sun." Nancy was smiling down at her Romeo when Jack Randolph came into the garden. She closed her window and drew her curtains quickly and was sitting at some distance from them with a book in her hand when Jack rapped on her door.

"Father Tucker thought I should come and see how you did."

"How kind of him. You may tell him that I thank him and keep quite amazing well."

Jack looked around the room appraisingly. "It's a bit smaller than you're used to, but it seems clean enough." With the tip of his crop he lifted the curtain aside and looked out the window. "I can easily see that you don't lack for entertainment or—" he weighted the word—"companionship."

Nancy warned him against the drawing of conclusions, and Jack assured her that he would not and after the briefest possible exchange of civilities he was gone.

She had only one other family visitor in her months at the Pryors'. Tudor was allowed a day away from his school in Richmond to attend a performance of *Pizarro* and have tea with her afterward.

"I liked Mr. Therkell best," Tudor said. "Especially his helmet and the sword fights. But his wife didn't look any more like an Indian than you do, Aunt Nancy."

"She's not his wife, Tudor." Nancy said absently as she poured their tea.

"It says on the bill, Mrs. Therkell as Cora."

"That's just a way actors have. It's more convenient."

Tudor was far more interested in the plate of cakes that Mrs. Pryor had sent up "for the young gentleman." He took off his coat to feed more comfortably and a rustle of paper reminded him. "This is for you." He handed her an envelope. "I'm to say it's from Mama."

"But it's not from your mother, is it?" Nancy asked after one look inside. "Was it your Uncle Jack?"

"It was Uncle Jack gave it to me, but he said it came from Mama."

"He must think me a proper fool. As if I'd believe for a moment that your mother would let a ten-year-old boy wander around the streets of Richmond with a hundred-dollar note in his pocket."

"I'm eleven," Tudor said indignantly, "and I didn't wander around. I came in a hire carriage and I'm going back in one."

"Nevertheless." Nancy took out her needle and thread and sewed the envelope securely into Tudor's pocket. "I never heard of anything so risky. You have your schoolmaster's wife pick out these threads so you don't tear the cloth and give the envelope to her to keep until the next time you see Uncle Jack. Do you understand me?"

"Yes, but he'll be angry."

"But not with you. You did just as you were told. You tell him that I am managing very well and have no need of his help or that of any other member of his family."

Sending the money back gave her a great glow of self-satisfaction at the time but was a gesture she would regret a few months later. The money from Tom which had been arriving promptly on the first of the month did not come one month until the twentieth and didn't arrive at all the month following. Mrs. Pryor, whose pleasure at having Nancy as a paying guest had considerably diminished once she discovered that Nancy was not going to provide an entré into the best society of Richmond, was even less pleased at the prospect of Nancy as a nonpaying guest. Only her husband's intervention prevented her from bundling Nancy out and she made her attitude painfully clear.

Nancy wrote frantically to her brother, describing her situation in the most drastic terms, and Tom sent back a bank draft sufficient to cover her debt to the Pryors and very little more. "I was sorry to hear of your embarrassment," Tom wrote, "and trust that this will take care of your most pressing debts. However, I am afraid that it has turned out quite impossible for me to promise you a regular stated income when my own is quite uncertain. I will continue, of course, to send you whatever I can spare when I can, but perhaps it would be best if you would decide to give up this experiment of independent living."

"I sometimes think Tom must live at several removes from the real world," Nancy spluttered to Dr. Meade when he called on her. "Experiment in independent living, indeed. Does he really think I live this way by choice? And if he does, I'll warrant you that Martha knows better. It would make a pretty scandal for her father if her sister-in-law was found starving in the streets."

Dr. Meade quieted her, promised her that things would never come to that dire a strait, but privately he shared her concern. His worry was not made any less sharp by an encounter with Mr. Pryor on his way to his carriage.

"If it was just myself I'd be happy to have her stay on, but there's Mrs. Pryor to be thought of and she's taken against her ever since the actors were here. She won't say anything as long as there's the money for the room every month, but she's just waiting for an excuse. I've been thinking there's a lot of men in this town who were good friends of Colonel Tom. I think it's time someone went to them. They wouldn't any of them want to see his daughter in trouble."

Richmond was indeed full of old friends of Tom Randolph, most of them shocked at Dr. Meade's description of Nancy's circumstances, but none of them at all enthusiastic about the prospect of Nancy as a permanent dependent. They would put their hands in their pockets once for old Tom's sake, but not every month for God only knew how long. "She's still a young woman," one of them pointed out. "It would be better if you could find her some sort of position in which she could earn her own way, governess in some house full of girls, for instance."

Dr. Meade hesitated. "The problem there is that while I know Nancy as well as anyone and have the highest regard for her character, there does still hang a faint color of the old scandal around her name. I doubt if there are any Virginia houses that would risk it."

"Then you ought to go further afield. Out of the state. Even up north. Maybe find her a decent widower with some daughters needing instruction. She's still a good-looking woman, maybe she could make a permanence out of it."

When the network of old friends was extended, it was successful in a matter of weeks. "I don't believe you've ever met him," Dr. Meade told Nancy, "but he was acquainted with both your father and your grandfather, and he was a very good friend of Mr. Tucker."

"But I don't know that I could do it. Teach in a school. What if they wanted me to teach the mathematics?"

"Dr. Johnson's is a school for girls. I don't suppose they go very heavy on the mathematics. And I know how great a part you played in teaching young St. George to read and write. If you can do that you should have no trouble with children without disabilities."

(353)

"But Connecticut. It seems a very long way away. How would I get there?"

"You'd take the packet to New York, where Johnson would meet you and escort you the rest of the way. You always used to talk about sailing away on your adventures. Here's your chance to finally take ship."

"I used to be very young and very foolish, didn't I?" Nancy smiled. "I haven't even enough for the fare, Dr. Meade. And I've nothing left to sell except my books, and I don't think they'd fetch enough."

"Don't worry. It's all been taken care of and a bit over for any other expenses."

When she protested, he hastened to assure her that it was not his money, that he acted only as an agent in the matter. It was not Judith's either, her next concern. "Just let's say that it's from old friends who wish you well."

More likely old friends who want to make sure that if I'm finally forced on the streets, it will be far away enough not to embarrass them, Nancy thought. She trusted Dr. Meade and knew that he acted only out of kindness. There was nothing more for her in Richmond, that was clear, but still she had the uncomfortable feeling that she was being hurried away, that this was just a continuation of the night that Jack had asked her to leave Bizarre. Now it was a city, a whole state, that seemed to feel crowded by her presence.

She thought it better to be under obligation to someone known, rather than the mysterious benefactors represented by Dr. Meade, so she wrote to Jack and asked him to lend her fifty dollars, half the amount she had impulsively returned to him by Tudor. She had no reply, and it was Dr. Meade who escorted her on board and placed her under the protection of the captain, making certain that as a lady traveling alone she would still be treated as a lady.

"No last-minute advice for me, Dr. Meade?"

"Not really. Just try and be happy, Nancy. It's nearly past time for it."

* 2 *

Much to her surprise she was happy at Dr. Johnson's Academy for Young Ladies. Dr. Johnson himself had a rather grave and dusty look, but his smile was kind and he was immediately sympathetic when she told him, on their way to Stratford, that she hoped she would not be required to teach either Latin or the mathematics.

"I couldn't teach numbers myself; my wife does that. She's a perfect wonder at it. Can't think how she does it. And I do the Latin and the Greek for any girls whose parents want it, and Theology too, although I don't suppose you even gave that much thought."

Nancy confessed that she hadn't.

"Don't know why I bother really, probably shouldn't touch it not being a man of the cloth myself. But there it is. Mrs. Johnson and I started this school with the notion that we would try to give young ladies the same sort of education that their brothers get. So that means Latin and Greek and Theology ... would have been Hebrew too, except that's no earthly use if you aren't going into orders and want to read the gospels, and I don't expect any of our young ladies are planning on going out to preach. But the truth of the matter is, Miss Randolph, that the girls don't want their brothers' education and neither do their parents. They want them nicely mannered, able to make a pretty little sketch with chalks or colors, play a tune on the spinet and read and talk a little French and Italian. What history Mrs. Johnson teaches them and what classics I give them scales right off on their holidays. But it's a fine school nonetheless and a happy one. Some people might think it a comedown after Columbia College, but I'll tell you the most fortunate day of my life was the one when I resigned the President's office. Wouldn't have lived another year if I'd had to stay in New York City. Came back to Stratford and was a new man in six months. Married Mrs. Johnson, started our school and fifteen years later here I am, still going strong. Would you believe I'm eighty-one years old?"

Nancy said quite truthfully that she would not have thought it possible and he beamed at her. "I expect you think I'm a rare old chatterer. Truth to tell, I thought you were looking a bit uneasy. Natural enough. Coming so far from home to strangers. Thought I'd give you some time to get acquainted with me. Not frightened now, are you?"

She was so far from being frightened that she asked him the one question that she had thought she would most scrupulously avoid. "Dr. Johnson, how much do you know, how much did they tell you about me?"

"Know all I need to know just looking at you. It's plain to see that you're a lady and a cultivated one. If you mean your—" he paused, hunting for a word—"your troubles, that was a long time ago and I can remember reading the newspaper accounts at the time and thinking what a very brave young girl you must be to put yourself in jeopardy that way."

Nancy's eyes filled with grateful tears. "And Mrs. Johnson?"

"You'll find as you get to know us that what Dr. Johnson knows, Mrs. Johnson knows as well and agrees with every particle."

Mornings at the academy began with the young ladies, boarders and day students alike, gathered in the main hall. Dr. Johnson would read the text set for the day and then glare upward and briskly instruct God to watch over their labors on this day. What a blessing it would have been, Nancy thought, if poor Mr. Leslie had learned from Dr. Johnson.

For the rest of the morning until the dinner break, Nancy was in charge of the younger half of the school, eight little girls from six to ten, frowning earnestly at their slates, reading aloud in clear treble voices. She fell in love with them all, individually and collectively. It was like having her darling Jenny back again. The children sensed her feeling and responded to it, clustering around her in their free time. The one or two of them who were boarders soon insisted that Miss Randolph and only Miss

Randolph could hear their bedtime prayers and tuck them in for the night.

When the girls were asleep Nancy joined the Johnsons in their private sitting room. Dr. Johnson sat nearest the fire, his head nodding over a book, while his wife and Nancy talked softly of the happenings of the day. It had been a very long time since Nancy had enjoyed an easy relationship with another woman. Despite the difference in their ages, Mrs. Johnson standing in years midway between Nancy and her husband, and their positions in the house, they were soon warm friends.

"I think perhaps I should warn you, Nancy, not to fall into the trap that waits for all unwary schoolmistresses. You mustn't get too attached to your charges. They are only on loan to us from their parents, and if we forget that, the parting can be very painful."

"But it's impossible not to grow fond of them. They are such a delight."

"I know, and if you didn't feel that way you wouldn't be half the teacher that you are. You have a real gift for it, did you know that?"

"Do I really? I thought it was going well and certainly I was enjoying it, but I couldn't be sure."

"Trust me. Dr. Johnson and I are both very pleased. We know that you came to us thinking it would be only temporary, a stopgap until something else could be found for you, but we've grown very fond of you and hope that you'll stay on with us for as long as you can. That you'll think of this as your home, just as we do."

"If I try to say anything at all, I shall cry."

"Then don't try, and we'll take the bargain as made."

The hours that Nancy spent with the older girls were not as markedly successful. The music went well enough, taking the girls one at a time at the spinet, but the sewing class was another matter. The first sight she had of twelve girls bent over their needlework in grim silence was so unnerving that she promptly relaxed the rule against talking in class only to discover that the faster their tongues wagged the slower their needles went. She harvested a cornucopia of complaints and excuses, pricked fingers and headaches and strained eyes. She remembered so well how much she had loathed her needle at their age that she hadn't the heart to enforce the lesson. For the few who really wanted to learn she showed all the tricks she knew, how to stroke the back of a bullion knot to make it lie flat against the linen, how to work an eyelet from the outside in. The rest of them she let gossip and chatter or gaze moonily out the window until the day when the door burst open and Dr. Johnson, his glasses pushed up on his forehead, his finger still holding the place in the book he had been trying to read, hushed them all. "Bless me, I thought twenty monkeys had come off the boats and taken up residence in my house. I never knew sewing to be such noisy work."

For the next week all of the older girls were models of decorum. A few of them even finished hemming the napkins that had been assigned to them. Nancy congratulated herself and hoped that it would last over their midwinter holiday.

The New Year's Day custom that Nancy knew, the gentlemen riding out on visits to the neighborhood while the ladies received their guests at home, did not hold in Stratford. The Johnsons held open house, and all of Stratford's best people came to pay their respects to their most distinguished townsman. Several of them identified themselves to Nancy as parents of one or the other of her little girls. There was only one awkward moment. A guest who had some acquaintance with Virginia and Virginians tried to find friends or relations in common. It was soon established that most of her acquaintances were in the Norfolk area, and Nancy could say quite truthfully that she knew very few people there.

"Still, I feel I should know you," the woman persisted with a frown. "Nancy Randolph. The name seems so familiar."

"I expect," Mrs. Johnson interposed smoothly, "that that's because half the inhabitants of Virginia are named Randolph, or so it has always seemed to me. Do come try the seedcake, Mrs. Stanton. It's nowhere nearly as fine as that at your house, but I've despaired of ever persuading you to give over your secret."

She felt the difference on the first afternoon after the girls returned to school. When she entered the room a hush fell. It was not the same industrious murmuring quiet that Dr. Johnson's visit had inspired. Now the girls sat as silent as stones. Even when she asked them questions about their holidays, their answers were brief and constrained. She supposed that she might congratulate herself at having suddenly imposed discipline on a very unruly crew, but she felt only uneasiness. She had had enough experience of children to recognize the quiet that precedes a piece of mischief-making, and she waited. They were a little old for the frog in her sewing box or the sign pinned to the back of her skirt, but something was brewing. It was the same the next day and the day after, and then, as she bent over to help the youngest child in the class untangle an enormous snarl in her thread, she felt the girl shrink away from her. When the same child made a shambles of a song she had played perfectly before Christmas, Nancy put the cover down on the keyboard.

"Are you sickening for something, Molly? Do you feel a little feverish?"

"Please, Miss Randolph, I'm fine. I'll do better next time, I promise."

The child's terrified, Nancy thought. She was only eleven and as flat as a board, but even so perhaps her monthlies had started. The question was how to approach the subject. "Is something bothering you? Has something happened to you that you don't understand?" She put her hand in a gesture of comfort on the child's shoulder, and once again Molly shrank away as if stung.

(359)

"Please don't hurt me, Miss Randolph, please don't."

"You surely can't be frightened of me, Molly. What's gotten into you girls?"

Between sobs and protestations of disbelief the story came pouring out. "Betsy Stanton says you killed a lot of little children in Virginia and ran away up here so they wouldn't hang you for it. And she says she's all right because she goes home at night, but the rest of us are like to be murdered in our beds. But I didn't believe her, I promise, I promise I didn't believe her."

"Molly's very young and not overly bright," Nancy said to the Johnsons. "I don't suppose any of the others including Betsy Stanton believe the tale at all. They're just titillating each other, making a drama. But I had to bring it to you. I don't know what I should do."

Dr. Johnson's solution was to keep the whole school assembled in the hall after their morning prayer while he delivered a sermon on the evils of scandalmongering, to the bewilderment of the younger girls and the elaborate indifference of the others. He firmly believed that once the error of their ways had been pointed out to them, the matter would be over. Neither his wife nor Nancy shared his confidence in the natural goodness of young girls.

Mrs. Johnson had her carriage brought round and paid a call on Mrs. Stanton, from which she returned with a formally worded note of apology for Nancy, and the news that family matters would keep Betsy Stanton at home for the rest of the term.

"It won't do," Nancy said. "I'm more grateful to you both than I can say, but it simply isn't going to work out. Betsy garbled something she heard at home, and even though no one with any sense would believe the story she told, still there will be questions and you know as well as I do that no school can withstand scandal hanging over its staff. I'll have to leave you. It's foolish to even imagine anything else."

Dr. Johnson was prepared to defend Nancy's right to teach

until the last pupil had been snatched away by worried parents. "I won't hear of your leaving. It's a violation of every principle I've lived my life by, and I'm not so old that I don't have at least one more fight left in me."

Mrs. Johnson was equally determined that Nancy not be forced away, but she was a practical woman and not given to the grand gesture. "You must stay on with us, Nancy. We can't let you go . . . unless, of course, it's for a pleasanter situation."

The two women smiled at each other, understood each other. One way or the other a pleasanter situation would be found for Nancy.

* 3 *

The January meeting of the trustees of Columbia College droned on. Gouverneur Morris shifted in his chair and gazed out over Trinity churchyard pretending not to see the dumb show of his old colleague, William Johnson, urgently pantomiming that he wanted private conversation with him after the meeting. He supposed that he was about to be asked for a contribution to the school in Stratford, which would pose a pretty diplomatic problem. It was a case of the truth sounding so implausible as to be more insulting than a lie or an unexplained refusal. His father had carried his lifelong loathing of Yale to the grave with him and forbidden any of his heirs ever to attend or contribute to any place of learning in the state of Connecticut. On the whole, it would probably be better just to give Johnson some money in a friend's name, avoiding the letter of the injunction. Its spirit would be well enough served as long as not a penny of the Morris fortune went to the institution at New Haven.

And in return, he thought, I might ask him what his secret is. It must be going on twenty years since he gave his resignation to a grateful board, and here he is. He's outlived nearly all those trustees and seems well on his way to outlasting these.

Funny, I remember thinking him an old man in Philadelphia in eighty-seven and treating him with deference in the committee meetings and then ignoring his suggestions when it came to the actual drafting. He can't have been much older than I am now, and I suppose those two young men at the far end of the table think much the same way about me and can't wait for us to leave so they can get down to business. Well, mustn't let that depress my spirits. Whatever they may think, I know I'm just reaching my prime, years of useful work ahead of me, and a great many pleasures as well. I wonder if old Johnson feels the same way. Maybe no one ever seems old to himself. At least as long as there's someone around who's even older.

Johnson waited for him to stump down the path between the graves to the gate on Wall Street. "I need your help, Morris, because I know you to be a man of the world . . ."

Good God, Morris thought, the old goat's been caught with his hand up some pupil's skirt.

". . . and because you have a wider acquaintance here in the city than I have these days. You knew Colonel Tom Randolph in Virginia, didn't you?"

"I stayed at Tuckahoe with him during the Constitution debates. But it seems to me I heard he was dead, some time ago while I was in France."

"That's right. Do you remember his daughter, Nancy?"

"As I remember, the Randolphs had a houseful of daughters."

"She would have been thirteen or fourteen."

"That doesn't help much. Wait a minute. There was a dark-haired serious girl, a bit older than that, and there was one with fair hair . . ."

"That would be Nancy."

Morris smiled. "Isn't that strange? I do remember her very well, though I don't suppose I've given her a thought in all these years. She sat a horse better than her brothers and had a laugh like a spring brook. A charming child and a very special pet of her father's. Come to think of it, I did hear something

(362)

else about her later on. She got herself into some sort of scrape with one of her cousins, didn't she? I don't remember too much about it."

Dr. Johnson assured him that whatever he might have heard about Nancy, she was a woman of the highest character, a victim of unfortunate circumstances and in need of help. He told Morris the situation at Stratford. "Neither Mrs. Johnson nor I wish her to leave us, but she feels that she cannot stay. But we can't let her go unless we are certain that she will be safe and treated as someone of her position deserves. I thought you might know of a family here in need of a governess, a highly qualified one, a family that could be trusted with her story and not take advantage of her or expose her to gossip."

"I don't at the moment think of anyone. Most of my intimates are well past the age of having young children still at home. But I can make some inquiries . . ."

"Discreetly," Johnson warned.

"Of course. In the meantime, come with me to Fraunces' and I'll give you a letter to take back to her."

That first letter, the briefest of notes, a courteous acknowledgment of old acquaintance and a hope that he might be of some service to her, was followed in rapid order by others. Almost before Nancy had time to reply to one, another was placed in her hand.

If the Johnsons were aware of the direction in which Morris's letters were tending they said nothing of it and waited for Nancy to come to them.

"Mr. Morris has asked me to come to Morrisania to be his housekeeper."

"But that's out of the question." Mrs. Johnson was shocked. "I don't know what he can be thinking of."

"He assures me that I will be treated with every courtesy. It is in fact partially because of who I am that he wishes me to take the position. He says that there have been problems with some of his other housekeepers because they took on the airs and privileges of a lady without being one."

"I don't care what he says about it. You cannot go into his employment."

"If truth were told, Mrs. Johnson, there have been times in my life when the title of housekeeper would have been a distinct step upward."

"And after all, my dear," Dr. Johnson interposed, "being the housekeeper in the sort of grand establishment that Morris keeps is nothing like being a servant in the ordinary way."

"And even if it were, I can scarcely afford the luxury of pride," Nancy added.

"You neither of you understand me, or else you choose not to. You both know perfectly well that I don't believe any honest labor to be beneath the dignity of the most exalted person in the land, and if Gouverneur Morris had a wife I would give my blessing most willingly. But he does not, and the position of housekeeper in a bachelor establishment is an equivocal one at best."

Now it was Dr. Johnson's turn to be outraged. "I've known young Morris for well over twenty years. He couldn't have been much over thirty when I first met him, and I can tell you that I have as great confidence in the man's integrity as I do of any man on earth, and for you to insinuate as you have is as insulting to me as it is to him."

"I'm sorry that you must find yourself so offended, but surely you can see that a man may have a reputation for the greatest probity and honesty in his dealings with other men and in the world in general and still fall somewhat short of that in his dealings with women."

"You have no reason at all to say such a thing about Morris."

"Don't I indeed? What of the stories about his leg? I never heard of him denying them."

"That was thirty years ago. He was a boy. You can't hold a man's youthful follies against him."

"He wasn't a boy when the scandal broke over Adele dewhatever and Talleyrand."

"But that was was in another country," Johnson protested.

And besides the wench is dead, Nancy quoted to herself. "Please, dear friends," she said, "don't quarrel. The last thing I want is to bring disharmony here, and in any event, I shall have to make the decision myself."

"But there's no hurry," Mrs. Johnson said. "You'll not do anything rash, not without thinking about what I said. Something else will turn up, I'm sure it will."

Nancy was not all sure that something would. She did not even hope that something else would come along. Later that same evening she wrote to Morris and accepted his offer.

On the whole she thought that Mrs. Johnson might very well have the right of it. She did not believe for a moment that a man who wrote to her about how well he remembered her golden curls was entirely interested in how well she would supervise his servants.

Nevertheless, she told herself as she blew out her candle, if the worst should come, I am neither so young nor so virtuous as to make it a very great fall from grace.

* * * * * * * * * *

Morrisania

* * * * * * * * * *

Despite her husband's attempts to stop her, Nancy read Jack's letter over again, slowly, unbelieving, forcing herself to accept its reality.

MADAM: When at my departure from Morrisania I bade you remember the past . . . my object was to tell you that the eye of man, as well as that of God whom you seek not, was upon you; to impress upon your mind a sense of duty towards your husband, and, if possible, to arouse some dormant spark of virtue, if haply such should slumber in your bosom. The conscience of the most hardened criminal has, by a sudden stroke, been sometimes alarmed into contrition and penitence. Yours, I see, is not made of penetrable stuff. . . . You now live in daily and nightly dread of discovery. Detection itself could be hardly worse. Some of the proofs of your guilt . . . those which in despair you sent me through Dr. Meade, on your leaving Virginia—these proofs, I say, had not been produced against you, had you not used my name in imposing upon a generous man, to whose arms you brought pollution. . . .

Cunning and guilt are no match for wisdom and truth; yet you persevere in your wicked course. Your apprehensions for the life of your child first flashed conviction on my mind that your hand had deprived of life that of which you were delivered in Oct. 1792, at

Randolph Harrison's. This child, to interest his feelings in its behalf, you told my brother Richard (when you intrusted to him the secret of your pregnancy, and implored him to hide your shame) was begotten by my brother Theodoric, who died at Bizarre of a long decline the preceding February. You knew long before his death that he was reduced to a skeleton, that he was unable to work and his bones had worn through the skin—such was the inviting object whose bed you sought. . . . To screen the character of such a creature was the life and fame of the most generous and gallant of men put in jeopardy . . . His hands received the burden, bloody from the womb and already lifeless. Who stifled its cries? God only knows and *you*. His hand consigned it to an uncoffined grave. To the prudence of Randolph Harrison . . . refraining from a search under that pile of shingles, some of which were marked with blood—to his cautious conduct it is owing that my brother did not perish by the side of you on the same gibbet; and that the foul stain of incest and murder is not indelibly stamped on his memory. . . .

My brother died suddenly in June 1796, only three years after his trial. I was from home. Tudor, because he believed you capable of anything, imparted to me the morning I left Morrisania his misgivings, lest you might have been the perpetrator of that act. . . . I too had my former misgivings strengthened. If I am wrong, I ask forgiveness of God and even of you. A dose of medicine was the avowed cause of his death.

Nancy looked up from the pages in her hand. What in the name of God would lead him to think that I murdered Richard? He was the only thing that made life tolerable for me in that house. And Tudor was two years old when his father died. If he has suspicions about it, they can't have originated with him. She found her place in the letter again:

When he was no more, you gave loose rein to your inordinate passions. Your quarrels with your sister, before fierce and angry, now knew no remission. . . . She endured you as well as she could, and you poured on. But your intimacy with one of the slaves, your dear "Billy Eller," thus you commenced your letters to this Othello, attracted notice. You would stay no longer at Bizarre. You abandoned it under plea of ill-usage. . . . Your subsequent association with the player, your decline into a very drab, I was informed of by a friend in Richmond. . . . When I heard of your living with Mr. Morris, as his housekeeper, I was glad of it, as a means of keeping you from worse course . . . the idea of his marrying *you* never entered my head. Another connexion *did*. . . .

Chance has again thrown you under my observation. What do I see? A vampyre, that after sucking the best blood of my race, has flitted off to the north, and stuck its harpy fangs into an infirm old man. To what condition have you reduced him? Have you made him a prisoner in his own house, that there may be no witness to your lewd amours? Have you driven away his friends and old domestics, that there may be no witness to his death? . . .

I have done. Before this reaches you it will have been perused by him, to whom, next to my unfortunate brother, you are most deeply indebted, and whom, next to him, you have most deeply injured. If he be not both blind and deaf, he must sooner or later unmask you, unless he too die of "Cramp in the stomach." You understand me. If I were persuaded that his life was safe in your custody, I might forbear making this communication to him. Repent, before it be too late! May I hear of that repentance and never see you more. John Randolph of Roanoke.

Her husband took the letter from her hands and turned toward the fire with it. She took hold of his arm. "No, you mustn't burn it."

"Nothing more surely ever belonged in the fire, unless it's Jack himself."

"It's addressed to me. Surely I may do as I wish with it."

"Of course you may, but I would hope that you'd let me guide you."

"Not in this, because I already know what your advice will be. You'll want to ignore it, to go on just as we always have as if nothing had changed. And in the meantime God only knows how many people Jack has spewed his poison to. You've told me of Decatur and Beecher because they came to you. How many others are there who don't have the courage to face you? How many of your enemies will seize this chance to attack you, an old fool, with no more sense than to take a murderess to his bosom?"

"However many there are, they cannot touch us. No one who knows you, no one we care about will believe it."

"David Ogden believes it. Or what was your quarrel over?"

"He doesn't believe it. He would pretend to believe that you were a cannibal with a ring through your nose if he thought he could profit by it."

"What possible profit is there in this for him?"

"For an intelligent woman you are still astonishingly ignorant about the power of money. Look around you and see what David and my other relations see and remember what they saw five years ago before I married you. An old man, with no wife, no children, and so much money that even cut up between them there'd be more than they ever had. They borrowed up to their earholes on their expectations. And then I marry you, which is bad enough, though it only cuts their shares in half, and then our son is born and they see all that money melting away like fairy gold." Morris gave a mirthless laugh. "Believe Jack Randolph? My God, Nancy, they have probably been feeding him lies of their own. David gambled that I would be dimwitted enough to let this nonsense affect me, that I might turn you out, might even disavow my son.

"If you want revenge, think about what high hopes he rode out here with this morning and what a miserable man is making his way back to the city. He's thinking that he has not only lost any chance of ever being my heir, but also that I can wipe out the little he has of his own with one word to his bankers."

"Do you mean to tell me that he would conspire to destroy me, who has never shown him anything but kindness, just for money?"

"Precisely."

"I would rather he hated me."

"He hates you well enough. You stand in the way of what he loves best on earth."

"Then he's as great a monster as Jack."

"Not at all. He's a perfectly normal greedy man." Morris bent and kissed his wife's forehead. "Now will you take my lead and forget all this as quickly as you can?"

"Surely you can see that that's impossible."

"It's the only reasonable way to behave."

"Then I am not a reasonable woman. I spent nearly fifteen years of my life under a cloud of scandal. I know what it's like. Do you think I want my child to grow up dogged by rumors that his mother was a murderess, a concubine of blacks, an incestuous whore? You're a proud man. Do you want your son to be any less proud?"

"What do you think has been torturing me most in the days since that letter was delivered? The fact of the matter is that there is nothing we can do about it that will not make matters worse. What would you have me do? Call him out? In view of my prominence and your cousin's it would be a national scandal, even a political one. An action at law? That would also just give the matter greater currency."

"Then I'm helpless? Jack is to be allowed to spread whatever lies he chooses about me?"

"Nancy, the whole of our world knows your worth. They

also know that Jack Randolph is erratic to the point of being half mad. No one of any consequence to us will credit this filthy raving. What do you care for the rest of the world?"

"I care a great deal. And as for people not believing it, you may know a lot about money, but I know a lot about gossip, and people will believe anything at all if it makes a good morsel to chew over."

"And in time they will grow tired of it and there will be a new scandal . . ."

"That's not good enough. I want Jack punished. I want him to crawl to me for forgiveness and then I want to refuse him."

"Even if you destroy yourself in the process?"

"I've nothing more to lose. If I don't fight back it will be taken as an admission of guilt."

"You don't understand. Listen to me. You say that I don't know anything about gossip, think about this leg of mine. The whole world believes I lost it jumping from my paramour's window when in fact it was a driving accident. The story persists because there is a large element of truth in it. I didn't break my leg jumping from a window, pursued by an irate Philadelphia husband, but I could have and more than one. The truth is that the accident with the phaeton happened because I was driving far too fast and far too recklessly just to show a particular married lady what a very devil of a fellow I was. The point being that the only way to nail a lie is to tell the whole truth and I never bothered to deny the stories because the truth was not much better."

"I don't see what all that has to do with me."

"This letter and whatever else Jack has been saying around the city are on the face of it preposterous, a mixture of lies and distortions, but if you try to sort them out, only the complete truth will serve. Are you ready for that?"

"I told you. Was that foolish?"

"It was very brave. I'm not sure that that isn't very nearly the same thing. Do you truly want that story made public?"

"If it's the only way I can make the world see what a monster Jack is, then yes, I do."

"No matter who is hurt? Yourself, Judith, some old friends who skated very close to perjury for you, even me?"

"Gouvero, that is an unfair advantage. You know that I don't want to do anything to hurt you, but . . ."

"Then at least think about it," he interrupted. "Don't act hastily. Wait and see what happens. Randolph's own excess may destroy him. His reputation is already in question. People are beginning to recognize his mad streak for what it is. If you let him, he will destroy himself, and these stories about you will be considered just one more evidence of his madness."

"Do you really think so?"

"I am sure of it."

"And you feel that I should just go on as if nothing has happened?"

"Exactly."

"Then I'll tell you what I think. I think that Jack Randolph was quite right in one thing. He said that he had underestimated your generosity of mind, that he considered you to be without protection from me because you didn't understand my true nature. Gouverneur, I don't want to wait for Jack to destroy himself. I want to punish him. I stopped being a forgiving person many years and many betrayals ago. I am not a gentle lady from Tuckahoe. I haven't been for a very long time. I want to kill him and if I had the means to do so, I would. You're right, there is a germ of truth. I am not a murderess, but I could be and right cheerfully. If you won't help me, I'll do it myself. I don't know how just yet, but I'll find a way."

"Nancy, I beg you to consider . . ."

"Oh, I will consider. It will take a lot of thought and time."

* 2 *

On the next day Nancy wrote to Judith at Bizarre, telling her the substance of Jack's charges with particular emphasis on those concerning the circumstances of Richard's death. She did not have long to wait for an answer. "Judith says she hadn't an inkling of what Jack intended when she left him in New York and is shocked and horrified beyond words," Nancy told her husband. "She reminds me that he has made false accusations before, only to have to retract them, and promises to do everything in her power to scotch any stories that reach Virginia. All in all, a very satisfactory and affectionate letter."

"I'm glad, although I wish that you hadn't found it necessary to burden your sister with it."

"I need her nailed firmly down on my side and I knew she wouldn't want any speculation abroad about Dick's death and a dose of medicine. She knows I never held the keys to the medicine cupboard at Bizarre." Nancy drew a deep breath and thrust her chin out in determination. "If someone writes you a letter, Gouvero, that letter belongs to you and you may do anything you like with it, isn't that true?"

"Within limits, yes. If it contains confidential information, then there would be ethical if not legal grounds against publishing it. But, Nancy, I thought that I had your promise that you would wait and think carefully before . . ."

"I have waited and I've thought of nothing else. And I can tell you right now that my mind is firmly resolved and nothing you can say, much as I love you, can change it. I intend to write a reply to Jack's letter, examining every sentence, every lie, every distortion, and telling exactly what happened, and when I am through I shall have copies made of his letter and of mine and I shall send them to everyone of importance in his life. I'll send it to his colleagues in Washington and to all the most important people in his constituency. Let them see what sort of man they have been electing to represent them. A liar or a madman or both. He accuses me of lying. Very well, I shall tell the truth. And I'll also tell of his lies and false promises, not just to me but to others. Everyone will at last know the truth about me, but the truth about him is far more damning."

"And you want my blessing for this?"

"I would like it very much, more than I can tell you. But I shan't deceive you. I shall go ahead with or without your blessing."

"If I gave it, it would be most reluctantly."

"I know, and I'm sorry. I would never willingly do anything counter to you. But I must. Once and for all to clear up the shadows. Everything spread before the world, no more whispers. If I must confess to my sins, at least let them be the real ones, not those that Jack has manufactured."

During the weeks that Nancy Morris worked on her reply to Jack Randolph, reading through old journals and letters, she found herself thinking often of Aggie. There had been promises made. Perhaps the time had come to redeem them, and besides, she told herself, it might be better for Aggie to be at Morrisania when her mistress's letter reached Virginia.

"I can't bring a black slave into my household," Morris said. "It'd be a scandal."

"But Aggie's mine. It would have nothing to do with you. Other people bring their body servants with them when they come north for a visit. And there are people in New York who have slaves themselves."

"Very few, and there'll be none at all in five years' time, when the final provision of the law is in effect."

"And what'll become of those poor old people then, I'd like to know? I think it's a disgrace, throwing them out on the street with no one to care for them."

Her husband pulled his spectacles down his nose and looked over them incredulously. "You don't mean to tell me that you think manumission is a bad thing from a slave's point of view?"

Nancy frowned and considered the problem. "I suppose not," she said slowly. "Slavery's bad, so freedom must be good. But one thing I can tell you, because I've seen it myself, freedom doesn't always work out the way people think it will. I remember Aggie herself telling me . . ." She broke off, struck

by a wholly new idea. "I could free Aggie, couldn't I? I couldn't
ever sell her, even to Judy, because Grandpa Cary gave her to
me, but that doesn't mean I couldn't free her."

"You not only can, you must. I would have insisted that
you do it five years ago if I'd any notion before today that you
owned anyone."

"It didn't seem important—there were so many servants in
this house already—but I would have told you if you'd asked.
It wasn't a secret. I would never have a secret from you."

"No secrets, perhaps, but a multitude of surprises."

Morris agreed to act as her lawyer in the matter, drawing
up the papers that would set Aggie free. "And her children,"
Nancy suddenly remembered. "I own her children too, I think.
She had two boys when I left, but there may be more now."

Her husband blinked. "I'll just put down 'and issue.'"

"What a horrid word for a baby. Even a black one. Though
Aggie's boys must be nearly grown by now." Nancy clapped
her hands in delight. "What a good idea. I can't imagine why
I never thought of it before. You must send her a purse, you
know, when you get the papers all done legallike, so she can
take the packet from Richmond. Judy will see that she gets that
far on the cart. And I'll write her what to do when she gets to
New York. How long do you think it will take? I didn't know
how much I missed her. It will be like having part of home
here with me."

"Nancy, don't excite yourself so," her husband warned.
"The paper will free her. She may not wish to come to you."

Nancy stared at him in blank surprise. "But of course she'll
come. She belongs to me."

*   3   *

"The trouble is," Nancy said to her husband, "that I
have the ideas in my head but the words won't come."

"Not an uncommon problem, I assure you."

"I've been trying to sort out in my mind what to say about

my leaving Bizarre. Everything he says about it is false, but I can't just say that. He can't ever have believed that I was forced to leave when my intimacy with Billy Ellis became known. Aggie was fond of Billy when he was alive, but she could have picked him up and put him in her pocket. Nobody would ever have cast him as Othello, the way Jack says."

"I don't think that approach will serve you very well," Morris offered tentatively.

"I do know," Nancy said quickly. "I tried it. Whatever I wrote sounded as if I were protesting overmuch, or left the way open for someone who didn't know me to think if it wasn't that particular black it might have been another one. I knew I had to close the door completely and I thought of the letter Judy sent me after she left here."

"Judy's letter?"

"I have it right here." She pulled out a page from the papers in her lap. "See, here where it says that although she was prevented from spending the winter with us she is proud of the honor done her by the invitation. So, what I thought of this morning and had just finished writing when you came in was a few sentences about using my sister's name in connection with my alleged conduct and told him about the letter and quoted that bit about the honor of the invitation, and then I wrote . . . Listen to this and tell me what you think." She began to read. " 'With this letter before me, I should feel it an insult to her, as well as an indignity to myself, if I made any observation on your filthy slander respecting my conduct at Bizarre. No one can think so meanly of a woman, who moves in the sphere of a lady, as to suppose that she could be proud of having been invited to spend the winter with the concubine of one of her slaves. Nevertheless, though I disdain an answer to such imputations, I am determined that they shall appear in the neighborhood under your hand, so that your character may be fully known, and your signature forever after be, not only what it has hitherto been, the appendage of vainglorious boasting— but the designation of malicious baseness. . . .' " Nancy took a long satisfied look at her creation and then turned to her husband. "What do you think of that?" she asked proudly.

"I think the idea of using Judy to refute him is a very good one." He paused and chose his words carefully. "It may be a little over elaborate."

Nancy was crestfallen. "What part don't you like?"

In the course of his career, Gouverneur Morris had had to deal often with the wounded vanity of amateur authors. The skills that had served him well in the heated committee meetings of the Constitutional Convention were now brought into domestic use. "I like it all very much indeed," he assured her. "I'm perhaps not quite sure what 'appendage of vainglorious boasting' means."

"It means that ridiculous way he has begun to sign himself as 'John Randolph of Roanoke.' Like he was an English lord or something."

"Of course, stupid of me. Appendage refers to his signature. Perhaps it would be wise to explain that."

Nancy waved away the suggestion. "I don't think so. I mention it in another part of the letter. Do you like 'disdain an answer to such imputations'?" She didn't wait for his answer. "It means the same as saying that you wouldn't stoop to answer something, only I thought it sounded more dignified."

Her husband nodded his agreement. "Quite so. Much more dignified." If he thought that not stooping to reply was dignified enough and a deal clearer, he also thought it wiser not to say so.

"Thank you, Gouverneur, you're being such a help to me. Then that settles the matter of Billy. I think I know how he got that notion lodged in his head. The state he was in that night and the way she was raving. She wouldn't ever have told him the true reason for our quarrel. She couldn't. She must have said something about the note, but she couldn't have shown it to him. I had it when I left her room. I remember throwing it on the fire. He might have thought there was more in it than there was to make her so wild." She stopped, frowning. "Still you'd think he would have asked her later, when she was herself again. She'd have told him the truth of it."

"Perhaps some spark of delicacy inhibited him."

"You may be right. Even Jack might find it awkward to ask a lady if it was true that one of her servants was—what's Shakespeare's word?—tupping her sister." Nancy laughed. "It's ridiculous on the face of it. But people up here seem ready to believe almost anything about plantation people and their servants. They think the path from the master's bedroom to the quarters is as well-traveled as a post road. Look at the way they seized on those absurd lies about Cousin Tom. Not that it doesn't happen sometimes," she added hastily. "I had the evidence of it close by me for years. But only men. I never in my life heard any scandal about a Virginia lady and any of her servants. Maybe in Georgia, but never in Virginia."

* 4 *

Nancy Morris did not look up from her desk when she heard the door behind her open. "Aggie? I told you to go to your bed. I'm quite able to take care of myself."

"Are you so engrossed in your scribbling that you cannot recognize your husband's step?"

"I wasn't expecting you. I thought you and Mr. Bleecker were making a night of it down there, and Aggie has been in and out all evening. I'd forgotten how she used to fuss over me."

"Bleecker's halfway to the city by now on the late tide. It's gone past eleven, you know."

"Has it really? I didn't think more than an hour or two had passed since I came up."

"It occurs to me that more than the time of night escapes you when you sit down at that desk." Morris stirred up the fire and lowered himself into a chair beside it. Something in his voice or the weary slope of his shoulders filled her with compunction. She put down her pen and hurriedly shuffled her papers together. She pulled the hassock over beside him and sat leaning against his chair, her hand on his knee in a gesture of conciliation. He picked up her hand and ran his fingers over the inkstains and put it back without comment.

"Aggie settling in all right?" he asked after a moment.

Nancy smiled. "She'll do very well. She feels the cold some and she nags me for being too thin, but that's an old refrain for her. I sometimes used to think that she would never be happy unless I grew so plump I had to go through the door sideways."

"She's a good, sensible woman. And she's not the only one who thinks you've grown too thin. Bleecker asked if you were ill."

"Well, I'm not. And you may tell him so when you see him next."

"Nancy, haven't you looked in your mirror? Your face has gone so hollow and your eyes are so bruised that you look like a woman ten, even twenty, years your senior."

"That's not the most flattering thing you've ever said to me."

"It was not intended to be. If I had known you meant to ruin your health and lock yourself away from me and your son over this letter of yours, I would never have given my permission."

"I am sorrier than I can tell you that you feel neglected," Nancy said slowly, "but as for my son, it's his future as much as my own peace that I am thinking of. Besides, I am very nearly finished with it."

"You said that before the new year turned."

"But this time I mean it. There are just a few trifling changes and a clean copy to be made and you will have it to censor by dinnertime tomorrow."

"If that's true, I will be heartily glad of it. Not so much to have it in my hands but to have it out of yours." They sat in silence for a while, watching the fire die. It was Nancy who broke the spell.

"Do you know how miserable it makes me to think of all the trouble I've brought you? You can't have dreamed of the consequences when you gave Dr. Johnson that note to carry to me."

"Then you must think instead of the joy you've brought to me."

* 5 *

True to her promise, Nancy had a copy of her letter ready for her husband's eyes by dinnertime the next day. He looked at the bulky closely written packet with some dismay and suggested that she give him an hour to read it and then join him in the library. She had hoped to have him read it while she leaned over his shoulder, pointing out the more felicitous phrases she had labored over, or, even better, she would have liked to read it aloud so that she might by a scornful or sarcastic tone convey that emotion that even the most impassioned underlining could not express. Instead she waited in the hall like a supplicant watching the hands of the clock move toward her appointment.

When she came into the library she found him at his desk, the letter before him interleaved with scraps of paper bearing notes in his hand. Something in his manner made her think of poor Mr. Leslie struggling to make sense of the smudged and tattered papers she used to bring him when he had set her some problems in mathematics. There was nothing of Mr. Leslie, however, in Morris's affectionate greeting, or in his kiss, or in the way he made sure of her comfort in a chair beside him.

"To begin with, let me assure you that I think it a remarkable production. Quite astonishing, in fact. It has the ring of truth that only real, deeply felt emotion can produce."

Nancy thanked him and waited.

"Having said that, I trust you will understand me when I ask you whether the weeks you have spent writing it have not served to relieve your emotions, so that we can now put it behind us and go on with our lives as if we had never heard of John Randolph."

"What do you mean?" Nancy was incredulous. "Do you mean not to send it?"

Her husband nodded. "That was what I hoped for, yes."

"Then it's a vain hope," she said firmly. "Not only do I intend to see that John Randolph is answered, but every hour I add another name to the list of those to whom it is to be circulated. As for relieving my emotions, the only possibility of that would be to have Jack Randolph come crawling on his belly to plead for my pardon in front of the highest in the land, and I'm not at all sure that that would be sufficient."

"Is there nothing I can say that will make you reconsider?"

"Gouverneur, I love you dearly. I would yield to you regarding anything else on earth. But not in this. I'm truly sorry, but there's no other answer I can give you."

He shrugged in resignation. "I don't suppose I had any real expectation of another answer. Perhaps I might even have been a little disappointed if you had yielded to me, even though I think it the wiser course. But having said that, I now want you to give me a hearing on some trifling modifications."

Nancy agreed but with an unspoken reservation that she would decide whether or not the changes were indeed trifling. Certainly the first suggestion that he made seemed to her far from a minor one. She had liberally salted her letter with references to her husband's kindness, love and generosity to herself, to young Tudor, to John Randolph himself. Now, on what she considered grounds of irrational modesty, he wanted them removed.

"You can hardly expect me to reply to an accusation of planning your murder without so much as mentioning your name," Nancy protested.

"I'm not asking that. When you actually address yourself to that issue, when you point out how different your behavior would be if you were either untrue to me or planning my departure, it seems to me very well said, but there are passages in here that would seem excessive in a funeral oration and are intolerable when everyone will know that I permitted you to write them. I am far from being a saint. I cannot permit you to set me up as one."

Nancy was unconvinced, but on this one point her husband was immovable. The only concession that she could gain from him was permission to say that he had forbidden her to speak of his kindness. Reluctantly she picked up her pen and lined out the offending passages. "What else must I do?"

"There is nothing else that I can insist on. Nothing that directly concerns me." He took the pages of her letter from her and referred to them as he spoke. "I think you have handled all the charges he makes about your conduct before and after you left Bizarre with the proper blend of dignity and outrage. I am especially pleased with the directness with which you answer him on the one damning thing of which he has evidence." He read aloud from the letter. " 'I was left at Bizarre under the circumstances of a girl of seventeen, with the man she loved. I was betrothed to him and considered him as my husband. He was my husband in the presence of the God whose name you presume to invoke on occasions the most trivial and for purposes the most malevolent. We should have been married, if death had not snatched him away a few days after the scene which began the history of my sorrows.' " He put the papers down and looked at her affectionately. "I do not think that anyone could read your words about the origin of the child that was born at Glenlyrvar and not be affected."

"As well as I can remember those are precisely the words I used in the letter I wrote to Jack when I left Richmond. They don't seem to have softened his heart overmuch."

"Nancy, why in the name of God did you ever put such a weapon in the hands of a man like John Randolph?"

"I don't know. I've often asked myself the same question. I was leaving Virginia. I didn't know whether I would ever see any of them again. I didn't know what Judith might tell him and wanted him to have my story to counter her. Richard allowed himself to be tried for murder to protect my reputation. I didn't think Jack could fall so far short of his example. He very nearly worshipped Dick, I thought he deserved the truth. And besides—it seems beyond belief now—I thought he loved me." Nancy sighed and looked down at her hands folded in her lap. "I think that might be a fitting epitaph for me. Time after time, despite all past experience, I am astonished to discover malice or indifference where I thought love lived."

"If it's a fault, it's one that comes from your own warm heart."

"I should like to think so, because the only other conclusion, looking back over all my years, is that I must be the stupidest woman alive."

Her husband assured her that he had as high a regard for her intellectual capacity as he did for her courage. "I don't quite understand why you are so insistent that the baby was born in September rather than October first."

"You would if you were a woman. There's not a woman I ever heard of who doesn't count the months off on her fingers when she hears of a suspicious birthing."

"I see." He bent his head and studied the page before him so intently that it occurred to her that men had the ability to count to nine as well and that the exercise of it by this man could very well lead him into matters that were best left unexplored.

"But you approve of the rest of it?" she asked quickly and turned the page, her finger pointing out a paragraph. "Here, where I talk about the trial and how Richard was acquitted and everyone cheered. 'Shouts of exultation' I call it. I particularly like this part." She read aloud. " 'This passed in a remote County of Virginia more than twenty years ago. You have revived the slanderous tale in the most populous city of the U.S. For what? to repay my kindness to your nephew by tearing me from the arms of my husband, and blasting the prospects of my child—poor innocent babe, now playing at my feet, unconscious of his mother's wrongs. ....' I think that's rather good," she commented judiciously. "It puts a certain emphasis on how wicked it is of him to bring it all up, rather than ... "

"Rather than how wicked it was of you to have anticipated your vows," Morris finished for her when she hesitated. "You don't need to persuade me in this matter. I think everything you said about the birth, the trial, the role that Richard Randolph played as your confidant is well said and utterly damning to Jack in its truthful simplicity."

"But there is something still troubling you, I can tell."

"It's not so much that it is troubling me as that there is something that seems to me unworthy of you. Something that I cannot believe represents your true feeling."

"Show me. What is it?"

His eye went quickly over the page. "Here, where you reply to his suspicions about Richard's death. Where you say 'it was not my hand that delivered the fatal dose.' "

"That's perfectly true. It wasn't."

"I don't doubt that. But can't you see, when you phrase your denial in that way it leaves a clear implication that someone else did deliver a fatal dose?" Nancy turned her head away and studied the far corner of the room with great interest. "Nancy, I do not believe that you truly think your sister murdered her husband, and if you don't, it puts you on John Randolph's level to raise such a suspicion."

"I wasn't the one who brought it up. Maybe when he sees that the shadow will fall on Judy he will think twice before he says anything again. And for all I know she did kill him. Jack may have the right of it when he says that it was a dose of medicine that killed him. And why didn't she send for the doctor until it was too late?"

"You don't believe that," Morris said gently.

Nancy sighed. "I suppose I don't. At least not that she intended it. But I'll tell you one thing. She is afraid that she caused it."

"If that's true, then she must have been in torment all

the years since his death. You don't want to add to her anguish."

Nancy pulled her hand away from his. Her voice trembled with the effort of keeping herself in control. "If she was in torment, she made sure that I shared it with her. Why should I spare her now?"

"Because you have a husband who loves you and a fine, healthy child and she has neither. And because I had hoped that the happiness I had brought you had overcome all the old bitterness. Do you want me to feel that I have failed you?"

Then, amid tears, protestations of love, reassurance and apologies, an agreement was reached. Nancy would say nothing of the circumstances of Dick's death. The words she had written concerning his nobility, kindness, and honor would stand as sufficient proof that she could never have been responsible for bringing them to an end. When she was calmer, Morris made a halfhearted attempt to bring some coherence to her attack on John Randolph's political life. Nancy had a dim recollection of once having heard something of the Yazoo settlements and was aware that there had been some disagreement or other in foreign affairs, but as far as she was concerned John Randolph had turned on Jefferson and nearly succeeded in tearing apart the Republican party, solely because he had hoped and planned to be sent as an Ambassador abroad and Cousin Tom and Jemmy Madison had passed him over. It offended her husband's sense of historical propriety, but Nancy knew what she knew.

"He's still angry over it," she said. "Didn't you see how sulky he was when you talked about your years in France?"

"Believe me, Nancy, political matters, matters of state do not hinge on things of that nature."

"Maybe they don't in New York—though I could remind you of Mr. Burr—but they do in Virginia. Always have. John Hancock would have been President instead of General Washington if Patrick Henry had had better manners."

This blithe summary of the Virginia ratification battle served to convince her husband that any further discussion of political matters was futile. But he had one more suggestion to make. "I cannot refrain from noticing that better than a quarter of these pages concern trifling transactions between you and Tudor. Monies you lent him while he was here to pay his servant or to purchase stockings and handkerchiefs. Don't you think that such a wealth of detail, especially concerning such minor matters, rather obscures your point?"

Nancy could spare it only a moment's thought. "No, I don't. It's the detail that makes it so convincing." There was, however, one other matter that he could help her with. "The letter wants an ending, something grand and devastating, like the last bit of a political speech that makes everyone cheer."

"See what you think of this," her husband said later and read to her in what she always called his "speechifying" voice. " 'I observe, sir, in the course of your letter, allusions to one of Shakespeare's best tragedies. I trust you are, by this time, convinced that you have clumsily performed the part of "honest Iago." Happily for my life and for my husband's peace, you did not find in him a headlong rash Othello. For a full and proper description of what you have written on this occasion, I refer you to the same admirable author. He will tell you it is "a tale told by an idiot, full of sound and fury, signifying nothing.' "

"*Macbeth?*" Nancy asked. Her husband nodded. "Very fitting," she said. "And then I'll sign it Ann C. Morris, so he'll know I'll never be Nancy to him again."

* 6 *

For the next few days Nancy was engaged on making clear copies of Jack's letter and her revised reply. None of them was sent to her friends, although a trusted few in New York were allowed to read them. They went instead to political figures in Virginia, enemies of her enemy. He had met defeat for the first time in his last Congressional race. Nancy confidently expected that her revelations of his true character, whether he was considered vicious or simply mad, would be sufficient to gain him permanent political exile. She sent off her bombs and waited for the explosion. And continued to wait.

Later that year, John Randolph was elected to Congress. Nancy took the news with equanimity, helped by her husband's admirable restraint in failing ever to mention her political misjudgment. Privately she may have thought it a prime example of the conspiracy of men, but she never said so. She turned once again to the task she found most rewardiing, the making of a comfortable, contented life for her husband and child.

For Gouverneur Morris it was a happy year. He had the full attention of his adored wife. None of his old friends had deserted him in their trouble and now could be found once again enjoying his hospitality. The government that he had helped found seemed to have weathered the worst of its early stresses. His son grew brighter and bonnier every day. He was rich, respected, and loved. In a little more than a year after Nancy sent off her reply to Jack Randolph, Gouverneur Morris was dead. Quite peacefully and with a last encouraging smile for his Nancy.

Nancy Morris never remarried and never returned to Virginia. She spent the years of her widowhood in a fierce guardianship of her son's estate. Forewarned by her husband, she fended off the jackals and displayed a grasp of matters financial that would have both surprised and delighted him. Through it all she was sustained and consoled by Aggie, no longer bound to her by law but by the chains of affectionate habit.

* 7 *

The two women, fair and dark, mistress and servant, stood at the upper window and watched as young Gouverneur Morris mounted his horse on the gravel drive below.

"Aggie, I defy you to say that you have ever seen a handsomer boy," his mother said. "And so strong. Thank God he takes his constitution from his father and not from me."

"You're not so weak as you think you are. Never were. The other baby, yours and Mr. Richard's, he would have been a fine big one, too."

Nancy's shoulders stiffened. "Mr. Theodoric, Aggie," she corrected.

"Miss Nancy, you forgot I was there? Mr. Theo had been a long time in his grave when that baby started. Poor little thing. He wasn't nowhere near ready to be birthed, but he was trying."

Nancy watched her son out of sight down the drive. She wished herself out of the room or back in time, anywhere away from the echo of Aggie's words. She turned slowly away from the window to face her maid. What must I look like? she thought. I've never seen Aggie frightened of me before. Her lips moved, but the question she was afraid to ask would not be spoken. She cleared her throat. Her voice was a strangled whisper. "It was alive?"

Aggie backed away from her until she was halted by the corner of the mantelpiece. She seemed to cower and held out her hands in appeal. Nancy stood still and waited. "Mr. Richard had it in his hands and made to give it to me, but I was afraid to touch it and I picked up the pillow and he put it down all bloody and went back to you."

"It was alive," Nancy repeated unbelievingly.

"He kept opening and shutting his mouth like he was trying to cry and his little arms and legs were moving, no bigger round than a pencil. And I thought, Poor little mite, you won't live to see another midnight, just long enough to bring disgrace down on your mama and papa and drive Miss Judith crazy wild, and I put my hand under him and turned him over very easy on his face and he stopped moving, so I put the towel over and I told Mr. Richard it was dead and he looked very sad but said perhaps it was as well." Aggie drew a long shuddering breath and appealed to her mistress. "Did I do wrong, Miss Nancy? Did I do wrong?"

Nancy closed her eyes and felt herself returning from the dead. It wasn't Dick who did it, she thought gratefully. I should have known it couldn't have been. She took Aggie in her arms and held the sobbing woman close to her, stroking her hair.

"Dearest Aggie," Nancy Randolph Morris said to her aunt. "You always did have more than enough of family feeling."